PANAMA...

A love story of unparalleled magnificence—of
Philippe Bunau-Varilla, the engineering genius,
and Madelon Grabralet, a beautiful and passionate woman. They shared a love that
spanned decades and ranged from the tropics
of Panama to the stately mansions of Paris
and Washington.

Here is the gripping tale of the men and women
whose lives were shaped by the monumental
task of linking two giant oceans. It is a powerful story that captures all the flavor and perilous adventure of an era when history was made.

PANAMA

by

Ashley Carter

FAWCETT GOLD MEDAL • NEW YORK

PANAMA

Published by Fawcett Gold Medal Books, a unit of CBS Publications, the Consumer Publishing Division of CBS Inc.

This is a fictionalized version of the French years in the Panama Canal Zone and does not purport in any way to be an actual biographical depiction of the life of Philippe Jean Bunau-Varilla.

ISBN 0-449-14025-3

Printed in the United States of America

10 9 8 7 6 5 4 3 2 1

For Mauri Grashin

PROLOGUE

Canal Zone, Panama, 1914

The speeches droned endlessly. Each speaker proved more longwinded than the last, all determined to be eloquent, expansive and complete. Everyone who could be praised, thanked or commended must be acknowledged by name and deed.

Philippe Jean Bunau-Varilla blew at a fly buzzing about his sweaty face, fought to conceal a yawn, and tried to blink away the drowsiness weighing down his eyelids. But these voices, even when they singled him out for extravagant homage, were sleep-inducing, and the torrid sun made the atmosphere blisteringly hot. The stars and stripes, the tricolor, and the hastily created Panamanian flag, all sagged lifelessly above the daïs where he sat.

"Bunau-Varilla dedicated his life, his career, his fortune—"

The faint bow of acknowledgment, the rigid smile. He struggled to keep his wits about him enough to respond with a humble nod of the head when his name was intoned. *Mon dieu,* would it never end? Thirty-four years digging the big ditch; it looked as if they'd spend the next 34 years here in this pitiless sun recounting this greatest engineering triumph of mankind's recorded history.

Triumph it was, but he was exhausted.

"The late, sorely lamented John Hay, our magnificent

Secretary of State, said of Philippe Bunau-Varilla—and President Roosevelt echoed his words—'Many men will build the Panama Canal, but without this one man, this Philippe Bunau-Varilla, we can say this canal may never have been built at all.' "

Bunau-Varilla nodded his head, feeling his face flush to the roots of his graying hair. John Hay had indeed paid him this tribute, but he had done it in less spectacular surroundings.

Exhaling, he gazed out over the harbor, alive with ships, as modern a facility as one would find anywhere on earth. The new Canal Zone city gleamed in fumigated splendor. Sodded and bordered walkways offered controlled shade. The whole region shone antiseptically clean and vigorously busy. Fresh, white stucco hotels displayed huge signs, theaters glowed with lights, shops displayed latest fashions.

"It is not given to many men—as it was to *M'sieu* Bunau-Varilla—to render such service to three nations and to the civilized world—"

The smile, the nod. He watched the S.S. *Cristobal* standing at anchor in the harbor, ready to move through the sea-level entrance from Limon Bay into Gatun, a channel seven miles long that linked two oceans.

"Live forever then, *M'sieu* Bunau-Varilla, in our memory, in our undying gratitude—"

Until now, weighted under accolades and laurels, he had not truly known how tired he was. Fifty-four years old! Was it possible? Where had the time gone?

He gazed at the dignitaries along the sun-blasted dais. Senator Morgan of Alabama, no less proud and obstinately opinionated than ever. Goethels, Gorgas—all those who had contributed so much and lived to tell it, they were all present.

Near him, under the tricolor, Ducrot Bazaine, still the martinet, stiff-necked, inflexible, staring straight ahead, unblinking in the blaze of tropic sun.

On the front row, Clee sat, grinning and crying openly at the same time. Clee, the young brigand, now a respected Panamanian bureaucrat, clutching the dark hand of a lovely young wife. And Myti, that monolith of strength and inner goodness—dressed to the teeth, flashy jewelry and gold tooth winking back at the sun.

"Because of Bunau-Varilla and Colonel Gorgas, all those valiant heroes, we can look forward today, not only with pride and hope but—"

Bunau-Varilla acknowledged the smattering of fatigued, sun-stunned applause, but his interest was only polite. At last, this ditch was for him a finished project. It was behind him now; he was finally free of its challenges and crises.

But he admitted he would never truly escape it.

They crowded unseen around him, those vital, driven people who had given their lives before reaching this momentous hour of dedication. John Hay, Secretary of State under both McKinley and Roosevelt; the kingmaker Mark Hanna of Ohio; Jean-Paul Galludct, director-general of the Panama Canal program under the French; President Roosevelt, who refused to be deterred or delayed; the amiable, politically impotent McKinley.

He saw them all in his mind, but even more vividly and hurtfully, he saw Guido De Blasio, terrified of the yellow jack but refusing to run from the plague. And the lovely, sensuous Anouk Bazaine—a casualty, too. As was Claude-Bruce Grabralet, though he never came within three thousand miles of the canal. And the saddest casualty, Vicomte Ferdinand Marie de Lesseps, the aged Lion of the Suez.

"We dedicate this great Canal, not to the glory of the United States, or to the new Republic of Panama, but to the whole community of all the great nations of the world, now brought closer together than ever through this magnificent engineering accomplishment—"

As the future tugged at them, Philippe's mind bore him backward against the floodtide into that violent turmoil of the past. The speeches fulminated on, unreal, remote, distant as summer thunder, gray monotone upon gray monotone, while inside his mind, the furies raged, the voices clamored, rising, demanding, strident, driving out this present, bringing it all cascading back, clutching at him. . . .

ONE

Paris, 1882

[1]

Philippe recalled in sharpest clarity that morning of the duel. It all seemed to begin there. The duel itself was not significant—a stupid child's game of honor for grown men—played out with real guns. He recalled it so vividly because that day he first encountered the only woman he could ever truly love.

"A beautiful morning," he said. "Isn't it, Toine? A beautiful morning."

Antoine Montivilliers caught his breath, stunned. He stared at Philippe as if he were insane. Antoine's youthful face was pallid, haggard. Obviously, the poor fellow had not slept for two nights at least. His voice choked, a croaking sound in his throat. "How can you say that?"

Philippe grinned and shrugged. Perhaps it was pushing credibility a bit to call this false dawn beautiful. It was nothing really, a lost hour between darkness and daybreak, a veil of gray mists clotting the green park beside the Seine. Horse-chestnut trees wept great droplets. Distant gas lamps spun pale halos in the fog. A chill gnawed at them through the comic-opera costumes that were *de rigueur* for this deadly charade—black suits, black top hats and black, lined capes.

Antoine moaned audibly and staggered slightly on the path. Philippe caught his arm. "Come. Don't let them see you're afraid."

"If you are not afraid, Philippe, it is because you are too reckless to recognize danger."

"I simply haven't thought about it."

"How in God's name could you *not* think about it? We face—what? Death at the worst. Only ruin can issue from the most reasonable settlement. A painful bullet wound. Disgrace. Unable to go to a hospital for treatment without risking jail for violating all ordinances against public violence, against dueling. Even if all went well, which I dare not even hope, Depuits et David sacks any employee engaging in this illegal offense."

"They'll see the fear in your face, Toine. They'll smell it on you."

"Let them! Damn it, why are we here?"

"Because Aubrey de Fecame insists on dying for his honor."

Their opponent, his seconds and referees were already on the mall. They loomed like black-attired wraiths in the thickening fog. Silent and aloof near the carriages stood the doctor, gripping his medical kit in his fist.

They shook hands all around. When Philippe offered his hand, Aubrey de Fecame, a slender aristocrat with sharp features and prominent overbite, refused to touch it.

The referee made a faint clucking sound of disapproval at de Fecame's lack of courtesy. He motioned the adversaries to face each other before him, each with his second at his shoulder. Philippe wished Toine Montivilliers would clamp his mouth shut so his teeth wouldn't chatter.

"Gentlemen." The referee's voice was low, chilled. "I am bound under terms reached by your seconds, and as a gentleman of honor, to inquire if you cannot reach satisfaction through compromise?"

De Fecame stiffened, tilting his head. "I remind you. No apology is permitted in any *duello a la mazza* until after the first shot has been fired."

The referee's tone remained cold. "I ask you again,

m'sieu. Will you accept an apology as satisfaction from *M'sieu* Bunau-Varilla?"

"No. It cannot be satisfied in that manner," de Fecame said.

"I'm afraid not." Philippe shrugged.

"I am required to ask you once more," the referee persisted. "Count Aubrey de Fecame, you come here as the aggrieved. Can you not find it in your heart to accept an apology from your adversary?"

"My honor has been damaged. Only blood will wash away the stain," de Fecame said.

"Oh, for God's sake, de Fecame," Philippe said. "Wake up. There is no need for this."

De Fecame flinched, but straightened his wiry shoulders. "I have placed my life in jeopardy in this *duorum bellum* of my own free will, well aware of the risks. A man cannot live without his honor."

"Your honor is intact," Philippe said. "Your pride may be a little piqued, that's all. I don't know what Yvette told you, but—"

"Yvette told me *everything, m'sieu.* Everything, do you understand?"

"And you still want to duel?"

De Fecame flushed through his pallid cheeks. "I warn you. I realize you are no gentleman, Bunau-Varilla. No gentleman would mention a lady's name in this place."

"Gentlemen. Gentlemen. This is not the site for debate. If you swear and declare before God that your differences run so deep, are so irreconcilable that they cannot otherwise be accommodated, I ask you to select your weapons."

A second man stepped forward, his face solemn and rigid, his austerity somehow marred by a streak of egg yolk along his chin. He extended the set of dueling pistols in their velvet-covered case.

Philippe could not help admiring the polished beauty and craftsmanship of the dueling guns, this finest example of the gunsmith's art. He could almost find his reflection in the brass mountings. When he had taken the gun remaining after de Fecame had chosen, he found the weapon perfectly in balance, with its ten-inch octagonal

14

barrel, front and rear sights, locks of excellent workmanship, finely shaped and finished half-stocks. Fifteen inches long overall, it used round lead ball with a light powder charge and was deadly at 25 paces.

Philippe and de Fecame stood back to back, though Philippe was a head taller than his opponent. At the slow, tolling count, they paced forward. Philippe held the pistol beside his face, and drops of moisture glistened on the barrel.

Through the mist, he heard the solemn voice of the referee intone the word, "Fire."

Instinctively, Philippe turned, angling his body sideways to present the slimmest target. He let his gun hand hang at his side, almost negligently.

De Fecame, in sudden panic, jerked up his gun and pressed its trigger. The weapon lurched in his grip. The explosion was sharp, its brief flame quickly muffled in the enveloping mists. Philippe felt the bullet whistle past his cheek, stinging slightly, like the grazing slash of a vagrant wasp.

He winced. So close had he come to dying because he was fool enough to indulge these idiots in a "war of two" on a chilled "field of honor."

Rage gorged up through him. But he was no more enraged at de Fecame and these other clowns than at himself. It took two to waltz. These adult delinquents could not have contrived a duel without his compliance.

Slowly, seeing de Fecame shrink into himself, Philippe raised his dueling pistol. He pointed it high and fired above the treetops.

He heard the exhalations of relief from the other men. Toine exhaled as if he had been holding his breath for hours, as if he had forgotten how to breathe. For the first time the doctor relaxed near the carriages. De Fecame's second looked as if he might faint from sheer relief.

Twenty-five paces away, de Fecame howled in agony. He stood immobile for one long moment, staring at the pistol in his hand. Then he hurled it away.

He ran sobbing in rage toward Philippe. He caught the ruffled front of Philippe's white shirt in his trembling fists. He stared up at Philippe, his face twisted, and his eyes glittering in mindless despair.

"Damn you, Bunau-Varilla. How dare you play games with me, with my honor?"

"The whole gambit is a game, de Fecame. A stupid child's game."

"This *rencontre* has been settled in an honorable fashion," the referee declared.

De Fecame ignored him.

The seconds stepped forward. Toine cried out, "Do I need to remind you, *M'sieu* de Fecame, that firing into the air is tantamount to apology?"

De Fecame raged. "No apology can settle this matter. I demand, *m'sieu,* that you fire as affirmed in our exchange of cards. There are strict forms of conduct—"

"Do you want to die then?" Philippe asked calmly.

De Fecame's eyes filled with tears. "Even La Chateigneraie died at the foot of his loving king rather than survive in defeat. Let me—a gentleman, an aristocrat—do at least as much."

"For God's sake, de Fecame," Philippe said. "That was two hundred years ago."

"When you agreed to a duel, *M'sieu* Bunau-Varilla, you agreed to abide by formal rules of conduct."

"It's over," Philippe said.

De Fecame glared around him wildly. Not even his own seconds would meet his eyes. His voice crackled. "You bastard! They say you are a bastard. Now you prove it. You are no gentleman, *m'sieu*. You have humiliated me, treated me with contempt, spat upon my honor, and left me to live mocked in disgrace."

"Oh, please, de Fecame. It's not all that dramatic or world-shaking. Sure, I'll know you for a fool, but I've always known that."

"These men—" De Fecame swung his trembling arm. "These men have seen you mortify me, mock my good name, seduce my wife, abase me before my peers, and you dare to laugh at me, you arrogant bastard."

Coldly, Philippe caught de Fecame's bony wrists and removed them from his shirt front. "Be thankful I am a bastard, de Fecame. If I were a so-called gentleman like

16

you, you'd be dead. Instead, you can return to your wife."

De Fecame sank to the ground and sobbed. "You've left me nothing, nothing! Nothing to live for. A man without honor."

"You're still breathing, still talking too much. Nothing has changed. Thank Yvette that you're still alive, de Fecame."

"Yvette." De Fecame's body quivered visibly. "You dare mock—"

"I mock nothing. I was never more serious. It is because of Yvette I did not kill you. You were willing to die for her. Surely you're willing to live with her."

[2]

Philippe sat and watched Antoine Montivilliers approach.
Toine walked along the rows of desks, drafting stands
and drawing boards, the wan light gleaming on his cuff
protectors.

He paused before Philippe's desk, looking troubled, his
eyes weak behind thick-lensed glasses. Philippe could see
a brilliant future for Toine at Depuits et David. Toine
spoke only when he was spoken to, he never made waves,
he offered no suggestions on anything, he delayed over
every minor scrap of work as if giving it deepest consideration. It might take Toine three days to answer a
letter requesting information on materials. This pleased
the upper echelon. They liked to say, "Young Montivilliers is coming along beautifully." No one delivered a
message in house better than Antoine Montivilliers.

"We're due in a staff meeting, Philippe. Something big,
I suspect. We're to be in the staff room right away."

"Why? Junior engineers are never permitted either to
speak, think or squirm in chairs."

Antoine tried to smile, but he checked nervously over
his shoulder. "They want us to learn to be silent. Old

18

David always says a young engineer learns most with his own mouth shut."

"Old David gives me a pain in the ass."

"My God, Philippe. Someone will hear you. Listening and not interrupting is simply one of their rules here."

Philippe did not stir from his chair. "I think I'm losing the capacity to communicate verbally."

"Oh, come on. For God's sake, just don't make waves. You move upward here as they decide, and that's the only way. You know that. Accept it."

"I'm gut sick of having to sit in a staff meeting and pretend I'm as stupid as some of these senior engineers, simply to get along with them."

Toine's earnest young face flushed red. He glanced around again. "Philippe, there's nothing you can't accomplish in engineering, and with Depuits et David. My God, they're rated right at the top. They just have their rules. They've brought along a lot of junior engineers in the last thirty years, and maybe they've learned how it should be done."

"I'll bet Paul-Jacques David said that, too."

Toine laughed in spite of himself. He stopped smiling at once and glanced around one more time to be certain they were not overheard. "Have you—heard anything?" He leaned forward across Philippe's cluttered desk.

Philippe leaned forward too, mocking him. "About what?" he whispered in that conspiratorial tone.

Toine winced. "About the—'walk in the fields'—of course."

"No. Why should I?"

Toine flushed again to the roots of his hair. "There have been rumors. I heard in the *pissoire* that old Depuits was inquiring—"

"You're getting to be quite an old maid, Toine."

Toine shrugged. "If I'm getting gray, it's your fault."

A few moments later, Philippe was slouched in an uncomfortable chair near the foot of the conference table. Toine sat stiff and erect beside him. Beyond Toine was an ancient senior engineer smoking a cigar. When the smoker finished with the soggy butt, he dropped it into a brass spittoon between his chair and Toine's. Earlier someone had disposed of paper in the spittoon. This debris ignited almost immediately and a steady pall of acrid smoke flowed upward and across Toine's face. Paul-Jacques David was speaking and Toine was too timid to push the spittoon away with his boot. He sat there turning a beet red, his face expanding as he struggled to keep from coughing.

Philippe concentrated on David, biting at his underlip to keep from laughing aloud at Toine's predicament. If Toine didn't let go and cough soon he was going to turn purple and explode. Toine's eyes were running, and his nose was beginning to leak, too. But he continued to sit stiffly, unmoving, his coughing now held deep in his chest.

David was a squat animal of a man. His large head even looked muscular to match his brutal shoulders and extraordinary biceps. His chest was keglike, his legs short thick blocks. His cheeks and chin were darkly shadowed five minutes after he shaved. When he talked he bent forward aggressively at the hips.

Armed with a three-foot pointer, David discussed the blueprints tacked to the large easel beside him at the head of the table.

Beside David, in the only other really comfortable chair in the staff room, sat Alexandre Eiffel, the famous structural engineer. He had graduated—David had stressed this in introducing him earlier—with highest honors from the Ecole Centrale des Arts et Manufactures. Three years later he completed the railway bridge across the Garonne River at Bordeaux. Philippe stuck his tongue in his cheek—one thing was certain, Alexandre Gustave Eiffel hadn't begun *his* career at Depuits et David. If he had he'd never have been responsible for building *anything* within his first three years out of school.

"For those junior engineers so busy knowing it all that you don't know what is going on around you," Paul-Jacques David said, glowering toward the lower end of the table, "for those of you, I will briefly review the background of this project which Alex Eiffel has brought to us. Projected to be built in time for the Paris Exposition of 1889, is a 984-foot-high tower, its piers constructed of iron lattice work and 330 feet square at its base. It is to be located at the western extremity of the Champ de Mars, at a cost of more than one million.

"This beautiful structure, Alex assures me, will command a view of 85 miles. It will of course be the tallest structure in the world. The fact that no monument, permanent structure or church spire in the city rises above ninety feet will add to the grandeur of this new tower.

"This brings us to that section of this magnificent structure which *M'sieu* Eiffel has entrusted to Depuits et David to plan and execute. This is the concrete-base, reinforced wall which will support the tower."

Moving his pointer over the draftsman drawings, David explained in detail the measurements, the materials and the construction. He showed the steel pilings driven like taproots into the earth, the massive walls, the added supports which, as drawn, would angle out at intervals all around the lower piers of the tower.

The more David went into detail about the below-ground and first-tier construction, the lower Philippe slouched in his chair, the more he squirmed. Beside Philippe, Antoine Montivilliers was approaching apoplexy. He was choking, but he sat so still that David ignored him.

Philippe wished he were in some other hell. He could no longer glance at Montivilliers, who would rather explode than disturb a superior. If he looked at Toine he was going into raging laughter that might lose Depuits et David all credibility with Alexandre Eiffel. It would certainly end his career with the firm.

Montivilliers nudged him with his elbow, but Philippe was afraid to glance toward Toine, for fear he would laugh at that lobster face and distended neck. Oh God, let this meeting end!

"M'sieu Bunau-Varilla." David's heavy voice impaled him from the other end of the room.

Philippe heard Toine's gasp of anguish. At least the poor devil had been forced to exhale. "Sir?"

David's voice crackled with sarcasm. "Something about my presentation disturbs you, *M'sieu* Bunau-Varilla?"

"No, sir. You're doing fine. If *M'sieu* Eiffel is pleased, I am most happy."

"What in hell is that supposed to mean?"

"Nothing, sir. You asked me. I told you."

"Then are you sitting on a pincushion? Why can't you sit still?"

Philippe drew a deep breath. "It's just that those steel poles need not be driven so deep. They won't help structurally, anyway. Nor do you need those studs to brace all around the base of the first tier of the tower."

"Oh?" The sarcasm dripped. The older engineers turned in their chairs, their eyes fixed in cold disapproval upon Philippe. "I dislike having to waste *M'sieu* Eiffel's time."

"No," Eiffel said. "Please go on. It concerns this structure. I'm most interested."

David hunched those shoulders forward, supporting himself upon his fists on the polished tabletop. "I'm afraid, *M'sieu* Eiffel, our young engineer can't have much to say of interest to a man of your experience and knowledge. We invite young junior engineers into these meetings to *learn* from us—not to air their untried theories."

Philippe's voice was firm. "I know only what I've studied."

David's voice raked him like talons. "Your recent study in the Ecole Polytechnique has provided you only one thing as far as I am concerned, Bunau-Varilla. A diploma." David was obviously enjoying himself. "That diploma earns you *only* the right to come to Depuits et David and learn engineering on the job. Here."

Philippe nodded and shrugged again. David continued to glare at him until Philippe slouched back in his chair. It was Eiffel who said, "I'd like to hear the young engineer's suggestions, *M'sieu* David. If we may?"

David smiled, thinking that Eiffel was enlisting on his side to cut the upstart down. He said, "We do not encourage *suggestions* from our junior engineers, Alex."

"All the same," Eiffel persisted, "out of the mouths of babes . . ."

Seeing that Eiffel was serious, David spoke in cold anger. "Go ahead. Please, Bunau-Varilla, instruct the foremost structural engineer of the world. Please. You have the floor."

Philippe drew a deep breath and stood up. "It seems

22

to me, *M'sieu* David, and forgive me, *M'sieu* Eiffel, that too much material is going into the base of the structure, too much attention is being given to supporting the first tier."

"We don't want another leaning tower, like the one in Pisa, do we?" David inquired and all senior engineers laughed dutifully.

"Mathematics have proved the stresses of the tower itself are its best support. As it is rendered there, the tapered needle shape will support itself. This has been worked out mathematically."

"We work from what experience has taught us here," David said in an exaggeratedly mild tone.

"Yes, sir. I know. But *M'sieu* Eiffel was kind enough to ask—"

"Oh, please, *M'sieu* Bunau-Varilla. Proceed."

"Well, I could work it out for you. It would take time, but in the first place, a masonry wall to give the tower support."

"Masonry, eh? Support for a 984-foot tower?" David's fists quivered on the table. "We prefer to work only as materials are developed, in use, and thus improved—"

"But progress is being made in understanding the strength, resilience, unit weight—all factors important in the equation which shows that available materials—"

"Do you have anything more to say about this structure? I assure you, what we don't need is a lecture on engineering materials."

"All right, sir. Then I have nothing more to say." Under the confusion caused by the sardonic applause led by David, Toine managed to expel a fit of coughing. He nudged Philippe, urging him to sit down. Philippe said, "Except, sir, that the stress resulting when a known force acts on a body of given shape and size has been worked out mathematically. You are not risking anything."

"You're suggesting that we build the tallest structure in the world on the basis of some mathematical probability? Against information known from experience?"

Philippe was silent.

David's face was almost as red as Montivillier's.

Apoplexy threatened at both ends of the table. David managed to speak with cold, belittling calm. "Is that all?"

"Yes, sir. That's all." A loud exhalation around the table. Philippe added, "Except—"

"Yes, Bunau-Varilla? Except what?"

"Except that those supports planned for the first tier of the tower are not only esthetically offensive. They are structurally unnecessary."

"My God," Eiffel said. "My words exactly. You recall, David, that I said all along—"

"You will recall, my dear Eiffel, that you bowed to the majority opinion of a panel of consulting engineers, the best minds. You recall that."

"I recall I never agreed with them," Eiffel said. "Or with you." He smiled down the table toward where Philippe stood alone, ashen, but defiant. He was damned if he was going on playing this game of *I'm stupid because I'm young and you're smart because you're old.*

David swore volubly. At last, he heeled around and jerked the prints from the easel. His hands whitened about the knuckles as he ripped the paper across and hurled it from him. "We will go back to the drawing board," he announced, fury making his voice quaver.

No one spoke. Eiffel nodded, and smiled at the stunned men.

"Excellent," Eiffel said. He nodded his head enthusiastically. "Excellent idea."

"I want all this worked out. All of it. Down to the least possible chance for error. The final possibility, do you understand me? I want it worked out not only so it meets with the approval of *M'sieu* Eiffel, but goddamn it, it's got to satisfy me. Is that clear? This meeting is adjourned."

Montivilliers sat at the table beside Philippe long after the room was deserted. He pushed the spittoon half across the floor with his boot. He sat, head back, gasping like a fish out of water, while with one hand he clutched at Philippe's arm. At last, he whispered. "Jesus, Philippe. Why can't you learn to keep your mouth shut?"

"Because I don't intend to choke to death from fear of expressing myself."

"Oh, Christ. They'll sack you now, for sure."

"For what? For thinking? For speaking the truth?"

Toine looked ready to cry. "For rocking the boat. Depuits et David will tolerate almost anything else."

$\lceil 3 \rceil$

With Antoine Montivilliers at his heels, Philippe stepped into the early evening chill outside the offices of Depuits and David. Around him, crowds exited hastily in the dinner-hour rush. He loitered at the entrance until Toine chose a course, then he set off, walking swiftly in the opposite direction, ready to explode with rage against all authority. The hell with them, what he needed was a good rousing roll in the hay.

An urchin on the corner hawked newspapers. Philippe bought a late edition and walked slowly along the busy avenue. He read the latest dispatch on the Isthmus of Panama, finding in it a small release for the passions seething inside him.

Another landslide had destroyed all progress hacked out by the Canal Company in the past six months and caused a loss of heavy machinery estimated in the millions of francs. Damn! It was a national disgrace. His restlessness intensified and his impatience mounted. There was only one quick way to erase all this from his mind.

A closed hack pulled in at the curb. He stepped into it and found it redolent of perfume from a previous occu-

26

pant. He gave the driver the address and sank back against the seat rest, thinking ahead to Anne-Margot's bed.

Later, after she had settled a small matter of five hundred francs which were urgently required to settle accounts with that horrible ogre of a greengrocer from the corner, Anne-Margot put the money Philippe gave her into a teapot and trained her total attention to the needs of his body.

She was a healthy peasant of a Gallic girl, full in the breasts and rounded in the hips. She confessed she'd been initiated, in her eleventh year, to the wonders of physical encounter, by an obliging uncle who neglected no facet of her biological education. By the time she was thirteen, he swore he had never been nursed more voluptuously by the finest whores of Paris.

Anne-Margot pressed Philippe back among the scented cushions on her downy sheets and slowly removed each article of his clothing, kissing and licking him wetly as she bared his flesh to her avid gaze.

"You are so beautiful," she whispered. "Do you know how beautiful you are?"

"Don't talk so much," he teased.

She laughed up at him. "You have deeply missed your Anne-Margot today, yes?"

"Let me show you."

When he stretched naked across her bed, she inventoried his slender body, the cablelike muscles, the hairy chest, the athletically trim hips, the long legs and the heated youthful glow of his flesh. Her eyes glittered as she moistened her lips with the tip of her tongue. "So nice," she whispered. "So nice, so rough, so rugged. So hairy like a young bear."

Her eyes devoured him. "I want to *feel* you inside me," she said, "then I want it in my mouth, in my throat. I want to taste you, to drink you, to lose not a drop."

"I don't think we can start an argument that way," he said, his hands moving roughly in her hair, about her ears, upon her throat.

She touched at the dark brown hair growing to a widow's peak at his forehead, the classic line of his profile, the jutting strength of his chin.

"So perfect," she kept whispering, like an incantation. "So strong. So beautiful. You *are* beautiful, *mon chéri*."

She drew her moist, heated lips along his cheeks, across his throat, to the dampness of the black hair matting his chest. Her lips found his nipples. She nuzzled them until he bit his own underlip in a torment of ecstasy. She moved her mouth tantalizingly along the muscles of his chest to the flat planes of his belly and down, down.

She left him drained, as if he had lain with a hundred succubi and not just one. He lay for some moments watching her when she drifted down on her back in complete exhaustion. He smiled. She slept with her mouth parted, making weary little puffing sounds. He let his gaze revisit the pleasant escarpment of her full breasts, the pink mound of her stomach, the dark triangle at her thighs.

Then, feeling renewed and invigorated, he got up, dressed, and gently kissed the nipple of her left breast.

Anne-Margot stirred deep within the warm confines of exhausted sleep. She whispered, "When you wake up, all hard, we'll really get down to making love, eh, *chéri?*"

He had already put her out of his mind as he strode the narrow walkway that led him along the boulevard, across an arched bridge, through one of the ancient city gates and into his own short side street.

Whistling a mindless little love tune under his breath, he removed his hat, feeling the wind drying his sweat-dampened hair. He yawned, listening to remote laughter wafted from the *caboulot* across the narrow street. The bistro remained crowded until curfew and beyond. A *poule* strolled past, smiled, and for a moment revived his mistress in his mind.

He was content with this arrangement with Anne-Margot. Often, she pleaded to be permitted to move into this apartment on the Isle St. Louis with him, promising to serve him as well as cook and housekeeper as she now serviced him in her bed. But he only laughed and shook his head. His mother would go into mourning if she found a girl like Anne-Margot sharing his pension.

He grinned ruefully. He himself would go into decline

if he lived caged in the same apartment with Anne-Margot for more than two or three brief hours a day. If he truly loved her, she said, he would want her where he could watch her. Every girl of her acquaintance had a jealous lover—they were jealous because they loved so passionately it dróve them mad, the thought of other men in their sweetheart's arms.

It had never occurred to him to work up the least twinge of jealousy. He simply did not care. There was a great deal to Anne-Margot, sexually speaking. One man. Ten men. One would never know unless she told. No, any risks of losing her were outweighed by the convenience of going to her when he needed her and then walking out when it pleased him.

The existence was ideal as it was, and he didn't care to change it. It was pleasant. Nothing permanent, of course. But, for the present, he was quite satisfied. He had Anne-Margot where he wanted her and, unfortunately for any plans of hers, she was *never* going to get him where *she* wanted him—under her thumb. He laughed, bounding up the stone steps to the courtyard entrance gateway.

Someone stepped from the darkness of the small court. It was as if a shadow emerged from a shadow. It was also upsetting, as if someone had been waiting for a long time.

"Philippe."

Claude-Bruce Grabralet stepped into the vague light from the street lamp. He graced Philippe with his most disarming smile. "Oh," Grabralet said. "We meet again."

[4]

Philippe stared at the député across the small table. The sounds of the crowd in the neighborhood bistro lapped at them like a tide at ebb on a shore.

Philippe could not pretend with Claude-Bruce that this was an accidental meeting. He recalled the frightened look in Grabralet's face when they had first met and exchanged a few public words in the courtyard. He was puzzled and disturbed by this overt display of friendship. Somehow he still felt his initial aversion to the man, though he could not explain why, for he found the young politician cultured and of a noble family of the *ancien régime*. Grabralet was extraordinarily handsome—too comely, really—with long sooty lashes and fine lips. He was a modern-day aristocrat, with the sharply hewn features of the patrician and the slender graceful body of a ballet dancer.

After a moment, Claude-Bruce murmured with a sardonic smile, "One hears you sometimes take the walk in the field, that you hotheadedly defend your honor against aspersion?"

"Is that what you hear?"

Grabralet laughed. "Not really. I was merely trying to

see what reaction I might draw from you. No, I did hear that the young fool de Fecame called you out, and that you shot at the sky when you could have killed him."

"My God. How things get around."

"De Fecame is a menace. His wife is a menace. They will keep on until some innocent man is killed."

Philippe sipped his wine. "I wasn't all that innocent."

"Yvette de Fecame is quite famous in Paris, Philippe. You don't have to apologize."

"No apology intended."

Claude-Bruce smiled. "What other interests do you have, Philippe, except dueling pistols? Do you like sailing?"

Philippe nodded. "I was a summer sailor all during my boyhood. We used to spend our summers at the seashore. During the winter we were a long way from the sea, but near the Seine. I looked forward to the spring and the small catboats. I've always loved boats and the sea."

"As have I. How about riding? Do you like horses?"

Philippe shrugged. "I gave up riding horses when I discovered the whores of Paris."

"Is that where you have been all evening?"

Philippe glanced up. It was none of Grabralet's damned busisness where he had been and he didn't bother answering.

Claude-Bruce smiled and gazed at Philippe who felt the prickling of mild discomfort under the caress of those doelike eyes. He shrugged his jacket up on his shouders.

Grabralet said, "I suppose women find you terribly attractive."

This appeared to call for no reply and Philippe made none. He poured chablis for both of them. If there were something Grabralet wanted, why the devil didn't the fellow get to it?

The silence stretched so thin between them that Philippe felt a twinge of guilt. The man was trying to be neighborly. It was not his fault that Philippe had experienced an initial distaste for him. Philippe spoke. "You asked about my interests. I'll tell you my true interests. I get my daily laughter reading about old de Lesseps and that infernal canal. Do you know anything of this massive fraud?"

Claude-Bruce sat forward, his face brightening. "Fraud? How can you call it a fraud? The old Lion of the Suez, in his final years—"

"In his dotage—"

"—hacking a canal from that torrid earth! If ever there were a project worthy of a man's blood and guts and energy and mental capacities! Such a project as only a de Lesseps could undertake! Why, to me there is music in the very name! De Lesseps. God, what a name, what a legend. Holy Mary, what a magnificent man."

"God only knows how old he is."

"But you see, despite his great age, de Lesseps brings greater zeal to this project than even he expended—in his youth!—upon the Suez. I admit, the obstacles are fearful."

"Insurmountable is a good word."

Claude-Bruce sighed. "It is coincidence that you find the project of keen interest."

"I said a great source of humor."

"I have been assigned to serve—in a modest way, of course—on the Parliamentary Committee of Eleven. This is an oversight commission charged with monitoring the canal program and keeping the government abreast of its accomplishments or failures."

"You'll need reams for its failures." Philippe laughed.

"You underestimate the old Lion."

"They are pouring the nation's resources into that ditch. As fast as they dig, the porous soil caves in upon itself. Malaria is killing more laborers down there than soldiers who died in the Prussian war."

"Things are bad."

"They are badly planned. They have begun to dig at least five years before they are ready. The Old Lion, as you call him, thinks he's back in the Suez. Well, he's not. This calls for a new approach, new machinery, new thinking."

"Why aren't you with them?" Claude-Bruce asked.

"I don't care for failures, and this is a doomed project."

"God knows I wish I had something to offer."

"You're joking."

"I was never more serious, *mon cher*. To help old de Lesseps make his most fantastic, incredible dream come true. Ten years of my life? Twenty years? What would it matter? What sacrifice would be too great?"

"You talk as if there were some chance. Going down there is a good way to die, horribly. Hundreds of the ablest who've gone with such high hopes are now dead of yellow fever, malaria, dysentery, and jungle rot."

"I admit there are problems, but, *m'sieu,* there is also old de Lesseps," responded Grabralet. "Surely, you don't class de Lesseps as a crooked promoter?"

Philippe shrugged. "Many do. Many in high places. Others say he is only a dupe, a figurehead, a very old man who is misled by his own eagerness to add to his glory as the builder of the Suez Canal. Perhaps this is nearer the truth."

"I can't believe it. I admit our commission finds there has been waste of materials by the Canal Company—and some demonstrable dishonesty among its promoters. But not one drop of this scandal reaches de Lesseps."

"Still, if you people were smart you would refuse to pour another cent down that sinkhole."

"A canal across the Isthmus would be the most magnificent accomplishment of this century," Grabralet said.

"If it were not an impossible task. My dear Grabralet, surely I don't have to tell you that tropical disease—malaria alone, for which there is no known cure—is decimating the program, making it impossible, even if the engineers had tools and machinery huge enough for so vast a project."

Now, Philippe was fully engaged in the conversation. He and Claude-Bruce were arguing as loudly as any of the grocers, bakers or laborers at the other tables. They were among the last to leave the bistro. Philippe found himself too excited and too drunk to sleep.

His mind spun with all the information Grabralet had imparted. As the wine flowed and state secrets were divulged, Grabralet's reticence evaporated and he spoke with confidence, enthusiasm and almost reverential adulation for de Lesseps. As a member of the oversight commission, Grabralet was in the center of the controversy. He insisted that somehow de Lesseps would succeed, against all odds, against the greed that had infected many of the Company underlings.

Grabralet had spoken with great sadness, yet terrible indignation. "We have seen the errors into which greed and corruption have led the United States in its dealings with Colombia, with Great Britain, with anyone concerned in the economics of that part of the world, and now we are seeing what greed can do to Frenchmen."

"The whole program is fraud and greed, and that goes all the way to the top," Philippe said.

"How can you call it greed that men, inspired by de Lesseps, go there and die?"

Philippe laughed. "The greedy do not go there, my friend, nor do they die, except from bloated guts. No, my great young deputy, there is too much flowery talk of accomplishment—to the glory of France, for God's sake—as if huge profit played no part. Only patriotism."

"You are wrong, *mon cher*. There is patriotism."

"There is patriotism in every public address by de Lesseps, and they continue spending money as if it were water. Millions of francs already washed away in that ditch. And millions upon millions more will follow before they are through, unless someone has the guts and strength to stop them. It is a nightmare."

"And yet, despite all obstacles, all opposition, all controversy, old de Lesseps strides forward. He will not stop. He will not be stopped. Doesn't this inspire you at all?"

"Not at all. The engineering is so poor that I want to vomit. De Lesseps is squandering the savings of the Republic, just as we're trying to recover from the war. He could bankrupt the nation. But when rational men try to tell de Lesseps this, what does our Old Lion do? He launches into impassioned diatribes about the glory of France. God knows, I am not inspired at all. I am appalled. I am infuriated that he is permitted to continue this impossible undertaking."

"The canal will be built. France must build it."

"Oh, Christ."

Lying on his bed now, remembering, Philippe smiled.

At least he'd put aside his early aversion for his young neighbor. Now he even looked forward to long debates with Grabralet. Maybe if he could make even one deputy see the truth about that fraudulent canal program, they might rise up and close the thing down before the republic itself collapsed.

Yet he knew what Grabralet's answer would be. Old de Lesseps had so many detractors, so many enemies in high places, he needed strong and vigorous defenders, men who could make that desperate project a success despite all the terrible odds.

Philippe yawned. It was well past midnight. He had to sleep or the day would be lost at the office. But when he closed his eyes, he saw only mudslides, inadequate machinery, men falling dead of the yellow jack. He saw the jackals baying at de Lesseps' heels and the Old Lion fighting them off, as alone and lonely as Prometheus himself, with only slender young deputies like Claude-Bruce Grabralet to defend him against his enemies. The Old Lion was worse off than he knew.

Then, into his consciousness seeped a sound he would have sworn he had never heard before, and yet there was a haunting, familiarity about it. It was a distant sobbing, the saddest sound Philippe had ever heard in his life. He wanted to weep when he heard it. Never had there been such crying of heartbreak.

He sat up in bed and listened. The sound seemed to come from the walls themselves, as if this old house wept for someone or something lost in the irrecoverable past. No, it wasn't coming from inside the house. Somewhere nearby, someone was crying. The sobbing was muffled, as if the cries were buried in a pillow, but they penetrated his room, permeated it, engulfed it.

He listened until the weeping stopped, and when the heartbroken sobs had faded in forlorn gasps. He was stunned at the depths of silence into which he was hurtled. It was as if a vast blanket of stifling quiet settled over the house, the courtyard, the island, the sleeping city.

He lay, shattered emotionally. He stared, waiting and wide-eyed, at the somber shadows across the ceiling, sleepless and deeply troubled.

[5]

Philippe stood at the casement window of his bedroom for a long time in the chill of first daylight. His breath smoked from his lips, his heart pounded oddly as he considered the weeping, anguished woman whose muffled sobs had disturbed and troubled him in the night. Where was she? Who was she? For what did she weep in the darkest hours before dawn?

Everything looked so fresh and tranquil in the sunlight. The stone-paved courtyard, the small gurgling fountain, the beds of flowers, the clipped angles of buildings, and shard of sky, with only the memory of last night to mark the moment his life was utterly changed.

He turned away and tried to forget. He dressed, shaved, drank his coffee and glanced through the *Tribune*. He went out and crossed the courtyard, not at all astonished to see Claude-Bruce Grabralet emerge from the foyer across the court.

"See you this evening, *mon ami*," Claude-Bruce called out.

"Why not?"

The days passed swiftly, as if the whole world had boarded a doomed runaway express on which everybody

36

laughed too much, drank too much and carefully ignored the truth. There was no engineer and they thundered toward tragedy. Philippe admitted this was a melodramatic idea, but he also had come to believe that time speeded up when trouble lay ahead, as if the gods couldn't wait to watch you squirm.

Each day he trudged reluctantly to work in an office where the tensions were almost tangible. By six he was drawn fine, ready to explode. He hurried off to Anne-Margot, who seemed always armed with sensual new weaponry with which to overwhelm, subdue and pacify him. Then home to find Claude-Bruce waiting with fresh gossip from the parliament, the canal, the oversight commission. And finally to troubled sleep, filled with the sounds of muffled sobbing from across the courtyard. These two things filled his mind, those desperate night sounds, and the lively debates with Claude-Bruce.

Philippe had to admit there was something engaging, even endearing about the warm young *député*. Grabralet knew how to attract and influence people. Philippe could almost see Claude-Bruce as the president of the Republic one of these days. He was too young, of course, but time would remedy that flaw, and in politics nothing was more important than an ingratiating manner, a smooth, unyielding smile and a mellifluent voice. Claude-Bruce might well make it to the President's palace.

Grabralet truly believed de Lesseps a man worthy of adulation, respect and support. Even when he admitted the oversight commission found proof of fraud in the machinations of de Lessep's canal company, he continued to defend the magnificent Old Lion. Philippe could not move him from his position, bend him from his admiration. They talked, in Philippe's apartment now, many nights well past midnight, shouting, declaiming and ending in laughter.

Philippe was enormously amused at the idea of two strong-willed men, each trying to convert the other to his viewpoint. He struggled to show Grabralet that fraud and greed, not patriotism, motivated the Interoceanique officials, including de Lesseps himself. Grabralet as passionately attempted to prove that de Lesseps was too honorable, too honest, too dedicated and too old to want to defraud *anybody*, least of all the nation to which he had devoted his entire adult life. De Lesseps was not only immortal, Grabralet declared, but might even yet succeed in an impossible task.

"Impossible in itself means it cannot be done," Philippe reminded him. "Why can't you see the truth?"

"Oh? You have the truth?"

"I think so. I have now only to convince you."

Grabralet laughed, shaking his head. "My old grandmother always said, *mon cher:* who is convinced against his will is of the same opinion still. Why don't you admit I'm right?"

"Why don't you go to hell? Even a politician ought to be able to smell the deceit immersed in that last refuge of scoundrels, patriotism."

"Are we then reduced to quoting clichés at each other?"

"You may be quoting, I'm yelling."

They laughed and drank more wine.

Grabralet's ingrained reserve, no matter how much he attempted to follow its cautious dictates, quickly melted away under the warmth of their mutual laughter. "How happy I am," Grabralet often said, "to have a man near my own age in this courtyard. Some one, dear friend, with whom I can forget the—" he shrugged, "unpleasant aspects of my life. I know I am here too much. I talk too much, drink too much. Yet, this is the happiest time of my day."

For the next few weeks, he and Claude-Bruce were often together in the evenings. Grabralet made it a habit to drop in to Philippe's apartment late, after Philippe returned yawning from Anne-Margot. Anne-Margot, the minx, she knew ways to rouse a man from the dead! Some nights Philippe devoutly wished his neighbor in the hole beyond hell, but Claude-Bruce looked forward in anticipation to these visits; often he brought wine and fancy cheeses; he seemed to have no other interests outside the parliament and his politics. Philippe recalled that Claude-Bruce had declared he and his wife were blessed with many friends, but Philippe was aware of few callers in the old house across the way. Madame Grabralet's parents, Monsieur and Madame Grenet, came with some regularity. They were a haughty couple whom Philippe sometimes glimpsed hurrying across the courtyard, looking as if they smelled something unpleasant.

Once in a while he encountered the willowy young maid of Madame Grabralet. The girl's name was Fanny LeBeau. She crept tautly across the courtyard, as if in eternal terror of rapists lurking in every shadow. She almost wept when Philippe spoke to her at the gate, racing past him as if trying to press herself into the walls to escape him, her chalky, milk-white face ready to shatter, her thin slash of red mouth poised to scream. He wondered that even a girl of Fanny's meager education could dwell so long in Paris and remain so naïve.

As to Madame Grabralet, she remained invisible. Though occasionally Claude-Bruce mentioned Madelon, Philippe never met her nor even glimpsed her as far as he knew. He became curious about her. Was Claude-Bruce so in love, or so jealous, that he kept his Madelon a prisoner in their home?

But Philippe had his own problems; he didn't have time to wonder about the young couple across the courtyard. Nothing went well at Depuits et David. Anne-Margot began again to importune him to permit her to share his apartment. And each night he was haunted by the heartbroken sobbing in the gloom.

His friendship with Claude-Bruce became his main pleasure. Sometimes, in the late afternoon, Claude-Bruce would bring out his swords and they would fence in the courtyard. Claude-Bruce had been a master of the *epées* in the university, but Philippe was taller, his arms longer, his recklessness ample compensation for Grabralet's superior knowledge and technique.

They fought with their rapiers all over the courtyard, laughing, shouting, taunting, challenging. They leapt acrobatically across stone benches, over boxed plants, up on the fountain walls. Neighbors gathered to watch from stoops, doors and windows; passersby congregated at the stone pillars by the gates. Only one person in that small cosmos never came out to watch: Madame Grabralet.

Philippe found it unusual that Claude-Bruce never discussed any woman except Madelon. Recently he had spoken of her great beauty, but he never once boasted of his prowess with *les femmes*. Where most of the young men Philippe had known at the Ecole Polytechnique spent most of their waking hours talking, planning or boasting about their females, Claude-Bruce never talked about women. One night, Philippe suggested that Claude-Bruce might, if he cared to, accompany him to Anne-Margot's apartment. "Anne-Margot has a pretty little friend who lives on the same floor. If ever a woman would please you, I'm sure little Rose would do it."

Grabralet's refusal was curt. Then he managed a brief smile. "You forget, Philippe, I am not a bachelor like you. I *am* married, you know."

"Married, yes, but not buried."

"Ah, but I have such a fine beautiful wife. I am quite satisfied, you see." Claude-Bruce glanced at the old Swiss clock against Philippe's wall. He shook his head. "Almost one. Here I've kept you up half the night. Madelon will be exasperated with me again. She says I must bore you, and, by the way, she has invited you to dinner on Tuesday next. She says she will not take no for an answer."

Philippe only laughed. "I don't know where I'll be Tuesday."

Claude-Bruce paused at the door. "It is no use to refuse. Madelon says she will send you a formal invitation."

Exhausted, Philippe undressed as he staggered into his bedroom. Too much wine again tonight, up too late. He fell naked across his bed and slept at once, face down.

He wakened in the deepest darkness, chilled to the bone. He got up from the mattress and located his nightshirt without lighting a lamp. Still he shuddered with cold, his teeth chattered. He found his silk bathrobe and tied it at the waist.

He huddled for a moment on the side of the bed. He hugged his arms across his chest. Then he heard it—the remote mewling sound of muffled weeping.

He got up from the bed and walked to the window. He stood, with the night chill penetrating him to the bone, listening.

It was out there somewhere, somewhere in the darkness. The sound would fade, and then increase faintly in volume, as false dawn hurled pink rims around the cornices of the buildings. He searched the courtyard.

He saw her. His eyes widened and he stared, incredulous. The woman wore a pale yellow peignoir with a cape thrown over it and she sat huddled on one of the stone benches beside the small fountain.

Philippe backed away from the window. His heart hammering, he shoved his feet into slippers. He ran across the apartment, flung open the door, and went swiftly down the stairwell.

He forced himself to move cautiously, letting himself out the foyer door. He did not want to frighten her away. He had to know who she was—this nocturnal woman who broke his sleep and his heart with her weeping.

He stayed close to the building, deep in the shadows as long as he could. When he was within a few feet of where the woman sagged, hands pressed against her face, a light suddenly illumined the foyer of the mansion across the court.

The woman lunged upward to her feet at the exact instant Philippe stepped from the shadows. For a moment they stood, in tableau, staring at each other.

Philippe's heart lurched and seemed to break its moorings. His belly went empty. She was the most beautiful woman he had ever seen.

She tilted her head slightly, and diffused light lowered across her features. Even in this wan glow, Philippe thrilled at the chiseled perfection of her profile; her face was etched, an olive-tinted cameo against the framing of autumnal golden hair.

He drank in huge draughts of her beauty, as a man dying of thirst might slake his needs. The curved arc of her brow, violet depths of her eyes, the finely sculptured rise of delicate cheekbones, the full, lustrous red mouth and daintily rounded chin. He had never encountered such gentle beauty before. Who was she? God knew, he had to have that answer! Did she live in this court, or did she flee some distant cruelty hoping to suffer here unheard?

He was aware he had not breathed. His chest ached, his throat burned. In this murky glow, he recognized her now, the one woman he wanted above all others. Overpowering desire burned through the pity he felt for her. This shock of recognition had charged through him at his first glimpse, and it was stronger than ever now. Damn him! What was wrong with him? A young girl wept in a sorrow too deep to be repressed or concealed and he stood wanting her, because despite her melancholy she was incredibly beautiful, alluring. He did want her. She would haunt him forever.

She had stood immobile. Now she stirred, looking around as if trapped.

"Who are you?" he whispered. "What's your name? What's the matter?"

She gazed at him, face taut, stricken. She looked so slender, so dainty, so fragile. She only shook her head, backing away.

"Wait," he begged. "Please. I didn't mean to frighten you. I want to help. I only want to help."

She only shook her head. Suddenly, she spun around and ran into the shadows across the court.

He strode after her, taking long steps, his arms outflung. Then he slowed. He took another step forward and stopped, feeling disconsolate. She had disappeared into the last blocks of darkness, even the sound of her running footsteps was gone. Philippe stood unmoving, afraid, now that she was gone, that it was all part of an old nightmare or dream, that he had not really seen her at all.

[6]

Someone rapped lightly on Philippe's locked door, but he remained sprawled in an easy chair, stockinged feet propped up by the fire waiting for the intruder to go away. He didn't want to talk with anyone. Somehow, he had struggled through a hellish day. He did not know how he had made it. The reality of the office receded, diffused against images of the woman crying in the dawn, running away from him, disappearing. It had been unbearable when her heartbroken sobs had unsettled him in the night. It was infinitely worse now knowing how lovely she was, how desperate and lonely, how fearfully she needed someone. The loveliest creature he'd ever encountered.

The rainy afternoon had dragged interminably. Philippe returned from his office directly to his apartment. He did not detour via Anne-Margot's place, though he recognized she would weep hysterically in her accusations and self-abasement the next time he saw her. He was too disconsolate to submit to her sweet violences. He asked nothing more than to lie here with his jagged thoughts, his eyes closed and a large decanter of wine to sustain him.

That faint yet determined tapping continued. Whoever

it was, was female; the timid touch too frail for any masculine fist. It suddenly occurred to him it might be the weeping girl. What if she had come to explain her nocturnal anguish, to plead for his help in some villainous situation?

He found his silk robe, slipped it on and secured its belt at his waist. He walked across the parlor to the corridor door, panting as if he'd run a mile. With all his heart he hoped it was the lovely vision from the courtyard; with all his reason, he prayed it was not.

"You!" he whispered. He stared in dismay at Fanny LeBeau's slug-white face, the elevated black brows, the enormous staring eyes, the thin body in maid's uniform apron and dust cap. One might have laughed at this unexpected comic valentine, but he had no laughter in him. "What do you want?"

Fanny's teeth chattered, her lips trembled. She stood, like a hummingbird poised for flight. "Oh, please, sir," she whimpered in abject terror. "I didn't like to bother you."

"Then why did you? Why did you keep banging on my door?"

Fanny looked as if she might faint. "My mistress sent me. We knew you were in. We saw you come home. She insisted that I come, sir."

Curiosity drove everything else from his thoughts. "Madame Grabralet saw me come in? She sent you?"

"Yes, sir. I'd never have come, but she sent me. Indeed she sent me, sir."

"Why?"

"This," Fanny blurted the word. She thrust out a gray envelope, and when he reached out to take it, Fanny jerked back her hand to avoid any contact. She was already retreating, backing away toward the stairs.

"Wait a minute," he ordered.

Fanny managed to nod, swallowing with difficulty and pressing her knotted fists tightly against her stomach. Philippe went to his wallet, extracted a ten-franc note and offered it to her. "Oh, no, sir, I couldn't take this."

"Why not?"

"I just couldn't, sir. I couldn't take money from a strange man."

"You better learn to take money from strange men. It's easy income sometimes. Take it, Fanny. Buy yourself a new *chapeau.*" He forced a smile. "You showed great courage, coming all this way from the next house, actually knocking on my door."

"Yes, sir." She nodded, agreeing with this estimate. It had required great courage. She reached out trembling fingers, took the ten-franc note and pressed it into a wad in her fist. Then she backed away to the newel post and practically dissolved behind it.

He stood for a long time with the note, a perfumed correspondence from the wife of Claude-Bruce. Then carefully, he opened the flap, removed the note and read:

My dear neighbor, I write now to invite you to dinner Tuesday next at seven o'clock. I do pray you will not disappoint us. If you do not come, you will indeed greatly inconvenience me, and I have verily gone to vast expense to entertain you, the cost of meat rising beyond reason. Please, Madelon G.

Tuesday dawned and Philippe watched the rising sun paint clouds of orange, purple and cerise across the roof of heaven. For the past several nights no anguished weeping had broken through his sleep. Still, he had thought almost constantly of the beautiful apparition from the courtyard. His only escape from his feelings of love and longing had come in his obsession with the dispatches from Panama. As the day dragged on, he found new confirmation for his doubts about this disastrous project. Unseasonal tropical storms had washed heavy equipment and hapless laborers into the sea. The dreaded plagues of malaria and yellow fever killed off the strongest men as if they were flies. Now, checking the Swiss clock as he dressed for the evening, Philippe saw minutes ticking away, each etched full-season in the scheme of time.

At seven, he rang the bell of the house where the Grabralets lived. Fanny LeBeau opened the door and announced his name in a tremulous, fluting voice.

Claude-Bruce came bounding from the double doorway of the formal parlor, his arms extended.

"Philippe, *mon cher.*" Claude-Bruce embraced him. "How good to have you in my home at last."

"I got an official summons."

Claude-Bruce laughed. With an arm about Philippe, he convoyed him through the parlor to a small bar where cheese, condiments and extravagant hors-d'oeuvres were appetizingly displayed. He poured Philippe a drink, brimming the glass. "I don't have to inquire your favorite, after all this time, eh, dear friend?"

Accepting the cognac, Philippe looked around in awe. Though his grandparents' estate at Argenteuil was imposing, this interior decor glittered with an elegance that seemed to belong to the age of Louis XIV—more splendid than habitable.

A brilliant chandelier dominated and illumined the room. A spinet rack held sheet music. The elaborately carved and brocaded furniture exemplified cultivated taste and profligate purse. The place looked lovely, but Philippe felt ill at ease.

Claude-Bruce spoke. "I believe there is coming up an event of extraordinary interest to you, Philippe. On Tuesday, Viscount de Lesseps and his son Charles appear before the *Senat*. I have arranged for you to attend as my guest."

"Thank you. That's most thoughtful."

"I want to please you, Philippe. If I can."

Embarrassed, Philippe glanced toward the doorways, the polished foyer, the wide and silent stairways. He was spared having to answer by the appearance of Madame Grabralet. Relief fled through him, a relief that changed quickly to disbelief, and then to shock.

He stood up, aware that Claude-Bruce came slowly to his own feet beside him. Philippe stared at Madelon Grabralet. He shook his head, feeling as if he'd been struck brutally in the solar plexus. He wanted to laugh, to cry, to yell out in despair and protest. He was helpless to speak at all, powerless to move.

She paused in the doorway, an incredible vision. Her lovely face tinted a delicate red, her violet eyes, for one

46

instant, swirled with panic. It was she! The woman sobbing in the night was Madelon Grabralet.

He wanted to run to her, to reassure her, to touch her, to kiss the fabric of her gown, to let her know she need never cry in the night again. He did not move.

Claude-Bruce extended his slight, manicured hand to her and Madelon walked toward them.

She was so slender, so dainty, so fragile. The ice-blue evening gown she wore flowed about her ankles, and her pointed slippers winked from beneath its hem. The bodice of her gown, with a touch of lace, cut low across the alabaster rise of her breasts. He raised his eyes and found her smiling, composed, at ease.

Through the surflike pounding of blood in his temples he heard Claude-Bruce making introductions. Philippe was aware he presented a sorry, awkward sight, but he could not help his emotion. "Why, you—you are Madelon," he murmured.

"I must be." Her musical voice teased him. "I know I've heard that name somewhere. And you—at last—the brilliant Philippe Jean Bunau-Varilla, of whom I have heard so much, and seen so little."

He sagged, stunned, unable to recover. His mind spun with it, her weeping, her anguish, her identity! The wife of Claude-Bruce Grabralet. Sobbing, heartbroken in the night. Now, smiling, as if no care touched her spirit. "Oh, my God," he whispered.

"Philippe," Claude-Bruce grasped his arm. "Are you all right?"

Why should he lie? Why should he even try to lie? He would never be *all right* again. He had strode through life to this moment anticipating the best, accepting the cream of everything as his right if not his heritage. And all the time the malicious fates had been devising this moment.

He felt sick. He wanted to cry out in protest. It was wrong. All wrong. Not fair. For he knew in that instant, as he'd felt from the first moment he beheld her fleetingly in the courtyard, she was the one woman he wanted above all others. He knew without equivocation, this woman had to be his! Wars had been fought, plagues endured, ships built and cities raised so that he and Madelon could encounter one another in a brilliantly lit old villa on a Paris side street. It had to be that way. There was no other explanation for the evolution of man on this whirling globe.

Now that he had found her, he could not walk away and forget her. Here was the only woman he would ever want for his own. No concubine, no mistress, no other female would ever please him again. He knew it as he knew his heartbeat and the breath of life. Without Madelon Grabralet his life held no meaning, no promise. No matter what great achievements he accomplished, no matter what rewards he earned, or what good fortune was heaped upon him, life would be empty for him if Madelon were not by his side.

He wanted to howl in outrage. For he could never have her. Here was fate's cruelest jest of all! At night, she lay only a few yards from him in the darkness. He heard her anguished tears. He shared her heartbreak. But there was a wall between them. He had a sudden and terrible premonition: there would always be walls between him and Madelon Grabralet.

He moved his gaze from her face. Well, the puzzle, as to why Grabralet had been so pained at meeting him that morning after Madelon's heartbroken sobbing had wakened him, was now plainly and fully answered.

No wonder Claude-Bruce had hesitated, glancing around like a frightened rabbit, wanting to retreat when first they met. He must have wondered how much Philippe had heard in the deep night silence across that narrow courtyard.

Claude-Bruce was speaking. "May I pour wine for you, Madelon?"

"Make it cognac, Claude-Bruce. I want to laugh. I want to have fun. After all, *chéri,* how often does a girl get to dine with the two handsomest men of the Western world?"

She was the perfect hostess—gracious, vivacious, interested, with precisely the quality of reserve to be maddening. She appeared forever just out of reach, like a butterfly whose very elusiveness makes the fingers covetous.

At the dining table, she spoke lightly of the theater—a new production of *La Dame aux Camélias*. "Of course, Dumas *fils*'s play is at least twenty years old, yet it is still the finest production of the season—and I've seen them all! It still plays well, as if it is ageless, don't you think? It may prove to be one of those tragedies which go on and on, loving selflessly, coughing helplessly and dying nobly."

Her laughter rang with the pure clarity of silver against crystal. The more enchanting she became, and she was almost giddy after three cognacs, the more dour Philippe felt, heavy-handed, stupid, humorless, a clod.

The courses came, a crystal clear soup with flecks of celery, fish lightly golden and spicy, and they were removed. Philippe remained numb, insensitive to taste or quality.

His throat felt constricted. He barely touched his food, while across the bright table, Madelon ate hungrily and with relish. He heard her chatting about the facelifting the poor city was undergoing. Wasn't it shameful, the way they ripped out the last vestiges of the old fortifications which had made Paris unique, a walled city?

Claude-Bruce laughed indulgently. "The Republic has learned, my dear, that walls don't keep an enemy out. Those new, wide boulevards they're building will be a hundred times more esthetically pleasing, and a thousand times easier to police."

"Still, it's shameful," Madelon insisted. "Don't you agree it's shameful to destroy the heritage of our lovely city, *M'sieu* Bunau-Varilla?"

"God knows," Philippe said.

[7]

Madelon Grabralet slept well that night but Philippe did not sleep at all.

He lay, sleepless, upon his rumpled bed, restless and hot-eyed. He heard every cough and every rattle of the big Swiss clock. He held his breath and listened for some sound of Madelon across the narrow courtyard. There was none. It seemed another jest of the demonic gods that once all tranquility was destroyed in the life of Philippe Bunau-Varilla, then quiet could settle upon the chambers of his neighbors.

By daybreak, Philippe had reached only one conclusion. He would break off any relationship with Claude-Bruce Grabralet. There was too much he did not understand, too much he hated, too much he did not want to know of the intimate affairs across that courtyard. But for the moment, he could think little about the elegant politico— his mind churned with thoughts of Grabralet's wife. He wanted her as he had never wanted anything in his life.

Though he had actually been in her company only a few hours in time, they had shared weeks of sleepless nights, across that shallow canyon of the courtyard. He knew her agonies better than anyone else in the world. If she had known any happiness with Grabralet, he would know about that, too. Oh, he knew her far better than many men knew their wives of a decade.

He would go to see her. The hell with Grabralet. His heart pounded, palpitating at the prospect of being near Madelon, sitting on a couch beside her, touching her hand. Somehow, her husband would cease to exist, and he could drink in her beauty, if only for a little while. He could look at her, hear her voice, woo her laughter. He could be near her. Every part of him longed for her.

And then the cold, muted voice of reason intruded and he faced the sobering truth whether he wanted to or not. To see Madelon at all was only to torment himself. She was not the type for a sordid hideaway romance; she was no Yvette de Fecame. Anyway, as incredible as it sounded in his own ears, this wasn't the way he wanted her. He wanted her in his arms, belonging only to him.

Yet the hard fact was that for him to remain near Madelon was to court scandal, perhaps tragedy. As his need for her burned whiter, as his desire erupted more fiercely, as his hatred for Claude-Bruce deepened, what fool thing might he do? He saw no chance for happiness, but rather every opportunity for catastrophe. This further torture Madelon didn't need. She already wept in the night.

He got out of bed and poured a cognac. He stood at his small window and stared through the darkness toward the Seine, toward infinity. He sipped the alcohol, feeling it burn his throat and his empty belly. There was every reason he should depart this place in all haste. He finished off his drink. He told himself he would clear out. This should have made him feel better, but it did not. He had to be near Madelon, should she call out to him, or need him. That day had to come. Madelon and Claude-Bruce were bitterly unhappy, mismated, and at terrible odds. She *would* need Philippe. He had to be near.

Damn it, how could he pretend friendship with a man who kept a young wife isolated, miserable and weeping into her pillow, while he strode about full of smiles and self-esteem? What brand of sadistic cruelty did Grabralet practice upon that fragile girl across the court? Why did she prowl during the night, sleepless and desolated, unable to stifle her sobs? How could Claude-Bruce Grabralet emerge each morning from that abode of bitter sadness, bright-faced and smiling?

Philippe shaved, bathed and dressed, filled with dread for the day ahead. He made coffee, brought in the newspaper and loaf of hot bread from the corridor. He ate without appetite, read without reaction an interview with Charles de Lesseps. On another day, Philippe would have responded with vigor. This morning he felt nothing but fatigue—a residue of sadness that pervaded his bedroom, his apartment, his life.

This morning he delayed, hoping that Grabralet would go off to the parliament so they would not have to meet in the courtyard. As he had been the last person Grabralet had wanted to encounter that first morning, so now he dreaded the prospect of his meeting with his neighbor. He took up his hat, and went out the door. But inevitability had assumed control of his existence.

Claude-Bruce exited his own door as Philippe crossed the courtyard toward the street. Claude-Bruce barely met his gaze. Well, thank God, the pretty bastard had the sensitivity to feel contrition.

"Bonjour, mon cher Philippe. Did you sleep well?" The beardless face flushed slightly.

"Yes, thank you." Philippe replied, and they went down the wide stone steps in silence. At last, as they reached the walk, Philippe said, "As to next Thursday, I won't be able to attend the de Lesseps hearing, after all. My mother—suddenly ill—I must go out to Argenteuil."

"I quite understand."

"Please express my gratitude to Madame Grabralet. She was most gracious last evening."

Claude-Bruce hesitated. The faint pretense of a smile disappeared completely, replaced with cold annoyance not directed at Philippe at all, but toward Grabralet's own wife. "It is not important," he said. "What she thinks—and whether she thinks at all—is not important."

Grabralet nodded his head almost curtly and strode away, slender shoulders straight and set rigidly, along the morning street. Shocked, Philippe hesitated a long moment on the lowest step, surrounded by early-day sounds, and stared after him, hating him, yet more puzzled and disturbed than ever.

"Oh my God, Philippe, Depuits wants to see you," Toine Montivilliers said, looking ready to cry. "I was afraid of this."

Just when he'd congratulated himself on having made it through one more day in the unnatural tensions of this office, the day was prolonged. When he'd fought off sleep with every throb of the clock, when he'd decided he had to clear Madelon Grabralet somehow from his mind, and forever, or throw over all the traces and carry her away forcibly, he was yanked back to the real world.

Philippe determined to face the senior partner defiantly. He walked slowly, crippled by fatigue and the tension which had intensified since Paul-Jacques David had torn up the prints on the Eiffel project. Now David scowled when they met accidentally in corridors or offices. All Philippe's work since that day had been triple-checked by a team of senior engineers. Still, if he were to be dismissed, an underling supervisor would have been assigned the task. Neither Depuits nor David ever bothered with details such as hiring or firing.

Outside Depuits' office, he pressed his hand along his temples, smoothing the slight curl of his hair. His fingers touched at his chin where a late-afternoon shadow of beard deepened. He checked his polished boots before he rapped on the door.

André, the thin, stoop-shouldered little man who served as Depuits' personal secretary, opened the door and motioned without speaking toward the inner depths of the sedately furnished office.

This niche was a new experience for Philippe—leather couch, deep book shelves, a massive framed portrait, ornate desk and judge's chair in which Depuits sat, checking his fat gold watch.

As if to reinforce Depuits' inquiry, a wall clock coughed and struggled drily, then slowly chimed a quarter to six. Depuits motioned Philippe to the least comfortable of the Louis XIV chairs placed near his desk. Obviously, the interview was to be brief. It had been twenty years since Depuits had been seen to remain in his office past six P.M.

Depuits pressed his pince-nez onto the bridge of his hawk nose and lowered his head, studying the young engineer as if he had never seen him before.

"Well, Bunau-Varilla, I hear you found fault with Paul-Jacques on the Eiffel project," Depuits said.

"If you want an apology, I'm afraid I have none."

Depuits' aged face almost crinkled into a smile. "I was young once myself," he said as if speaking to himself. "Full of vinegar. Well, I don't have to defend Paul-Jacques, do I? He's quite capable of taking care of himself. You see, he's a great man, but he forgets young engineers study a hundred things we never even heard about when we were at school. I dare say in sixty years, there will be a thousand new studies, none of which are even hinted at in the best engineering schools of the world today."

Philippe waited. After a moment, Depuits nodded. "You're bigger than I recalled, Bunau-Varilla. You're more the romantic novelist's image of the engineer than most of the men I deal with. Most of us are quite ordinary souls!" He laughed at his pleasantry. "I've learned to mistrust the superficial values of appearance."

Philippe felt somehow he should apologize for his six feet of slender height, his yard-wide shoulders and long legs. He merely smiled.

"Best engineer I ever worked with looked like an orangutan," Depuits said. "In fact, he still does. But if you tell Paul-Jacques David I said this, I'll not only deny it, I'll discharge you."

"Your secret is safe with me, sir." Philippe's spirits lifted slightly. Depuits could not have anything very unpleasant on his mind, or he would not broach such subjects in this light-hearted fashion. "As I said a moment ago, most of the engineers I deal with, most of them we employ here at Depuits et David, are content to move upward by rote, according to a routine established by this firm over the past thirty years—and if I do say it, quite successfully."

Philippe nodded. "I understand the rules, sir. I've tried to abide by them."

Depuits cleared his throat. "Yes. Well, really this won't take long. I won't waste your time. A little chat. That's all. One I've been meaning to initiate these months you've been with us. Yes. You've been on my mind. A talented young engineer, champing at the bit."

"You're most kind, sir."

"Yes. Well, I don't mean to be. Kindness never built a bridge nor spanned a chasm." Depuits laughed self-consciously. "You may write that down if you like. You may quote me."

Philippe laughed aloud, finding suddenly that he liked this aging executive. He recalled the stories he'd heard in outer offices about Depuits—distant, chilled, reserved, self-centered, arrogant, egotistical—and he discounted most of them. Depuits did wear that air of self-esteem characteristic of most vital and important personages but, Philippe saw, he was quite human and warm—even likeable.

"I won't dissemble, Bunau-Varilla," the aging man said. "We are proud of the work you are doing here. You're an engineer with a creative and inventive mind. Most of us prefer to go by the book. This is not always the most rewarding, but it is safest. But, without dreamers, the men who demand to know not *why*, but *why not*, engineering might well be in the dark ages."

"Thank you, sir."

"Yes. Well, this is not my evaluation. Rather it is the opinion of the orangutan—pardon, of my partner, Paul-Jacques David." They smiled together. "But David is an orangutan who would rather steal bananas from you than to speak a word in praise. He asked me to pass along his evaluation for what it was worth to you."

"I do appreciate it deeply, sir."

"He didn't really want to say anything about it. We are not a firm to encourage junior engineers too hastily, or to pressure them into areas beyond their depths. But we have also concluded, at least David has concluded and passed the word to me, that you are dissatisfied here at Depuits et David."

Philippe shook his head. "I'm not dissatisfied, sir."

"Only impatient, eh? As satisfied as you could be at any job which offers as little physical activity and challenge of responsibility as this? We have, as I said, been thinking about you. We are willing to offer you a position that ordinarily we would not even consider for any of our engineers under five years in experience."

"Sir?"

"We all have our dreams, young man. Eh? All of us. Me? I always longed to ride the wild horses across the plains of western America."

"And fight Indians?"

"No." The old man touched at the ends of his waxed mustache with the backs of his fingers. "Robbing stage-coaches was more to my taste."

"There is much to recommend a career like that."

"And perhaps there is much to recommend this opportunity we want to offer you. We have projects in Tunisia and in Algiers. If you headed them up for us, we believe you'd be happier than sitting in an office in Paris."

Philippe sat in stunned silence. He should have been yelling his joy, but instead, he felt the twist of a dull knife in his gut. All he could think of was Madelon. Madelon. Madelon. Here was his opportunity to clear out ahead of disaster. What was he delaying for? And yet exile from Madelon looked like a kind of death, even if it were impossible to have her.

He swallowed hard. "Must I—give you my answer now?"

Depuits frowned slightly, then shook his head. "Of course not. Think about it. Think it over tonight. We'd like for you to have the position. Of course we can't hold it indefinitely."

"Of course not. I deeply appreciate your trust. I do understand."

Depuits stood up. He was almost as tall as Philippe and the faint memory of rebellious youth still smoldered deep in his faded blue eyes. "Yes. Well, I won't keep you any longer. We all are proud of you here, and offer all our cooperation to make your life what you want to make it. Young fools aren't the only ones who make huge mistakes." He laughed, gazing at the colored globe beside his desk. He gave it a twirl with his finger. He stopped it with his hand somewhere near the equator. "Look at old de Lesseps. An octogenarian, though he probably lies about his age. He's going to open that ditch between the Atlantic and Pacific, and then what?"

Philippe laughed with Depuits. "Then all the water in the Pacific will run through that big ditch to the Atlantic and the Luxembourg Gardens will be oceanfront."

They laughed together, shook hands and parted. Depuits was out of the building ahead of Philippe, who moved slowly, in a daze, wanting more than anything else to break down and cry.

[8]

Philippe staggered along the Rue de la Huchette. Passersby —tourists, tramps, artists, dark-skinned Arabs, Algerians, even blasé Parisians—paused to gape and laugh at him. Every forward motion was most painstakingly and cautiously executed, as if he were climbing extraordinarily steep and wide-spaced stairs. Pedestrians and horse carriages existed only as dim, dancing wraiths before him and he tried to walk through all of them. A stout, militantly sober woman refused to give way. Though she was swathed in mink and glittered with rhinestones, her vocabulary would have served a fishmonger or dock worker. She raged at Philippe in no uncertain terms, explicitly detailing what she thought of him, of anyone who stumbled in the public streets as helplessly and contemptibly as he.

Philippe bowed so gallantly and so low that he almost fell on his face. "A million pardons, madamoiselle, but I am just as drunk as you are!"

Rage and laughter spewed around him as he continued his erratic forward progress. He had set out to get drunk, so totally drunk that Madelon Grabralet's face would be washed forever from his mind and her memory from his heart. He succeeded admirably, at least in part. He was exceedingly drunk. His eyes felt as if they were bursting from their sockets; he reeked sourly of wine and he cursed the fates which had let him look for one brief moment upon the one woman who might have made his earthly existence a paradise but instead could only prove it a hell.

A prostitute had made her way through a crowded bar to his table. "Would you like to buy me a drink, *chéri?*" she asked. "Perhaps later we would find pleasure upon my bed?"

He gazed at her through an occluding haze. It didn't matter that she was pretty enough for a girl in her profession. It didn't matter that there was an odd space between her two front teeth. It didn't matter that her eyes looked tired and somehow chaotic, or that her mouth turned down at the corners unless she laughed and laughing for her was an effort. What did matter was that she was not Madelon. He said, "Does your mother know you are out?"

"You may be certain she does, *mon cher,* since it was she who kicked me out."

"I'll buy you a drink," he said, "because I think no one should be without a drink. But as for the rest of it—" he shook his head.

"Why? What's the matter with me?"

"Why should anything be wrong with you? There is nothing wrong with you. I am sure you are quite expert, *ma'm'selle.* It is nothing personal."

"Are you one then who prefers another man instead of girls?"

"No. Nor little boys, nor old men with beards. I just don't want *anybody.* I am trying to give it up. Give it all up."

She laughed and sipped the cognac a waiter placed before her. "Why would you do that? A beautiful man like you?"

"It's too long a story. Too long and too sad."

"A woman." She nodded sagely. "Some woman has broken your heart."

"No. It is not that easy, *ma'm'selle.* Not at all. The truth is, some woman has spoiled me for all other women."

Now she laughed without restraint. "Come now. Only

children believe there is but one woman for one man. There are many women, some better than others."

"Then I am a child. Because I believe that myth."

"Perhaps I could change your mind. It would be a great favor to you. It might help you see things as they really are. And I can always use the money."

He smiled sadly. "You are most charming, *ma'm'selle*. Most persuasive. I would go with you now. But I would fail you, and fail myself, and hate both of us. I despise the idea of ever growing to hate you. Here, five hundred francs. No hard feelings?"

She could only stare at him . . . and take the money.

He had sat alone for a long time, led, by his talk with the street girl, to a momentous decision. The time had come for him to break with Anne-Margot. He would never want her again; her bed would never entice him anew. Nothing she could do would rouse the slightest response in him. If perhaps it were possible to close his eyes and dream that she were Madelon—but no; he wanted *only* Madelon. If he didn't have Madelon, he wanted no woman. This made only one course clear. He had to be rid of Anne-Margot. Madelon had walked into his life and wiped away the entire past. Though he had believed he had known happy moments in Anne-Margot's chambers, he would never want to go there again.

It was a long and difficult passage from the Montmarte bistro to the chambers of his mistress. He dreaded the moment when he would come for the last time into her presence: Anne-Margot would likely dissolve into hysteria. Ah, she was capable of hysterics. When he did not appear at the hour she expected him, she wailed, accusing him and berating herself, castigating him for worrying her— she had no way of knowing he did not lie dead in an alley somewhere. Her own *father* had disappeared in this way, with a broken skull. She would weep. She would throw things.

He must be considerate, compassionate, understanding, but above all, *firm* in his resolve. He must make her see this parting was as much for her own happiness as for his. He could no longer make her happy. He could not promise ever to appear at her door again. Though she swore that she loved him, he would make her see that if she truly loved him she would not want to make trouble for him. She would not want to prolong something that no longer could have the old sweetness, or meaning, or pleasure. He knew that finally it would come down to a matter of francs. How much was he willing to pay for his freedom? Ah, he dreaded the scene ahead, even fortified as he was by drink.

Sighing, he navigated the final corner, entered the brick building where she lived and managed to mount the stairs in less than ten minutes. When he knocked on her door, she called, "Who is it?"

"Who are you expecting?" he asked.

The door flew open and she reached for him. It had been a long time and Anne-Margot was a girl of ravenous appetites. Her hand went in under his coat as she drew him to her. Her fingers moved along his vest, tripped over the gold watch chain, found his belt and, not being repulsed, slid down to grip him tightly. "Oh, I've missed you," Anne-Margot whispered. "How I have missed you."

He wanted to pull away. This was the time to be firm, to set the tone for this whole final interview. But her heated fingers closed and loosened, kneading, and he found himself responding physically, if not emotionally, despite all his decisions. She kicked the door closed behind them and by this time she had his trousers unbuttoned.

"Oh," he said. "Oh, no. I can't stay. I can't stay at all."

"Why not? And why have you been drinking so heavily?"

He drew a deep breath. "I have been building the courage to tell you good-bye, Anne-Margot."

They must have heard her wail a good two blocks away. She stared up at him, distended eyes brimming with tears. Then she whirled around and threw herself across the rumpled bed. It didn't help matters that her peignoir parted, falling back across the milk-and-pink expanse of her behind.

He followed her to her bed and sank down beside her. The old memories swarmed up in his mind, stirred by the heated fragrance of her pillows, her body, her chemise. Oh

God, these scenes were never easy. He tried to console her, to stroke her back, but, despite his best efforts, his hand sank to the alabaster rise of those cheeks. A woman's behind was a beguiling sight! He had never realized before how exciting a bare *derrière* could be.

"Please," he said. "I'd never want to leave you."

"Then why must you?"

He floundered. "Please. Understand. I would never leave you. But I have been warned. My mother's—uh, delicate health—you admit I've mentioned how delicate her health is? I have been told definitely that if she even suspected or were told that I had such a liaison with you— with any woman outside wedlock—I'm sorry, Anne-Margot. You cannot ask me to murder my own mother, even for a body like yours."

"But if we were discreet?" She wept.

"Who can ever be that discreet, *ma chérie*? One has enemies. The jealous. The greedy who might hope to gain by betraying an intimate secret. Nothing else would make me leave you, but I cannot come again." His hand cupped that rounded cheek, slid into the deep cleavage. "I want you to know how much all this has meant to me."

"Will I never see you again?"

"I'm afraid not. I am sorry."

She wailed again; this time the pictures on the walls quivered and people stirred restively in the corridors. The door opened and her neighbor Rose peeked in quickly before silently retreating.

Anne-Margot turned on the bed. This time the dark triangle of her femininity was revealed, the shadowed inner thighs, the knees. She did not care. "And what is to become of me?"

"You'll be all right, Anne-Margot. You may stay here— rent-free. Yes, rent-free. A year . . . until you find another liaison . . . as long as you like. You won't find me ungrateful—or stingy."

"But what am I to do to live? Return to a bakery?"

He hadn't known she had worked in a bakery. He had never inquired. He had never cared. She began to cry again, alternately sobbing and screaming. She pleaded with him, she clung to him, she lost her voice in helpless choking sobs. She loved him. She had never loved another. She would never love another man. No. Not as long as she lived. She would be lost without him. Ruined. Abandoned.

From his coat he took a bank draft and wrote some figures upon it. She fell into fresh paroxysms of weeping but she clutched the paper, folded it carefully and thrust it with Gallic caution between her heavy breasts. "And so I am to be paid? That is what I've meant to you. Now you pay me some francs and walk away. Is that it?"

"Not at all. I am trying to help, not to be cruel."

"You are cruel. All men are cruel."

"I can't argue with that, Anne-Margot. I can express only my own situation. I beg you to understand. I cannot see you any more. It breaks my heart. It breaks my heart to see you carry on like this. But it cannot be helped."

"And so I must return to the bakery." She whispered it. "If you wish."

"Perhaps . . . if I owned a bakery—it would not be so terrible."

"Owned a bakery?"

"Of my own. That I could run. I could manage it better than many are operated, I can tell you. I would not waste. I am very frugal. I should make it pay." She sat up, staring at him. "Perhaps if I spoke to your grandfather, he might be kind enough to help me find such a business for myself."

Now he laughed. "Perhaps he would. But why don't you let me talk to him about it? No sense endangering my mother's health by permitting her to suspect." He scribbled the name of an attorney on a card and slipped it into the molten chasm between her peach-colored breasts where his bank draft rested secure. "You find the place you want, decide the amount you need to see you safely embarked as manager of your own bakery. Then see this solicitor and I vow it will all be handled for you."

She did manage to shed tears, she did cling to him, she did falter and sniffle as he prepared to leave, but actually, she seemed anxious to see him gone, for she called in Rose and they were chattering feverishly about a bakery of

Anne-Margot's own before he reached the stair at the end of the corridor.

A rush of damp chill air swept over Philippe as he stepped into the street. He turned up the collar of his great coat to keep out the mist of rain. A bakery. Anne-Margot was not only a fantastic concubine, she was also a sensible, pragmatic Gallic girl. Well, for good or evil, he had broken it off.

He looked around in the darkness and sighed heavily.

A hack pulled into the curb and the cabbie called, asking if he cared to ride in this miserable weather. Philippe hesitated, then shook his head. The rain increased, but he did not care. He strode along the dark street, seeing the lights leaping in the muddy pools, needing a drink, but glad to be alone and unburdened.

As he crossed the court to his own apartment building the door of the Grabralet apartment opened and Claude-Bruce stepped quickly out. His limpid eyes widened and he stared at Philippe. "What's the matter, Philippe? Are you all right?"

Philippe tried to push past him. "A little drunk, that's all. Nothing I can't handle alone."

"Where have you been? I've been ill with worry."

"What concern is it of yours? My coming, my going, they are none of your affair."

"You're drunk."

"I certainly hope so! I'd hate to think I'd consumed all the alcohol I have and appeared sober. Now, if you'll excuse me." With great dignity but complete ineptness, he fought to insert the key in his door lock.

Claude-Bruce laughed at him. "You better let me do that."

Philippe wheeled around, standing tall. "Don't you understand? I don't want you to do anything for me. I want you to stay away from me. We are no longer friends, if we have ever been. We are from this moment mere acquaintances. And the merer, the better, from this night forward. Is that clear?"

"I'll undress you and put you to bed. You must get out of these wet clothes or you'll have pneumonia."

Philippe sagged against the wall, frustrated and helpless.

He swore bitterly. "Don't you understand? I want you to get away from me. Stay away from me. You and your wife and your problems and your smiling and your politics, all of it. Get away! Get away. I want you to leave me alone."

[9]

Philippe swung his arm wildly, but the blow was wide of its mark, and he fell against the door-frame. Claude-Bruce gently removed the keys from his numb fingers and unlocked the door. He drew Philippe's arm about his shoulders and staggered under his weight across the threshold.

Philippe had not realized how exhausted he was, how near the ragged end of his rope he'd come. He sank suddenly to his knees. Claude-Bruce almost fell, dragged down with him. On his knees, Philippe tried to crawl toward his bedroom. He did not make it. He fell asleep with his nose pressed into the handloomed Persian rug.

He awoke, chilled, to find himself lying naked across his own bed. The cover was turned back. Dimly, through a wreathing of pink clouds he watched Claude-Bruce making a neat stack of his wet clothing and soggy boots. "Get out," Philippe whispered and sank again into sleep.

He awoke once more to find Claude-Bruce kneeling beside his bed, whispering, crying, "Oh, Philippe. *Mon* Philippe."

He was not entirely conscious but he was aware of

66

Claude-Bruce's hands—softer than Anne-Margot's ever were and far more insistent—moving inside his thighs, cupping him, tenderly kneading. Repulsed, he tried to pull away from those heated hands; he tried to swear but there were no words, no responses to his mental messages. His legs were too weak to support him, his arms as watery as whey, his body a helpless lump across the mattress. He could not even push Claude-Bruce away. There were only those slender, heated hands fondling and caressing him, that hot, parted mouth kissing hungrily at his inner thighs. He tried to turn away and could not. "Don't," he managed to mutter.

Claude-Bruce tilted his flushed face, his eyes brimmed with tears. "Oh, *mon* Philippe. Can I desire you so fiercely and you not care at all?"

"Yes. Hell yes."

"No. I will love you as no woman ever could, Philippe."

"Leave me alone—"

"I only wanted Madelon to—to attract you, Philippe, because I need you so terribly. Oh God, Philippe, don't you understand?"

Philippe gathered all his inner will and tried to lift himself. He could not. He swung his arm wildly.

"I love you, Philippe. I would do anything for you, anything, no one will ever love you as I do." He closed his hands on Philippe's hips, massaging and caressing while he dipped his head against Philippe's thighs, his breath hot and passionate.

"Damn you." Philippe's head rolled back and forth. He felt Claude-Bruce's moist lips close over him, nuzzling and tightening. He tried to fight, but it was as if he were trying to struggle free from an engorging quagmire, only to be pulled relentlessly down, down, down.

He awakened with the brilliant shafts of early morning sunlight lancing through his tightly closed eyelids to the most vulnerable chambers of his brain. He remembered, against his will, much that filled him with disgust and revulsion.

"I only wanted Madelon to attract you, Philippe, because I need you so terribly." Good God! How ironic!

67

Had Grabralet really said those words or were they shards from some fragmented delusion?

His head throbbed. Each pulsation of blood in the distended veins of his temples threatened to derange him again. He clawed at the mattress in a rage. After an eternal time, he got up and found a pitcher of water. He turned it up and drank from its mouth, spilling it along his naked body. The water traced chilled lines down his fevered flesh.

He shuddered in disgust, the memory of disgust, fresh and hot and vile. He despised himself. He cursed the memory of Claude-Bruce Grabralet, and he cursed too the achingly sweet recollection of Madelon's lovely face— lost to him! Eternally lost to him.

He prowled the room, naked, anguished. He could not have Madelon; he could not forget her. He couldn't then continue to exist in any dimension of sanity across the courtyard from her. How could he even stay in Paris? Yet the thought of being distantly removed so that he never saw her again, even accidentally for a few moments at a time, made him want to cry as he had not wept since he was a small boy.

He stood at the window, staring across the morning court. Sounds from the streets raked at him, but he was only barely aware of them.

Perhaps it made no sense that he could have fallen so desperately in love with Madelon the first moment he saw her. But it happened like a stroke of lightning. He believed with all his heart that God meant for him to have Madelon. But something had gone wrong. Something had surely gone wrong—it was Madelon's *husband* who wanted to be his lover!

He drew the back of his hand across his chill-sweated forehead. "Madelon," he whispered toward her window. "Oh, Madelon."

He stared at that restored old mansion, willing its walls to dissolve and reveal her standing beyond, arms outstretched to him.

He laughed sardonically at himself. Because he had gone out of his mind for her did not imply that she felt anything for him. If she understood anything of what her

68

husband was, she might well think him Claude-Bruce's lover, for God's sake!

He stood helplessly, torn apart inside between laughter and anguish, feeling completely caught up in a wild farce worthy of Molière himself.

[10]

Philippe dressed quickly. He would *see her. Now. This*
morning. For a little while he would drink in the sight of
her, hear her voice, stir the music of her laughter. What
could be more wondrous, after a time of lonely need, than
to be admitted into the full glare of her smile, into the
orbit of her heady fragrance? No matter where his roads
led him, he would have this moment to treasure and no one
could take it away from him. Grabralet's prior claims to
her would not detract a gram from his pleasure. He knew
what Claude-Bruce was, and that was beneath his concern.

He gulped a long swig of cognac to quiet the quivering
in his stomach. He felt as awkward as a schoolboy. His
face was flushed, his hands cold and clammy. By the time
he stepped through his doorway, crossed the courtyard and
rapped on the facing of her door, he held himself under
leash only by exercising a total discipline he hadn't even
been aware he possessed.

He knocked again, listening for movement beyond that
door. For a long breathless moment there was none,
then the door was opened most reluctantly.

Fanny LeBeau stood there. Her great round eyes were
filled with tears. Her bleak face was rigid with a look he

could only interpret as hatred. She wore her square heavy shoes, an unflattering cloth coat—and a new chapeau. She nodded her head stiffly.

Philippe stepped into the glittering parlor and forgot Fanny Lebeau. Madelon entered from the dining room and gathered all the light in the place. He stared at her, his passion increased a thousandfold. She was lovelier even than his most heated fantasy. The crinolines of her morning frock crinkled and whispered when she moved. She smiled and her smile made her seem younger than ever, more vulnerable, more exquisite. Her bare arms and face were pale olive, and those deep violet eyes shimmered in a glow which highlighted her luminous skin. Her full underlip was the only excess in the cameo perfection of her features—it was the slight flaw which made her irresistible.

Fanny LeBeau said, voice quavering, "Are you sure, madame?"

Madelon's gaze seemed to move reluctantly beyond Philippe and she nodded impatiently. "I am quite sure, Fanny. The day is yours."

Fanny bit her lip and looked as if she might break into tears again. Then, sighing heavily, she gathered her coat about her and fled past Philippe. She closed the door behind her in a sharp gesture of disapproval.

Madelon bestowed upon him her loveliest smile. "Poor Fanny. She is afraid to leave me alone with my neighbor."

Philippe drank in her loveliness. He would not have minded had she told him that Fanny's head would be chopped off and served as an hors-d'oeuvre. His heart battered at his rib cage. *He was alone with her*. He didn't know what he'd done to win this favor, but he uttered a swift and silent prayer of thanksgiving.

Madelon motioned him to a brocaded loveseat beside the high-backed divan. She placed a decanter of wine on a silver tray before them and sat near him on the edge of the satin-covered couch. "Well, here you are at last," she said.

He sipped wine, not tasting it. "I've been as near as just across that court all this time."

"Yes. Haven't you? All the months of my marriage,

you have been there." She gazed directly into his face, and her violet eyes touched his.

"I don't know why we didn't meet months ago."

"Don't you?" Now she took up her small silver goblet of wine and sipped. A droplet of chablis sparkled for an instant on that full underlip and he watched it, fascinated. Her head tilted. "I didn't meet you because I was ashamed."

"Ashamed? Why, your beauty places you beyond shame."

"Do not flatter me, *m'sieu.* I dislike pretense in all its guises. Politics is the art of pretense. Surely engineering is more direct. More honest. We should be most uncomfortable with each other if we had to pretend."

He did not see how he could be more uncomfortable than she made him with her complete, yet somehow impersonal honesty.

Her gaze held his. "I have decided, Philippe, for the rest of my life to say only what is true. Only what I feel. Only what I believe. I am through with pretense. Because I have made this decision, I find myself at ease with you."

He watched her refill his small goblet with wine. She sat back, and he took up the vessel, his fingers trembling. Was she revealing her innermost self to him, or merely making polite conversation. He could not say. "Would you prefer that I dissemble, Philippe? I know that art well."

"Oh no."

"Because if you would, then you are less than I perceived you to be when we met. It was meeting you that helped bring me to this resolve."

"I don't believe you could ever lie."

"But you are wrong. I have done nothing but lie all the months of my marriage. I suppose you see what the world is allowed to see, the charming young *député* and his happy young wife. Don't misunderstand. I would do nothing to harm Claude-Bruce's career; it means everything to him. I have done all I can to help foster that career. But this is the extent of my lying. From now on, I shall have a life of my own. Friends of my own. Friends like you."

"I am not a friend of yours."

"Aren't you? How unkind."

"You know I'm not your friend. You know I could never be."

She bit her lip and seemed somehow more aloof than ever. "Isn't that sad? I hoped for a friend like you. I needed such a friend."

"Stop it. Stop talking about friendship. I love you, and I've loved you since the moment I saw you in the courtyard, without even knowing who you were."

"Please. You mustn't say such things."

"Why not? You were the one just praising the joys of complete honesty."

"But—is it completely honest to speak of love to me?"

"Yes. I am telling you I love you with all my heart."

"But you must not. I am married to Claude-Bruce Grabralet, in the church. . . . I am forever married to Claude-Bruce Grabralet. Until death do us part."

"Is that why you cry your heart out every night?"

"Perhaps I have the tears of any bride, once in a while."

"Don't lie. You know I've heard you. All these months. It has broken my heart, as I believe your heart is broken."

"Oh, no, Philippe. We must not even talk like this."

"What's happened to the truth you championed so passionately?"

Her eyes filled with helpless tears, but when he reached out to her, she withdrew. Her dainty chin tilted. "Perhaps the truth you so bravely demand would be too much for you, *m'sieu*."

"You must tell me."

She spoke to the backs of her trembling fingers. "Claude-Bruce wanted me to—seduce you. He wanted me to come to your apartment with him and make love to you. He even wanted me to send for you, pretend he was delayed at some meeting, and seduce you, while he watched from the cloak closet there. He made such plans as I would not even hear. And so I would not come near you."

He did not trust himself to speak. He merely nodded his head.

"While I am being so truthful, I may as well confess. I have watched you go striding off to your work every morning, from that window there. I watch you walk along the avenue with your great shoulders back as if you owned the world—and not only owned it but meant to remake it in your own image."

"Are you jesting now?"

She smiled sadly. "I wish I were. I wish it were that simple, *m'sieu*. With all my heart. I know I am a fool to confess to you my innermost feelings. But I have been forced into a heartbreaking situation by my husband. He asked me to do things I could not do, would not do, had never even suspected went on in this world. That is why I wept, *m'sieu*. That and the loss I found in my marriage where I had hoped to find ecstasy."

"I am sorry. Truly sorry."

"So you see, Philippe. I do need a friend. A confidante. Claude-Bruce believes I need a lover. Perhaps I do. I don't know. I know only that such a thing is impossible and insulting. And, anyway, I don't know that much about lovers and loving, but I do know about being alone and lonely, of having no one to talk to."

"My heart has broken, Madelon, at the sound of your crying. I wanted to help you, to console you. Yet there was nothing I could do."

She reached out and pressed her soft, chilled fingers on the back of his hand. The charge shot through his body. "Now there is." She tried to smile. "Now you can be my friend, the thing I need most on this earth."

"But you know I can't be your friend. I love you too deeply, want you too terribly."

She seemed to refuse to hear the anguished need throbbing in his voice. "How badly I need someone to confide in, to advise me. Someone I can trust. I have no right to burden you, and yet we have shared those ugly nights, haven't we? If you wish, we may spend a polite hour, and part. Or you may come into my life, as I have prayed you would, as my friend."

"No," he said. "You have felt as I have. The need, the desires."

"Please, Philippe. All I know is hurt. I have been hurt deeply. I need comfort."

"Oh, Madelon, at the sight of you in that courtyard—without even knowing your name, I knew I could never

74

want another woman. I would be happy to be alone with you for the rest of my life. I would be empty without you. I knew all of that at once."

"How beautiful. Oh, my dear Philippe, how *terrible*."

"I am here. If you need me, I am here. You have only to speak my name."

"Philippe," she whispered.

They sat for some moments with Madelon clinging forlornly to his hand, not as a lover might, but as a child, frightened.

He wanted desperately to reach out, draw her into his arms. Her golden fingers were chilled, soft and gleaming against his dark fist. But upon that hand her wedding band glittered, winking maliciously at them both.

"Madelon, say you return my love. I know you do. You know it in your heart. I want to hear you say that you care for me."

"Oh, Philippe, such talk can lead only to destruction. I do care for you. As I have never cared for another human being on earth, but it can go no further. I have my home, my marriage, my family. No matter how empty my life, we could only destroy ourselves and those around us."

He did not speak.

She exhaled heavily. "Don't you see? I was a young girl. Young and stupidly innocent. I saw only that Claude-Bruce was prettier, far lovelier than I. This was all I could see. All I could think was that we would be so beautiful kneeling at the altar in our wedding ceremony, two beautiful people, surrounded by fern and lace and candles and a church full of friends. What young girl could ask more?"

He watched her full underlip tremble. He turned his hand over and closed his fingers upon her hand. "Do you not see, Philippe? They told me nothing. They allowed me to guess at nothing."

"I do understand."

Her face was suffused with blood, to the roots of her autumn-gold hair. "Yes, you do understand. If only I had understood. If only I had been given some hint that I would not—could not—be happy with Claude-Bruce

. . . that he would break my heart a hundred times, that he would not even want me—I might have been spared."

There were no words to console her.

"My mother told me the night before the marriage ceremony that the first night might be an ordeal, that my husband might make demands upon me, that I might even hate and loathe what happened to me. Well, how right she was, but for all the wrong reasons.

"Oh, if only I had suspected that Claude would *never* want me. My pride would have saved me then. I would have refused to marry him though the world insisted. If only I had known, but I knew nothing at all. Nothing. Nothing of good marriages between people who love and desire one another. Of dreadful unions between people like Claude-Bruce and me, I who loved him and he who never wanted me."

She lowered her face, pale with shame and humiliation. He moved to sit beside her on the divan. It was most uncomfortable, another part of the Grabralet existence intended for appearances only.

He drew Madelon to him and placed his arm around her slender shoulders. She shuddered, her whole body quivering, but then suddenly she pressed herself against him as if seeking to draw some faint strength from the reservoir of his muscular frame.

"I could tell no one else all this, Philippe. But I can tell you because you already know how bitter my life has been in this house. I thought my honeymoon with Claude-Bruce would be a romantic time. My husband could ask nothing that I would not willingly, anxiously give if I could. Only, he didn't want anything.

"When I tried to show him how much I loved him, how devotedly I cared, how anxiously I wanted to please him, I only drove him off. When I tried to devour him with kisses, to caress him as I wanted him to caress my body, he pushed me away. When I touched him, I shivered with anticipation. But he put me off. He was impatient with me. He told me I was acting like a fool."

She told it all, sparing neither of them. She had wept in her bed that night until daybreak, as she had been crying

76

out her heartbreak ever since. "We did not have one happy moment together," she confessed.

He touched her face with the palm of his hand, gently, holding her against him. Her voice became taut and she cried out. "Is this all life holds for me? Is there no more? Am I to exist in agony all the rest of my days? Is that what I can hope for?"

Her hands dug into his arms. She trembled and pressed herself upon him. He held her against him but she hardly knew what was happening to her. She responded to the touch of his hands but seemed not to know that she had roused him until he was quivering with desire.

"If only Claude-Bruce wanted me." She shook her head. "But he does not." She moved away from him and he felt a chill of loss. "Do you suppose he has some other woman?"

He stared at her in shock. She still did not truly understand what was wrong between her and Claude-Bruce! She knew only that he did not want her, and for this she blamed and berated herself—the lack must in some way be hers.

"He must have another woman," she persisted, "because he appears to want to share his guilt with me."

Philippe frowned. "His guilt?"

"Yes. He must be trying to ease his conscience because he tells me, lying in our bed at night, that I am free to have a lover—or lovers—he would not protest as long as I was discreet." She cried out in a burst of agony. "Am I so undesirable then?"

He could only hold her gently, try to console her. When, because he could not resist, he lifted her against him she sagged upon him. He fought to control the passions raging like fever in his blood. He wanted to clasp her hips in his hands, move her upon him; he wanted to push his hands into the open bodice of her dress, to spill those beautiful breasts to view, to caress and fondle them, to gaze at the pink of her nipple as the jeweler stares into the rarest ruby.

She laid her head back and he kissed her. Her heated mouth parted and he thrust his tongue deeply between her teeth. His hands moved instinctively to her breasts, caressing. Her breathing quickened, her body quivered.

Then, all of a sudden, the front door opened, and Fanny

77

stood inside the door, staring at them. She cried out, "Oh, madame, I was so worried. I had to come back. Thank God, I made it in time."

Philippe sagged back on the divan, caught between tears and raging laughter. The wall between him and Madelon had not been removed. It was still there, and higher than ever.

[11]

Philippe stood up. Fanny's bug eyes were riveted on the bulge warping his trouser front and, as stupid as she appeared, the maid well knew what reared there. Horror crawled like maggots deep in those swollen pupils. She felt righteous; more than that, self-righteous. She had disobeyed her mistress by returning here early but in doing so had saved her from a fate worse than death.

As for Madelon, she sank back on the divan, her clothing in disarray, her hair loose about her pallid face.

Looking at her, Philippe felt the agony of loss. Fanny's precipitous return reminded him forcefully that Madelon was Madame Grabralet, another man's wife. She could never belong to him except in stolen moments that would eventually destroy her. He owed Fanny LeBeau a debt, whether of curses or thanks he did not know.

He bowed toward Madelon, walked quickly past Fanny LeBeau, and closed the Grabralet door behind him. He had learned a terrible and exquisite truth in Madelon's parlor, upon her divan, in her arms. If they were near each other, they would be lovers. Nothing except distance could frustrate their frantic need each for the other. She had been married almost two years; two years of starvation.

Two years married to a man and still innocent of a man's natural response to her loveliness. Had Grabralet then never even been tumescent in her presence? Was the fellow so completely affronted by females that he was unable to respond at all? Was his impotence total in loving women? God help them all. This girl had been married for two years to Grabralet. She believed she knew what she needed but she had no idea what it was she wanted.

When he thrust open his own door and stepped into his silent parlor, loneliness engulfed him. He did not see how he could stay in this room, in this building, in this city. He had to leave Paris. Nothing else made sense. If he stayed where he could see Madelon, he would see Madelon. One could talk of self-discipline, strength of character, moral codes, laws, all abstract virtues, but the driving need of a man for a woman was as old as man himself. Along with thirst and hunger, desire had motivated man long before he created law or invented morals, or submitted to marriage.

He poured himself a glass of cognac, the liquid sloshing over the brim of his glass. His hands shook as he lifted it to his mouth and drank deeply.

"Philippe."

He wheeled around and faced Claude-Bruce Grabralet. He said, "What do you want?"

Claude-Bruce smiled and closed the corridor door. "I want to talk to you, *mon cher*."

"About what? What have we to say to each other?"

"I have just returned home. De Lesseps and his problems had no appeal for me this morning. I have talked to Madelon. I must apologize for her outburst. She must have embarrassed you. How sorry I am."

"She said nothing that embarrassed me, nothing I did not already know, or suspect, at least."

Claude-Bruce's face flushed. He loosed his cape and let it fall to the floor. He set his cane, gloves and top hat on a side table. When he turned he was quite composed again and smiling in that easy manner which might yet make him President of the Republic.

"Yes. Madelon confessed to me that she poured out her heart to you. She burdened you with matters intimate to

Madelon and me. Matters which are concerns of no one but her and me. I do apologize for her."

"I don't want your apology. I listened to all Madelon said to me. I was saddened. Deeply affected. But I warrant that it will go no further. No one will ever hear a whisper of it from me. Isn't that your real concern?"

"Naturally, it's important. My career is important. My career could be destroyed overnight. Impropriety. The very appearance of impropriety."

"You have my word."

Grabralet laughed. "Oh, my most dear Philippe! How little you know me. Don't you realize I had no fear of you? I knew the whole matter was safe with you. I know you, Philippe. I love you for what you are."

"I'd rather you didn't love me."

Grabralet laughed. "When one begins to hear the truth, my dear Philippe, it is not always easy to choose what truth one will hear, what one will reject. Madelon has wept, confessing to you how she has suffered. I, too, have suffered. I have lain dreaming of you, wanting you, needing you. In all this time I have been permitted only once to touch you and love you, and then only when you were unconscious, unaware of how terribly I wanted you."

"What are you leading to, Grabralet? Where do you expect this dialogue to take us?"

"To the truth, Philippe. The total truth. Madelon's family wanted a marriage between their daughter and a social equal. I was certainly that. My family is as old as the Grenets. Older. We are financially stable, if less affluent than they. In every way, we were a correct marriage, in the eyes of our families, the Church, the state."

"Why did you do this monstrous thing to her?"

"Because she swore she loved me. I am not a monster, Philippe. I have hurt Madelon, but it was not intentional. I thought we could live together, she with her life and I with mine. I needed the protection of a good marriage if I were to succeed in public life. Madelon presented that opportunity for security. I have given her in return my name, my fortune, my support."

"You have put her in hell."

"I never wanted to. How was I to anticipate her vora-

81

cious sexual appetites? I thought Madelon was a gentle young girl who would be pleased to be free of the ugly demands made between a brutish man and his woman. I truly believed this. I tried to convince her that she had every reason to be happy with me. Thousands of women would have welcomed and reveled in her freedom. I knew she loved me—as an innocent young girl loves. I knew she understood nothing of sex. I believed we could have a marriage of convenience."

"Of your convenience."

"For the sake of appearances. I would be discreet. Within reason, I would be tolerant of her behavior. As long as she were discreet. I realize now that I failed."

"You needn't worry about any further indiscretion. I'm leaving this place."

A cry broke across Grabralet's lips. He shook his head and ran forward. "No. No. You must not go. You must not leave me."

"I'm not leaving you. I was never with you, but I am leaving Madelon. I will not destroy her in my way as you have in yours."

Claude-Bruce burst into tears. "I beg you, Philippe, *mon* Philippe, don't leave me. Don't destroy me. You may have Madelon. I swear it. As you wish her. No one need ever know. All I ask in return is that you let me come to you, let me show you how deeply I love you. There is nothing I won't do for you. Oh God, Philippe, don't leave me."

Weeping, Grabralet sank to his knees. Philippe retreated a step, but Claude-Bruce cried out and clutched him about the hips, closing his slender arms fiercely. He pressed his face against Philippe, and sank to the floor, wracked with his crying.

"Don't do this, Philippe. For God's sake, don't throw me out."

"Get up. Act like a man."

Now, Grabralet did pull himself to his knees. He still breathed raggedly, his face was splotched and contorted with his crying, but he stiffened there, defiantly. "Do you think me not a man?" he said. "Because it would kill me if you leave me? I am more of a man than you know, Philippe, and I warn you, with more influence than you ever imagined. If you leave me, I swear I'll make you regret it, to the last day you live."

TWO

Algeria, 1883

[12]

The morning sun of North Africa climbed out of the sea and thrust its pitiless feelers between the shutters.

Philippe opened his eyes unwillingly, blinking helplessly against the light. God knew there was no such sun as this in France; that faint pale orb north of *mare nostrum* was only a weak-eyed cousin of this fiery star.

Philippe shifted restlessly beneath the canopy of netting. Great liquid marbles of sweat formed in his armpits and trickled along his ribcage. Rivulets of perspiration ran from his hair down into his eyes and seeped the salty taste of his body into his parched mouth.

He stretched and yawned, his naked flesh seeking one cool spot on the sheet and finding none. As he had done throughout the eternal exile of this past year, he began his day with thoughts of Madelon Grabralet. Madelon—in this alien clime her memory had been his keel as well as his torment. Thinking about her, gazing north across the miles to verdant France, he found every day a thousand lonely hours, but without her memory to cling to, he'd probably have joined most of the other Europeans condemned to Algeria, on opium, hashish, or alcohol. In these months he'd found that few Europeans ever truly oriented themselves to this sun-blasted crucible. Only the thought that Madelon might need him, might send for him, kept him from sinking totally into that apathy and dissolution he saw all about him.

Finally fully awake and acclimated to the burn of the sun, he watched a chameleon skitter across his wall, leap to the windowsill, and race along it. This land remained strange to him, a place the likes of which he'd never even imagined in those civilized years back home in Paris. The heavy furnishings, the thick fabrics, the oddly woven rugs on stone floors, it was all like the setting for a nightmare—and this was what his life had become. Daily he grew to hate himself more fiercely, with a rancid loathing that embraced everything he had accomplished, here and in Tunis, and all he had left undone. He hated this place and everyone in it, himself most of all. He dreaded his self-imposed exile; it proved to be nothing he wanted. He was 23 years old and life was a thankless job in a land where he wasn't even wanted.

The nude Ziri girl on the bed beside him whimpered in her sleep and turned toward him. She settled her full breasts against his hard biceps and after a moment slid her leg over his so that her sweated thighs nestled against the rise of his pelvis. He turned his head on the damp pillow and gazed at her dark form. Her crisp, black hair spilled across the white sheet. Her skin was the color of unburnished brass in the blaze of sunlight. Her breath was still redolent of sweet hot wine from last evening. He hated her almost as deeply as he hated himself. He tried to edge away from her to find a cool breath of air, but his movement awakened her. Her dark slender hands closed on him, her brilliantly painted nails dug into his shoulder. He cursed her silently. "Stop it, Sahyin. You're worse than a tigress."

The red lips pulled back from glittering teeth. "Sahyin is a tigress, my lord Philippe. She is your tigress." She bent her head and bit his left nipple viciously. He shoved her away, but she toppled back on the spread laughing. "Sahyin leaves her mark on you."

"I'll send you away. I'll send you back to your people." He said it casually. It was a threat he'd learned from De

87

Blasio, who used the warning to keep her and all other bonded servants under his thumb.

Sahyin sat up crying out like an animal in distress.

"What the hell's the matter with you?" he demanded.

"My lord no longer loves his Sahyin."

He kept his voice chilled. "I no longer love you, Sahyin, because I never loved you. Can't you understand that? You are my servant. My slave. My bed wench. You are a convenience that I could not exist in this place without, but don't get confused in your mind. You belong to me. You were a gift to me from patron De Blasio. But I don't love you."

Sahyin wept inconsolably. He let her lie huddled up like a fetus on the heated mattress. He disliked seeing Sahyin cry but he disliked a great deal more her growing possessiveness. It had to stop somewhere.

When he did not respond to her crying, the bronze-skinned girl ceased weeping as suddenly as a summer rain dries up in sunlight. She sniffled a couple of times and pressed her face against his belly, tickling his flesh as though her tongue were a feather. He responded whether he wanted to or not. Damn him. Was there no woman he could resist? Was he an absolute slave to his lust? He wanted no woman but Madelon Grabralet, but though his mind and his heart could deny all other women his hot rushing blood could not.

She opened her mouth, kissing him. Biting down on his lips, he caught both sides of her head in his hands, pressing her down upon him, surrendering to her. "Oh God, forgive me," he whispered, and then, "Oh, God, oh God, oh God almighty. Almighty God."

She shivered in an ecstasy of pleasure and excitement and, he recognized, her renewed sense of possession. In the months he'd had her, Sahyin had forgotten who was slave, who was master.

A sharp rapping on his door battered somehow into his conscious mind but before he could answer, the door was thrown open and De Blasio strode across the room to the bed. Helplessly, Philippe watched the stout young Italian approach, his eternal cigar clenched between his dark lips. De Blasio was under medium height, balding, olive-skinned and at least fifty pounds overweight. He wore boots, jodhpurs, a cotton blouse and sweat-discolored sun helmet. He caught Sahyin's ankle and yanked her roughly off the bed.

Sahyin wailed in savage hatred and protest but De Blasio ignored her. He said to Philippe around his cigar, "You up yet?"

"Obviously, my dear De Blasio, I'm *up*, but you've managed to barge in here and destroy my hope for relief."

De Blasio shrugged. "On your feet. You can achieve your release in rage. We've got trouble."

Philippe sat up slowly. "You name me one morning in this hell-hot place that has not begun with trouble."

De Blasio nudged the slave girl with the toe of his boot and jerked his head, ordering her out of the room. He said, "I'm not talking about minor inconveniences, my boy. Work in the harbor has stopped. Dead. And it may stay shut down."

Philippe stared at De Blasio. The young engineer was deadly serious. Philippe exhaled heavily. "Let me shave."

"No time for that. We can both shave at our leisure in Paris, after the tribes throw us out of here."

De Blasio had not exaggerated the seriousness of the trouble. When they arrived at the harbor, Philippe stared in disbelief. All work on the docks and in deepening the port had ceased. Even along the breakwater the native laborers no longer dumped the random-sized riprap against the encroachment of the tides. Drays stood idle and empty, mules and other beasts sagged in the fly-infested heat. But the work stoppage was only the tip of the problem. Armed men wearing ash-colored burnooses lined the docks. They stood with their rifles beside their camels, implacable, immovable, inscrutable.

"Who is in charge of this insurrection?" Philippe said. "Don't they know we're trying to help them into the nineteenth century? Don't they know we represent France here? Don't they know we have the Republic behind us?"

"They don't seem to give a shit." De Blasio shrugged.

"You mean these tramps have stopped us, just like that?"

"Looks like it. We are checkmated, for the moment at least."

Philippe stared along the quay. The desert men remained unmoving, all seemingly alike. "Somebody has to be in charge here."

"Why?"

"Because uprisings like this are well-planned, directed, and carried out for some reason, usually ransom, bounty or bribes. They don't just happen. These rascals came in from all over the country, from God knows how far. They arrived on schedule. We had no hint they were coming. This is a well-planned maneuver."

De Blasio glanced around, squinting in the metallic sunlight. "One way we can find out who is in command."

"All right."

"All we have to do is order these Bedouins out of here and then try to enforce that order."

"The two of us against this rabble? Unarmed?"

"The odds are indeed unattractive, I grant you. The alternative is most alluring. We can return to the hotel, order drinks and wait."

"For what?"

"For the French bureacracy to send in troops to help us."

"That could take six months."

"Time isn't too important here in the desert. Rome left some of its legions over here for two hundred years, on temporary duty."

Philippe thought of the months he had been in Algiers, the months before that improving roads and harbors in Tunis, the hot months ahead of him before he could hope to see Madelon again. "Time is important to me," he said.

De Blasio nodded casually. "Then let's try to run this riffraff out of here."

"Have you noticed their rifles? They'll kill us."

"I didn't promise it would be easy."

"Oh, hell." Philippe looked around, found a pitchfork standing in a pile of green camel dung. As he took up the fork, blue flies swarmed upward in a humming cloud. "All right," he said to De Blasio. "Let's go."

Without waiting to see if De Blasio followed, Philippe

approached the nearest armed man, the prongs of the pitchfork glittering. "Get out," Philippe said, advancing.

The man winced. His black eyes darted. He looked about in confusion. By the time he lifted his gun upward, the tines of the pitchfork were poised against his chest.

Philippe jabbed with the pitchfork. The man retreated, dragging his camel with him, until he bumped the soldier next in line. All the way along the quay the tribesmen broke ranks and stepped forward to watch the disturbance Philippe created by herding the herdsmen ahead of him. Walking in Philippe's shadow, De Blasio moved forward with a dung-smeared shovel raised threateningly above his head.

From far down the wooden pier a man yelled. His voice raged in the silence and the heat. He lunged out of the ranks and strode at a half-run toward where Philippe and De Blasio continued to heckle the tribesmen along the dock toward open water. Many of the dark-skinned men raised their guns but something in the imperious manner of Philippe and De Blasio evoked the ruthless power of the Republic in their minds; they hesitated to fire their weapons at French nationals in the absence of a direct order.

Philippe paused and watched the man stride toward them. The fellow was attempting to hurry, in order to stop the intimidation before it infected his troops and at the same time to walk with a dignity befitting his rank. His gray *cloak* parted as he walked, revealing a faded Foreign Legionnaire's tunic and trousers. He was even shorter in stature than De Blasio, and as thin as a desert jackal. "I am Mohammed Bin of Tlemcen," he said. "Do you wish to be killed, attacking my men in this way?"

"You are the intruders here, *M'sieu* Bin," Philippe said. "We have been sent here as French civil servants to deepen this harbor and improve its dock facilities. Your troops are trespassing and you're delaying government work."

"We are halting it altogether." Mohammed Bin waved his arm. "We do not wish it done."

Philippe laughed helplessly and without mirth. "Just like that?" he said. "You have taken it upon yourself to stop the forward progress of the Republic?"

"Not at all have I taken any decision unilaterally," Mohammed Bin said. "What affects Algiers and Algeria affects the tribes of Algeria, and to stop this rape of our country is the decision of the tribes of Algeria: the tribes of Maghrawa Arabs, the Ziris, the Almohades, the Ziamids of Tlemcen, the Merinids of Fez."

"And you are the commander of these combined forces?"

"Not at all. I am a captain only in direct charge of these troops of His Imperial Majesty. All our tribes are united in following the dictates of the Emir Adel Kader. It is his decision that work will cease which destroys the natural harmony of the harbors of our country. We here today simply offer our lives to carry out his command."

"Where is this—this—" Philippe stopped when De Blasio caught his arm, tightening his fingers like a vise.

De Blasio said, "I know Emir Adel Kader, and you are right, *Capitaine* Bin. We—even as servants of the Third Republic—are powerless to oppose the wishes and dictates of the Emir Adel Kader."

Philippe stared at De Blasio. It was unlike him to knuckle under to anyone, especially some desert chieftain. "Are you joking?"

De Blasio winced as if he'd been struck across the face and shook his head sharply back and forth.

"Certainly not. The word of the Emir Adel Kader is as sacred as the readings from the Koran, or as the word of Allah through Mohammed to His people, Mohammed from whom the Emir descends in a direct line. Rest easy, *M'sieu* Mohammed Bin. We bow to your injunction. Come, Philippe, we are powerless unless our petition can alter the position of Emir Adel Kader." He caught Philippe's arm. Mohammed Bin smiled in triumph. When they were three feet away, De Blasio swore under his breath. "That corrupt, money-grabbing son of a bitch. We're stopped, Philippe."

"I can't believe you're going to let France be stopped by—by this bunch of desert rats."

"We'll have to see Emir Adel Kader."

"Where is he?"

De Blasio shrugged. "Who the hell knows? We'll have

to find him. Oh, he'll let us find him, when we let him smell our money."

"Whose money?"

"All right. Perhaps we'll have to use a false scent. But we can at least let the Emir Adel Kader smell the *promise* of money, can't we?"

[13]

The narrow-gauge train left the station at Algiers and climbed through the broken terrain between the sea and the desert. The engine gathered speed and the land raced past the crowded, unglassed window spaces of the open coaches. On the unpadded bench beside Philippe, De Blasio cursed the heat and the rebellious tribes. "Damn these godless assassins," he muttered around his cigar. "Trying to disrupt everything France attempts to do for them." They even bombed schools and hospitals unless they were paid enormous tribute. "It's money this dog Adel Kader wants now. He doesn't give a damn about the harbor."

De Blasio swore he'd seen the terrorists hack men's arms and legs off when they came upon workers unprotected in fields. They chopped at the victims with their huge knives until the workers were helpless, and then threw the crippled bodies to the wild dogs. "Did you know that when the Berbers ruled Algiers their entire government revenue derived from piracy?" De Blasio demanded. "These native rulers are still thieves and thugs. It would be no less than they deserved if France pulled out and abandoned them, let them all sink into the sand."

Philippe shrugged. "It's not our decision to make."

"It should be our recommendation. It would be mine. Meantime, we ride in this abominable heat and body-stench. For what? To deal with this scabrous Adel Kader! An Algerian patriot? Hardly. An opportunist with his filthy hand out. He'd sell the soul of this poor land for a sou."

"How can we deal with him? We have no authority to speak for the Republic."

"You know that. I know that. Must the desert bastard Adel Kader need to know that? What does he want? Money. All right, we promise him money. What do we want, you and I?" He exhaled a dark wreath of smoke and answered his own question. "To improve those docks, deepen the harbor and get the hell out of here, right?"

"Amen."

"There are two ways we can get that work completed. Get the protection of the French army—which might take months—or . . . buy Adel Kader off."

Philippe grinned. "And that will take money we haven't got, money we haven't the right to obligate."

De Blasio shook his head vehemently. "That's where you're wrong. We—you and I—have the right to underwrite any amount that will insure our being allowed to complete work that Adel Kader had no right to stop in the first place."

"That's involved thinking."

"If you're going to accomplish anything among complex people, you'll have to learn involved cerebration," De Blasio said. "You put the truth in perspective. You speak it and you exchange it only where it is justified. We're dealing with a first-class son of a bitch here, and we'll just have to be sons of bitches."

"I'm afraid I don't have the experience to deal in such intrigue," Philippe said. "You handle it, I'll watch—and try to learn."

"That's where you're wrong, my boy." De Blasio grinned sourly. "You're going to handle it all. The whole diplomatic swindle. This Adel Kader is the son of a dung-tailed camel. He professes to be a direct descendent of Mohammed Himself. He is the goddamnedest, foxiest bastard that was ever born with a pair of brass balls. I'd trust him no further than I would a Venetian, and if you knew what we of the south of Italy thought of those northern— Well! But just now we are stymied by the bastard. He's holding aces and we're drawing to treys."

"This calls for your style of bluffing," Philippe said. "I've played poker with you."

"Not for stakes like this, old fellow. He can stop us permanently. He can stop us until the army is sent in, if ever. Or he can join us in seeing that we get that harbor deepened for the progress of Algeria and the glory of Emir Adel Kader. Along with money to fill his slippery paws. That's what you're going to promise him, old bucko."

"Why me? He'll know I'm lying."

"He'd better not. If he suspects either one of us of lying, we'll never get out of his camp alive. And I don't look forward to being hacked up and thrown to the wild dogs. That's why you are going to be the suave diplomat. You are going to find out what his demand for tribute is, and you're going to agree to deliver it, once his troops are pulled out of Algiers."

"I'll never get away with it. No. You'll have to do it, De Blasio."

"For hell's sake. I told you! He *knows* me! We're old enemies. But I think he respects me enough to let me in his tent, if I prostrate myself and kiss his toes."

"I'll never do that."

"The hell you won't. You'll do it, and you'll smile while you're doing it. Be glad for this opportunity with a desert-rat chieftain. Someday you may look back on what you learn here as the most important training of your engineering career."

"I build bridges and docks and waterways," Philippe protested.

"Learning to deal with greedy crooks like Adel Kader is as important as knowing the difference between stress and a hod bucket," De Blasio said. "You don't build bridges by going out and finding chasms that need to be spanned. You are permitted to build roadbeds by finding the right palms to grease."

"God. I never heard such cynicism."

"You're out of the Ecole Polytechnique now, young man. You're now learning the real engineering facts. Facts that have nothing to do with engineering you learned in school, but everything to do with engineering in this world. Maybe you don't know a goddamn thing about dealing with powerful crooks in high places. Well, Professor De Blasio will teach you. In this engineering lesson, the ends justify the means. Make an equation out of it if it will soothe your conscience. But learn it! And learn it well!"

"You're a real son of a bitch, aren't you?"

"Just older, just more accomplished, more experienced than you, my boy. That's what makes me look like a gold-plated son of a bitch. At heart I'm soft as lasagne. But right now I'm trying to think like the ruthless bastard we've got to outwit. You're going to his camp, wherever that proves to be, not as Philippe Bunau-Varilla, the wet-behind-the-ears engineer, but as *M'sieu* Bunau-Varilla, chargé d'affaires, envoy from the consul himself. Use your wits. Make him believe what you want him to believe. After all, you've got a lot going for you. You look young. You look honest. You're pretty and well built, and I can tell you, Emir Adel Kader likes well-built young Europeans. He's developed a real taste for them as bedmates."

Philippe drew a deep breath and held it, as much against the smell of this project as against the malodorous humanity crowded around them in the coach. This railway line from Algiers to Oran was always overcrowded, as if droves of peasants rode the new conveyance to escape their own lives or simply for the thrill of movement. Many carried their worldly goods wrapped in goatskin bundles and concealed their meager dreams behind flat black eyes in solemn, expressionless coffee-colored faces. Besides people, the train transported cattle, sheep, chickens, goats, wool hides and grains and, Philippe supposed, contraband guns for the desert men.

The train wound tortuously upward through the hills, often seeming to perch precariously on a rock ledge, the glittering stone wall rising sheer beside it. They crossed high, rickety trestles above dry rivulets. Philippe looked down on tops of Aleppo pines, clumps of false acacia, and dead gray oaks, leafless perches for vultures in that barren and fallow land. Even these uplands, once the only really fertile area of Algeria, had been laid waste by drought and herds of goats.

From the slowly climbing train, Philippe watched villages of low, gray, stone huts with thin slit windows, the drawn dark faces of people crowded around doorways of their *gourbis*. Beyond their fallow fields, the dry springs, the sheep and goat sniffing in the hot sand for a blade of esparto grass. They rolled past groups of tents, those small, permanent settlements of Moslem kinsmen who formed self-sustaining *douars*. Philippe winced; these were the desolated and abandoned people for whom they tried to improve the quality of life, only to be obstructed by the greedy and corrupt men like Adel Kader.

The train stopped in a small village at the rim of the desert. It was an unscheduled stop. The passengers closed their arms tightly about their belongings and stared out at the armed horsemen along the tracks. Two men came along the coaches studying the passengers until they discovered De Blasio and Philippe. One of the men, small and wizened, spoke in polite French. "You will debark here."

Philippe hesitated, but De Blasio nudged him with his elbow. They swung down. One of the horsemen waved his arm and the train pulled away into the rocky uplands. Horses were brought and the little man nodded, motioning Philippe and De Blasio to mount.

They rode most of the afternoon. Nobody talked much. They left the caravan trail and followed an old goat path into the foothills. Tall pines and ash trees threw long shadows over the encampment—tents made of goatskins stretched taut over cypress poles.

A splendid purple carpet was spread across the dung-mottled sand from the exact center of the encampment to the entrance of the largest tent. A rising wind from the desert stung their faces and riffled the fabrics at the entrance. The native horsemen motioned Philippe and De Blasio to dismount. Their horses were taken from them. They were not permitted to go directly to the chieftain's tent as Philippe had naïvely desired and hoped they might. He saw that the accomplishment of their mission would be achieved only by the most circuitous route; he alone seemed to be in a hurry to get about the business of fortifying the harbor at Algiers.

They were led to a smaller tent where they were bathed by eunuchs, their naked bodies then rubbed with palm oil by young girls. Philippe almost fell asleep under their ministrations; the ointment was a rich orange yellow in color and gave off a pleasant aroma. Dressing in fresh clothing, Philippe admitted he felt refreshed, if more than slightly aroused. He felt at least capable of facing the desert sheik.

But it was well after nightfall before he and De Blasio were led out to the center of the encampment and permitted to walk along the royal carpeting toward the entrance of Adel Kader's tent. In the meantime they had dined on rice, mutton, zucchini squash, topped off with fresh fruit in syrups and washed down with a dry red wine. There was much to recommend this business of state diplomacy. Your clothes were always clean whether your hands were or not.

As they approached the draped entranceway, dark hands appeared from within to retract the fabrics and open the path to a dazzling display of opulence. The entire tent, a complex of smaller sections closed off by heavy damasks and bright silks, was carpeted with a single huge, intricately designed Numidian rug.

Emir Adel Kader sprawled upon a deeply upholstered chair completely camouflaged beneath rich silks, colorful satins and damasks. The room was illumined by innumerable candles set in gold and diamond-encrusted holders.

Philippe and De Blasio hesitated just inside the entrance of the royal chamber, escorted on each side and at the rear by huge, bare-chested blacks armed with scimitars. The emir lifted his hand in a limp gesture of welcome and, like a tug nudging a reluctant vessel in strange waters, De Blasio steered Philippe toward the pillowed throne.

Philippe stared at their host, this desert sheik who dared challenge the might of France and the authority of the Third Republic—for blackmail. Adel Kader was perniciously thin, a balding man with Arabic features. His dark flesh seemed to be stretched painfully over his protuberant bone structure. He looked like a desert jackal, and it was impossible to guess his age. Philippe realized he had not until this moment recognized how deeply in jeopardy their work at Algiers was.

The huge, armed blacks who had accompanied them suddenly hesitated and stopped twenty feet from the man on the throne. Trembling, they dropped to their knees, eyes lowered. Philippe considered the emir one of the least imposing male specimens he'd ever encountered. The contrast between the huge, muscular slaves and the papyruslike fragility of their master was incredible, yet the mammoth servants shook visibly, terrified in the emir's presence.

The chieftain sat gazing at his guests without speaking. He was elaborately dressed, swathed in silks and bathed in a heady cologne which did not lose its bouquet even to the heavy incense burning in brass pots. A single diamond gleamed like a cyclops' eye on the emir's silken turban. His hands glittered with precious stones set in heavy gold. Only his washed, scented, pink feet were bare and unadorned. They extended with ugly, gnarled toes from his silken pantaloons. De Blasio approached, sank to his knees and kissed the emir's toes. Philippe was revolted. Damned if he could do that.

He felt those black eyes fixed on him. He met that gaze for an instant and saw the emir was reading his thoughts. Wincing, Philippe moved to fall to his knees, but before he could do it, De Blasio rose and caught his arm, holding him in place.

"Who is this man, *M'sieu* De Blasio?" Adel Kader said. "Why does he not kiss my feet as you have done? Does he have no respect?"

"This is your servant, Count Philippe Jean Bunau-Varilla," De Blasio said and Philippe bit back a smile at the title bestowed upon him. "He humbles himself before the son of Mohammed, as I do. But, my lord, as the representative of France itself, it is not fitting for him to crawl before any ruler, not even one as mighty as you."

100

"Then why does he intrude into my presence if he does not mean to pay me homage?" The emir's tone was chilled, but Philippe saw the sheik was eyeing him with some pleasure, the kind of look he had seen in the doe eyes of Claude-Bruce Grabralet!

"As a private citizen, my lord, Count Bunau-Varilla pays you every respect. It is the Third Republic which you cannot ask to bend its knees, even before you."

"This is indeed true, my lord Adel Kader," Philippe heard himself saying. Inwardly, he was thinking, the ends justify the means, make an equation of that. "I heard of you—and your beneficent rule of your people—long before I came to Africa. I came without the hope of ever meeting you in person. I am indeed privileged and honored, and I do humble myself before you."

Adel Kader got up suddenly. He was tall, but standing did not alter the first impression of him as a hungry jackal, a swaggering scavenger, a hyena laughing at starvation. He came down the wide, silk-draped steps and embraced Philippe, letting his bony hands stroke Philippe's buttocks before he withdrew. Philippe saw De Blasio's wicked grin. The odor of cologne from the immaculate garments was almost overwhelming. Philippe breathed a sigh of relief when the sheik released him and returned to his throne.

"I welcome you, Count Bunau-Varilla," Adel Kader said. "My land, my heart, anything within my power is yours. I am pleased to have you as my guest."

"And I am pleased to be privileged at last to come into your august presence," Philippe said. "Though I am unhappy because of the reason for my visit. I hope it will prove a minor unpleasantness, quickly removed."

"I hope so." The emir spoke in a bland voice and waved a ruby-encrusted hand. "The French have done much to depress and destroy the Allah-bestowed good of my poor land. If you have come to redress those wrongs, I welcome you a thousand times."

"I do come to redress a wrong, my lord," Philippe said. "Or perhaps we should name it a mistaken impression. France has no wish to harm or to exploit your land or your people in any way."

101

"And yet, this is what you do. This is one of your crimes. Once my people lived reasonably well. Now they are victims of actual hunger. Well, France is a rich nation. France carries away much of our wealth. France can well afford to help my people."

"We are indeed here to help you, my lord. If your people seemed once to live well, it was in a different world. The world was then agrarian. Today the world is becoming industrialized. France wishes, my lord, to help your people enter the nineteenth century, to use modern equipment, to compete on equal terms with the advanced nations."

"Suppose we do not want our peace, our tranquility, our natural resources altered? Suppose we want a land where our people may follow the dictates of Mohammed, to lead their lives as they've always led them?"

"Sire, that is a beautiful ideal. But it is the way to self-destruction. It is the way to decay. No nation today can crawl into its own womb and hope to exist. A land must be opened to trade and commerce. For example, its harbors must be deepened to accommodate the larger ships now plying the seas."

"We have a beautiful and spacious harbor at the Bay of Algiers. We like it as it is."

"Sire, Algiers is indeed lovely, but as a harbor it is no longer adequate in world trade."

"Then we shall have to be content as we are, shan't we?"

"Sire, a good harbor must be closed against the common direction of violent gales. In order to accomplish this, the artificial breakwaters must be strengthened. A harbor must have sufficient depth to accommodate deep-draft ships at ebb tide. Algiers must be deepened in order to do this. A harbor must have a bottom providing good holding ground for those big ship anchors. On this single quality is Algiers harbor passable."

"Ships have always used our harbors as they are. As they are we want them. As they are, they will remain. We do not fight progress so much as we fight against the alteration of the face of our nation by outsiders who hope only to rape us."

"Sire, nations and people have been improving their harbors since the first sails were invented, since the first trading ship sailed from one place to another. Civilization followed the trade routes and flourished where the harbors invited shipping."

"We have no wish that Algiers should be modernized, as you call it, made ugly in the image of French ports. We wish to live in peace, unchanged."

"Sire, you are a brilliant man. A practical man. You know, I'm sure, that a good harbor can be protection against those who would attack you by sea. Our ports have played an important part in repulsing foreign invaders. You do want protection for your subjects?"

For the first time the emir remained silent. He watched Philippe thoughtfully.

Thinking, hoping at least, that he was making some impression on the chieftain, Philippe continued. "If you are to become stronger, your nation greater, sire, you must depend on trading by sea. A protected inner harbor with a narrow entrance makes possible cargo loading and discharging free from violent waves. To have a good harbor we must govern the height of waves by the fetch, or distance, from the upwind shore. Without an adequate breakwater, the exposure to violent elements will render your harbor useless."

"Why must your people, under this man De Blasio here, tear away our native structures along the quays and replace them with great French-style barns?" Adel Kader inquired. "Is this progress or is this disfigurement of my land?"

"Dock facilities, sire, including piers, wharves, bulkheads and basin, all must be upgraded unless Algiers is to remain rooted to the days when ships had drafts of ten to fifteen feet instead of twenty to forty feet as they do now."

The emir rose again. He stood poised, and the image of the jackal trembling to be at its prey raced through Philippe's mind. He stared for a brief instant at De Blasio. The emir's gaze struck Philippe and moved over him, devouring him. Then he came down the steps and embraced Philippe again, that odor of cologne now stronger and mixed with body musk. Philippe permitted himself to be held close. At last the sheik stood back, holding Philippe's arms and gazing raptly into his face. "I am not impressed with your facts or your cause, but your argument, your power and emotional integrity have moved me beyond words. I would plead with you, Count Bunau-Varilla, to remain here as my guest, and then to become my economic adviser. I don't know you well. But I know you well enough to trust my future to your integrity, my welfare to your brilliance."

Philippe was speechless. At last he managed to murmur, "I am flattered, my lord, naturally, but—"

"That is why I invite you to remain as my guest, a few weeks, a few months. For whatever time you need to make up your mind that your future, your destiny is here in this land which needs you, with me who needs you."

"My lord Adel Kader—" Philippe started to speak but suddenly realized that his and De Blasio's lives might well depend on his careful choice of words. The sheik was fascinated by him, ready to share his power with him, but at the wrong phrase, he could as quickly change as violent storms came up without warning in the desert. He had no intention of remaining here with Adel Kader any more than he had money with which to bribe him, but these were delicate matters.

"All you might wish to bring about," Adel Kader said, "would be within your power. With you to advise me, I would become a God in this world. Poets would speak my name for a hundred generations."

"Forgive me, sire," De Blasio said. "You are taking a most unfair and hurtful advantage of the count. M'sieu Bunau-Varilla cannot answer as you wish him to reply— no matter what might be in his heart. You are speaking to him as a private citizen, as a man. But he is here as the sole representative of the Third Republic. He cannot speak as Philippe Bunau-Varilla, only as the representative of his country. I hope you appreciate this."

The expression on the emir's face did not change, but he retreated up the silken steps to his throne and sagged upon it, watching Philippe.

104

"As honored as I am by your generous offer, sire," Philippe said, "as any man would be, I do represent my country."

"Then state your business." The emir nodded curtly.

"Let me speak one more time, if I may," De Blasio said. "We want to continue the work on the harbor and docking facilities at Algiers. We have no wish to deface, destroy or in anyway harm the natural beauty of your native land. Is there no way we might convince you to let us proceed with what we see as urgent work, for your own benefit?"

The emir spoke in that same curt tone, without looking at De Blasio. "There is no way you will receive my permission, and there is no way you can continue without it, unless you are willing to shed more blood than the French have ever spilled before."

Philippe said, "My lord, I understand your position. I do not, as envoy of my government, necessarily agree with it, or suggest that it is the correct one. But from your standpoint, I certainly see its validity. Still, without the improvements we plan to make on the harbor, you will in the long run be the loser—you, your people, not France. France has other great ports and harbors. You have Algiers. Still, there must be some accommodation. Suppose my country would be willing to pay some reasonable sum for what you see as a wrong, reparations for any damage done. We admit to none. We see none. But we are willing to adjust our view as far as possible to agree with yours."

The emir sat perfectly still, watching him without speaking.

"Suppose my country invested an amount, named by you, for you to use to rebuild, restore, or modernize anywhere in Algeria as you wished?" Philippe suggested. "In exchange, we want the right to proceed with what we see as vital work in the bay at Algiers."

"Your country would be willing perhaps to settle upon the tribes which I represent a stipulated amount, for our cooperation in this matter?"

"Exactly, sire." Philippe was sweating. The emir's black eyes had not faltered or moved from his face.

De Blasio said, "If you named an amount which my government could recognize as reasonable, Count Buñau-Varilla has come with the authority to accede to your requirements, to accept and approve."

For the first time the emir's eyes moved from Philippe to De Blasio, and were illumined by a new glitter.

"You are prepared to deliver the sum I require, as reparations, here and now?"

"Of course not." De Blasio's voice sharpened, and Philippe could see both of them hanging by the toes; then his voice lowered, softened, mellowed and sweetened. "My lord knows better than this. Unless you are making some small joke at our expense."

"I assure you, I never joke."

"I didn't believe you were joking, sire. But as you are a practical man, so is our government pragmatic and demanding. You know, sire, we could not deliver you any amount until you had removed your troops from Algiers."

"Suppose I will agree only that I *will* remove them, only upon receipt of payment?"

De Blasio shook his head. "Our government will not agree to this any more than you would. But it will agree to send a troop, led by Count Bunau-Varilla, if you so stipulated, to deliver the funds once the troops were at a prearranged distance from the area with the assurance they would not return."

The emir smiled faintly. "Suppose I named an amount as reparations. You agreed upon it, and I insisted upon holding Count Bunau-Varilla here as my guest—until that money were paid, and my troops removed."

De Blasio retreated half a step. This was an eventuality, Philippe saw, which De Blasio had not considered. Philippe said, "I would gladly stay, sire, as your guest. But as envoy of France I could not. It would create—an incident. It might well cause troops to be sent in by my country."

The emir considered this. De Blasio dampened his lips and spoke quickly. "Yes. This is certainly true. It would be as Count Bunau-Varilla describes. Nothing but the safe conduct of the envoy, Count Bunau-Varilla and

106

myself, would be acceptable as good faith by our government. This must be clear to your highness."

The emir shrugged. "Perhaps it is as you say. Would your country pay reparations to me of a hundred million francs?"

Without hesitation, De Blasio nodded. "When your troops are removed. When we have your signature upon an agreement that they will remain twenty leagues from Algiers until all work on the harbor is completed. I am sure you have the Count's word of honor on that."

The emir's black eyes darted back to Philippe's face and rested there. Philippe nodded. "I would be prepared to sign such an agreement here and now."

The emir did not move. "Suppose I request the amount of five hundred million francs? What is your answer?"

Philippe saw now how right De Blasio had been all along. Adel Kader's maneuver had been a cold-blooded and calculated attempt to collect tribute. It was blackmail. No tribute, no work on the harbor. Philippe was ready to tell him to go to hell, but he felt De Blasio's sharp elbow nudge him in the side and he nodded, unwillingly.

"And a billion francs?" the emir suggested. "A billion francs might be a small amount to pay for my friendship and cooperation."

Philippe did not answer and even De Blasio hesitated. In the long run, Philippe saw, De Blasio realized they were not dealing in counterfeit money. Nothing would keep Adel Kader from destroying the works at Algiers unless he were paid whatever was agreed upon here. Philippe felt a sudden need to vomit. Adel Kader was not the only one who was being duped here; De Blasio had been using him as well. The game of statesmanship, set up as a phony action to deceive a gullible desert chieftain, was in reality an action in which they were actually obligating France to pay reparations or blackmail or tribute, or bounty, to this thug in silks and cologne. De Blasio was simply buying time. They would get from Adel Kader his demands for tribute. They would also get from him an agreement to permit work to proceed. The crews would work in Algiers while he and De Blasio—or perhaps De Blasio intended to send him alone!—tried to convince French officials that the money had to be paid! All De Blasio gave a damn about was getting on with the engineering work. The ends justify the means! Make it an equation so it was palatable enough to live with. It didn't matter what you did, as long as you achieved your goal.

Philippe said, "Forgive me, Your Highness. But your latest demand far exceeds anything I am empowered even to discuss with you."

The emir shrugged. "Then we have nothing more to say, because you are far from reaching a figure upon which I will even consider negotiations."

De Blasio's voice shook. "When could we hope to get a firm agreement from you?" He did not bother to put humility and homage in words or tone.

The emir shrugged. "We will have an agreement when all my demands—and all my *desires*—are met."

[14]

With the desert sun painful against his eyelids, Philippe
awoke the next morning, aching with fatigue and sour
with failure.

He and De Blasio departed from the encampment of
Emir Adel Kader in low spirits. They were led by armed
horsemen down the goatpath and along the ancient caravan trail to the place where it intersected the railroad.
When the long train puffed and strained up the rocky
incline, the horsemen halted it and Philippe and De
Blasio boarded for the long ride back to the coast. Adel
Kader had not bothered to say good-bye. He had said all
he had to say the evening before.

Philippe sensed that he was far more depressed over
the failure of their mission than De Blasio was. De Blasio
was pragmatic; he never wasted time on the past—failure
or success. He had tried; he had failed; what the hell.
"I'll try something else," he told Philippe from behind a
cloud of gray cigar smoke.

"What else? You know as well as I do that the work
on the harbor is suspended until Adel Kader's demands
are satisfied."

"Yes. We are stopped. But that doesn't mean we have to quit."

"Do you have a plan? What are you going to do?"

De Blasio shrugged. "First, I'm going to have four slave girls give me a bath, three of them give me a massage, and two of them go to bed with me."

"It's not like you to let a greedy savage stop you."

"How do you know what I'm like? I see things as they are," De Blasio blew a thick wreath of smoke. "Not as I wish they were. Hell, cheer up, my boy, you did one hell of a job. Adel Kader was impressed. *I* was impressed. Me. You said some clever things. Perhaps some of them hold the solution to our problem. I don't know. You did a fine job as a diplomat. Perhaps you missed your true vocation, though you are a damned fine engineer, too."

"When I get a chance to be."

They rode silently in the crowded, sweaty coach. After a little while, Philippe saw that De Blasio was asleep. He tried to sleep, but the smells were too putrid, too pervasive, the seat too uncomfortable, the noise too intense, the sense of failure too disturbing. He had been bred to look upon failure as something disgraceful. When one admitted failure, one admitted others were superior, their minds sharper, their wits faster, and he was damned if he would ever admit that greedy desert barbarian was his better. And that harbor work had to be completed; it could not be permitted to languish at the whim of a tribe leader with a itchy palm. He would not stop. They had appealed to the decency and compassionate instincts of a man who possessed neither. The machinations of the Third Republic moved slowly, as De Blasio charged, but he would get them moving.

Philippe had never suspected that he possessed any aptitude for the subtleties of statesmanship or the deviousness of diplomacy, any desire to attempt to sway and influence other men to understand, accept and act upon his own views. He had always acknowledged and appreciated the straightforward honesty of engineering. One faced a problem and one found the answer in the quickest, most direct fashion. He had found a new kind of excitement and challenge in dealing with Adel Kader. Not even the total failure of his mission affected the exultant feeling that had spurred him in dealing with the chieftain. He despised the fact of failing in obtaining permission to renew the vital harbor work program, but instead of admitting defeat, he determined to go on fighting, with a driving need to win that surprised even himself. He had to find new arenas of argument, new areas of attack, new maneuvers.

He arrived in Algiers feeling more hopeful, though he still did not know what he would do, or what he could do, only that he would do *something*. He was damned if he'd sit idly and accept failure. Still, the sense of emptiness persisted. He admitted his lack of experience, his ignorance about dealing with either diplomats or bureaucrats, and most of all his desperate need for expert advice and practical help, and this seemed to bring him inevitably back to De Blasio.

De Blasio refused to be any help at all. He clapped Philippe on the shoulder as they parted and said, "Forget it, *paisano*. Go home and get in the covers with your bed wench. We made a good fight; we've nothing to be ashamed of."

Walking to the hotel through the crowded streets of the old town, Philippe pushed thoughts of the failed mission from his mind. He hurried through the mobs of loiterers, beggars and children, hoping against reason that there would be a letter from Madelon awaiting him.

He had written to her constantly, and his letters went unanswered.

He hurried to his rooms each evening, going first to the mail Sahyin had laid out beside his chilled whiskey. Each night his anticipation mounted, only to be dashed. His heart slugged and his belly went empty with loss and rejection. He felt helpless. There was never a letter from her.

Perhaps the passionate fervor of his missives had frightened and repelled her. Or, perhaps, even if she did love him, she despaired ever of being free of her marriage vows. Perhaps her proud nature refused to permit her to carry on a love affair—even across five hundred lonely miles. Whatever the reason, she never wrote.

111

Faced with Madelon's silènce, Philippe existed in a black world of doubt and loss.

He walked into the moldy-smelling lobby of his hotel, aching with fatigue. The desk clerk handed him a parcel of collected mail.

Philippe's heart lurched. He could smell the fresh scent of Madelon!

"I held all your mail here at the desk, *m'sieu,* rather than give it to your slave girl as usual." The clerk smiled obsequiously.

Philippe barely heard him. His mind spun with pleasure and relief. She had written to him! He tossed the clerk a franc.

With his mail in his fist, his heart pounding erratically, Philippe climbed the stairs to his room on the shadowed upper floor. He laughed inwardly, debating whether to tear open Madelon's letter first, or to save it until he'd had a hot bath, a cold whiskey, and time to savor every word.

When he inserted his key in his lock, he heard squeals from inside his room.

He hesitated with his hand on the knob. He didn't look forward to Sahyin's frenetic ministrations. He didn't know whether he was getting old, simply exhausted, or attacked by guilt. He remembered what De Blasio had said, joking and yet not joking at all: "Forget it. Go home and get in the covers with your bed wench."

Any other day, this would have been his only hope of heaven. But now there was the letter, the enormous need to be alone with it, whatever it said.

He pushed open the door and Sahyin sprang upon him like a cat. She threw her arms about him, kissing his neck, his chin, his earlobes, the loosened knot of his tie. However, he was aware that Sahyin, even in her frenzied welcome, was calculating enough to grab the bundle of mail from him and hurl it across the room.

Chattering at him in her native tongue, she drew him after her to the bed, pushed him down upon it and hurled herself upon him again. He lay back under the sensuous pressure of her voluptuous body and the frenzy of her kisses.

As always, as anxious as he was to get to Madelon's letter, he fought a losing battle against Sahyin's body, her mouth and her hands. His mind could reject her—at this moment his mind rejected her totally—but he felt his body betraying him, surrendering to her heated lovemaking.

He sagged against the covers and permitted her to remove his clothing. After all, she would pester, nag and nibble at him until he surrendered. When she was sated and his own body soothed, then he would lie with Madelon's letter in his hands.

Sahyin kissed squealed her delight over each new area of his body she uncovered. By the time she threw herself, nude, across him, he was rigid and quivering with need. He gave himself over to the frantic ritual, almost like a dance, in which she tried to destroy both their bodies with the heated assault of her thighs.

The room spun, and nothing else was important. What did a harbor at Algiers matter? What did Algiers matter? *Faster, Sahyin, faster.* She was like a belly-dancer, enthralled by unheard rhythms. *Faster, Sahyin, faster. Harder, damn it, harder. . . .*

But a chill settled over him at the very moment when he should have been spinning mindlessly to the crest of ecstatic delight, he wasn't thinking of Sahyin and her flailing hips at all. He was seeing Madelon Grabralet.

He lay upon the bed in exhaustion when it was over. Sahyin understood instinctively something was wrong.

"My lord didn't like Sahyin?" She crawled over him, sweaty and persistent.

"Get away and let me alone, Sahyin."

"My lord, please. What's wrong? What has Sahyin done that has failed her master? Please, sire, there is nothing I would not do to please you."

"Except be silent."

"Why do you hate Sahyin? Sahyin wait. So lonely for you. Sahyin lives for you, but Sahyin no longer pleases you? Please, before Allah, my lord, be kind. Tell me why?"

"Because you talk too much." He was almost asleep.

"Sahyin will never speak again if that will please my lord." She wept, writhing upon him, her full breasts heated

113

and heavy upon his chest. Their wet skin adhered. Suddenly, more asleep than awake, he shoved her away.

Sahyin hung for a moment on the edge of the mattress and then fell off the bed, landing loudly on the floor. But Philippe, freed of her musk and her sweat and her body, escaped into sleep. He heard nothing of her weeping.

Philippe never afterward knew what woke him, the prickle of chill in the breathless heat, a sense of wrong that permeated the room.

He opened his eyes and sat up in bed, looking around. He hardly knew where he was, how long or how briefly he'd slept.

His gaze swept across the room. Then he saw Sahyin in the gathering dusk of afternoon. She walked, like a condemned person on her way to a firing squad, toward the oblong patch of sunlight through the balcony door.

She was naked, but this did not stop her. She walked through the doorway out to the balcony. He stared, incredulous. Women of her tribe *never* appeared in public unless their faces were veiled. Yet, there was Sahyin un-self-consciously nude on his balcony. Then, his mind clearing, his gaze focusing, he saw what she had in her hand.

Even from across the room, he recognized it. The letter from Madelon. Sahyin had ripped it open. She threw away the envelope, spitting after it, and then, before he could react, she ripped the letter paper into pieces and threw it into the wind.

Philippe lunged from the bed. "Goddamn you," he yelled.

She spun around, bracing herself against the grill of the balcony. He ran across the room, stood in the doorway, as naked as she, trembling with outrage. "You bitch," he said. "I ought to kill you."

Sahyin sprang, catlike, and curled herself up at his feet. She kissed at his ankles, his toes, his instep. He stepped back, leaving her sprawled facedown on the flooring, sobbing.

"No." She spat the word at him. "Letter from *her*. Letter from that one, stinking of perfume. No."

114

Sahyin slithered across the carpeting, moving out of the sunlight like a serpent toward him. She came upward fluidly on hands and knees, her hands reaching for him like fangs.

"Damn you." He slapped her across the face, and she went sprawling on the floor again.

"Her! Her! Her!" Sahyin wept. "I hate her."

He stared down at her. "What do you know of her? How do you know that letter is even from a woman? You can't read."

"Can smell! Yes! Stinks of her perfume. All her letters —stink of her perfume. Her letters make you no want Sahyin. I tear them all up."

He trembled with rage. "You're damned right. I don't want Sahyin."

"Please, my lord. I never speak again of this woman. Never touch another letter. Never breathe stinking perfume." She crawled forward, clutching her arms around his legs, pulling herself upward, pressing her hot, tear-streaked face against him, pleading, her whole body quivering. Her breath seared his flesh.

He caught her hair in his fist and tried to pull her away.

Sahyin clung tighter, pressing her face upon him, her mouth molten and swollen. She nuzzled at his thighs and kissed him, using every wile that had worked so well before. But he felt no desire for her. He did not want to kiss her. He wanted to kill her.

"Get dressed," he told her, his voice savage.

She continued pressing her mouth upon him. He shoved her away. "I mean it, Sahyin. Get dressed. Now. Right now."

Sahyin dressed, delaying as long as she could. He put on his own clothes, and then led her into the crowded street. Shopkeepers were closing for the day. Voices called from the minarets. The street was a cacophony of sound, of smells of vegetables, fruit, dates, dried fish and smoked mutton. All the noises seemed strident, discordant and protracted.

Sahyin paced herself behind his left shoulder, moving in a fluid motion as his shadow might pursue him. Her veil was drawn up across the bridge of her nose. Only her olive-black eyes were exposed to the gaze of strangers, yet men turned to follow her with approving glances, knowing by some instinct that she was young and lovely.

As they approached De Blasio's small stone and stucco cottage, Sahyin began to cry. Philippe knocked on the door. She wailed loudly.

"Shut up." He spoke curtly across his shoulder without turning to look at her. "A scene won't make this any easier on either one of us."

De Blasio seemed preoccupied. As Philippe explained that he was returning the slave girl, De Blasio seemed to be only half-listening, his mind turned inward.

"Tired of her, eh?" De Blasio said.

Sahyin wailed. Neither Philippe nor De Blasio even glanced toward her.

"I find her vicious," Philippe said.

"I beg your pardon? I'm sorry. What did you say?"

Philippe stared at De Blasio. He'd never seen the little man like this. "I said I don't want her any more."

"Of course." De Blasio nodded emphatically. "We all need a bed wench. I can send over another girl. I agree, variety is the spice—"

Sahyin was wailing loudly and helplessly by now.

De Blasio tossed her a casual glance. He nodded. "I'll be glad to have her for a while. She looks good. Yes. She'll add a nice touch to my menage."

Philippe winced. Despite what he knew of the customs of this place, the way slaves were treated as subhumans, he disliked discussing Sahyin as if she were chattel. She had been good to him, pleasant and compliant in his bed, more than pleasant, more than compliant. But destroying Madelon's letters! My God! How many? For how long? She was certainly no animal but a true woman—possessive, conniving, and dangerous.

He spoke with a forced coolness he did not feel. "I don't give a damn what you do with her. Just keep her away from me."

"Of course, dear boy," De Blasio said. "Of course I will." And he seemed to sink again into that deep reverie.

Philippe turned and walked toward the door. Sahyin

116

stood unmoving, almost as if in a trance. Then, suddenly, she flung herself after him, digging her long, tapered fingers into his clothing and screeching.

"Please, sire! In the name of Allah! Take me with you. I'll be good. I swear I'll be good."

Philippe twisted away from her, pushing her back into the room with one hand and reaching for the doorknob with the other. She clutched at him anew every time he pried her fingers loose.

At last De Blasio seemed to become fully aware of what was going on in his parlor.

"Go ahead, old fellow," he said. "She'll be all right. They forget fast."

De Blasio caught the girl roughly about the waist, dragged her back from the door and flung her across the room.

His voice lashed at her. "Behave yourself now, damn it, or I'll flog your hide off and send you back to your people for dog meat."

Sahyin sprawled on the floor and stared up at De Blasio in terror. She shuddered, quivered and then subsided into small sobs.

Philippe exhaled heavily and went quickly through the doorway. Well, now it was over. He squared his shoulders and hurried away.

He spent a restless, sleepless night. He rolled and tossed on the bed. He listened to the sounds from the old town, and when finally the city grew quiet, noises and exotic music from the Casbah drifted in on the night wind.

He shifted miserably under the netting. In his mind he saw Madelon's face, Madelon enslaved, her loveliness concealed by a veil, weeping in the darkness. He felt as if he were fettered, somehow trussed up and constricted on the mattress. He couldn't get a full breath of air. He wanted to escape. He wanted to run to Madelon. He tried to think about the harbor project, idled workers standing at the whim of a desert chieftain. But he kept coming back to Madelon.

In the deepest dark hour before the dawn, he finally fell into fitful sleep.

[15]

At first he thought the disturbing sound was thunder, earthshaking tremors of the storms of his boyhood at Argenteuil. It didn't make sense, a northern-European rainstorm in the desert. Yet nothing else explained the fearsome rumble of thunder. Even more unusual was thunder without lightning. Gradually, as men's voices rose, the shouting mixed with the roaring of thunder brought him fully awake.

He lay still for some moments, listening. He felt disoriented, puzzled by the repeated clap of thunder in a still, hot morning. And those men shouting, the steady rumbling, the creaking of leather and metal. He swung off his bed and ran across the room to his small balcony.

Unable to believe his eyes, he stared down at the army dray wagons loaded with soldiers, trappings and equipment, all the accoutrements of a military occupation. The tricolor, snapped in the wind on scores of staffs in the pink sunlight of early morning. Behind the wagons marched the Foreign Legionnaires, four abreast, in full pack and parade dress. In the distance, he saw the cavalry, the glittering scabbards, the prancing horses, the riffling plumes. What was the purpose of this military parade, this display of French war might, at six-thirty in the morning?

He stood for some moments watching the infantry, troopers and artillery striding past. Then he returned inside his room and dressed quickly. The supply wagons were still rumbling through the twisting, cobbled streets of the old town.

Before he had crossed the musty lobby he learned the reason for the display of weaponry, manpower and arms strength. Sometime during the night, the French consulate had been forcibly entered and the Consul himself kidnapped. A note had been left behind, rumor had it, demanding the incredible ransom of ten billion francs for the safe return of the official representative of the Third Republic in Algeria. An international incident was threatened.

Philippe hurried through the streets, finding French soldiers and weaponry stationed everywhere, with liaisons already springing up between the combatants and the native women. Algerian shopkeepers displayed tricolor flags. Many mothers had sent their children off to school carrying lunches, books and small French flags so there could be no doubting the allegiances of the young. Flags and false smiles flew everywhere in the sultry morning. Many ordinary citizens had not heard of the kidnapping; they did not know why the army was occupying the city, but they were taking no chances. They declared their loyalty to France, they displayed it in every obsequious way they could recall or invent. Others saw a chance to profit from the influx of soldiers. They hawked fresh bread, cheeses, wines and souvenirs along the walk. There was the carnival atmosphere of impending combat in the air.

When Philippe finally pushed and shoved his way through the streets to the temporary engineering offices at the harbor, he stopped in stunned shock. The sight that greeted his eyes was incredible. The troops sent in by Emir Adel Kader had completely, silently and totally dissolved from the waterfront. They had disappeared before the invasion of the French troops.

Philippe stood on the wharf in the blazing sun, feeling

a sense of exultation even in the midst of a threatened catastrophe. Every evil wind blows in some good. Adel Kader's men were cleared out before the superior forces of the French. But the sickening thought occurred to him that the French Consul may well have been spirited away with the greedy emir's troops during the night. Since he had met Adel Kader, it was precisely the action he might anticipate from the desert scavenger.

He found De Blasio prowling the offices, barking out orders around a large cigar. De Blasio was armed, a gun in holster at his hip. It was not like De Blasio to resort to halfway measures. "This whole scurrilous country is an armed camp," he told Philippe, smoke clouding his swarthy face. "If you're smart, you'll go nowhere without a gun."

De Blasio moved to walk away but Philippe caught his arm. "Listen. I know who did this."

"What?" De Blasio heeled around, face taut.

"The kidnapping. I know who is behind it. It has to be Adel Kader. He must have plotted the whole thing."

De Blasio scowled and gave Philippe an odd look. At last he shrugged. "It may be." He didn't sound convinced or particularly interested.

Philippe was incredulous. "It must be Adel Kader who ordered this crime. Who else?"

"I don't know. I don't care. It's not my job to know, to care, or to find out."

"You know Adel Kader. He might kill the consul if his demands aren't met."

De Blasio shrugged again. "He might."

"My God, De Blasio. This is a man's life."

"Oh, hell, my boy, it's a political power struggle. Nothing else. If Adel Kader has the consul you can bet he won't let anything happen to him. He doesn't want the French army chasing his ragtags across the Sahara. If he wants anything he wants money."

"Ten billion francs, I heard."

"Did you? I heard twenty billion. But what the hell, it's not our money."

"It's our country being mocked, flouted, threatened."

"Oh, shit! Does anybody believe that patriotic slop any

more? Next you'll be waving the tricolor and singing the *Marseillaise*. I've got work to do."

"But, De Blasio, we know where Adel Kader is."

"Correction, my dear boy. We know where he *was*."

"We can go to the military authorities, offer our services, lead troops there."

De Blasio laughed at him. "Suppose we set off as you suggest, Don Quixote and Sancho Panza! Suppose they sent troops and we led them into those hills. Do you know what we would find? A few uncovered latrines."

Slack-jawed, Philippe stared at De Blasio, unable to believe what he was hearing. "We've got to do something," he said uncertainly.

"The hell we do! This place is bristling with three-quarters of the French troops occupying the country. They've installed generals and majors and secret police and spies, the whole military network is in action. I'll tell you what we've got to do. We've got to take advantage of the best possible break we could have gotten, military protection for work on the harbor. That's what we've got to do, get to work and finish that job while we've got all this expensive protection." He laughed. "The troops aren't here to protect us or our project, but no one is going to interfere with us while they're here. So let's get off our butts and get working."

Stunned at De Blasio's attitude, Philippe found himself nodding weakly in assent. He set out to take up the repairs and expansion exactly where work had been halted by the arrival of Adel Kader's camel troops. The laborers fell to, anxious to get back on the French government payroll. Neither Philippe nor De Blasio left the waterfront, sleeping and eating in the offices. They lived on bread, cheese and black coffee. Neither of them shaved. Each morning they checked, Philippe holding his breath, as to whether the consul had been rescued and the troops recalled from occupation of the city. De Blasio put his laborers on extra shifts and promised bonuses. Philippe argued against this rash move. They had no authorization for adding workers or promising extra pay. "The hell with that," De Blasio growled, his swollen eyes red-rimmed. "Let the government auditors worry about that."

Under De Blasio's unrelenting dominance and Philippe's ever-present oversight, the work moved swiftly toward completion. Sometimes in the late afternoon, Philippe would take a breather. He didn't walk away from the harbor. Instead he strolled the long wharves which marked the west bank of the Bay of Algiers. The artificial shelter made the port one of the finest in North Africa. The new piers and docking facilities provided ships protection from the elements and promised fast loading and unloading. He laughed aloud with the pride he felt in his accomplishment. He walked along the gleaming piers, touching hawsers, chains, tackles, uprights, watching the waning sunlight find its reflection in the new storage buildings.

He returned one afternoon to the office to find De Blasio drinking from the mouth of a whiskey bottle. The liquid ran through his beard and stained his shirt. De Blasio didn't care. He took a long drag on his cigar, blew smoke toward the distant heavens almost defiantly and then drew in long drafts of raw liquor. Philippe stared at him. "Are you trying to kill yourself?"

De Blasio put his head back, laughing. His beard was wet. He even looked as if he might have poured champagne over his own thinning hair. "I'm celebrating, you brilliant son of a bitch! The army is pulling out!"

Philippe's eyes widened. "And this is something to celebrate? What will we do for protection?"

"Who the hell needs the army now, dear boy? We've done it, you with your genius for knowing the right answers, and me for being able to translate those answers into hard, sweaty work."

"But why is the army pulling out?"

"Because we don't need them any more. Sure, we're not quite finished, but there remains only the finishing touches. The big stuff is done. Adel Kader couldn't stop us now. Nobody could stop us now. God Himself—couldn't stop us now. We made it, Philippe. We made it."

"Yes." Philippe nodded. He took the bottle and drank from it, but he still felt uncertain, troubled. "What about the consul?"

De Blasio drank again, sloppily. "What about him?"

"Is he dead?"

"I don't think so. He's been returned. He's back in the consulate; we didn't have to pay a sou to get him returned. He's happy, we've finished the harbor, and all's right with God's world."

"Returned. Unharmed. Without payment?"

De Blasio laughed loudly, the sound rattling the building. Philippe stared at him, unable to believe what he now saw as the truth. He shook his head. "You," he whispered.

"What?"

"You son of a bitch. There's nothing you wouldn't do, is there? What do you say? What's your equation? The ends justify the means. Huh?"

De Blasio grinned and drank again. "I don't know what you're talking about."

"The hell you don't. You son of a bitch, *you* kidnapped the consul."

"Me?" De Blasio waved his arm and shook his head vigorously. "Why, I've been here, working at your side, dear boy, the whole time."

"Oh, you didn't actually kidnap the consul. Hell, I suppose nobody did, really. Did they? Where did you have him spirited off to? Some castle on the Mediterranean? He lived on chicken breasts, caviar and vintage wines while this whole city teetered on the brink of war. Jesus. Is there *anything* you wouldn't do to accomplish your goals? You couldn't get the army in to guard a harbor project, but you brought the whole force of the French nation to look for a *kidnapped* consul."

De Blasio bowed his head in mock humility. "Hell, the consul agreed to the total concept with one proviso."

"Yes?"

"He agreed to the *kidnapping,* he could use the vacation, but he stipulated that if anything went wrong, you and I would be the scapegoats. Governments always have to have scapegoats in matters like this."

"Me?"

"Well, after all, as I explained to the consul, it was your idea."

"Damn you! We never discussed such a plan, ever!"

123

"No. You and I didn't. But you put it in words. You made me see how it could work."

"What in hell are you talking about?"

"Your organizational, creative genius. You told old Adel Kader that if he held you, Count Bunau-Varilla, against your will, as his guest, it would create an incident and bring in the French army."

"I—did that?"

"Right. You put in words, with your usual clarity and vision, the quickest way to get troops, a whole army, into Algiers. A request would take six months, an *incident* would bring them in overnight. And you were right, dear boy, it did."

Philippe sagged into a swivel chair. He sat staring at the floor. He could not yet believe it. He and De Blasio could have spent the rest of their lives on Devil's Island if anything had gone wrong. Any small flare-up might have caused a pitched battle between French forces and tribesmen. But De Blasio didn't give a damn, as long as he got his harbor project completed. The ends justify the means.

De Blasio offered him a drink, but he shook his head. He saw that his studies at the Ecole Polytechnique had been merely basics; his degree earned him the *right* to become an engineer. His months at Depuits et David had developed his engineering skills. He had put these skills into practical application at Tunis. But here in Algiers, under the expert tutelage of De Blasio, he had won his doctorate. He would never again accept anything at its face value. He would see that the straight line might be the shortest distance between two points, but the circuitous route was often the quickest. He wondered if he would ever meet a more complex, devious and tenacious soul than this drunken, laughing, bearded De Blasio. He could devoutly pray that he did not, or that if he did come upon such a man, he would be on his side, and not his foe. With a friend like Guido, a man didn't need enemies.

"You look a little gray around the gills," De Blasio said, pacing back and forth before Philippe's chair. "Why don't you go back to the hotel, get a hot bath, shave, and relax for a few days? There's nothing around here I can't handle."

"There's nothing anywhere *you* can't handle," Philippe said, half in admiration, half in exasperation.

He walked along the narrow streets of the old town. As suddenly as they had arrived, the French troops had pulled out; the small tricolor flags that had blossomed everywhere had now disappeared completely. The littered streets were sadder and dirtier than usual. The whores had drifted into bars, cafés or temporary honest employment. The ancient city displayed the total exhaustion that Philippe felt. He kept putting one foot in front of the other because if he made it to the hotel he could have a hot bath, clean socks, and uninterrupted sleep. If he fell on the cobbled walk, he would be robbed, walked on, or sent to a local hospital, a fate frequently synonymous with death.

He crossed the mildewed lobby, finding the odors not too much more unpleasant than those of the street. It was an interminable climb up the dark stairwell to the second floor. He came off the top step and sagged a moment against the wall before continuing along the dust-caked carpeting. At first, he thought he'd stopped at the wrong room because his door was ajar, but even to his be-numbed mind the number was right. He entered, aware that someone was in his parlor. He stopped inside the door, stunned. It was Madelon.

[16]

Madelon!

"Madelon," he whispered, afraid even now she was a figment of his fatigued imagination, a trick of the mind, part of the release from the volcano of excitement in which he had existed these past weeks. But no, it was she. It was Madelon. Thank God, she was standing there, smiling, holding out her arms.

For a moment, he stood immobile just inside his door. He gazed hungrily at Madelon, his reddened eyes brimming with tears even while he laughed aloud with joy. How long he had dreamed of the moment when he would see her again, hold her again. Now suddenly, inexplicably, she stood before him, as if through some miracle, lovelier by far even than in his lonely fantasies. How beautiful she was! Her beauty was so breathtakingly perfect—that delicately chiseled profile, the flawless olive-tinted skin, the lustrous golden hair, violet eyes and full-lipped, smiling mouth.

If he were dreaming, if exhaustion had totally incapacitated him, so be it! He didn't want to wake up and find her gone.

"Madelon?"

Like a wraith materializing from shadows, Madelon advanced a hesitant step toward him. She was dressed in fragile white, adding a further touch of unreality. She looked as if she'd been waiting a long time. Feeling foolish, but troubled, he glanced about for the comic-valentine face of Fanny LeBeau. Madelon seemed to follow the flow of his thoughts. "I didn't bring her with me, darling," she said, laughing.

He caught her up in his arms, wanting to hold her tenderly, wanting to crush her savagely against him, to somehow imprint her upon him so she was part of him, so they could never be torn apart again. He kissed her and the sweetness of her mouth, the swollen softness of her lips, the passion that flared, ignited by their touching, threatened to explode him into oblivion. For a moment the room spun about his head. He was afraid he was going to stagger and fall from exhaustion and relief. He clung to Madelon, drawing strength from her presence.

"I'm so—filthy!" he protested. "I haven't bathed or shaved in—in God knows how long."

"I don't care!"

"I wanted everything just right when we met again."

"Everything is just right! You are here. I am here, close in your arms."

"I must smell. I do. I stink. My God."

"Philippe! I don't care." She laughed up at him, caressing his dark beard. "Do you think anything matters, except that at last I am here, where I have always wanted to be since the first moment I met you?"

"But, the dirt . . . and the smell—"

"I do care about your exhaustion. You look ready to fall. Oh, darling, I've heard about your wonderful—incredible!—achievement in upgrading the harbor. Against such terrible obstacles! A tribal war threatened all around you. The army brought in, and yet you completed your work. Everyone is talking about it. You're a hero, darling. A poor, exhausted hero, ready to fall flat on his dear sweet face."

"No, no." He shook his head, forcing himself to stand straight. "I'm all right. Just let me hold you, if you can

127

stand it." He laughed. "Maybe if you stay upwind from me—"

"Oh, darling! Your beautiful laughter. It's so good to see you."

He shivered suddenly in helpless exhaustion. She caught him in her arms. "You listen to me. You order a hot bath, someone to shave you. Rest. I'm just down the corridor. The truth is, I'm next door. I'll order dinner sent here in an hour."

"I can't stay away from you for a whole hour."

Madelon laughed, touching his lips with the tip of her finger. "It may be your last hour of freedom, darling. Make the most of it! Oh, I've so much news. So much to tell you."

"I just want to hold you. Kiss you." But he staggered when she moved away from him.

"You go in there and start taking off your clothes. I'll send up a barber, someone to bathe you."

He tried vainly to protest but Madelon pushed him gently yet insistently toward the tiled room in which mirrors reflected his weariness and a square metal tub awaited. He kissed her longingly. She withdrew and closed the door behind her. The barber and the servants, carrying buckets of hot water, found him slumped on the floor against the bronze tub, fast asleep.

He was vaguely aware of many things, fully cognizant of nothing, for a long time. He tried to stir vigor and energy inside himself. Madelon had come to him, she awaited him. But in his stunned agony of fatigue it was not real. No matter how hard he fought, he found himself plunging into exhausted sleep. By some painful discipline of will, he forced himself upward, coming awake to find the room candle-lit and Madelon sitting on the bed beside him. She smiled uncertainly and he drew her to him and kissed her.

She trembled when he touched her. Heavy bolts of excitement and desire flared through his body. His lips parted her mouth and he pressed his tongue between her teeth, tasting her sweetness. She lay back, shivering as if frightened, but accepting his thrusting tongue, sucking at it.

128

"Do you really want me as terribly as I have wanted you?" His whisper came from the depths of lonely months without letters from her.

She pressed her heated face against his freshly shaven cheek. "I've never wanted anyone else. I have lived for the moment when I could come to you."

"I could never love anyone but you," he told her. And this was certainly the truth. At that moment he understood the difference between his love for Madelon and the vagrant desire he felt for other women, for the Sahyins and Anne-Margots of the world. He wanted Madelon as he wanted no other woman—forever . . . spiritually as well as physically.

But there was such excitement at her nearness. His hands slipped into the bodice of the fragile gown she wore beneath her negligee. Gently, but hungrily, he fondled and caressed her breasts. She pressed closer, her hands moving on his muscled chest, her pleasure so exquisite she quivered.

"Oh, Philippe, I am really here, with you at last, aren't I?"

"You really are," he said.

From the old city beyond his open window and balcony came the calls from the minarets, and from somewhere nearer in a dusty garden the low-hushed vespering song of a finch. Stillness rode in on the pale light from the town, seeming to waver in the wind.

"I love you so terribly," Madelon whispered. "Forgive me—if I can't show you how much. If I don't know anything. If I'm stupid."

"Oh God, Madelon, I want you desperately. But you are still married. We cannot do this! Grabralet might use it against you, faithlessness, adultery—it could ruin your reputation."

"My reputation? But I wrote all that to you—in my letters."

"I never received them. Your letters never reached me."

She gasped. "My poor Philippe. Then you never knew, never knew how much I missed you, how much I longed for you. And you don't know—the most important thing of all."

129

Overwhelmed with anticipation, he drew her close, then held her lovely form at arm's length. "Tell me," he said breathlessly.

She caressed his cheek with her fingers. "I had terrible pains in my stomach after you'd left Paris. My mother took me to the physician. While examining me, he discovered that I was a virgin—I had never—been penetrated. He told my mother and has sworn to it. In writing. My parents took it up with the bishop of our diocese. My marriage has been annulled by the Church."

Stunned and exultant, Philippe closed his arms around Madelon. She struggled, talking against his mouth. "On the strength of the doctor's sworn statement, before witnesses, that my marriage was never consummated. Because it was never consummated, it is as if it never existed, as God knows it did not!"

He could only stare at her, his passion rising.

She kissed him, moving her hands on him in a way that set him wild. "Claude and I haven't lived together for months," she said. "As I wrote to you, I returned home to my parents. Claude-Bruce has his own apartment, his own life, his own friends. He is still successful. I suppose I could hate him, but I don't. He simply does not matter. He has not mattered since I met you. He matters not at all right now."

"Will your being here like this affect the annulment?"

Madelon laughed. "No one will question me further unless *you* want to. I was a virgin then, and I am a virgin at this moment, in your hands. That's all I care about. I've waited long enough, too long. I won't wait any more."

"When can we marry?"

"Stop talking. Please stop talking."

"Tell me, when? How long?"

"It doesn't matter! We're together. We'll be together. What can come between us now, darling? Please, please don't make me wait any more."

He was wide awake, alert now, throbbing with life, blood pulsing through his veins. He lifted her easily and removed the gown, the negligee. He caressed and stroked and fondled the exquisite perfection of her nude body. She was even lovelier than his fantasies had promised.

He lifted her body then and brought her under him on the mattress. Voices from the minarets filtered in like sounds from some distant chorus. A breeze riffled and filled the curtains at the balcony doorway. Madelon opened her arms and her body to him, embracing him, drawing herself up to him. Yet she was so nervous and unsure of herself that she gasped for breath.

Philippe felt the charged rasp of shock. How innocent she was! She wanted him with all her heart. She didn't even attempt to hide that. Like him, she was overflowing with desire, and yet she was frightened. She clasped his rigidity in her hand, and her eyes widened with anxiety at the size and hardness, the promise and the threat. But need and excitement drove everything else from her mind. She held her fingers tightly on him, drawing him to the fiery liquidity at her thighs.

He tilted her head back, her golden hair spilling across the pillows. He kissed her lips, parting her mouth widely with his tongue, teaching her and learning the agony of need in the same instant. The aching demands of his body boiled from his toes upward, agonizingly sweet and violent. Madelon's whole body glowed, fevered, the bed was warm with the heat of their bodies, yet he felt as if he'd die of chill if he didn't thrust himself closer to her, closer inside her, deeper and deeper.

He tried to move gently as he thrust upward into her. At first there was resistance, and she gasped in pain, even while her hips whipped wildly, and she cried out in agonized rapture.

With him inside her, she could not lie still. Her trim hips jerked and tossed, always churning. Her legs instinctively parted wide. Breathing through her opened mouth, she closed tightly about him, responding and yielding to every desire within her. Her arms and legs locked about him, and Philippe felt as if he had never lived before, never before had a woman.

Grasping the round globes of her hips, he brought her savagely up to him, their bodies merging in a frantic act of taking and yielding, wilder than lust. It was as if they were driven by primordial needs to become one in body and flesh. His mouth covered hers. She sighed and moaned, deep in her throat, her fingers digging into his shoulders. She bucked her hips faster, the convulsions mindless and unbridled. Her whole body palpitated. He bit down on her full underlip, trying to hold back the vehement eruptions, trying to prolong this ecstasy, but they were swept along on a torrent of delight and pleasure and release.

She lay beneath him, shaken, unable to speak. "I've dreamed of this," she whispered against his throat, "but not even in my wildest dreams could I know the exaltation I feel. Nineteen years of loneliness, and none of that matters any more."

They lay unmoving, enveloped in each other, yet this was not enough for her, even now. She closed her lips, her arms, her legs, upon him, trying to keep him, a most intimate part of her, straining to bring him closer.

He kissed her gently and sagged upon her, exhausted. A misting red fog clouded her vision and she trembled. "Oh, Philippe," she whispered. "How have I lived without you? How can I stay away from you ever again?"

"You won't," he whispered in exhaustion. "We'll never part again."

She laughed. "The very sound of your voice makes me all hot and wet inside again. Makes me weak with wanting you, again."

He tried to laugh. "My God. You'll have to give me a few minutes to recover."

"How can I? I'm on fire, and it's your fault."

He smiled and caressed her. "You've been starved too long, that's all."

"I don't think so. I'll always be like this with you." Her seeking hands closed on him. She shivered. "Do you think perhaps—now that I have you—I'll ask too much of you?"

"God knows I hope so," he said.

He held her for a long time, feeling the raging needs rekindled deep in his loins and flaring out through his body. He traced the gentle rise of her youthful breasts.

He nursed the pink nipples until she sobbed in bittersweet pleasure, his mouth releasing all her long-denied hungers.

"Please," she whispered. "Don't make me wait any more."

He pulled her to him, but in the pleasant stillness, a discordant rustling sound intruded. It was like a mouse in the wall, a fluttering of a small bird, and nothing like that at all. It was like a serpent gliding across the flooring in the shadows. Philippe went taut, poised above Madelon, listening. It was Madelon who screamed, "Philippe! Look out!"

Philippe lunged around on the bed, poised there, naked, vulnerable. He stared at Sahyin and the knife glittering in her fist.

"Sahyin," Philippe said. "Don't be a damned fool."

"Me kill her," Sahyin said. "Me kill her."

She leaped, trying to fight her way around Philippe. He sprang at her as she brought the knife upward.

He felt the blade slice into his lower abdomen. A numbing sickness gushed through him.

Sahyin screamed. "No, my lord, no!"

She hurled the knife away and fell on the floor beside the bed, wailing out her remorse.

Philippe slapped his hand over the wound. Blood seeped, between his fingers, sticky and hot.

Sahyin went on sobbing out her lamentation. She had never wanted to harm him. She loved him with all her soul. She didn't want to hurt him.

Philippe ignored her. Nor was he thinking about the knife wound, the pain, or the blood smearing his hand and oozing down his hip.

All he could think of was Madelon, rigid and unmoving beside him on the bed. Her mind, her heart, and all her thoughts had been for him, for that moment when they could be together.

He wanted to acknowledge his evil, his unworthiness, beg her to forgive him for the wench, for his faithlessness, which now was exposed to her in the blood staining his hand and leaking along his body.

He took up a pillow, shook it from its case. He folded the pillow into a pad and pressed it over the hot wound.

Holding it there, he sucked in a long draught of air and held it until the room stopped spinning around his head. He spoke to Sahyin, his voice harsher and colder than De Blasio's had ever been. "Listen to me. Get off that floor and stop that sniveling. You get down to De Blasio and send him here. At once, do you understand me?"

Sahyin stood up. "I am your slave," she whispered. "I never—"

"Get out of here. Don't waste another minute."

Sahyin nodded, still crying, and ran across the room. The door closed behind her.

Philippe looked at Madelon. Her face was as cold as marble. Her eyes were flat, dead. The room spun crazily about him. He wanted to beg her forgiveness, but he could not speak. The last thing he heard her say before he fainted was, "I never want to—see you again."

THREE

Paris, 1884

[17]

Philippe rattled the brass knocker on the thick door facing.
He had lost no time upon his return to Paris in riding out
to Neuilly and presenting himself at the Grenet house.

This was not his first visit. Getting inside this imposing
old mansion had so far proved impossible. But he had
been unable to stay away. He had been deeply troubled
since the last time he'd seen Madelon, three months ago
in Algiers. All those weeks of convalescence, he had
dreamed ahead to the moment when he would see her
again. After his return to Paris, he'd been badgered by a
sense of wrong, something which could not be set right
unless he saw Madelon in person, held her in his arms,
reassured himself that she was all right. But he had not
been welcomed at the Grenet home. Madelon refused to
see him; the butler was always stiff and cold as he relayed
her message. Philippe had stood across the street watching
for her; he'd written her dozens of letters. Her answer
had been chilled silence. How could he reassure himself
that she was all right, how could he present his case, if he
were not permitted inside this formidable front door?

Empty-bellied, he relived these recent rejections as he
rattled the brass knocker again. Across the street loomed

that lonely place where he'd stood, watching this house, hoping for a glimpse of Madelon, his heart and his hopes sinking.

After a tense wait, the door was opened. He and Fanny LeBeau stared at each other. It was difficult to say who was the more shocked. Yet, in a way it was good to see Fanny. It at least meant Madelon was near.

Fanny's chalk-white, comic-opera face, with its black eye sockets, sagged and then grew taut. She retreated a step as if she'd encountered the devil himself.

Philippe laughed. "It's only me, Fanny."

She nodded curtly. He handed her his card. Fanny took it without looking at it. "I want to see Madelon," he said. *Oh God, how I want to see her.*

"Yes, *m'sieu*. I'll see if she's in."

Fanny went away up the curving staircase and left him standing alone in an ornate foyer large enough to accommodate a modest state reception and splendid enough to grace a musical theater. The house was silent as if poised for polite but unyielding combat. He glanced about at the portraits of Grenet forebears. Idly studying them, he wondered where Madelon inherited her delicate, heartbreaking beauty.

He shifted from one leg to the other, lost interest in the portraiture, and was reduced to counting the patterns in the Persian carpeting. Waiting. It seemed he had been waiting for Madelon all the years of his life. Without her, he was nothing, he simply existed, despite his busy career, drifting from day to day, rudderless. Waiting. A stately old Swiss clock urbanely tolled the seconds and the minutes for him.

He watched Fanny return down the wide, gleaming stairway. She came off the lower step and crossed primly to him. She held out his card. "I'm very sorry, *m'sieu*, but Mademoiselle Grenet sends her regrets. She cannot see you."

"Why, Fanny, this is the first time I ever saw you smile." He turned toward the door. He hesitated, stopped, swung about. Fanny caught her breath and retreated. "I want you to deliver a message to Mademoiselle Grabralet,

Fanny. Say to her I shall come every day to this door until she agrees to see me."

Fanny stared at him. "Yes, *m'sieu*. I'll tell her."

"Now, Fanny. I'll wait for her answer."

Fanny was gone an even longer period of time now. She came at last to the head of the stairs, pausing for a moment with her hand on the newel post. She descended slowly, trailing her fingers on the banister for support, and finally, standing stiffly on the bottom step, she said, *"M'sieu* Henri Grenet requests that you await him in the library, sir. He will join you there."

Philippe grinned coldly. "All right, Fanny. I'll talk to *M'sieu* Henri this time, if that's the best you can do. But you tell madame, she can send her mother, all her siblings and her cousins, but I'll keep coming back until she agrees to see me. In person, Fanny."

Within minutes Monsieur Henri Grenet joined Philippe in the book-lined study. Philippe sat in a deep wing chair at his host's invitation, but he refused either wine or cigar.

Madelon's father was somewhere in his forties, thin-shouldered, flat-bellied, long-legged, with the casual elegance of the well-born. His graying mutton-chop beard was closely clipped against his grim jawline. He listened, stone-faced, while Philippe spoke with forced calm, of the weather—cloudy, ominous, wet for this time of the year—of the state of the government and, finally, of his deep love for Madelon.

Henri Grenet scowled. "You appear to feel you have earned some—some right to see my daughter, whether she wishes to see you or not."

"I have no wish to harass her."

"Yet, that's what you are doing, isn't it?"

"I have loved Madelon for a long time, sir. A long time silently. I can be silent no more. I loved her, sir, when she was living as *M'sieu* Grabralet's wife. Though they lived next door, I hid my devotion as well as I could, and tried to deny it. I realized how improper, impossible my love was then. But much has changed. Everything has changed, except that I love her still, more than my own life."

Monsieur Grenet scowled at the back of his hands. He went on sitting stiffly in the overstuffed, peacock-backed chair, his face a mask which revealed nothing. At last he rose slowly and paced the well-worn Persian carpeting.

Finally, he turned and stared down at Philippe, poised on the edge of the armchair. "I confess to some sense of shock, *M'sieu* Bunau-Varilla."

"Shock, sir?"

"Impropriety in this whole matter. You seem to feel some right to call upon my daughter, to visit her, in this house."

"My appearance here may seem precipitous to you, sir. But I assure you, it has been a long and unhappy two years for Madelon and for me. We have openly avowed our love for each other, sir, even when her sense of duty to you and Madame Grenet forced us to deny our emotions."

The tall man gazed down at Philippe, eyes chilled. "What you are saying, or almost saying, is there has been a liaison between you and Madelon since that time you scrupulously denied your feelings? My suspicions then are correct. It is true. Madelon went to Algeria for one reason. To see you."

"We met briefly, in Algiers, sir."

"She knew in advance you were there."

"We wrote to each other. Yes."

"She knew she would see you if she went there?"

"I suppose so."

"You suppose so. Damn it, Bunau-Varilla, a moment ago you sanctimoniously declared you and my daughter had denied your—love—for each other."

"The only important thing is that Madelon and I love each other now."

"It seems the least important consideration of all, young man. And even you must recognize that she refuses to see you."

"Yes, sir. But it's all really very simple. She's angered, a misunderstanding. We could clear it up if she would see me. It can be blown into something complex and difficult, but it is as simple and natural as love itself."

139

Monsieur Grenet shook his head, totally rejecting this. He paced again and at last returned and stared down at Philippe. "We don't know you."

"I don't believe I'm either a rogue or a scoundrel, sir, and I think you know that."

"Oh, I'm quite privy to your achievements. You have returned to Paris something of a celebrity. You undoubtedly accomplished a great deal of good in Tunis and Algeria, against formidable odds. All of this was in the newspapers. But what troubles me is the matter which was kept out of the newspapers, but has a wide circulation via gossip in the most exclusive clubs of Paris. I am alluding, of course, to that unfortunate incident involving a native girl who tried to kill you with a knife in some kind of lover's brawl. I don't ask you whether it happened or not. But it is not a pretty picture, young man. It grows no prettier as it circulates in whispers. You have a certain fame, perhaps, but as far as I am concerned, it is far outweighed by a kind of infamy."

"I won't pretend to be other than I am." Philippe's voice sounded empty in his own ears.

"Then you will permit me a certain skepticism concerning your—moral character." Monsieur Grenet's voice was scathing. "I don't give a damn that you are acclaimed for your harbor-building down in Africa. Engineering is your career, your work, and you did your job commendably. I see it as no more than that."

"Nor do I, sir."

"But I do care, and I do oppose your presence here in my home, because you were scandalously involved with a native woman. This concerns me because it concerns my daughter. But far more important are the facts, hidden from me until this moment, that you lured my daughter to Algiers, that the affair between you is far more potentially scandalous and ruinous than any drunken fight in a whorehouse."

"If I could only talk to her, sir—"

"That is no longer even a consideration, *M'sieu* Bunau-Varilla. As long as my daughter resides in my home, you will not see her. You will not be welcome here."

"You don't understand, sir."

"It is you who refuses to understand, *M'sieu* Bunau-Varilla. Oh, I understand. I now understand a great deal I didn't fathom before. I like it less, but it's clear to me now—the way Madelon behaved when she suddenly returned from her—vacation—in Algiers.

"She appeared on the verge of nervous collapse. We were deeply puzzled. In agony. We knew she was unhappy about her annulment, but this was something she had wanted. Something else ate at her, drove her, sickened her. She confided in neither her mother nor me. She behaved almost erratically, hurling herself abruptly into fevered social activity when always before she'd been most reserved, modest, even retiring, despite her great beauty.

"From a girl content to stay at home, she became a party-goer. Day and night. Night after night. As lovely as she is, she quickly became the rage of Paris society. Yet none of it really touched her, or pleased her, or lifted her spirits. She acted as if she were afraid to slow down, afraid to stop and think. She had to hurry out, to have a good time, even if it destroyed her.

"From a soft and gentle girl, she became hard as a diamond, with a sheen of bitterness in everything she did. It was as if she even chased after pleasure in a cold fury. Thanks to you, I know now *why* she behaved as she did. I know now it was because of you. You have hurt her beyond any possible hope of forgiveness. You have destroyed her health. Made her ill. Lately, physical illness, an indisposition in the mornings, unwilling, unable to get out of bed. Nauseated. Gaining weight though she barely touches food. Languishing. Apathetic. Haven't you done enough?

"It seems to me, *m'sieu,* that even you, insensitive as you must be, even you would have compassion on her, even you would understand that you have hurt her enough. Even you would want to leave her in peace."

Philippe stood up and their gazes clashed. "You don't care that I love her?"

"I don't give a damn. Not for anything you think or do, except where it may concern my daughter. And I feel with all my heart, *m'sieu*, that you have done enough. Enough. I wish you every good fortune, *m'sieu*. But I love my daughter above all else on this earth. Who hurts my daughter has me as his implacable foe for eternity."

M'sieu Grenet waited, but only, Philippe saw, for him to leave. Exhaling heavily, he took up his hat. His hands quivered and he gripped the hat tightly to conceal his trembling.

Henri Grenet remained standing immobile in the middle of the study. The doors opened and his wife entered, followed by Madelon, looking pale and melancholy. She wore an air of indifference, like a protective mask.

"Did you forbid him the privilege of entering this house again?" Madame Grenet said.

M'sieu Grenet nodded. He sighed. "The hell of it is, despite everything, I liked him. He didn't have horns after all. He seemed quite sincere and, at the last, quite— humbled."

Suddenly Madelon cried out, an agonized, wounded sound from deep inside. She sank to the floor, one fist pressed into her solar plexus, the other covering her mouth. She gasped and then retched helplessly.

Fanny, *M'sieu* and Madame Grenet stood for a moment in shock. Then Madame Grenet recovered. She ran to Madelon and sank beside her, cradling her in her arms. Madame Grenet jerked her head up. "Don't stand there, Henri. Or you, Fanny. Get the doctor. At once."

[18]

Philippe entered the Bois de Boulogne precisely at two in the afternoon and strode along its bright pathways. He had not been inside the park for a long time. For years it had been a place of sadness. It still showed scars where many trees of the old Rouvray Forest had been cut for fuel throughout that freezing winter of 1870 during the war with Prussia. The vast grounds, extending from the river to the old fortifications between Neuilly and Boulogne-Billancourt, provided woodlands, lakes, restaurants and playgrounds.

Philippe followed the winding walkways toward a small café near the *Jardin d'Acclimation,* which housed the zoo and conservatories. Before him, the long, flowered incline stretched out, bordered with ornamental greenery and splashed with delicate tints and bold hues of clustered flowers. Somewhere near the end of the terrace, a fountain frothed in the sunlight like tossed silver coins. The air was filled the cloying scent of hothouse plants.

Philippe hurried along the promenade searching for a glimpse of Madelon or the somber figure of her chaperone. He had walked out of the Grenet home, sick with defeat and more troubled than ever about Madelon. Grenet left him little hope that Madelon would ever see him again willingly.

And yet, when he'd finally determined that nothing kept him in Paris any more except a futile yearning after something that could never be, the chalk-cheeked Fanny LeBeau had appeared at his apartment door.

They stared at each other. Fanny trembled in terror and quaked with ill-concealed antipathy. She extended a note which, she said, came from her mistress, Mademoiselle Grenet. Fanny's voice quavered, her nostrils flared and her entire body pinched tight in disapproval. "And *ma'm'selle* says she will be in the Bois de Boulogne zoological gardens tomorrow at two in the afternoon, and *I'll* be there, too." Exultant, his heart pounding, incredulous at this sudden reversal, he'd grinned at Fanny. "Tell your mistress I too shall be there, unless, dearest Fanny, you prefer that I kept a rendezvous with you alone."

She'd gazed at him in frostiest hostility, gathered her black skirts, tossed her head, and strode away. He closed the corridor door and leaned against it. He clutched Madelon's note, able to think only that soon, within hours, an eternity of waiting, yet a finite time, he would see Madelon again, look into her violet eyes, touch her fingers, kiss her soft lips, make her believe he loved her alone of all the women in the world.

His hands trembling, he broke the seal on the small, scented envelope. For one brief instant that scent brought back the loneliness and despair of Algiers. He shook the flaring images from his mind as he read: "I will see you. I don't know what good it will do either of us. But an hour in the park surely can't ruin us. M."

Many early afternoon visitors strolled the winding walks which stretched ribbonlike in every direction. He had spent a sleepless night and, striding along, he hoped against hope that Madelon had come alone. Her note had not promised much; in fact, it promised nothing, but it had been a long lonely exile for both of them.

He saw her seated on the garden café terrace. She glowed, a fragile splash of color under a brightly striped parasol at a small table near a low stone balustrade. In one violent, shattering instant he felt the sharp pang of pain, the throb of need, the aching end of despair, the thrill of finding her again, the end of waiting.

She had not seen him yet. She spoke softly to Fanny LeBeau, posted as a disapproving sentinel at a table a few feet away.

He paused, staring at Madelon. She looked thinner, less happy than in Algiers, but far lovelier than he remembered. Yet her eyes were shadowed. About her there was a brilliant hardness, an unreachable lightness of manner that he'd never seen before. She waved continually to people—men who tipped top hats and ladies who bowed and smiled warmly. But her smiles never reached her eyes.

Still, it had been a long hungry time, and he stored this bright image of her, as a storekeeper might, or a miser, or a doomed lover afraid of losing her even as he found her again.

"Madelon." He held his hat in his hand.

She caught her breath, for an instant held herself tense as if afraid of flying apart, and then looked up at him.

For a moment, as if benumbed upon the axis of a storm, with the violence and agitation swirling about them but not touching them at all, they gazed at each other. He watched her violet eyes fill with tears, and inwardly he wanted to rage out his own loneliness, his need, his wild pleasure at finding her again.

He stood unmoving in the thick silence of the garden.

"Oh, Philippe." She whispered, her voice taut in her throat. She put out her hand to him and he took it. Her fingers were like ice.

He sat on the edge of a small chair facing her under the parasol. People, faces, forms, shadows without substance, swept around them like chaff in the fragrant atmosphere.

He looked around helplessly. These unreal masses were people, the sounds were subdued laughter, muted calls, the remote harsh cries and sibilant hissing and prowling of distant birds, serpents and beasts, discordant and intrusive. "We can't talk here," he said.

She shrugged. "There are some things we can say better in public."

He flinched, seeing only continued rejection, polite and formal and chilled, as proper as this place. He ordered

145

wine and had a glass deposited before Fanny LeBeau at the adjoining table. Fanny inclined her head without smiling, acknowledging his courtesy; she did not touch the drink. "I'd hoped you'd forgiven me," he said to Madelon, his voice agonized and empty.

Her smile was almost disdainful. "Oh, I have forgiven you, Philippe. A poor, shallow, vain and empty man. I have forgiven you."

He stared at her. "My God. How you hate me."

She was like marble, untouchable. She laughed again in forced lightness, returned the greeting of a passing couple, twisted the stem of the wine glass in her fingers. "No, Philippe. I don't even hate you any more. I was—deeply hurt. I admit that. Jealous. Torn apart with jealousy. That girl, she loved you with such violence, such savagery. I cannot forget you meant so much to her, she would kill to have you."

"She—meant nothing to me."

"No. I suppose not. No more than I did. Neither of us really meant anything to you, did we? I risked my reputation coming to Algiers to you. But you didn't give a damn, did you? Why should you? You had your own resident whore. On the premises."

"No one ever mattered to me except you." His voice, pitched low, quivered. He looked about miserably. "I won't pretend I didn't use her body for release. She was— my slave. It was a stupid custom of the place. Madelon, I had little hope that I'd ever see you again."

She bit her lip and at last nodded without looking up at him. "I am sure this is a satisfactory absolution in your own mind."

"I don't try to justify. I only swear I love only you."

"Well, don't. I've heard all the lies from men I ever want to hear."

"I want your forgiveness."

She shrugged and spoke as if tossing him a sou. "You have that. You are forgiven."

He stared, deeply troubled at that unyielding smile, that withdrawn and inflexible tilt of her head. It was as if she said defiantly, *You can't reach me, and if you can't touch me, you can't hurt me.* He wanted to weep, but he tried to laugh. "No. I want much, much more. I want your love."

"Well, I'm sorry."

"What are you saying?" He tried to keep his voice down.

She continued to smile that brittle, surface smile, glancing about as if discussing nothing of more importance than the weather. "I'm saying I can't give you my love. It's too late."

"Madelon. Don't do this. Don't destroy us."

"But it's true. I brought you all my heart, months ago, all the way to Algiers. But that wasn't what you wanted, was it?"

"It was all I wanted. Then. Now. Forever. If as you say you forgive me, then you can love me and let me spend my life making up any hurt I've caused you."

She caught her breath and withdrew from him. Her hands quivered, and she'd knotted her handkerchief into a sodden silken ball.

"Didn't you ever make a mistake?" he said. "Didn't you ever learn truly to forgive?"

Now she was able to laugh, that defiant sound of disdain. "I've made mistakes. I have forgiven. I have forgiven you. But that girl in Algiers was no mistake. She was final evidence of your true carnal nature. I should thank her for teaching me in time. I shouldn't hate her. But I do. Perhaps I shouldn't hate you. But I do. I have forgiven, Philippe, but I have not forgotten. Because I cannot. She is between us now, as she stood there that night. She will always be between us, not as a person, but as a reminder of what you are and are not—inside."

"My God. Is that what you want me to say? I am as low as an animal? All right, I'm whatever I am. But whatever I am, I love you. I'll always love you. No one will ever love you as I do."

"Then God help me." She met his gaze defiantly, her eyes blurred with tears. "All right. I asked too much of you. Because I loved you with all my heart, I thought you could love me with all of yours. I found out the truth. Please, Philippe, let it go at that."

"What do you want?"

"What do I want? It seemed so very little. I wanted to

love one man and be loved by him alone. I was a fool. I asked too much. Well, I don't ask anything any more."

"I have failed you. But I love you. I won't fail you, Madelon. I swear. Not again."

"How sweet." That unyielding smile that didn't touch the melancholy eyes. "But it's too late for that. I have lost my capacity to care; I don't blame you; I do forgive you. But once I put all my faith in you. I needed you so terribly because I had been rejected by one man. But you see, you failed me, more terribly than Claude-Bruce ever did."

His shoulders sagged round. He spread his hands. "Then what is to become of us?"

"God knows," she said. She turned the stem of her wine glass in her fingers. Her laughter flared, hard, irreverent. "Perhaps we could go somewhere. Perhaps to your apartment. I don't love you, but I don't object to going to bed with you. As long as you realize it means nothing."

They hailed a cab outside the Bois de Boulogne. They were less than a vivacious trio. Stunned, Philippe had had to bite back a savage growl of protest. He sat as if she'd struck him across the face until she laughed at him again, the sound as hard as coins on a counter. Finally, he had nodded. They walked silently, with Fanny LeBeau a reluctant shadow in their wake. Inside the tonneau of the cab, Fanny huddled in a shadowed corner, sniffling, muttering through the kerchief knotted against her mouth.

"Stop mumbling, Fanny," Madelon said. "You know you won't tell my father."

"I shall," Fanny whimpered.

"You mention one word of *anything* I do and I shall send you away. Let's see how you like to slave on a farm somewhere." Madelon tilted her head. "I have my own life, Fanny. A new life. You may as well accept that. My old life is over."

Fanny cried out, weeping. "But why this, this wild man who may even hurt you? You had such a lovely husband. So kind. Gentle. Handsome. Oh, *ma'm'selle*, you had everything."

Madelon laughed. "Fanny, you're almost as stupid as I was. Now, not another word. No, not one."

Philippe sat cold, unable to speak.

They deposited Fanny at a table in a café near Philippe's apartment. Philippe remained stunned, not yet believing Madelon intended going through with a casual affair. Nothing in God's world was more foreign to her very nature.

Madelon told the proprietor to serve any and all of the displayed sweets—iced raisin buns, éclairs, tortes—as long as Fanny ordered them. Fanny remained stiff-necked, rigid in her chair, eyes stricken. But the prospect of an unrestricted orgy of sweets mollified her slightly and, before they reached the street, Fanny had begun to nibble upon a flaky puff filled with custard.

They walked along the narrow side street without speaking. They entered the apartment house and Madelon preceded him up the stairwell. He regretted bringing her here; she was reacting rebelliously against everything she had lived by, believed in, been taught. She looked vulnerable and dejected. But, inside his apartment, as he turned to close his corridor door, she tossed away her parasol, handbag and gloves. She turned on her toes in a pirouette. "Unbutton me," she said.

He stared at her. She was far more at ease than he. He pulled her into his arms, wanting to cradle her as one might protect and love a child, but she writhed her body against his, watching him with those diamond-hard eyes.

"There," she said. "Isn't this better?"

He covered her mouth, her cheeks and eyes with kisses. She struggled but she was not trying to escape him. She kicked off her slippers; they clattered half across the room.

His hands trembling, Philippe unbuttoned the row of tiny pearl buttons fastening her pastel green dress. Then he loosened the pins that secured the soft rolls of her hair. Thick golden locks showered down over her shoulders. His heart beat faster. He lifted those tendrils in handfuls and pressed his face into the warm fragrance.

She turned in a gracefully fluid motion, which released the full-skirted dress from her slender shoulders and let it topple to the floor about her ankles. Philippe held her face cupped in his hand and kissed her mouth, at first gently.

149

She clung to him and her lips lingered, pressing upward to his with savagery.

Their lips parted, but she did not move away, and he kissed her again, much less gently. He was still convinced she would confess her love for him. His tongue pressed its way between her teeth to the sweetness of her mouth. She opened her mouth wider to him and returned his kiss.

Still kissing her, he took her up in his arms and carried her to his bed. She lay close against him, accommodating her body to his. Without releasing her lips, he gently removed her underclothing—chemise, crinoline, fragile lace —until she lay naked to his hungry eyes. He wanted her ravenously. His breathing quickened, rasping and burning in his tight throat. His hands shook visibly.

She moved closer under him, murmuring meaningless words, whispering unintelligibly. Her hands moved on his fevered body, exploring, discovering and caressing.

The faultlessly smooth, heated softness of her skin kindled fires he hadn't even suspected existed inside him, needs he had never anticipated, voracious appetites he had felt could never be appeased. With a flaring of joy, he saw that her passion and desire matched his. Perhaps he could win her back, after all.

They rose to a savage crisis. Now at last they were not to be denied. He drove himself to her; she thrust upward, devouring him. Nothing could stop him from slaking his thirsts, or from convincing her beyond doubt his passion for her alone was real. And Madelon too, in this moment was possessed by a molten hot desire stronger than morality, older than civilization, fiercer than hatred, more basic than the hope of heaven.

For a long time neither of them moved. They remained locked in embrace. It was much later; they had no idea how much time had passed, how many kingdoms had toppled outside this room, how many cocks had crowed, how many éclairs Fanny had consumed.

Philippe closed his arms tighter. His satiety went beyond the physical. He was totally fulfilled, content, exalted. His eyes burned with tears, for all the time they'd lost, all the hours and months they'd wasted.

He took his lips reluctantly from hers. She unlocked her ankles, he withdrew from her and she fell away. She lay on her back, staring at the ceiling.

Watching her, he caught his breath, agonized. That old scornful smile twisted her mouth. "Thanks," she said.

Rage gorged up through him. "What are you talking about?"

"You. I am living by your rules now. I needed some fun. So why not you, for old times' sake?"

He stared at her, watching her slip beyond his reach though she did not stir on the mattress, the diamond hardness glazing over those violet eyes, a patina of bitterness over deep, irreparable hurt.

He caught her arms, stared down into her face. "You don't mean this."

Her smile was never meant to be shared. "I was never more serious. I learned much from you in Algeria."

"Damn it, don't talk like this."

She moved her shoulders. "Why not? It seems to me this arrangement should please you. No vows. No responsibilities. I can never love you. I won't stab you."

"Don't lie any more. You loved me with every part of your body."

"You're talking about this . . . just now. But this is not love. What I feel for you isn't love."

"Damn you."

"Does that mean you don't want me? No wonder I feel so unworthy inside, so unwanted, so empty. First, Claude-Bruce didn't want me, and now you don't want me."

"I'll always want you."

"Like this? Of course, but I'm afraid that isn't what I meant, dear heart. To be wanted, as a real woman is wanted, for herself alone. This is what I never had. This is what I have learned to face. But even if the two men I was fool enough to love were unable to *return* my love, this doesn't mean I can't find satisfactory substitutes for love, does it?"

"I won't let you talk like this."

"Of course not. I've upset you, haven't I? Well, I'll go now. No, you needn't even see me to the door. If you change your mind, let me know. I'm sure we can work out

151

something for our convenience." She laughed. "I'll save a few evenings for you."

Tears brimmed his eyes and ran along his cheeks. "Oh God, Madelon. Don't. You don't mean this bitter talk. I know how badly I hurt you."

She laughed again. "That's something you'll never know, *m'sieu*. You will never know how badly I hurt, because you have no real feelings of your own. Any woman will do for you. *Voilà!* Any man will do for me. That's my new philosophy, *M'sieu* Bunau-Varilla, thanks to you."

[19]

Six pernods at the bar in the Hotel Crillon did not make Philippe drunk, nor did the liquor make him forget the icy chill in Madelon's wounded eyes. He was helpless against her new steely facade, enraged by her attitude of smiling indifference. In black fury, he had returned downtown, cursing Madelon and himself. He was sick, lost and empty without her. He'd known she was deeply hurt, but he had not realized the cold hatred she felt for him. And yet, this afternoon she'd taught him one maddening truth: no other woman's body would ever enthrall him as hers did. He could never have her and he could never get her out of his mind. He was back where he'd been when Madelon was still Grabralet's wife. Nowhere.

He moved to get off the bar stool. All that liquor and he was still coldly, agonizingly sober. He wandered out of the elegant old bar and into the lobby. Then, some strange instinct drew him toward a throng of people gathered in an entryway. When he reached them, they quickly dispersed and took seats at the back of what Philippe realized was the grand ballroom of the Hotel Crillon. He looked in a daze toward the front of the huge room.

The first glimpse Philippe had of the legendary

Vicomte Ferdinand-Marie de Lesseps electrified him, despite the fact that he'd felt the whole canal project ill-conceived, badly managed, and poorly implemented.

He gazed in awe at the old man on the podium. Since his earliest boyhood, the name de Lesseps had conjured up, in Philippe's imagination, visions of a giant among men. He was not now disillusioned.

Here was the man who had built the Suez Canal against all odds, all obstacles, all estimates of learned men and the accumulated negative technical reports of centuries. De Lesseps had proved himself a warrior as well as a diplomat, promoter and statesman. To whatever he did, he brought the energy, strength and persistence of twenty men. Now old Ferdinand was locked in unequal combat with an unremitting and unconquerable foe: time.

Though he approached his eightieth year, his crown of white hair still waved healthy and full, precisely parted, brushed back from his forehead. Heavy gray brows bushed above his direct eyes and large nose. A carefully trimmed brush mustache accented the vigor and alertness evident in his round and remarkably unlined face.

Born in Versailles and educated in Paris, he'd entered the French consular service at twenty and dedicated the rest of his life to serving the public, building his image and fighting the entrenched reactionary. By 1833, he was French Consul at Cairo. His selfless combatting of a plague outbreak earned him the deathless friendship and gratitude of the Egyptian Viceroy Mehemet Ali and Ali's son, Said Pasha. This friendship led directly to his being awarded a concession to construct the Suez Canal.

De Lesseps seemed forever in the center of controversy, verbal combat and even armed conflict. In 1842 at Barcelona, he distinguished himself, and made headlines, protecting the foreign colony during a violent insurrection. He was forced to resign from the diplomatic service in apparent disgrace after a bitter failure in Italy. His protests were heard around the world. Long interested in linking the Mediterranean and the Red Sea via a maritime canal across the Isthmus of the Suez, he attained, by submitting, with grand simplicity and power, the advantages of this project, the concession from his old friend Said

Pasha. He struck immediately and headlong against the opposition of the English government and skeptical engineers who believed the project was too big, unwieldly, too costly. De Lesseps formed the Universal Company in 1858 and completed the canal in 1869 at a cost more than double the original estimates.

He returned to France a conquering hero, afforded at last that homage he'd always considered his due as a selfless public servant. In 1879 he was elected by a geographic congress in Paris to head the Panama Canal enterprise. Though he was then 74 years old, he hurled himself into the project with the energy and drive of a man thirty years younger.

Philippe slipped into the rear row of straight-backed chairs in the ballroom which had been converted into a lecture area, with raised dais, lectern and blackboard.

The Chairman of the Society of Civil Engineers was just introducing de Lesseps to a smattering of applause and some pointedly and tensely undemonstrative silence. A lesser man, as controversial as de Lesseps, may have had to endure those infamous, strident, mocking whistles typical of disapproving French audiences, but those brave enough to indicate their animosity toward him, manifested it only in chilled silence.

Despite the unenthusiastic reception, the almost tangible chill in the atmosphere, de Lesseps was, unfailingly optimistic on that dais, as he had always been over the years. He was pleased to report that work on the Canal was going along very well, taking discernible shape in the jungles and lowlands of that distant Isthmus. "We are, if not on schedule, not seriously behind it. I see no reason to doubt, despite doomsayers and detractors, completion of the canal in 1894, as per schedule. The first ships *shall* sail through that canal in ten years."

Someone in the audience called out scathingly, "Isn't it true instead, sir, that you are far behind schedule, far over in cost, that privately you admit the canal is a hopeless project and will never be completed?"

"No, *m'sieu*, this is not true."

"Isn't it true, Vicomte de Lesseps, that work has been, to all practical intents and purposes, halted because of in-

155

credible numbers of deaths from an epidemic of yellow fever?"

"I cannot deny there have been such deaths."

"Many such deaths, sir!"

"Sadly. Tragically. Many such deaths, when *one* death from disease is too many. But, gentlemen, we have faced catastrophe before. I see many familiar faces here tonight, men who gallantly faced disaster with me in the past, only to wrest victory finally from threat of defeat. We shall find a cure for yellow fever."

"And for malaria?"

De Lesseps spread his hands. "There have been deaths from disease on the Isthmus. I would be less than candid if I pretended the loss anything but heartbreaking. But this is wild, undeveloped swampland, the hottest belt of the Tropics. *Tierra caliente*, the natives call it. However, doctors now say they believe they have found the cause of malaria and yellow fever. I am pleased to be able to report this scientific finding to you. We are turning up this fetid land, the doctors say, and this surface material causes illness. We believe when this turned-up surface has been removed, it will be as healthy there as anywhere in any tropical country. And, after all, there are fifteen thousand men on our payroll out there. Naturally, deaths will occur, as if it were a town of that size. But to blame our disruption totally on yellow fever and malaria is to spread a new epidemic, a plague of terror through false information. May I remind you gentlemen that I have just returned from six months on site at the Isthmus. Will you demand a doctor to certify that *I* have not died of yellow fever or malaria?"

General laughter greeted this remark and the chairman rapped for silence. "Please show our distinguished guest the courtesy of permitting him to proceed with your full attention."

But before de Lesseps could continue, another engineer called out, "Where disease and death have not stopped you, have not landslides and floods totally disrupted progress?"

Voices rose across the room. The chairman banged his gavel. But every man knew that costs at the Isthmus were ruinous; a government administration, even national fiscal security, was at stake. Not even a man of de Lesseps' stature could be permitted to waive such serious charges casually. Nor did he attempt to do this. He nodded in sober agreement with the engineer's gloomy assessment of present conditions on the project. Floods and landslides were the reasons, he said, that he had come before this society of engineers. He had not come to hide these facts, but to present them as problems requiring answers from the best minds in the nation.

The audience fell silent. For the first time, publicly, in six years, de Lesseps admitted a potentially ruinous government program was in serious, perhaps even terminal jeopardy, a peril which could destroy a nation already bled white by the long and costly war with Prussia.

De Lesseps said. "Floods and landslides do delay the project and will continue to halt and destroy all work unless more engineers can be prevailed upon to go to the Isthmus, there to study, discover and provide methods and means to combat these natural catastrophes, these acts of God. We face serious delay. But we are not defeated. We are not destroyed. There *are* answers. We found new answers to our problems in the Suez peninsula, we will find them in Panama."

In order to reconcile "these temporary failures" in Panama with the long-range goals of the Company—"of France!"—the old statesman returned with zeal to his gaudiest triumph against overwhelming odds—the Suez Canal. "We followed the accepted wisdoms and logics only until we affirmed the opposite of all of what previously was universally acknowledged as fact, traditional conceptions, engineering verities. We were told from all sides that such and such facts *had* to be true. They had been accepted as gospel for thousands of years. Well, there was little that was revolutionary or new in our attempts to connect the waters of the Nile with the Red Sea, except that we succeeded where others had failed. And we succeeded precisely because we discarded immediately old conceptions which had caused the Suez project to be abandoned as impractical, expensive, even impossible.

157

From Darius to Omar, about twelve centuries, the canal project was viewed totally as a fresh-water canal.

"Why, the very idea of connecting sea to sea was never even contemplated! For a thousand years the need for a trade route from Europe to the East lay recognized, but without hope of accomplishment.

"Napoleon had the vision. With work directed by that illustrious French engineer, Monsieur Lepere, Napoleon planned to reactivate and complete the canal project. He might have put his incredible energy and indomitable will to work and accomplished his goal, had his military campaigns in Egypt been successful. Perhaps not. Even the brilliant Monsieur Lepere based his proposals on the error which had defeated all ancient plans. He accepted the concept that the Red Sea was higher than the Mediterranean by a mean height of 27½ feet. Monsieur Lepere proposed prohibitively expensive locks to govern differences in water height at various hours. Furthermore, the distance across the Suez Isthmus in a straight line is about 75 miles but, as surveyed, Monsieur Lepere planned a canal almost 93 miles long! I remind you that our project was 88 geological miles long, but only sixty miles are actual canal, 28 miles are run through three lakes.

"Again, as recently as 1847, the Egyptian Government proposed a canal from the Red Sea through the Bitter Lakes to Lake Timsah, through the lagoons of Lake Mensaleh to Tineh, or Pelisium, on the Mediterranean— all on the assumption that the levels of the seas, calculated by Monsieur Lepere, were correct.

"Then an eminent English engineer took a careful set of levels across the Suez Isthmus. His survey revealed there was *no* essential difference between the two seas at low water, and at high tide, the difference was no more than four feet! Rather than finding this knowledge helpful, he recommended that a canal could not then be kept open, because there would be no current through it!

"When the Khedive of Egypt graciously granted to me the concession of making a canal direct from the Red Sea to the Mediterranean, we proposed a waterway excavated to a depth of eight meters, a width at water level of eighty meters. We did not think in the old patterns, or use old facts which might be true under certain set conditions. We thought in new terms, boldly, and boldly we proceeded.

"Yes, the cost at Suez was high in lives and money. The cost was ultimately double our original estimate—but still a price the world views as one of the greatest bargains since time began!

"But our great expenses came from the unforeseeable, the catastrophic—what we are pleased to call Acts of God—those same acts, or natural disasters which harass us now in Panama. But we are the same dedicated men, our goals are as honorable, our ends justifiable. Our problems *are* enormous, though not insurmountable. But these problems, not graft, not greed, not dishonesty, not one ignoble thought, impede us and bring us begging for more time, more credit, more assistance from the best of our engineering intellects.

"Gentlemen, in 1854, when Mohammed Said signed the concession inaugurating a Universal Company to build that canal across the Isthmus of Suez, the English representative asked him how he expected the work could ever be accomplished. The Viceroy Said Pasha replied that the Company was universal, the benefits universal, the need universal, so all nations universally would be invited to participate. And so, in this year of 1884, we ask your faith, your prayers, your capital, your services, your contribution. We must not fail. With your help, we cannot."

Though considerable opposition and tension persisted, applause for the venerable statesman and his cause was warmer and more sustained than when he was introduced. Philippe helped to insure this through sheer physical display of enthusiasm. He stood up, applauding in what proved to be almost a one-man standing ovation. A few others hesitantly joined him and only a handful refused to applaud at all.

It was a small demonstration, but Philippe felt good about it. He had come here doubting and skeptical, but there was none who now could doubt where he stood. If the Old Lion, alone up on that lectern, needed an ally, he had him in the aisle at the rear of the room.

He felt as Saul of Tarsus must have on the road to Damascus. He had come to this place scoffing, mocking, skeptical, dissenting, suspicious. Not only had he been converted, he had found the dedication and direction for the rest of his life.

In the bustle and confusion after the charismatic old man left the podium, Philippe felt a hand on his shoulder and turned to look into the stern yet gentle face of Jean-Louis Depuits. The tall, craggy man, faded blue eyes warm behind pince-nez, smiled. Those early days at Depuits et David, flooded back across his mind, something from another time, another incarnation. They shook hands vigorously and Depuits clasped Philippe's arm as he might the arm of an equal, an old friend.

"My dear Bunau-Varilla. Still fighting those wild Indians, are you?"

"And robbing an occasional stagecoach, sir."

"You have won some acclaim, Philippe. We're very proud. I'm sure the orangutan—pardon, *M'sieu* David —would want me to add his congratulations."

"That's most kind of you and the orangutan, sir."

"Not at all. In a hellish brief time you've established an enviable reputation. It wasn't like that when I was young. Ten years at our drafting tables before we were permitted to lift our eyes or raise our voices. But then, we clung to the book."

"I'm sure you helped *write* the book, sir."

Depuits' eyes reflected his pleasure. "Well, you showed yourself an ardent and vocal supporter of old de Lesseps. I enjoyed your stubborn, one-man standing ovation. I thought then, that's our own Philippe. He has not changed. Still chasing cowboys." He took Philippe by the arm. "Have you met your celebrated hero, de Lesseps?"

"No. This is as close as I've ever been to him."

They moved forward to the base of the dais where de Lesseps was surrounded by grim-visaged men in heated discourse. As soon as he could break away, de Lesseps joined Depuits, Gustave Eiffel, Philippe, and Charles de Lesseps. They worked their way from the room and along the corridor to de Lesseps' suite. Charles, the great man's son, ordered drinks, cigars and food. Depuits introduced Philippe, extravagantly, Philippe felt. Gustave Eiffel added a warm word of approbation for him. "I was hoping to meet you, my boy," de Lesseps said. "Though I had no idea you'd be so damned young."

Depuits nodded. "That's what I've tried to tell him. Unforgivable. Talented. Accomplished. Handsome, and young. It's not fair to the rest of us."

De Lesseps laughed. "Yes. I'm sure there is legislation pending against me older than Bunau-Varilla. Eh?" He sank into a chair, gray with fatigue, looking older than God, exhausted. "I've been hoping you'd join us in Panama, my boy. We desperately need your kind of inventive mind down there.

"Yes. It's the place for you. You're young, creative, strong. France needs your skills. France must not fail with this canal. Our defeat in the war with Prussia cost us bitterly and left our people disunited. The success of the canal will not only provide a short trade route to the Pacific, it will bring the French people renewed hope, new pride, restored self-confidence. It will reunite them, revive and renew and reinvigorate our national spirit."

Philippe was aware of the other men—Depuits, Charles de Lesseps, Eiffel—and yet it was as if he were alone in this place with the Old Lion. As if from some muffled distance he heard de Lessep's voiec, speaking of the problems which by now obsessed him, the mounting weight of them, the cumulative crushing effect upon workers, investors and creditors.

It deeply troubled de Lesseps that representatives in the Assembly spoke increasingly against the program. "Men with great power denigrate the canal project as some fraudulent set-up supported by the government for the corrupt enrichment of a wealthy few. Nothing could be further from the truth. Nothing. There is even the foul slander that there was never a commitment to complete this canal, that it was a swindle from the first, that I in my dotage was persuaded to lend my name and reputation to afford it sanctity in the public nose, that I am not even kept fully informed of just how evilly things are going out there. God knows, I almost wish that were true. Every dispatch these days breaks my heart, humbles and destroys me.

161

"And, they shout, France does not need a canal half across the world. How nearsighted, how stupid can men allow themselves to become? France *does* need that canal. The first need is obvious. By canal the distance between the oceans is about fifty miles, against almost eight thousand miles around South America. France will profit materially and financially from a completed canal beyond the wildest comparison with the return from the canal in Suez."

De Lesseps gestured forlornly with his hand. "There is another truth worth your consideration. Six hundred thousand French families have invested their life savings in the Panama Canal. This is what I go to bed with every night. I don't have to suggest what failure will mean in personal hardship and ruin."

Philippe nodded. Financial failure of the Canal Company might topple the Third Republic, bankrupt the nation, throw it into anarchy unparalleled since the Revolution. How many times had he heard Claude-Bruce declaim on this subject!

He didn't flatter himself that his decision to go or refuse to go to Panama would make or break that project. But this magnificent old man needed him. He couldn't deny or ignore this. They crowded in on de Lesseps. His back was against the wall. He smiled, but every word was a desperate cry for help.

Philippe's mind spun. He was barely aware of how he got back to his apartment. When he entered, he saw the hand-delivered note on the carpeting, slipped under the door.

He picked it up, read it and grinned bitterly. An invitation to dinner at eight o'clock tomorrow—no, he checked the wall clock: three A.M.—at eight o'clock tonight at the Grenet house. His eyes burned, he felt empty, lost. God alone knew what he had to say to Madelon and her parents now, except good-bye.

[20]

Henri Grenet appeared no more than a meek, distant rela-
tive to the man who had so acidly denounced Philippe's
suit for his daughter's hand. Subdued, almost self-effacing,
anxious to please, eager to be liked, he seemed not yet
fully recovered from some recent and unnerving shock.
He invited Philippe into his study to await Madelon and
her mother. He offered Philippe a cigar, which Philippe
refused. Grenet then snubbed his own cigar out in an ash-
tray. He poured snifters of vintage brandy, but when
Philippe shook his head, declining a drink, Grenet smiled
diffidently and left the glasses untouched.

Philippe watched him, puzzled.

"We'll join the ladies in a moment." Grenet nodded.
His tone was apologetic. "Just a few things I wanted to
say. Eh? First. An apology, *M'sieu* Bunau-Varilla. I said
things about an alleged scandal. I repeated baseless
charges I should not have uttered. I permitted myself to
be influenced by rumor, idle gossip. I do apologize."

Philippe, mystified, moved his shoulders in a noncom-
mittal gesture. The tall patrician tried to smile without
spectacular success. "I don't want you to think that I am
any less totally pledged to my daughter's happiness."

Not knowing what to think, Philippe said, "I'm sure you're not, sir."

"But, though our talk was less than amicable, for which I was entirely at fault, entirely.—It was fruitful . . . very fruitful."

Philippe felt as if he were being asked to understand a puzzle from which all meaningful clues had been removed. Somehow, he'd liked Grenet better when he'd been rude. At least then he'd spoken plainly. "Sir?"

"Ah, yes. Yes. Very fruitful. A man may feel he is determined and be convinced of the rightness of his position, but we can all learn, even at my age, eh?"

Philippe waited. Last night, his mind befuddled with liquor, he'd understood what was going on around him better than he did now, cold sober.

Grenet shifted his neck inside his collar. "I have been persuaded, Philippe, that I was in error about you. Yes, and so I have reconsidered. I have talked with several men of highest moral character whose judgments and opinions I respect. They have the highest regard for you. And so, for these reasons, and my own personal liking for you—despite any differences which arose through misunderstanding, eh?—plus my wish that both you and my daughter will find happiness together, I withdraw my opposition to your—your suit." Grenet tried to smile affably again, failed, and a thick silence persisted for some seconds between them.

At the formal dining table, the situation became more clouded than ever for Philippe. Madelon seemed flushed, almost fevered, but she pasted a determined smile on her lips and met everyone's gaze squarely and brightly. Her eyes reflected light from the chandelier as the flat surface of a pond might. Her warmly tinted face was incredibly lovely, if gemlike in glaze. Philippe winced, unable to say why he felt an ache of compassion for her. She seemed completely at ease, but he knew better and he could only guess at what the effort was costing her.

He was aware that either Monsieur Grenet or Madame Grenet, or both, were speaking to him and that he had not heard a word. He had to force himself to attend either of

Madelon's parents, or to hobble along in the wake of their conversation. His eyes kept following his thoughts across the table to Madelon. Vaguely, Philippe realized that *Père* Grenet was proposing a toast, and he tried to care, tried to concentrate, tried to smile. "To your long life, my children. To your great happiness."

Everyone smiled except Madame Grenet, who blinked back tears.

Philippe frowned, moving his gaze from Madelon's ice-hard smile, to Madame Grenet's bland warmth, to Henri Grenet's stunned, but unyielding cordiality. Still holding his wine goblet aloft and relentlessly smiling, Monsieur Grenet reminded them that in the past day he'd been made extremely conscious of Philippe's reputation in the engineering world. "I am convinced Philippe has the brightest sort of future. Eh? He will receive those commissions which go only to the most respected engineers. I was assured of this again and again."

Philippe, more confused than ever, peered at Madelon's father, wondering why such flattering words sounded as if they were spoken by a man with a gun at his temple?

"Madelon will be truly happy at last, and that's all that really matters, isn't it, Henri?" Madame Grenet looked ready to burst into tears.

Yet, oddly, Madelon's parents' faces showed expectancy, delight and relief. As if after a long and bitterly secretive time in which they'd been forced to conceal shameful and unspeakable guilt, they could boast now expansively to all friends, acquaintances and enemies, but about what, Philippe had no idea.

"It will be a new and lovely time for all of us," Madame Grenet insisted, smiling around the table, her glow touching each of them like a benediction.

Philippe gazed, bewildered, from one smiling face to the next.

Finally, Philippe was alone with Madelon in a cozy music room, the door closed against intrusion. When she walked into the retreat, Madelon dropped her smile. Suddenly, it was as if she had never smiled.

She leaned against the piano and turned to face him. "You can still get out of it. You can still run."

"Get out of what?"

She stared at him, and then shook her head. "Don't you really understand yet?"

"I understand nothing. I was ordered to stay away from this house. To stay away from you. Suddenly, I am welcomed back like the prodigal son. No, I don't understand. What was going on in there?"

Her laughter was tainted with bitterness. "Why, they were being nice to you."

"I know that. But I still don't know why. In what way am I different from the last time I was here?"

"In no way. *You* haven't changed at all. Sadly, I suppose you never will."

"One argument at a time. Please. What were we celebrating in that dining room?"

"They've decided to announce our engagement."

Philippe gazed at her. She was not joking. There was not the slightest trace of pleasure in her voice. "Announce our engagement?"

"That was what you wanted the last time you were here, wasn't it?"

"Yes. But—"

"If that's not what you want, you'll have to forgive my parents for a false assumption. You've stood on my porch, knocking on my door. You've stood across the street. Written letters. What are they to think? They concluded that you did want to marry me."

"I wanted to. With all my heart, I wanted to."

"But you've changed your mind?"

"*I* haven't changed at all. But circumstances have altered. Conditions are not the same. You have changed. You swore you'd never marry me, could never love me again."

"None of that has altered. But, as you say, circumstances have altered."

"God knows I haven't understood one thing that's gone on here tonight."

"You haven't listened, darling," said that implacable voice.

"I've tried to."

"It's really very simple. My parents have welcomed you, as warmly as they could, into the very bosom of our family. *They* want you, after all."

"*That's* what I don't understand."

"Don't try to understand. They're not too clear about it, either."

"And what about you?"

She moved those beautiful shoulders in a slight shrug. "What I *want* is no longer important. If you still want me, *m'sieu*, I will marry you."

For a long time, neither of them spoke. The house itself seemed to hang suspended in a tense, waiting stillness. A carriage rattled past on the loose bricks of the street. Philippe was unsure whether he'd walked into heaven or plunged into nightmare. The words were what he'd prayed Madelon would say. But the tone was one of ridicule, and the voice a stranger's voice.

He sighed heavily. He reached out to touch her, but she evaded him with a slight twist of her body. His arms fell at his sides.

"But you don't love me? Any more now than yesterday?"

"I have not changed. I better warn you, I am not likely to change."

"Then what are we discussing?"

"Whether you want to marry me or not."

"God knows I want you. I've always wanted you. You. You, alone. No matter what you've decided. But there must be some rational explanation to this sudden reversal. What changed everything? What kind of charade is this?"

Her voice slashed him like a rapier. "Darling, haven't you guessed? I'm pregnant."

Again they drifted in a sea of silence. Philippe felt giddy, and had to steady himself against the ornate neck of a chair. She was as cold as the statuary in the gardens.

"Another little souvenir of my visit with you in Algiers."

He caught his breath. "Four—five months?"

"Yes. Perhaps this helps you understand my parents' total reversal of attitude. Soon I'll be quite visibly

167

pregnant. Clever seamstresses conceal the bulge. Of course, even when I'm naked, an unobservant man wouldn't notice."

"I had no idea. I was totally unaware."

"And, of course, totally indifferent."

He flinched but said nothing.

"You had what you wanted," she said. "A round little belly hardly got in your way, did it?"

His eyes filled with tears. "I am glad, Madelon. Pleased. This changes everything."

She stared at him, mouth twisted. "It changes nothing. You're still a liar. Cheat. Libertine. Rapist. Scamp."

"Who loves you." He forced himself to smile. "My God, Madelon. This is God's will. It has to be. Give us a chance. We can yet be happy."

"Can we? Would an alliance between us be a marriage, or a mockery of a holy estate?"

"I don't know. Give us a chance. We'll find out."

"Or will it be only a trap?"

Angered, he stepped toward her. A small muscle worked in the sharp line of his jaw. "A trap, eh? You're the one who speaks of traps. A trap, of course. That's why you met me in the gardens, why you went home with me, why you went to bed with me."

Her lips managed a disdainful smile. "Yes. I thought it wise, prudent even, to keep you interested."

"As one dangles a carrot to trap a rabbit."

"If you say so."

"And love? Love had nothing to do with it. You just wanted to keep me dangling, keep me available."

"That's right. I realized I might need you after all, when I could no longer hide my shameful little secret from my parents."

"Only fear of disgrace and public ridicule brings you to me?"

"I'm sorry, my darling. Morning sickness I could hide. But when I threw up after your visit, and they brought in the doctor, I was caught." She smiled. "Yes. In a way it's funny. The same doctor. The one who when I was married told me I was a virgin. And now that I am unwed, he tells me I am pregnant. But worse than that he told my parents."

"And so you set out coldly to arrange a marriage with me."

"That's right."

"You're totally without scruples."

She shrugged. "I learned that from you."

His eyes filled with tears, he glowered down at his trembling fists. "No. I'm damned if I will," he said. "You admit you don't love me. I'm damned if I'll marry you like this—in name only." He stared at her, eyes agonized. "Get one of your other partners."

She remained as cool as marble. "Sorry, my love. I'm afraid you're the only one so far."

Tenderness flooded through him. He reached for her. Though she resisted, he drew her to him. "I am the only one," he said. "As you are the only one."

Her eyes flared. "I said you are the only one—so far, *m'sieu*."

"Don't do this, Madelon. We've both been hurt enough."

She writhed free and walked back to the piano, leaning against it for support. She stared at him and shook her head. "You really don't understand yet, do you? I told you. The trap door is still open. You are free to walk out."

"You know I won't leave you to face this alone."

"You would if you were smart. Do not think I am marrying you for any fool reason. Love has nothing to do with it. Love, I've found, is for silly schoolgirls. And not even for them. For silly schoolboys, who are not taught any better. Our marriage would not be till death do us part. I see it only as an entirely civilized way to settle an unpleasant matter. We marry, we go away somewhere, long enough so that fool women who count on their fingers won't be able to laugh behind their hands. Then, you may go where you wish. I shall return to Paris to rear my child. All will be finished between us. That way, the public is deceived, our issue has a name, my poor parents can hold up their heads again. And our marriage exists, if at all, in the only way possible. In name only."

"You've got it all figured out, haven't you?"

"To survive and to protect my child. It's a woman's instinct."

"Suppose I tell you to go to hell with your marriage in name only. If you plan to walk out on me after our baby is born, you can stay in Paris—unwed. If you marry me, you'll go where I go, and be my wife, at my side—in my bed."

She sighed heavily. "Then perhaps you had better leave. Now."

"No. I'm still fool enough to believe that you are still Madelon, and that you do love me. In time, you'll admit it aloud. Maybe that's what makes this worthwhile. That—and a son of my own! No, my dear Madelon, you will marry me. But it won't be quite the civilized tea-party you have planned. You'll marry me. You'll stay married to me till death do us part. But not in the ease you envision. I'm on my way to Panama, my love, and by God, you'll go with me."

She stared at him, shaking her head. "You'd drag me into that hell?"

"There are all kinds of hells, my dear. There's the kind you planned to drag me into. Well, you may put me into hell, but you'll go into mine with me. I'll make it as good for you as I can, as good as you'll let me."

She shrugged. "You can marry me. You can take me into that hell to bear my child. But you can never make me love you."

He stood over her. "Oh, you'll love me all right. I'll make you love me."

She laughed at him, coldly, mocking. "You're too late, Philippe. I loved you once. A long time ago. In Algiers. Remember? Your slut's knife—it struck you. You survived. But my love died."

FOUR

Panama, 1884–1886

[21]

The long voyage began at midnight from the harbor at Saint Nazaire. Philippe and Madelon stood at the railing of the liner S.S. *Washington* and watched Europe recede in a frothy wake. The sound of ships' whistles, the barking of tugs, and the farewell cries of the passengers swirled around them. Even in that crush of boisterous voyagers Philippe felt alone. Long after he could no longer discern the crowd on the lighted docks, he knew that Madelon's face was warped with crying, her eyes swollen and red. And yet, at the same time, he could not deny a sense of hope. They were together. Man and wife. As long as they were together there was a chance.

Soon the ship steamed into a storm. The craft pitched and staggered, as it fought its way south and west across the wintry Atlantic. For the first few days everybody aboard existed in a state of agony. Philippe prowled the decks, watching the black sky and dark waters. He could barely see the plumelike tail of the ship's wake and the relentless belching of somber smoke. The savagery of the gales stunned him. The ship shuddered, tossed by hurricane-force winds, struggling to maintain a heading.

Cabinboys and stewards appeared only when summoned repeatedly. The passengers seen on deck were taut-faced, tight-fisted and withdrawn, as if holding in, under excrutiating self-discipline, the swill which roiled in their bellies and made them despise this ship, the sea, other human beings and most of all, themselves. Some were convulsively seasick, clinging passionately to the railings, faces a glaucous gray to match the pitching waves.

Stalking the decks, Philippe met the ship's captain who laughed about his particular brand of *mal de mer*. "You never overcome it, or escape it. You learn only to live with it or despite it. You somehow occupy your mind and keep it occupied or you can lose twenty pounds in a crossing. I know. I suffered it since the day I stepped aboard a brigantine as a cabin boy thirty years ago. I see sailors come aboard, throw up during a storm or afore they get their sea legs. Then they're fine. No touch of illness. I envy them, but that's not the way it is for me. The hot odors, the steam, the paint-smell that rides on even the freshest blast of air far forward or deep aft never lets me free. I've hated the sea, but I could never escape her. I was apprenticed and it was all I knew. I had to learn to live with it. It's a kind of imbalance in the inner ear. It turned me gall-bitter inside. Kept my nerves on edge, my temper riled. I was always exhausted, you see, and a little bit queasy at my stomach. Snappish, I was. Also, it made me me own man. Aboard my ship, I wasn't scared of no physical pain or thrashing nor hard labor. I wasn't scared of the divel himself. What could any man do to me that wouldn't be a relief and take me mind off that knot of sickness always simmering inside me." He shook his head, smiling, remembering. "The spleen I lived with made me a ship's captain. Nothin' else. Because I couldn't be scared or intimidated by nothin' nor nobody outside me own sick belly and dizzy brain, people learned to fear and then to respect me! I laugh about it sometimes, when I feel well enough, or if I'm sittin' ashore somewhere. Ship executive officer, and all because I never learned to throw up and get that sickness out of me."

Philippe tried to follow the captain's advice. He would

never like the sea; he could only learn to endure it. He forced himself into strenuous physical activity. He tried to study the canal blueprints and specification books but found no printed word vital enough to displace the squeamishness in his stomach.

Yet, his persistent sense of nausea was the least of his sorrows. Madelon tried to hide her own illness, but her face was gray and rigid. She fell across her bed. He tried to calm her, to touch her, but she pulled away. He lay down on his own bunk, caught between anger and a hunger which had nothing to do with food. He had believed that once he and Madelon were married they would begin their lives anew. It had to be like that. They were meant for one another.

Yet marriage had not changed the disastrous pattern of their courtship.

Philippe exhaled heavily, staring into the darkness. Madelon had looked lovely that day in the little chapel outside Neuilly, but she had been tense and cold. Most mothers of the bride cry at weddings but Madame Grenet's sobbing was full of despair. The thought that Philippe was dragging a pregnant Madelon after him to the tropic hell of Panama infuriated her parents. They spoke not a word to Philippe.

When at last Madelon came to their bed in a St. Nazaire hotel room, she was unsmiling. When he drew her to him, she remained icy, stiff with reserve.

He took her into his arms and pulled her against him. "Please, Madelon, won't you give us a chance?"

She allowed him to draw her down to the bed beside him. She lay rigid, her arms limp at her side. "Go ahead," she said. "I'm your wife. I can't stop you. You can do what you will. That I will hate it need not disturb you."

He stared down at her, withdrew his hands from her full breasts. "This is hell," he said, his voice anguished.

"Not yet, but we're well on our way," she replied.

He had dressed and stalked out of the room, slamming the door behind him. He stood in the dim corridor for a long time. But there was no sound from within their room, no calling his name, no sighs, no tears. He spent

174

their wedding night in the hotel bar. He was still badly hung over when they boarded the ship the next evening.

The rage built and swirled with the nausea inside him. He'd fallen finally into sweated, restless sleep when he heard Madelon scream out. She did not call his name. She screamed for Fanny.

He lunged off the bunk, bounded across the room and jerked open the connecting door. Fanny sprawled helplessly, her head toppled over the side of her bunk, moaning and retching into the gray bucket with each toss and pitch of the ship.

Madelon, too, was vomiting. Her head hung over the side of her mattress. She kept calling weakly for Fanny, but her maid was helpless to aid her.

Philippe walked to Madelon's bed, knelt beside it. "It's all right," he said. "I'm here, Madelon."

"Oh, no." She wept, rolling her head back and forth. "I don't want you. Where is Fanny?"

"I'm afraid Fanny is as helpless as you are," he said. He smoothed the sweated hair back from her forehead. "You'll have to let me help you. After all, I vowed for better or worse, remember?"

Day after day and through the endless nights, the violent pitching and yawing of the ship continued, intensifying Madelon's illness. Fanny's noisome infirmity only served to add to Madelon's suffering.

She fought to hold back her heaving and retching, but she had sufficient strength only to sag over the edge of the bunk and vomit. Across the room, Fanny lay in even worse agony, begging for dry land, pleading to be allowed to die.

Madelon's agony increased a thousand times as she realized it was Philippe who tenderly cleansed and changed and bathed her. She wanted him to suffer, but she didn't want him to see her in such a condition. She wanted to refuse his help, to drive him away, for she hated being dependent on him. But she was too weak, condemned to receive the tender ministrations of a man she despised.

175

Gradually, her condition improved. Her head rolled on the fresh pillow Philippe had brought her. When he sat beside her on the bed and touched her, because he could not resist touching her, she withdrew, thankful Fanny lay across the narrow room on the other bunk.

When she drew away from him, Philippe sighed heavily and stood up. He moved away from the bunk and stood looking down at her.

"I've sworn I'd be patient, I would give you time," he said. "I did hurt you. Badly. I owe you time to forget and to recover from hurt. But you let me see no hope at all for us."

She turned her face away to the wall, closed her eyes.

He spread his hands. "All right, my dear. I won't try to touch you again. You can stay in here with Fanny to keep you company. When you change your mind, you can come to me."

He turned and walked out. He did not see her lift her hand, reaching forlornly after him. But, even if he had seen, he may not have hesitated just then. He was too full of rage and despair to care any more.

sored. Yet her eyes were shadowed. About her there was a brilliant hardness, an approachable hardness of manner that

[22]

Philippe lounged alone at a table in the ship's salon drinking black coffee. He had no appetite, though his aversion to food had less to do with his persistent nausea than with gut-sickness as his hope for any conciliation with Madelon faded.

A mustachioed, middle-aged man, bowed and asked if he might join him. "My wife is indisposed. Violently. I asked if she'd like me to have dinner sent in to her, but she only told me in no uncertain terms to get out of her sight." He smiled. "She even told me where to go. I decided to come here instead."

Philippe nodded. To his chagrin, the man ordered fried ham, fried eggs in some sort of cheese casserole, and a meringue dessert. Philippe bit down hard on his underlip and managed to go on sitting there. He was ever afterward thankful he did.

Chewing lustily, the tall man smiled heartily across the linen-covered table. "Permit me to introduce myself. I am Jean-Paul Gallaudet, director-general of the Panama Canal Project. My wife and I are returning from a recruiting drive."

177

"I'm happy to know you, sir." Philippe introduced himself. "I'll be working for you."

"Yes. Pleased to have you. De Lesseps discussed his high expectations for you. Let me interject only a word of caution. Don't be dejected or defeated if at first you find failure—ah, that hated word—at the Isthmus."

"I realize how bad things are down there."

Gallaudet shook his head. "You can have no idea, until you have been there! So, if you are able to accomplish less than you hope, be philosophical about it. We face great odds. Fearful odds." Gallaudet tried to smile. "Visitors to the tropics denigrate the natives for apathy, negligence, indolence, procrastination, lethargic acceptance of good and ill. Perhaps these natives have evolved the only way to exist in equatorial regions. Life is lush and green, with food growing on every bush and tree. But disease pollutes the air, every drop of drinking water, it lurks in every bush, or hides in the folds of your clothing. Nature is erratic and moody. Everything grows in abundance, but destruction strikes as violently, and these people live with this capricious state of being. Then accept it, float along with it.

"But we outsiders are too brilliant, too civilized to do this, too ambitious, too energetic, too well-organized. We come down there and try to bend a violent nature to our bureaucratic will. We try to conquer it, force order into chaos. Perhaps for all our vaunted brilliance, we have not yet learned our best lessons."

Departing, Gallaudet touched Philippe's arm and smiled. "Have you met Monsieur Ducrot Bazaine, who will head the engineering corps?"

"No. I know him by reputation only."

Gallaudet inclined his graying head toward a bantam-sized man standing alone at the bar. "He is only forty, but he has an enviable reputation. We are fortunate to get him out here. We'll bring youth and strength to bear now, eh? His uncle is the same Marshal Bazaine who assumed command of the French army after our terrible defeat at Worth."

Gallaudet smiled and shook hands with Philippe warmly. "Ducrot is a leader. I hope he will provide the kind of inspiration and technical knowledge we so desperately need out here. Work with him, Philippe. Make the project move! God knows, my boy, I could use some good news to send home from the Isthmus for a change."

"It's good knowing you, sir. I hope we can make it all work at last."

"Introduce yourself to Ducrot. You two should have a great deal to discuss before we reach Colón-Aspinwall."

Philippe reached the bar just as the Negro bartender served a cocktail to Monsieur Bazaine. A sudden violent shift and shudder of the ship caused the black man to tilt the glass and spill some of the fluid on Bazaine's sleeve.

Bazaine's narrow, swarthy face went livid. His voice rasped, as brutal as a fist in the belly. "Be careful, you stupid ape-nigger. If you black bastards can't be taught to handle glassware properly, you at least ought to be kept where human beings don't have to be sullied by contact."

The bartender was too frightened to speak. His large eyes, white-rimmed with terror, he reached tentatively with a fresh napkin to blot the customer's sleeve. Bazaine lashed out, slapping his hand away. He knocked over his glass, spilling the remainder of the liquor and smashing the goblet. "Sorry, m'sieu. Sorry," the bartender said, his Bahamian accent unmistakable. "I'll get another drink. Right away, m'sieu."

"You certainly shall, you black jape," Ducrot Bazaine said, "which won't deter me from reporting your slovenly negligence to the head steward."

"Yes, m'sieu."

"And don't come grinning those goddamn white monkey teeth, expecting a gratuity, either, you clumsy black son of a bitch."

Standing only a barstool way from Ducrot Bazaine, Philippe stared slack-jawed at the diminutive package of outrage—this little man reacting insanely to a spilled drink. Philippe was reminded of a bantam rooster ruffling its tail feathers, cocking its crest and parading its spurs at the remotest hint of a barnyard challenge to its dignity. Watching Bazaine preening on the barstool, straightening his shoulders and caressing the tips of his waxed mustache,

Philippe realized the display was meant as a proof to the sparse crowd in the salon, and to Bazaine himself, of his own elevated rank among mortals.

Philippe turned away. He could wait to meet Bazaine at some later date and in the line of duty. Ducrot Bazaine was no one he cared to know socially. But Bazaine, turning his head, glimpsed him and said, "You, what did you want? Did you wish to speak with me?"

Philippe bit back a sour smile, thinking, *I'd like to break your ugly face. But we've got to work together. I realize you feel superior to all other races because of birth, despise all ethnic groups as inferior. Guido De Blasio, otherwise a good and decent man, an outstanding engineer, was as prejudiced.*

He sighed. He didn't have to agree with Bazaine, but he did have to work with him. "Monsieur Gallaudet suggested I introduce myself."

Bazaine gazed at him, brow tilted and thin-lipped mouth twisted. "Yes, I saw you buttering up the old man. Saw him point me out to you. Figured you to be a project underling of some sort."

"An engineer. Philippe Bunau-Varilla."

"Ah yes." Bazaine did not smile. "I've heard of you. Boy wonder. Some experience in Algiers. Almost got yourself knifed to death by some jealous black wench, wasn't it? Yes. I've heard of you. We'll have to keep tight rein on you at the Isthmus, no doubt."

Philippe's rage smoldered hotter. He forced himself to smile. "Monsieur Gallaudet suggested I introduce myself. I had no wish to force myself upon you. It was his suggestion."

"Why?"

"Damned if I know, Bazaine. Perhaps because he thinks we ought to be friends since we'll be working together in a strange place."

"I assure you, *M'sieu* Bunau-Varilla, being my *friend* won't buy you one damned special consideration or favor on this job. Any more than sucking up to old Gallaudet will land you easy assignments or preferential treatment. You produce. Do your job. That's all you have to do to get along with me. I have all the intimate and personal

180

friends I need. Kissing around because I'm executive in charge won't buy you anything with me except my contempt. Just work and keep your nose clean."

"You little son of a bitch," Philippe said.

Bazaine's lips pulled into a mocking smile. "I've always heard we ought never curse a man who may control our destiny."

"We'll worry about that, *m'sieu,* the day I ask a favor of you."

Bazaine grinned. "Well, you've gotten yourself off to a great start, haven't you, boy? And fresh from a brothel scandal on your last job."

Philippe gazed at Bazaine in total disbelief.

Then he turned and walked out of the salon. Bazaine's mocking laugh trailed after him as if the little man had spat on him. He strode up the ladder to an aft upper deck; he needed gales of fresh air. He found only one reassuring aspect in this strange and puzzling confrontation —he had completely forgotten his queasiness; he wasn't half sick at his stomach or even faintly dizzy. But he was trembling with rage. It was all so stupid, so gratuitously venomous. And this was the man he was going to work with.

Leaning against the deck railing, he became aware of a woman poised in a slender shaft of light. He had not seen her before. The wailing storm increased, something strange and upsetting cried in the darkness. The winds whistled from the black depths, across the shadowed deck, and into the vast abyss of water beyond. Yet the woman seemed not at all disturbed by the gale-force winds, the cold or the stinging mists. The dark night seemed part of her, or she part of it, as if she'd materialized in the deep shadows and would dissolve like gray smoke into them.

He felt her gaze fixed on him. The light from the companionway lantern wavered and flickered across her lovely face.

She smiled faintly. Some deep instinct recognized a danger signal like the wan flicker of a buoy light marking a shoal-pocked channel. At the same time his heart lurched. Her smile was an invitation as clear as any spoken word. He even had the sense that there was no need for words between them. The inner perceptions already existed there. The communication. Their eyes met across a dark narrow deck-space and everything relevant was said.

Two people—he didn't even glance toward them—emerged from the companionway and strolled past the woman, slowing and then disappearing in the darkness. She appeared unaware of them.

She watched him. He wanted to go to her, he wanted to run away. It was as if she'd known he would be alone out here, as if this blood-tingling isolation were somehow contrived. Yet, there was also an aloofness about her. One didn't walk up to this woman, and take her arm. In fact he felt that if he spoke to her she would rebuff him icily, anything he said would be the wrong thing.

Watching her, he wished he had more experience, that he'd spent less time building harbors and more in fashionable salons haunted by women like this. There was something he should do; the next move was his; but damned if he knew what it was.

She moved and he could not tear his gaze from her. An unreasoning flare of panic, fear of something within himself that he couldn't control, went through him. He was afraid she was going to leave, equally afraid she would not.

He went on peering at her from the depth of wind-swept shadow, but he was certain his eyes glittered with that curious telepathy that sometimes passes between strangers.

Her appraising and approving gaze gave him the courage to cross the brief space between them. He paused only a foot away from her. Even in gale winds, a warm and subtle fragrance emanated from her sable coat. Smiling, his heart pounding oddly, he bowed slightly. He waited but she did not return his smile.

"Cold," he said. He spoke in a mildly teasing way; she could take it as a comment on the weather or her unbending remoteness.

"Nights at sea are always cold when one is alone, *m'sieu*." Her classic face remained expressionless.

"Are you alone?" He asked it with the proper spicing

of concern, making it the innocuous question one traveler always asks of another.

Her red lips twisted. "Hardly. I'm afraid you misunderstood me."

His gaze held hers and he grinned. "Perhaps—may I introduce myself?"

"I already know who you are," she said. "I saw you. With your wife and her maid."

"Why didn't I see you?" She shrugged slightly.

He waited but she offered no information about herself. He said, "What is your name? Or must I call you only madame?"

"My name is Anouk. That's enough for you. I'm afraid we shan't see much of each other."

"Why not?"

She shrugged again. "I don't really trust in shipboard acquaintances. I believe such relationships are best left where they began, aboard ship."

"You're not being very encouraging, are you?"

"Why should I encourage you?"

He put his head back laughing. "Because the very sight of you encourages me."

"Does it? Or are you simply trying to escape mundane problems, *mal de mer*, frustration perhaps?" She left the thought unfinished as if she knew a great deal more than she said.

The ship lurched as the sea lifted and tossed it once more. Anouk leaned close against Philippe and steadied herself, her arm outstretched. For one long moment in eternity, her full, heated breasts pressed marvelously rich and warm against his arm. Philippe was breathless. The ship, the foul weather, his desperate future with Madelon, all disappeared. There was nothing in the world but the touch of this mysterious woman.

Suddenly, Anouk turned her head to look at something across the deck. When Philippe followed her glance, he saw Madelon frozen in a doorway. He stared at her, as if in a nightmare. Her eyes were glazed with fury.

She stared at him, then turned and half-ran, balancing against the bulkhead. Philippe felt sick at his stomach. He wanted to run after her. There was nothing in the incident. Anouk had staggered, he had steadied her. But everything was in their faces. He didn't try to lie to himself about that.

Madelon threw open her stateroom door and slammed it behind her. Philippe stood, staring after her. He heard Anouk's laugh. "Your wife saw it all. You see. I'm sorry. It's an omen. Nothing good can come of—our knowing each other. You just had a warning."

"It was an accident. You know that."

She smiled. "Yes. Wasn't it? Just as our meeting was accidental. We do know, don't we? But how will you make her believe that?" She let the rich fur slide from her shoulders, revealing her low-cut bodice. "It's too hot for this." She shook her head, her lips twisted now with a taunting smile. "She saw it, Philippe, but not as we did." She reached up, touched his face. "I know women like her. They see only what they want to see."

Angered, he said, "Isn't that what you're doing?"

She shook her head slowly, her face alive with that maddening smile. "You know better than that, too." Turning, she walked away suddenly. He watched her move along the long corridor, undulating gracefully in tune with the violent pitch and yaw of the ship.

Philippe entered his stateroom. The mysterious Anouk was driven from his mind. The fury in Madelon's eyes had been real. Final. He crossed the room, aware that the cabin lamp flickered and danced loosely with every roll of the ship.

He touched the knob of the door between the two staterooms. The door was locked. He wanted to kick the door down. With a herculean effort, he controlled his anger. He knew it was hopeless. His fists clenched at his sides. He turned away from the door raging, troubled, and sick with loss.

[23]

Philippe locked the corridor door of his cabin. He felt totally ashamed that he'd been bewitched at the sight and touch and scent of the fascinating Anouk. Good Lord! He owed Madelon fidelity. He had promised it. Yet here he was, enmeshed and snared in forbidden compulsions he could neither explain nor expunge. He couldn't get Anouk out of his mind.

He prowled the cabin, its walls pressing in upon him. He had to get Anouk out of his mind, keep her out of his mind. But the evanescent and inexpressible fragrance of her, the memory of that blurred silhouette, the brief pressure of his hand against her marvelous breast, all haunted him, as the very sight of that locked door between his stateroom and Madelon's, enraged and distressed him.

He undressed. Then, still restless, he stalked the cabin as if caged, filled with longings and needs and energies too violent and unbridled for the confines of this breathless crib. He kept seeing the first glimpse of Anouk on that storm deck. He thought ahead to the hot land at the Isthmus. He remembered Madelon's serene loveliness in that long ago courtyard on the Ile St. Louis.

The knocking on his corridor door was repeated twice before the sound truly penetrated his consciousness.

He crossed the room, opened the door and stood with it as a shield for his nakedness. His eyes widened and he stared, incredulous, at the woman standing there.

"May I come in?" The way Anouk phrased it, no question was implied. She wore that full-length sable coat and a diaphanous scarf over her lustrous dark hair.

"I was just going to bed," he said and flinched. How inane he sounded.

Anouk stepped through the doorway imperiously and slammed the door behind her. "Don't be a fool keeping me standing out there for the world to witness. Surely you're more experienced than that."

"How'd you know I'd be alone in here?"

She shrugged those fabulous shoulders. "Everyone on board knows you sleep alone, darling. And your child-bride with her nanny next door."

"That's nobody's goddamn business. Including yours."

She smiled. "Aboard a ship, my love, gossip, rumor, conjecture and even whispered slander become the only antidotes to boredom. They make existence possible in the enforced monotony of confinement and inescapable companionship of bores."

"I would have thought you avoided such chit-chat."

"I know what I know." She laughed. "What I need to know." She looked at Philippe, her smile slow and languorous, her lips heated and damp. Her eyes moved across his body, lingering, appraising, devouring. "You truly are a lovely young devil, aren't you?"

He shivered slightly under the unwavering inventory. "I'd offer you a drink," he said. "But there's nothing." He swung his arm to indicate the temporary nature of his lodgings in this room.

Anouk continued to gaze at him with unabashed pleasure and approval. "I've had a drink," she said. "Besides, you're far more intoxicating to me than alcohol. I saw you when you came aboard, with that silly blonde child clinging tearfully to you. Do you know what I said then?"

"It's late, Anouk."

"Not even close." She shook her head, smiling. "No.

186

I said, that beautiful young scoundrel is for me. I think I've been quite circumspect, as much as I intend to be anyhow. I've waited three days and three nights."

"You must go."

"Oh come now. You won't really help except in a transient way, because I really am on fire inside. I don't expect you to cool me down except for a little while. I don't ask too much of you." She smiled, tipping her tongue across her lips. "Only your best."

"Why'd you want to destroy me?"

Her gaze raked him. "Because you're built like a Greek god. Because I'm delaying, as civilizedly as possible, while you cast off any last foolish inhibitions."

He winced. "I'm afraid that *can't* happen." Inadvertently, his gaze touched at the interlocking door between his stateroom and Madelon's. He was almost insane with desire, but he wasn't crazy yet.

Coolly, Anouk walked over and shot the bolt on the door between the two cabins. "There," she said. "Is that better?"

He stood unmoving. She smiled at him, coolly and serenely self-confident. She shrugged her slender shoulders and the sable coat fell like a rag about her feet.

Philippe's eyes widened and he felt a painfully sweet constriction in his throat. She wore only a translucent gown of some pastel hue, a fabric of meshed lace.

Philippe stared at her, entranced. The saffron glitter of the lamps on her warm flesh was its own enticement. The rich blackness of her damasklike hair framed the pale, unearthly beauty of her face. She had stopped smiling. Her lips parted, as if in unspoken invitation. The lights trailed his gaze across the curve of her throat and breasts. The witchery of her lovely body held him entranced. He could not pull his fascinated gaze from the ruby points of her rigid nipples, the flat shadowy planes of her stomach, the dainty triangle of her femininity revealed enticingly through the sheer fabric.

When he remained unmoving, she inquired, almost coldly, "Now what are you afraid of?"

"You." But he was no longer afraid of her, only of

himself. He walked to her, cruelly aware of a stiffening erection, on which her eyes were now fixed.

She waited, expectant, but instead of touching her, he knelt and took up her sable coat, conscious of its richness and sensuous softness. He stood up and placed her coat gently but firmly about her shoulders.

Her mouth twisted and those dark eyes flared. "Stop being a fool," she said. Her heated hands caressed his bared chest, smoothed the flat planes of his belly until she touched the thrusting rod at his thighs. "We want each other," she said. "Now. And that's all that matters. We're strangers on a ship. Each with his own needs. We could mean a great deal to one another for this moment."

"No," he said, but as she went on stroking him with her hand, he knew he was not going to resist. He was unsure about the quality of the struggle he'd made against her, but it was a losing battle. His hands caught the lace bodice of her fragile gown and ripped it downward.

Her eyes flashed. "Oh God," she whispered. "You are going to cool me down, aren't you?"

His hands caressed her breasts. His breath rasped. His voice mocked her. "For a little while."

"Yes," she whispered. "Oh, yes. For a little while."

"You're lovely," he whispered against her face. "As lovely as you are reckless and dangerous."

"Oh, you're so good. I've been looking for a man like you all my life."

His twisted smile taunted her and himself. "And I'll bet you've looked in some hellishly interesting places."

"Don't be a bastard." She spoke against his mouth. Her breath was hot, intoxicating. "I don't pretend to be a virgin," she said. "But I am selective. Selective as hell." Her heated hands massaged him, hefted him, caressed him.

His hands smoothed the heated texture of her naked body. His fingers closed on her hips. He lifted her from the floor, bringing her thighs up to his own rigidity.

"We might as well be as civilized as possible," she said. "The bed is there."

"Yes," he said. "The bed." But holding her up from

188

the floor, he pushed himself into the fevered wetness. She gasped and dug her nails into him.

"Oh my God," she whispered. "Oh my God."

He thrust himself into her. "You started this," he said between his teeth. "And like it or hate it, you're going to get it."

She locked her arms over his shoulders, levering herself upward. Her long, sculptured legs entangled him and her ankles fastened him within a fiery embrace. Slowly, he sank to the floor. They lay lashed together. His hips flailed and she battered herself upward against him. The gales pitched and tossed and hurtled the ship, and they rolled with it, wilder than the storm itself.

[24]

Landfall. Excitement swept through the ship. Adults laughed and chattered like children restrained in those final moments before a school recess. They drank—to each other, to good health, good fortune, long life, the work most would be doing in some connection with the canal project. However, as the Isthmus materialized in the humid mists, an underlying tension crackled in the atmosphere. The ship steamed through sweltering heat into sight of the lowlands of Manzanillo. Beyond that warm fog, rising like a steam veil from becalmed seas, lay the unknown land, the ominous future.

The ship had slipped free of the storm at last and a kind of normal existence resumed among passengers and crew. Life became happier after the ship touched in at the Bahamas and moved on into the tropic waters. It was a pleasant passage and the voyagers forgot the storm and winter seas of the north.

Philippe left the door doubled-bolted between his cabin and Madelon's. Both Madelon and Fanny LeBeau recovered from their illness, but Fanny was unable to retain solid food and lost weight seriously. She cried a lot. Philippe was relieved to be out of her presence.

Though the seas lightened and the sun blazed, lifting the spirits of ship's company and passengers, Madelon remained utterly remote. She did take breakfast, lunch and dinner with Philippe in the salon. She made friends with Madame Gallaudet. Infrequently she would promenade with Philippe on the open deck, walking silently at his side, her hand on his arm—for support, he supposed, or for the benefit of strangers.

Philippe made no effort to locate Anouk aboard the ship, but she came to him night after night. The sound of her voice aroused and excited him. Her words were the obscene whispered promises of every wanton descended in a direct line from Lilith, making her a sister of Jezebel, Delilah and Thais. *I want to drink you. I want to taste you. I want you deep inside me. Deeper. Deeper.*

The last night she came to him aboard ship, she clung to him, kissing him, her eyes brimmed with tears, her mouth suckling and nursing at him until he writhed in intolerable delight. She lay close, her mouth upon his cheek. "I thought I'd never see you again once we left this ship. I was wiser then, younger, I didn't know then how *satisfying* you are. I leave you, stunned with weariness, and I sleep, and there are no dreams, no demons, no fantasies. You must not try to see me. But if I can see you again, somehow, I shall get word to you."

Philippe packed his steamer trunk and suitcase, leaving them on the cabin floor, and hurried out on deck, bareheaded, without a jacket, shirt open at the collar. He stood at the railing and watched the ship snugged into its berth at the Colón piers. Land, after an interminable voyage at sea! He'd escaped that smell of fuel, paint and varnish, the overheated odors from the galley and the ill. It was behind him. Vertigo. Nausea. The sense of being trapped. And in its place a whole new world lay dazzlingly green before him.

Never before had he seen such dense, lush forests climbing, clambering upward from incredibly white beaches in impenetrable masses of vines, trees and shrubs, to distant rocky headlands liquid with verdure to their summits. Over it all, the sun blazed in dazzling

191

whiteness, with intense, unyielding sweaty heat, a force the people simply ignored. He shook his head, disbelieving his own eyes.

He blinked against that blinding richness of jungle growth. The depth and shimmering brilliance of the rampantly spreading green swamp was almost like the green of gangrene, more like contagion than chaste beauty. Yet it was a riot of untamable beauty, overwhelming virescence of the land, the immense and cruel clarity of the sky, reflected in the lime blue of the transparent sea. In this luxuriant, uncontrollable mold, tumbling from remote plateau to waterline, men had hacked out roadways, homesites, villages and towns, only to wage constant battle against the ever-encroaching and clotting viridity of the creeping jungle.

Other ships moved into the harbor. Sea lanes were crowded with commerce, arrival of supply ships, outgoing cargo vessels laden with mangoes, cacao, coffee, rubber, mahogany, precious metals. Philippe watched the ships and then moved his rapt gaze to the white stucco houses built by the French, the masonry buildings and the crowds of people milling along the high-stacked wharves.

Monsieur Jean-Paul Gallaudet and Madame Gallaudet paused beside him at the railing. Madame Gallaudet was a graying, motherly woman in her forties. Some women are born matronly, and this was her ideal role, her sole interest. She had learned during other tours of duty in Panama to wear lightweight frocks and wide-brimmed straw sun hats. She managed to look cool in the sweltering heat.

Both Monsieur and Madame Gallaudet smiled warmly and invited him to visit at their home whenever he and Madelon felt lonely for Paris or wanted to talk about home.

Madame Gallaudet agreed they could not make the young couple feel at home out here in this savage place, but they would make every effort, they would love having young people and youthful laughter in their house again. Earlier, aboard ship, over cognac one night, Monsieur Gallaudet had confided that they had lost both their children—a son of twenty and a daughter sixteen—to the yellow fever epidemic in the three years they'd been in Panama. But, like de Lesseps, they believed in what they were doing. They had lost their worldly treasure now; there was no sense in running; they no longer feared malaria or yellow fever or anything else this hot land might deal them, except failure. Somehow, that canal must be built to the glory and benefit of France. Somehow. Perhaps now it was up to the young men like Philippe. Perhaps these young men were the answer to their prayers. They entreated him to visit often.

Philippe hesitated, wondering bitterly how Ducrot Bazaine would view such socializing between an underling engineer and the director-general of the entire project. Then, seeing the genuine warmth, and the desperately concealed sadness in the beautiful faces of those dedicated people, he consigned Bazaine to the hottest hole beyond hell and promised to visit often.

The big ship was snugged into its berth and made fast with huge hawsers in the hands of shouting, sweated men bared to the waist and blackened by the sun. Philippe remained standing at the shore railing long after the gangplank was secured and passengers debarked and native boys rushed aboard to offer their services as porters, guides or pimps. Amazed, he stared down at the crowds churning about on the quay. It was as if some frivolous-minded god had stirred a dozen races together, melted the tones and hues and features into a hybrid alloyage of races—mestizos, Negroes, Indians, whites, Orientals and mixtures of every variety.

"Here, boy! You, nigger boy! Yes, you. Over here."

Philippe recoiled, recognizing the strident voice of Ducrot Bazaine on the open deck behind him. He glanced over his shoulder to find the chief engineer thrusting his way through a sea of confused, on-rushing humanity near the gangway. Bazaine did not bother to glance in Philippe's direction.

The native boy at whom Bazaine yelled was shaking his head from side to side and trying to sidle past. *"Pardonne-moi, m'sieu."* The slender lad mouthed Spanish-accented French, eluding Bazaine's grasp.

"Damn you,". Bazaine's voice rasped. "My wife and I

193

need portage assistance. Are you so indolent and shiftless you don't even want to earn a few francs, you worthless scum?"

"*Je régrette. Régrette.*" The youth smiled but retreated steadily.

Bazaine cursed him, swung his fist futilely at the lad's head and then let him go.

Looking about, Bazaine found two broad-shouldered black porters who followed the chief engineer down the gangplank, sweating and bowed like beasts of burden, under dozens of huge and heavy crates and luggage.

Bazaine cursed the porters fluently and unrelentingly, warning them that he'd kill either of them who dared drop even one of those precious trunks.

Grinning, Philippe watched their awkwardly slow progress to the docks where open carriages awaited them.

When the last luggage was secured in the carriages, Bazaine ostentatiously tipped the black men, who accepted the francs, bowed and retreated and did not smile.

Bazaine then turned and, elbowing his way against the current of people, returned to the ship.

Philippe remained at the railing, watching the fevered activity under the merciless blaze of sun on the quays. People ran, shouted, waved and wept in the flaring of color, the pandemonium of confusion, noise and mindless activity.

At last, when some of the violent confusion had lessened, he turned from the railing to arrange his own debarking. He stopped as if he'd been struck suddenly in the groin.

His eyes wide, his jaw slack, he watched Ducrot Bazaine escort a woman from the cool of the ship's salon. Bazaine's wife was Anouk! Philippe gazed, incredulous, as Bazaine steered her, gripping her elbow, toward the gangplank. Anouk walked regally, tall beside her popinjay husband. She was strikingly attired in a fragile flowered dress, ornamented straw hat and dainty parasol. She caught the eye of every man aboard that ship.

Philippe felt the chilled sweat roll along his spine. Blood flushed upward from his neck and spread over his face to the roots of his hair. His heart pounded in his chest. Of all the alliances in this world, she had to be the wife of Ducrot Bazaine.

Philippe retreated a step, the railing biting into his back. Bazaine's cock-strut brought back all the red-flaring rages and hatred he'd felt for the man on sight. He managed to bow stiffly. He held his breath, waiting for them to pass. There is always one precise moment for retreat and his had come. This woman was poison. Worse than that, she was another man's poison, that of a man he despised.

Anouk Bazaine's smolderingly dark and slanted eyes touched at Philippe as she passed near beneath her bright parasol. Her faint fragrance clutched at him. Those ebony pupils glittered, her voluptuous lips barely parted in a smile so faint, so totally and exclusively for him alone that she may as well have screamed his name on the crowded ship.

He remained rooted where he was as Anouk and her bantam husband descended the gangplank and crossed the hot planks of the dock to the carriage. Bazaine helped her into the *tonneau* of a covered phaeton. He went around the other side and bounded in beside her. She appeared completely unaware of him. Rather, with her eyes fastened on Philippe at the ship's railing, she sat erect as Bazaine leaned forward and spoke to the driver. The carriage lurched forward, moving through the crowds spilling along the quay. She turned slightly in her seat and kept her gaze fixed on Philippe. It was not until the carriage passed the huge warehouse and turned on the street that she released him and Philippe exhaled a deep breath, realizing he had not breathed for uncounted minutes.

[25]

"*Guide,* m'sieu? *Carry your bags? Find you a carriage? Suggest a hotel? I know this town,* m'sieu, *as few will ever know it, from the best café to the cleanest* poule."

Philippe turned from the ship railing and grinned down into the impudent face of the native boy who had refused to serve Ducrot Bazaine moments earlier. "Thought you were refusing all jobs?"

"Clee never refuses work, *m'sieu.* Moral. Immoral. Wicked. Dishonest. This does not matter to your servant Clee, as long as the pay is right. I figure hell cannot be that much hotter than my homeland, eh, *m'sieu*? I reject only the man who may employ me. I have not yet been so hungry that I would enslave myself even temporarily for a few francs, to a cruel master."

Philippe laughed. "And how did you divine on sight that the man you refused would be cruel?"

"One finds mirrored in a man's face the image of his soul, if one only looks, masta."

Pleased with the little rascal, Philippe agreed to hire Clee. The boy looked to be in his late teens, of medium height, wiry and slender like most natives, as if the remorseless sun sucked all excess fat and moisture from

196

their frames. Clee's face was fair for this Latin country, his eyes oddly blue though his nose was Negroid, almost flat and wide-nostriled. His hair was a mat of bristly black curls. He wore open-strap sandals which flapped against his heels when he walked, white calf-length pants of thin muslin, caught about his waist with a brilliant red sash. He wore no shirt or hat. He grinned un-self-consciously as Philippe appraised him and finally nodded. "All right, Clee, you'll do. Let's get moving."

Philippe and Clee carried trunks and baggage out to an open carriage Clee had hired. When the vehicle was loaded, Philippe brought Madelon down the gangplank, followed by Fanny LeBeau.

Clee bowed and smiled at Madelon, staring at her fragile beauty in awe and instant adulation. "Your servant, madame," he whispered.

They rattled along the wharves toward Front Street, Clee on the box up front with the black driver, Fanny with Philippe and Madelon in the moldy *tonneau*.

As they moved away from the material-laden piers they quickly lost any trace of the salty, clean smell of the sea. This familiar odor was lost in the stench of dead fish, tide-level stagnant water, the offensive effluvium from open sewage and deteriorated and ramshackled privies.

Madelon looked ill. She tried to hold a parasol between herself and the blazing sun, but found the confusion of noises, the stench and frightening scenes of death and decay too much for her. She pressed back against the seat rest, eyes closed, handkerchief pressed over her nose and mouth. She looked ready to fly apart.

Philippe stared in disbelief at the sinkhole ugliness of the fetid town which sprawled on the mangrove and bindoree clotted shoreline. Discarded wine bottles lay everywhere, in sordid piles outside every open, unscreened shack window. The alley behind Front Street was paved with wine bottles, driven mouth-down into the soured mud. They passed a bottle dump which glittered, a roof-high monument. "Wine is much safer for *les Francais* than is our water," Clee said.

Prostitutes, black and white, prowled the mean streets

like stray cats. Uncrated materials rusted everywhere in great neglected piles.

Their carriage rattled along beside the railroad tracks on Front Street. Above them, buzzards glided in lazy, patient arcs on the wind drafts.

The stench of the town was unbearable. Madelon looked as if she would faint. She pressed her scented handkerchief against her nose as they drove deeper into the grotesque putrefaction.

Philippe shook his head, dismayed and sickened. Colón-Aspinwall was nothing he'd expected to find. A remote and almost uncivilized area, yes, but a garbage dump? After all, wasn't this the northern railhead of the Trans-Panama Railroad, the supply center and headquarters of the Canal company, a busy seaport?

From the ship Philippe had gazed upon a miragelike town rising through the warm mists—red tile roofing, white stucco walls, blue water and lush green plant life. Reality was a shanty town on a tide-level island, garbage-littered and unpaved streets, paint-peeled huts rotting in water-sour yards. The single permanent structure appeared to be the Catholic Church, its spires vaulting cleanly above the wet-rot, poverty and decay. The rest—ice house, railroad buildings, shabby hotels and jerry-built taverns—were little more than shacks, hurriedly thrown together, neglected and sagging. No screens covered doors or windows. Refuse littered every roadbed, bare-boned dogs and scruffy cats slunk from sunlight to shadow. It was as if the earth itself were diseased, with pollution, infection, contagion, pestilence, despair.

He could forgive the natives; they suffered the ills of superstition, oppressive and repressive religion, illiteracy, malaria and debilitating heat and humidity. But what of the changes promised by the Americans when Aspinwall and Stevens built the trans-isthmus railway? What had the French done to improve the sorry quality of life here in three years? He found few signs of upgrading. This pesthole held no promise that someday here two great oceans would be joined.

The carriage slogged through the quagmire, passing other slow-moving pedestrians, carriages, drays and carts.

Nauseating miasma of decay steamed up from the flooded streets. The further from the sea they rode, the more unbearable the heated stench became. Philippe was sweated down, shirt glued to his body, perspiration stinging his eyes. He read nothing but indifference and indolence in faces of outsiders among the natives. Who the hell cared about this hellhole? Whites were transients, here for the fast rape and the quick franc; they would take what they could grab and they would escape. In the passive faces of the natives was total resignation. Indian or black, they no longer opposed the terrible forces of nature; they let themselves be absorbed into it. They were like the reptiles, the peccaries, sloths and kinkajous; they were one with the palms, the mango trees, the breadfruit, the guazama bushes. They took the rain and the sun and the pestilence as they took the day and the night, as they came.

"Please, madame," Clee said, turning on the front seat to gaze worriedly at Madelon. "Patience. Do not despise my poor town. Soon it is prettier. Soon you will find much to like."

The carriage headed toward a lighthouse on the highest elevation north of the town. They drove along a narrow shell-paved lane, glistening and gray in the sun. Beside it, flowers blazed in a wild and brilliant profusion, of green, yellow, red, crimson. Mango trees sagged thick with orange fruit, avocados fell neglected on the ground, guazama trees, lions' ears, the palmlike leaves and large waxy, feathery limbs of the zamzia hid the ugliness of the coastal plain below.

Banana trees grew hedgelike along the narrow roadway. Gradually the stench and soured putrefaction of the town faded. The air was clean, fragrant.

The French had built white stucco cottages with red tile roofs, clustering them in a colony on the rim of the green foothill overlooking a white beach and the clear aquamarine bay. The cottages were well kept, freshly painted, shaded by palms in small, manicured lawns on winding cobbled streets. A world removed from Colón below. Beyond the French colony reared the larger residences of the white railroad officials and upper echelon employees.

Madelon straightened, breathing cautiously, but her face remained pallid, her eyes stricken.

They found their cottage only meagerly furnished, but cleaned and polished by a huge monolith of a mestizo woman named Myti.

Fanny trembled, entering the house. When a lizard ran across the floor, she screamed and retreated, shivering hysterically.

Madelon caught the girl in her arms. She held her until Fanny quieted. Fanny wept, pleading, "Oh, madame. This terrible place. You cannot stay here pregnant as you are. We must go back home at once."

Philippe flinched. The maid was right. This was the last place Madelon should be, pregnant or not. Her pregnancy only made it less suitable. Panama was no place to carry or bear a child. He had been a headstrong fool and worse, bringing her here.

But Madelon's voice was cool, almost firm and reproving as she answered her maid. "This house is pretty, Fanny. We'll be all right here. We'll do the best we can, as long as we can."

Clee insisted upon helping Philippe unpack and put his clothing away.

The boy chattered the whole time he worked. Clee had no parents that he remembered. His earliest memories were of sleeping in open doorways along Front Street, begging outside the *bodegas,* robbing the church poorbox in order to buy buns when he was too well known and too closely watched to steal them any more. He had pimped for whores when he was twelve. But, he warned the señor, most of the local *putas* were fireships, as dangerous as yellow jack itself. He boasted of his finest employment to date. He had been the full-time assistant to a young engineer on the canal project. When asked what happened to his former employer, Clee shrugged. "He died in the last Bronze John epidemic. We call yellow fever, the yellow jack, Bronze John, because one turns a bronze color at the last when it has him."

Clee spoke proudly of his late master. "He was one smart *hombre, m'sieu*. He knew so much. He was like a huge book walking around with all the knowledge in it. Sometime I think his head should be out to here, he held so much inside it. He taught me much. I could never work for a man I could not respect as I respected him, *m'sieu*. I handled all his funeral arrangements. Put him in his best suit when nobody else would touch him. I sent his things home to his family." Clee shook his head abruptly, putting all this behind him.

Clee suggested that Philippe never travel abroad without a straw hat. "Sunstroke is possible, *m'sieu*. A terrible thing."

When the packing was completed, Clee accompanied Philippe to the nearest bazaar, where he selected a white, flat-brimmed panama planter's hat. Clee haggled the price down two balboas from the marked cost.

Philippe set the hat jauntily on his head. Clee applauded enthusiastically. "One distinguished-looking *caballero*, señor! When people see me walking behind you, they will know we are somebody! *Sí! Las putas,* they will follow you in the streets like urchins wanting coins."

They returned to the cottage to find Madelon and Myti already rearranging the furniture. There was no longer any reason for Clee to remain, but the boy tarried. Philippe paid him generously and thanked him for his assistance. Still, the lad found little last-minute tasks which he assured Philippe could be handled by no one as well as he. He called to Myti and ordered the brass tub filled with tepid bath water for his young master.

"Hot water no good. Cold water worse. Tepid water when you bathe. You don't sweat so much," Clee said.

While Philippe bathed, Clee pressed and laid out his clothing so it would be ready for him the next morning.

It was a long, tiring day, the sun plunging into the sea southwest of them after nine that night. For a long time the sea, sky and jungle gleamed with vermilion which faded slowly into purple, shadowed darkness. Philippe found himself plunged into depression, deeply troubled about Madelon.

While darkness smoked in the tall windows and sudden

201

rain drummed the tile roofing. Clee spoke his thoughts. "*M'sieu* would do well to hire Clee as his manservant. The cost is small. My meals. A few balboas a week to buy a *puta*; only the strange ones interest me, and they do not come free, as many of those I have worked for would, you understand?"

Philippe grinned and nodded. Oh, indeed he understood.

"I sleep on a mat on the floor," Clee persisted. "Always at your beck and call, any hour of the night, for any mission, or in the hall outside your door, if you wish. You'll surely find, *caballero,* as my last master did, I earned each balboa paid me many times over."

"I'm sure of it, but—"

"A man such as you, *m'sieu*. Nobility. Of rank. Quality. Busy. Oh, he needs someone to tend his clothing and his boots so he appears at his best on the street, even in this heat and rain. His linens—I wash clothes as well. Iron. No laundry in town can compete with the elegance of my work—"

Madelon's screams broke across the boy's words. Both Philippe and Clee bounded across the room, ran into the parlor where Madelon was crouched on the floor, rocking in agony. She had thrown up and Fanny stood helplessly while Myti tried to clean up the vomit.

"I'll get a doctor," Clee said. He raced out of the front door, letting it slam behind him.

Philippe knelt beside Madelon, cradling her in his arms. "Such pain," she whispered. "I am in such agony."

"The baby," Philippe whispered, agonized. "Are you in labor?"

"If it is, it's a miscarriage," Fanny cried, her face livid with her hatred for him.

"The boy will bring a doctor," Philippe said, trying to reassure Madelon. He lifted her in his arms and laid her down on the couch.

She could not lie still, rolling back and forth in agony. Philippe's eyes filled with tears. "I'll send you home, Madelon. I swear I will. I'm sorry for all that's happened, with all my heart I'm sorry."

She chewed on her mouth, unable to speak. In minutes

—though it seemed hours to them—the front door was jerked open and Clee entered ahead of a French doctor from the Canal Company hospital in Colón.

The doctor ordered Philippe to carry Madelon into her bedroom where he helped Fanny undress her.

Philippe returned to the parlor. He thanked Clee for bringing the medic so quickly. Clee nodded. Nothing more was said about his leaving.

"The beautiful madame," Clee said. "She will be all right. Dr. Feuillet is a good man. A good man. He was with my last master when he died." Clee flinched. "You must understand, *m'sieu,* a pregnancy is unlike the Chagres fever. Eh? She will be fine. I know this in my heart. Can I get you something, *m'sieu*?"

"I'm all right."

"I am thankful I met you, señor. Sometimes a good thing like this happens and one almost believes again in God, eh? I will make you proud. The heat and illness has not sapped all my strength as it has many of my brothers. No malaria, no hookworm, yellow jack I had when I was a child. I lived. I am immune from yellow fever now. But I must confess, *m'sieu,* on that ship today, I studied all the new ones hard and fast. Clee chose you there for his master."

Philippe tried to smile, watching that bedroom door.

"*Sí. Es verdad.* I look into the faces of all the men who come to Colón to work for the Canal Company. I tell much, everything, from what I see in their faces. I can tell everything, even how long they'll stay alive in *tierra caliente.*"

"Fortuneteller, too, eh?"

"No, *caballero.* It is only that I know faces. I have had to learn faces to stay alive. I can see the smallness. Cruelty. Meanness. Most of all, I can see the fear."

"Fear?" Philippe turned from his vigil.

"*Sí.* Fear. I know fear. I can see it in the faces of the newcomers. I can smell the fear when they walk near. The fearful ones will die first out here, *m'sieu.* It's almost as if they are destined to early death. But it is also more than that. They are destined to early death because they doom themselves with their own dread. Ah, I have seen

203

them by the hundreds—dying these past three years of the canal. I avoid the fearful. I run from them as one runs from Bronze John himself. They lack the insides, the courage to face what is and to stay alive in this land that is so different from where they come. They have heard the stories, the rumors, the reports. They come in fear. They *fear*. Fear warps their faces and empties their eyes."

"Your late lamented master, wasn't he one of the brave ones? Didn't he die?"

"Bronze John does not respect the brave, *m'sieu*. It is only that the brave last longer, the brave who meet death, even Bronze John, when it comes, without fear."

The bedroom door opened. Both Philippe and Clee leaped to their feet, to meet Dr. Feuillet.

"Is she all right?" Philippe said.

"She is very sick," the doctor said. "I will watch her closely. She could lose the fetus. She must be most careful."

"She will be careful," Philippe promised. "I'll try to get her back to France."

Feuillet shook his head. "This would not be wise, in her condition. But do not worry. We have a good hospital here in Colón. We will give her every attention."

Philippe nodded. The doctor smiled and touched his arm. "It is you who must be most careful, most devoted. And yet, not too devoted at all, eh?" He smiled and shook his head. "I know this is evil on a young couple deeply in love and married less than a year. But, I must caution you, any sexual intercourse would endanger your wife's life as well as that of the child. It is a sad sacrifice, but one I know you will want to make."

Tropical sunlight and heat awoke Philippe early the next morning. He opened his eyes against the brassy light and found Clee already stirring about the room, fully dressed and energetically at work. The boy had meticulously brushed and pressed Philippe's clothing and cleaned and polished his boots, though this was an exercise in futility in this muddy, rain-sodden world. Philippe sat for a moment on the side of his bed and stared back at a green horned lizard while he oriented himself to time and place. The stench of the town, wafted in on a land breeze, reminded him forcefully where he was and why.

He walked through the deep-puddled street to the offices of the Canal Company. Clee slogged through the mud at a respectful pace behind him and yet close enough to demonstrate to all that he was Philippe's personal manservant. Clee had regained elevated status in the community because of his new employment; he wanted friend and foe alike to be aware of his great good fortune. He chased away the swarming street urchins who begged Philippe for coins, warning Philippe never to succumb to pity for the waifs. "If you do just once, they'll be after you every time you step on the street like pigeons. I know. I was one of them."

Philippe grinned. Clee had been one of the abandoned street children but he was the least compassionate of all toward them. "Let them make it on their own," Clee said, nodding sagely. "They'll be better off if you do, at last."

Philippe was mildly surprised to find the headquarters of the Compagnie Universelle du Canal Interoceanique was a converted warehouse, open, drafty, partitioned, on the noisiest section of the loading docks. There were few desks; most men worked at bare pine kitchen tables; wooden boxes served as filing cabinets. There appeared to be much fevered activity, but not much direction.

Bazaine's meeting for all engineers of the project began at 9 A.M. in an open space in which folding chairs, a lectern and blackboard had been set up. Monsieur Gallaudet was introduced. He spoke briefly and disappeared into a mildewed crib at the far end of the building.

Almost a hundred young, and some aging, engineers from many nations lounged in their chairs. Most wore lightweight cotton shirts and trousers already darkly sweat-stained. Many introduced themselves while they waited for Bazaine to appear.

"Welcome to *mañana* land," a young Canadian said. "We accomplish nothing here, but we will, as the natives say, *poco tiempo*—pretty soon."

"Whom the gods destroy they first send to Panama," said a British engineer, mopping his sweated, flushed face.

"We dig little holes and God fills them all up again," a U.S. engineer said. "Maybe He's trying to tell us something."

"We're getting nowhere, but we're glad to have you along," said a Frenchman. They all laughed, but there was a sense of deep frustration beneath their self-mocking laughter.

"Nobody wants to see grown men cry," the Britisher said.

All the engineering staff, including those who'd come in by train from Panama City on the southeast coast, the

206

Pacific division, were growing restless when Ducrot Bazaine finally strode in.

"Jesus Christ," Philippe heard the young Canadian whisper.

Bazaine was outfitted in a style and elegance which evoked choked snickers among the sloppily clad engineering crew. His boots shone, his jodhpurs were far too splendid and heavy for the environment. He wore a silk shirt, neck scarf and a pith helmet, which he removed only after having surveyed his complement of engineers for some seconds. Philippe supposed he intended to intimidate his audience.

"I've called you men here for several reasons," Ducrot Bazaine said. "First, to introduce myself and my goals for this project. I am Vicomte Ducrot Hélène-Marie Bazaine. Those of you who are French or German may be aware that my uncle was a military hero at Sedan in the Franco-Prussian war. I mention this only to underscore one fact: I am not here to trade on my uncle's name, or on any quality or capability but my own. These will be adequate. I was enlisted to turn around the failure of this project, and I tell each of you now, I shall do that with your assistance or without *you.*

"I am a capable engineer, a determined and unyielding leader. I was graduated in the top third of my class from the world's first organized school of engineering, Ecole des Ponts et Chaussées."

A smattering of applause interrupted Bazaine. Philippe recognized the clapping as ironic, but Bazaine was completely unaware that he was being mocked. He nodded and continued.

"I am not easy on myself. I shall not be easy on you. I have been brought here to wrest success from failure, and I shall do that, or by God each of you will answer to me personally."

"You might wish to interrogate God, too," somebody said. Nervous laughter rippled across the room.

Bazaine responded. "I am a bit surprised that you find humor in your miserable record of accomplishment out here. I hope you will laugh now because I can tell

207

you I will not tolerate laughter when you come whining to me of your failures from this day forward.

"I am not interested in your failures. I am not interested in hearing about them. Yours or anyone else's. You can pass blame among yourselves—I can't stop that—but I won't endure your coming to me with it. If you fail, the hell with you. You'll repair that failure, or you'll get out. It's that simple. I remind you. Your failures reflect only on you. But your failures on this project are *my* failures. And this I shall not tolerate.

"To get along with me, and get along well, you have only to do your job, do it well, control your subordinates, and get results I can see and report.

"My office door is closed to complainers. I do not want to hear your problems. I will not schedule any appointments for such exercises in futility. You have a problem? Solve it. That's why you were brought here. That's why you were taught rational method of design, why you spent five years being based in physical sciences, mathematics and the technical principles of executing theoretical designs. You are educated. You are experienced. You know by now what your problems are. Solve them. That's all I ask of you. That I demand of you.

"I needn't remind you that we have until this morning failed miserably in Panama. We have failed. France has failed. But I shall not fail. This means that you will not fail—if you wish to remain part of my project.

"My word to each of you is this: If you fail in your assignment from this morning forward, tell a priest, tell God, but don't come whining to me. If your job is too big for you, catch the next boat out of here, because you'll be replaced anyhow as soon as your ineptitude is exposed to me. Is this clear? Are there any questions?" He did not wait for questions; he ignored the raised hands. "I hope we shall work well together. But whether we do or not, I have a job to accomplish and I shall accomplish it—at all costs. Good morning, gentlemen."

Philippe went out that morning on a rail handcar to inspect the canal worksites. He was accompanied by

Korvache, Burns and Snelling, three engineers who had survived since the inception of the project.

These men were still slightly stunned by their first view of the new chief engineer. "I've heard of martinets, met plenty of them," Korvache said. "But this Bazaine is almost a caricature of the despotic little bureaucrat."

"You mean he's a prick?" Burns said.

"Exactly."

Snelling chewed at his unlit pipe. His narrow ruddy British face dripped sweat from beneath his battered, oil-stained planter's hat which had lost its shape in uncounted rainshowers. "At least we know where the old boy stands."

"I don't know." Korvache laughed. "He's such a short prick, I could hardly tell if he was standing at all."

"He was," Burns said. "He was standing exactly where I'd stand if I were in his shoes. He can't succeed. But he's laid it all out for everyone to see. He will pass blame for failure down where it belongs, to his subordinates who can never say they were not warned."

"Maybe he really is good," Snelling suggested.

"I don't think so." Burns spat with the wind. "If you're good, you don't have to rule by intimidation."

"Whether he's good or not doesn't really matter much, does it?" Snelling said.

"I'd like to have someone in charge whom I could respect."

"I say give him a chance," Snelling said. "When he fails, he won't be the first, will he?"

"When he fails?" Philippe said.

Snelling nodded. "That's the ticket. When he fails, old boy. Not if or where or why. Only when."

The handcar was stopped. The coolie handlers removed it from the tracks in what appeared to be impenetrable jungle. But Snelling assured Philippe the crews had worked in here for two years.

Philippe could find no sign of progress. He was apalled at the ineffectual diggings—little earth removed, no channels opened, shored or banked. He couldn't say what he'd expected to find; he had followed the catastrophic adversities faced by the Company in every newspaper:

disasters, calamity, accident, epidemic, flood, landslide, death, mismanagement. Still, millions of francs had been spent since work began out here in 1881. Millions—yet it was almost impossible to find what that money had bought —a jagged scar in the earth here, a decaying excavation deep in a trackless jungle, materials and equipment allowed to rust scabrously in sodden work yards and along the harbor piers, at rail sidings, and abandoned at deserted worksites. Four years! He had anticipated at least a traceable outline with patches where disaster had temporarily halted forward movement. Instead, he found only tentative slashes in the earth, wretched attempts already surrendering to lush jungle grasses and vines.

Philippe found the three sun-dried engineers watching him narrowly. He shook his head, staring at them. "Why won't it work?" He swung his arm helplessly, indicating the overgrown signs of trial and failure. "Why won't anything work?"

"Nothing works because we haven't yet found a way to *make* it work," Snelling said. "Man proposes. God disposes."

"Equipment," Korvache said. "None of our equipment is heavy enough. None of it. We can't stay ahead of limestone slides, mud slicks or flash floods because we can't dig fast enough or move enough earth at once."

"Native labor," Burns said. "Now there's a real problem. Most of the able-bodied natives simply refuse to work at hard labor. Why in God's name should they? Food grows in abundance on almost every tree, every bush. Dig into the earth an inch and find edible rootstock. And the sea? Good Lord! Fish, oysters, crabs, scallops, shrimp—anything out there can be steamed, boiled, turned into gumbo, soup, salad, stew, or eaten raw."

"Then there are those willing to work who can't because of illness." Snelling spread his hands. "These poor devils are infested with every intestinal worm known to man, hookworm, tapeworm, and worms you wouldn't believe. They're malarial or enervated by the heat."

"What about the Chinese?"

"Hell, there are plenty of coolies," Korvache said. "Lot of them came over to build Aspinwall's Trans-Isthmus

210

Railroad and stayed. They sent the word and every ship brings more Orientals."

"They work well," Snelling said.

"When they'll work," Korvache added.

"They're cheap labor. We must say that for them, chaps," Snelling said.

"Then what's wrong?"

Korvache laughed. "They're scared, these coolies are scared. And God knows I don't blame them. There is no poisonous spider, vermin, serpent or animal that doesn't reproduce madly and live well in this wet heat. Death hiding in every brush, under a dead stick. In your shoes in the morning. In the air you breathe—and for hell's sake, never drink the water."

Snelling nodded. "If a chink doesn't want to follow an order, say one he considers dangerous, he suddenly doesn't understand what is said to him. No follee Français, Spanish, English. No understandee Chinese interpreter. Chinese interpreter suddenly use wrong dialect. You can lose a lot of days like that. You can stand helplessly and see a dam structure washed away like that."

27

During those first weeks in the rain-sodden village, Philippe found himself in a constant state of conflict, inwardly and outwardly. No small part of that battle was against the bewitching and tranquilizing charm of the drowsy land itself. He constantly found himself fighting lassitude. Especially in those pleasantly languorous hours, noon to four every day, when the entire community sagged into the stunned slumber of the daily *siesta,* he struggled against lethargy and the urge to procrastinate.

One of his toughest battles was against his desire for Anouk Bazaine. During siesta time, her image would possess his mind, almost as she'd seemed to materialize from the dark night at sea. When the rest of the region lay drugged with sleep, he recalled the wild, secret parties he'd had with Anouk aboard ship. Which was before, he reminded himself in self-hatred, he'd known she was Ducrot Bazaine's wife. He tried to exorcise her from his mind. By night, things were no better. She filled his thoughts. He sprawled across his bed, exhausted by hard work and frustration, only to find his need for Anouk attacking him anew. He was truly sick with longing.

Sleep, when it finally came, was haunted by her face, her form, her passionate, unbridled lovemaking.

It seemed to him he stayed tired, frustrated and full of self-hatred, all the time.

Each evening he returned to the white stucco cottage without truly seeing the gradual changes taking place within it, though they were considerable and in many ways dramatic. He existed as if walking through a heavy red mist, in which nothing outside his own mind was clear. He sought ways to change the defeats which mounted daily on the canal project, the hopeless digging by shovel and pick, the inadequate machinery, the materials lost to floods or predators, to men who made their livelihood selling stolen property. How much had been lost to theft? Only God knew. None of the stealing was any more criminal than the complete absence of any effort to stop the thefts, to remedy or improve the deteriorating situation.

The house changed with—for Philippe—imperceptible metamorphosis from a meagerly furnished, rented cottage to a lovely home, under the tireless labors of Myti, and Madelon's creativity and ingenuity. She directed Myti's cleaning, painting, scrubbing and rearranging so carefully that Philippe's routine was not disturbed, his important papers seldom even temporarily displaced. Philippe was scarcely aware of changes occurring under his nose.

One of the bedrooms became his workroom, study, office-at-home. Its walls glittered with bright-headed little pins stuck in drafts, maps, designs, blueprints. Everything had its place and he went to it unerringly and without questioning the miracle that brought it all about. He did not know where Madelon and Myti found antique console tables, comfortable overstuffed chairs, bright carpeting. He did not inquire because each alteration appeared so gradually and with so little effect on his own routine that he was only vaguely conscious that it was hardly the same domicile at all.

Philippe didn't ask how the heavy furniture was moved about the house. Madelon told him in awe of Myti's incredible strength and endurance. Myti carried trunks and desks and tables as if they were toys. However, she learned even the most basic French slowly, painfully and unwillingly.

Philippe forced himself to observe the changes Madelon made and to comment on them. He wanted devoutly to thrust the rages of the long day from him, like a filthy cloak, doffed when he walked in the front door of the cottage each afternoon. It wasn't that easy.

His running battles with Bazaine exhausted him, added to his confusion, abstraction and conflict.

He was sprawled one evening on the couch, his arm across his eyes as if he could shut out the images reeling and spinning inside his brain. He heard Madelon's voice, cool and sharp, in the kitchen. "I won't have it, Fanny. No more. I'll send you away. This is our home. This place is our home because it is where Philippe is."

He felt chilled, the goosebumps rising along the nape of his neck. He felt a sense of exultance that flooded through him. A hundred times a day his common sense warned him that as soon as possible—after the baby was born—Madelon had to be sent back to Paris, away from this hot, dangerous land.

He sat up, looking around the newly decorated living room, smart now and even faintly elegant under the constant remodeling and renovation of Madelon and her devoted Myti. Somewhere, they'd found a *bergère,* an upholstered armchair, and hand-crafted endtables.

A warm vaporous fog rolled in from the bay. The wind that pushed it was damp and enervating and sinister. There was an eerie threat to the steamy heat, the misty zephyr. It was as if death existed in the very atmosphere. From somewhere in the colony, a piano and violin sent plaintive music to add another haunting quality to the unusual atmosphere. Philippe felt the unreasoning stirring of fear—the ever-present danger that something terrible might befall Madelon in this place.

He called to her. "Madelon." He was aware of the throb of panic in his voice.

She came into the parlor from the kitchen. She smiled wanly, her body growing round and ungainly. He held out his arms and she came to him. "What's the matter?" she said. "What's wrong?"

"I just remembered how much I loved you," he said. "I know I've got to get you away from here, but I wish—God, how I wish it were safe for you to stay."

She smiled up at him, uncertainly. "You know what I wish?" she whispered.

"What do you wish?"

"That right now I wasn't pregnant."

He laughed. "You wish that—for me?"

"No." She shook her head. "For me."

He awoke the next morning, still alone in his bed, but renewed and somehow even exuberant. He did not know how they could work it, but they would find happiness together. The unhappiness grew less vivid in Madelon's mind. Both looked forward joyously to the birth of their baby. Dr. Feuillet reported Madelon doing well; there was every hope that the delivery would be normal, without complications. "We must treat her like a fragile doll," Feuillet said to Philippe and Madelon, "but she looks much like a doll, and this makes it easier, eh?"

"I imagine it's real easy for you," Philippe said. And they all laughed. And it felt good to laugh, to want to laugh, to be able to laugh.

There was only conflict, indecision and defeat at work. Philippe did not succumb to the torpor and sloth around him in the canal offices. Rage kept him from sliding into the indolence of the engineers who'd been seduced by the environment and disgusted by mismanagement of the canal program. But he watched the project continue to slide down in ruin, feeling helpless even to delay the plunge toward total collapse.

He traveled the 48 rail miles across the isthmus on an inspection tour. The course of the future canal had been staked out to parallel the railway lines for one very practical reason. These tracks followed the best path through the gap between those volcanic ranges, the Serrania de Tabasara which rose out of Costa Rica and the Serrania del Darien which ran south through the jungle into Colombia. Since 1519, the Spanish and others had seen the need for a canal and recognized the route through the gap as the best possible site on the isthmus.

They found jungle which grew so thickly they could only hack their way through it. Jaguars, panthers and wildcats screamed in the brush a few yards from the train. Trees quivered, alive with chattering monkeys. Flocks of brilliantly hued parrots screamed aloft when the train rumbled past. And everywhere snakes slithered and dozed and wound themselves on branches and limbs, like Death waiting.

"This is why the work goes slowly up here," Korvache told Philippe. "Even the Jamaican blacks live in terror of these snakes, and God knows they're everywhere."

As he traveled, Philippe made a quick survey of work completed. He found little lasting accomplishment though canal promoters had been issuing regular reports of a monthly excavation of one million cubic yards. He discovered large areas littered with abandoned, discarded or wrecked equipment. He wrote a strong report demanding an immediate survey, followed by a program of retrieval, reclamation, repair and restoration of all company equipment and material. He tried to get into Bazaine's office to discuss his plan. The chief engineer refused to see him and sent him word that his letter had been filed. He'd been hired, Bazaine's note warned him, to produce results in excavation, not to waste time with hairbrained schemes for impractical studies and repossession which would be too wasteful in labor and money to be undertaken under the best of conditions—which, Bazaine need not remind him, were not present when engineers were wasting time in daydreaming rather than supervision.

On this train tour, Philippe learned that one of the key factors working against the canal project was the successful operation of the Aspinwall-United States-built railway from Colón to Panama City. The two oceans were already linked. The United States insisted that the most feasible route for a canal was in Nicaragua. So, with goods unloaded on one coast by cheap labor and shipped by rail to the other, there was little enthusiasm for the French project in Panama. Neither the U.S. nor Great Britain welcomed expansion of French influence in Pan-America.

After working with Korvache for a week, Philippe became convinced that the excavation and removal equipment in use was totally inadequate. The workers could not stay ahead of flooding or landslides. He wrote a letter to Bazaine suggesting purchase of heavy Scottish-made marine dredges, which offered quadruple the capacity of the best shovels now in Panama. Again, Bazaine's rejection was curt. He suggested that all matters of policy be left to the higher echelons and that Philippe and other malcontents concern themselves with on-the-job supervision, getting positive results with the equipment furnished by France's best engineering intellects.

On the job with Korvache, Philippe raged against Bazaine. The man was interested in one thing and one only, sending glowing reports of successful operations and record-setting excavations back to the Company in Paris. These reports were exaggerations, lies or distortions of small truths into major achievements. Word came back from France that de Lesseps was ecstatic, that he was using Bazaine's reports from Colón to silence his adversaries and to locate fresh sources of credit.

"The poor old son of a bitch," Korvache said.

"Why would he believe such lies?"

"Because he wants to. Because he's an old man, driven into a corner, and he *wants* to believe that Bazaine is working miracles out here."

"What I can't understand is why a man like Bazaine was put in charge in the first place."

Korvache shrugged. It was clear to him.

"He's in charge because he *is* a Bazaine. That's the best reason of all. The establishment believes one of its own can succeed where outsiders fail. He's in charge because he looks on failure and reports victory. Because he drives people and intimidates them, even when he's wrong. Look at yourself, *mon ami*. You know from actual inspection that equipment is inadequate, but what can you do? You can stand here and sweat. You can write a letter to Bazaine, and for your efforts be told curtly to go to hell."

"I'll go over his head!"

"And lose your own. That's all it would get you. You're not the first idealistic young engineer to come out here. Not the first to get sick at the waste, incompetence and mismanagement. But you may as well be the first to face

217

one fact, straight from Korvache. They don't want bad news sent up there above Bazaine. He's their buffer. They know the truth even when they won't admit it. They're not blind. They've tried good supervision, excellent, capable, dynamic men. Nothing worked. Now the martinet, the liar, the man with the glowing reports will hide the carcass until the stink reaches all the way to Paris."

Philippe stared at Korvache. "Do you think de Lesseps knows the truth?"

Korvache shrugged. "I don't know. I still believe he's honest. But, hell, no matter how honest he is, he's being used. He's old. He wants to be remembered as an immortal. He's 99 percent pride. Most men who really accomplish big tasks are. He *wants* to believe this thing will work, even yet. Hell, I don't know. The time to have stopped this start-and-fail process, and to find new ways, was two years ago, and they didn't do it. I don't know."

Philippe shivered in the blazing sun. He remembered Claude-Bruce Grabralet's earliest reports of charges in the Assembly that a senile old glory-seeker was being betrayed by the men he trusted. Claude-Bruce had passionately defended de Lesseps then and since Philippe had met the old hero in Paris he had believed in him completely. Standing on a pile of sandstone in the tropics, he felt the chill of doubt. He mistrusted de Lesseps' judgment. Perhaps the Old Lion *was* getting *old*. Would a younger de Lesseps have allowed himself ever to be pressured into accepting an executive on any basis other than superb qualifications for the job?

For a moment when Philippe entered the small cell which served as his office in the Canal Company building on Front Street, he was bat-blind after the dazzling brilliance of the sun.

He hesitated inside his doorway, aware of a presence in the small cubicle. He recognized Anouk in the slowly clearing gloom. His heart lurched. Again, he had the illusion of her materializing from the shadows. And most amazing of all, the world around them lay prostrate in the noon *siesta*. She had come to him as she had a hundred times before—in his heated fantasies.

She cleared into sharp focus, heartbreakingly lovely. The fragile dress she wore, and the delicate wide-brimmed straw hat, were perfect for the climate of Colón but would have been smartly eye-catching on the Champs Elysées.

Anouk gave him a warm and languorous smile. She leaned forward slightly, her loose bodice revealing the elegance of her breasts. He closed the door behind him, then stood awkwardly, gazing down at her while she looked him over, certain of her charms.

"You could get me killed coming here like this," Philippe heard himself saying. "You could get us both killed."

"You mean Ducrot?" Her smile licked at him. "He's far too egotistical and self-centered to be jealous of anyone, especially an *ordinary* engineer, even a young and good-tasting one, like you." She drew the tip of her tongue across her lips and it was impossible to mistake her meaning. "I didn't come here to talk about him. I don't give a damn what he does, as long as he keeps out of my way."

"Do you really think he won't hear about your coming here?"

"If you had come to me, *mon chéri*, I would not have had to come begging like a schoolgirl. Anyway, never mind what I tell Ducrot. I can make him believe anything I want him to believe. I always have."

He shook his head. "I don't need to add insane jealousy to his other obnoxious feelings toward me. I do have to work for him."

"But you're doing poorly anyway, aren't you? Perhaps you need my help if you're ever to get along with Ducrot. I could help you."

Smiling, she came near to him. The trace of heady cologne, drifting like some intimate promise from her warm cleavage, threatened to overwhelm him. He felt his stomach tie in knots, his hands shake, while she remained totally cool and at ease.

"I can be of great help to you, *mon chéri*," she whispered. "Of great pleasure to you."

"No. We can't do this, Anouk. You drive me insane. But it ends there. Madelon and I——"

"Spare me."

"All right. I don't need any more trouble with your husband than I've already got. I don't know what lie you told Bazaine about why you are here."

"Why do you care what I say to my husband?"

"Because he may follow you."

"Quite beneath his monstrous dignity." She laughed and tossed her straw hat on the chair behind her. "I've been—so hungry—for you. I want to drink you. I want to taste you."

He gazed at her, feeling the sharp constriction in his loins. He was helpless against her, no longer even wanting to fight against his need for her. Her dress seemed almost transparent, the clinging lines accenting the beautiful symmetry, revealing the warm ivory of her skin, the soft bloom of her breasts. Her dark eyes, her twisted smile, her heated body, her nearness lured him, promised, tormented him.

She pressed her body against his. He could feel the fever at her thighs. She spoke upward against his throat. "I've finally figured it all out. A small cottage on the beach, south of town. You can come to me there, at noon every day. We'll have the whole *siesta* time."

Realizing her fantasy had been the same as his, he clenched his trembling hands into fists at his sides. "That's the way to get us both killed."

"Can you think of a pleasanter way to die in this pesthole?"

"We can't do it, Anouk. I won't. God knows how terribly I want to. But I can't. Too much is at stake."

"Every day, Philippe, in each other's arms, alone, remote from the world. You and I, as it was on the ship, only more wonderful."

"You must leave, Anouk. Now. God knows I can't lie to you. I want you even more than you think I do—"

"Then stop being a fool."

"But I'm damned if I'll touch you. Now or ever again. If I can influence Bazaine, as you suggest, only through cuckolding him with you, the hell with him. If you think I'll trade my need to get a decent job done, for—for whatever you have to offer, the hell with you."

"You are as big a fool as Bazaine thinks you are."

He spread his hands helplessly.

Anouk stood there a few more moments, so confident of her charms she still could not believe he was turning her away. Remote sounds from the wharves washed in on sour mists through the tall windows. A ship's whistle called, lonely and distant in the harbor.

Their gazes clashed, locked together. He watched the smoky depths of her almond-shaped eyes swirl and cloud into seething venom. Her voice was flat. "I warn you, Philippe. I am a submissive, even slavish mistress, but I am even more an implacable enemy."

"I'm sorry."

"Sorry?" Her face paled, her eyes glittered. "You don't yet know anything about being sorry, *m'sieu*."

"It was you who suggested we leave our shipboard romance aboard ship."

"And don't patronize me, either. You should be smart enough to be careful of the enemies you make."

"Your husband said almost the same thing to me."

"Then perhaps you should be clever enough to heed good advice. I wonder, *m'sieu*, if you can afford two such powerful and unforgiving enemies as you will find my husband and me to be?"

Then, with a slight shrug, Anouk took up her floppy brimmed hat, turned and walked out of the room. She left the door standing open. He heard the sharp click of her heels on the flooring for a long time after she was gone.

[28]

A sudden cloudburst washed a giant excavator out to sea.
The lost machine, with more than twenty scoop-buckets,
was of the finest and latest design created by the French.
Steam-operated, its stacks reared four stories above a
lumbering body and cab sixty-feet wide. The buckets,
arranged with chains and pulleys on a movable metal
arm, brought the earth upward and spilled it in huge
mounds which would be used as dams or shoring. But
what happened—and had happened a dozen times before,
according to Korvache—was that water from the swollen
swamps, plus the foot of rain dumped in an hour, turned
the mountains of soil into mudslides which carried everything—even the iron and steel behemoths—into the river
and out to the bay.

Philippe and Korvache stood where the monstrous
shovel had recently rested on the bank of the river.
"Aren't the damned things ever secured?" Philippe asked.

"To what?" Korvache shrugged. "A machine bigger
than the Elysian Palace, mud that becomes a river and
then an avalanche."

"Twelve losses of machinery of this size should have
taught us something."

They returned to the office. Though Korvache advised strongly against it, Philippe wrote a passionate letter of protest to company officials and turned it in to Bazaine. He pointed out that common sense dictated moving the huge shovels each night away from the dangerous mountains of earth, the brink of excavation ditches, pits or waterways. Such transporting, though slow and expensive, was far cheaper than replacing these mammoth steam shovels, to say nothing of the incredible costs in delay, lost man-hours, and yards of earth unmoved.

Bazaine scrawled "Nonsense" across the first page of Philippe's letter and returned it.

Philippe found that the crews of dynamiters were moved on the rivers or lakes in small, overcrowded boats. A gang-raft would be safer and would provide space from which steel drills could be driven for dynamiting before dredging. He worked it all out to a mathematically calculated pattern. He drew detailed plans and specifications for the gang raft and driller. He submitted the papers to Bazaine. It was back within two hours, marked, "Harebrained."

Philippe was still raging when he picked up the second packet of official correspondence on his desk. He read the invitation to dine with Director-General and Madame Gallaudet. Madame Gallaudet's brief note invited him and Madelon to the Gallaudet home for "a comfortable, informal dinner. You and Madelon will be our only guests. We do look forward to seeing you."

Philippe's pleasure in receiving the note was tempered only by the realization that his socializing with the director-general would intensify the discord already crackling between himself and Ducrot Bazaine.

He hesitated thirty minutes before he accepted Madame Gallaudet's invitation. It was a long, tense half-hour for him. The enmity between himself and Bazaine deepened daily, and God only knew what Anouk had said to her husband about him by now.

Bazaine's attitude toward him deteriorated into derisive malice. No matter what went wrong on the project,

Bazaine managed to work into his staff-meeting talks sarcastic reference to "malcontented, novice engineers, uninformed on the total program, but infallibly opinionated in all matters pertaining to it." Perhaps, he suggested sardonically, if these men did their own jobs and left policy matters to policy makers, the rate of success on this project would rise sharply.

Philippe wanted to be friendly with the Gallaudets, but he was aware that he had to survive as a Bazaine subordinate on this project. Still, if he allowed the chief engineer to dictate his private life, he'd soon find himself reduced to servility.

He sat down and wrote a warm acceptance to Madame Gallaudet and sent Clee running across town to deliver it.

It was a small and oddly unpromising triumph over subjection, but he felt good about it.

The masonry home in which the Director-General was quartered, though larger, was designed much like his own. All the French colony houses had been fabricated to a pre-determined plan, evidence that the original program of the magnificent ditch had been conceived along disciplined lines of orderliness and economy.

The abandoned hundred-thousand-dollar home built by Dingler, the first director-general of the project, near Panama City on the Pacific coast, exemplified the profligate use of funds which set in as the program foundered.

The elegance of the Gallaudet interior was subdued. Heavy sofas, deep, overstuffed chairs and highly polished tables showed wear, that loving surrender to growing children. Though both the Gallaudet children were deceased, their memory permeated the home—their pictures, tintypes, books, careless mementos now lovingly preserved. There was an intangible sense of deep-rooted, hard-won serenity. They were at peace here, resigned and reconciled without being defeated.

Madelon carried her pregnancy low, as if concealing a watermelon in the fragile pastel gown she wore. Madame Gallaudet received her warmly and, while Philippe had wine with Jean-Paul, they chatted in the parlor. Philippe, hearing the remote rustle of their voices, smiled. They were like old friends.

At dinner—served by a native couple—Philippe found himself laughing and chatting as he had long ago among close friends and relatives at Argenteuil.

Madame Gallaudet said, "You two are such a lovely couple. Don't let anything tear you apart, ever."

Philippe met Madelon's eyes across the table.

"Stay near Philippe, Madelon," Madame Gallaudet said. "Despite the peril of this terrible place—believe me, *ma chérie,* there is no evil worse than separation—I suppose I could have stayed behind in France with my beloved children, and they might both be alive and laughing tonight, but I made my choice. I would go with Jean-Paul. I do not regret. I would do it again. We can forgive hurt, or slights, but we cannot recover lost time. There is no cold like loneliness. Time with loved ones is so brief." Her wan eyes filled with gentle tears. "Don't waste a moment."

Having wine and cigars with Gallaudet in the study after dinner, Philippe determined to unleash at least a few volleys of frustration regarding the canal project.

He watched the older man, resolved that if Gallaudet even introduced the subject tangentially, he would expose the criminal waste of equipment, the refusal to add innovative vessels, the need for heavier dredges, the lack of direction, surrender to the environment, growing apprehension of final failure, and the consequent alarming loss of morale among the engineers and laborers.

He waited like a duelist for his opportunity to lunge forward with his charges. But Gallaudet did not mention the project, even in passing. Either the older man didn't want to discuss it with an engineer on the line, or he never brought his workaday problems home, or he felt Philippe wished to escape the subject when he was off-duty. So Philippe waited, and sweated, and said nothing.

For whatever reason, Philippe returned home with Madelon at eleven o'clock with all the rages tamped inside him, tighter than ever, ready to explode.

At seven-thirty the following night, he presented himself at the masonry cottage assigned to Monsieur and Madame Bazaine.

For the occasion, Philippe donned a new suit of lightweight fabric. Clee polished his boots until they shone.

He set out across the compound. He wanted to arrive in style, looking his best. He meant to be received as an equal. He was not going with hat in hand, or with an obsequious smile pasted on his face. He asked nothing for himself, but there were matters which demanded discussion. Somehow, Ducrot Bazaine had to be forced to listen.

The Bazaine cottage was set on a small knoll above the street in a lush yard of sabal palms, bougainvillea, pink hibiscus, and luxuriant vines whose tendrils clambered over the walls and probed the eaves of the red-tile roofing.

A mestizo girl in a white cotton shift answered the door. Philippe gave her his name and said he'd come to call on the Señor Bazaine about a matter of some consequence.

The girl nodded and retreated. She was gone almost five minutes. At last she returned, held the door slightly open and hesitantly invited him in.

Philippe stepped into the foyer and the door was closed behind him. The half-breed girl fled. He was amazed at the elegance of the furnishings. He'd seen nothing in Panama remotely approaching this decadent richness. It suggested the profligacy of the Dingler mansion at Panama City.

He remained just inside the door until Bazaine strolled calmly in from the dining room, smoking an after-dinner cigar.

He did not bother to smile. "Well, I must say, after all that's happened, I'm astonished to see you here."

Philippe flushed slightly. There was no way to know what an enraged Anouk had said. He waited, but Bazaine merely shrugged and pursued the matter no further.

Madame Bazaine appeared in the parlor doorway. Philippe felt the constriction deep in his belly. She was sensationally beautiful. Excitement flared through him. He felt her gaze raking him coldly, as he noted how her silk gown followed the voluptuous lines of her body from the ripe rise of her breasts to the full curves of her thighs and hips, her sculptured legs.

Bazaine walked to his wife's side, exuding his pride and pleasure in the possession of this elegant piece of statuary. He took up Anouk's hand, raised it to his lips and kissed her cupped palm.

She accepted the gesture without a trace of emotion. Her dark eyes strayed across Philippe's face but she did not speak, even when Bazaine said, "I believe you have met my wife?"

At that moment the frightened *mestizo* girl arrived with some whispered crisis. Madame Bazaine left the foyer without speaking to Philippe at all. But at the last she gazed directly into his face as if looking for something. He smiled and gave her a small bow.

Bazaine shrugged. "The Vicomtesse does not like you, you know?"

"Oh?"

"It was her suggestion that we refuse to receive you in our home. Something about some crudity of yours toward her aboard ship." He smiled and his mouth pulled down in disdain. "Perhaps we may discuss it more fully at some other time."

"Perhaps."

"I told her you learned your manners toward women in Algerian brothels."

"Most kind of you."

Bazaine drew deeply on his cigar and waited silently.

When Philippe saw that Bazaine was not going to invite him into the parlor or extend the courtesy of asking him to be seated, he said, "I've tried to see you in your office about matters which I find untenable."

"My dear boy, any time you find anything out here untenable, there is an easy answer. We'll accept your resignation whenever you present it."

"You know I'm not going to do that unless I'm driven to it. I do not suggest I am the only engineer who wants to see this project successfully completed, but I do feel I have presented excellent suggestions for improving deplorable conditions, and you have chosen to ignore them."

"Doesn't this tell you anything? Doesn't it suggest that we know what we are doing and that perhaps you are not in possession of all the answers?"

"I know we have lost millions in equipment and material. Some of it is lost beyond recovery. But much could be reclaimed."

"You and I were not here when that property was abandoned or discarded, young man. Its loss is not our responsibility. We do have grave responsibilities of completing this task. This is all that matters, not what happened before either of us arrived here."

"New equipment arrives daily and is allowed to rust and deteriorate on the docks, or unused, uncared-for, on work sites. Soon it will be useless. We can surrender to the heat, the dampness, the jungle rot. Or we can stand against it. One way we must oppose such ruin is by keeping our heavy equipment painted, cleaned, in good repair, protected, always in top working order."

"Long experience down here, which you lack, sir, has taught our engineering staff that we must expect to lose a percentage of equipment and material to the atmosphere, to rot and decay. It's the nature of this hell-hole. What you suggest is impractical. It would require a crew of mechanics twice as large as we now have."

"Then we'll have to import them. Or we may as well close down. All of us on the line realize our best equipment is not heavy enough. I would put that down as our first reason for failure."

"Oh, is it your educated opinion that the canal project is a failure?"

"Yes, sir. It is headed toward final collapse."

Bazaine's voice was chilled. "If I felt like that, I would not stay aboard what I saw as a sinking ship."

"I don't say the project must fail, or even that it will fail—only that it will fail unless we correct such errors as the loss of millions in abandoned equipment we are allowing to rot. It is in our power to keep that equipment in good repair and we must do that. We owe it to the people who have invested millions in this program."

Bazaine drew hard on his cigar, waited and measured his answer. At last he spoke, his voice heavy with sarcasm. "All right, *m'sieu*. You have my permission. Reclaim all material you can. Repair all the abandoned equipment you can move into the yards."

Philippe stared at Bazaine. He could only murmur. "Thank you, sir."

Bazaine walked to the door, held the knob in his fist. He watched Philippe mockingly. "There is one proviso, Bunau-Varilla."

"Oh?"

"You may not pay one hour's overtime for this work. You must accomplish it, if it can be done at all, while keeping to your regular schedule. Otherwise, you have my blessing."

He held the door open and Philippe walked through it wondering why he had the damnedest sensation of having won the sortie and lost the battle.

[29]

Philippe cursed out loud as he walked downhill through a misting rain. He cursed Bazaine for arrogance, high-handed malice and brass-balled insolence. He cursed the sudden squalls, the tropics, the stench of failure and the whole canal project. Most of all, he cursed himself for having gone to Bazaine in the first place. How could he have been fool enough to believe that imperious and overweening man would respond to civility and urgency?

He was not through, but he felt impotent; at the moment he was checkmated. A carriage with sleek horse stood hitched outside his cottage. He was so full of rage he barely saw the vehicle. He strode, shoulders hunched against the pelting rain, up the flagstone walk. He opened the front door and stopped dead.

Anouk Bazaine stood in the saffron-lit parlor, a hooded cape over her white evening dress. A static silence crackled in the room. Madelon stood unmoving by the wall, her fists pressed against the round protusion of her stomach.

He went to Madelon and put his arm about her.

She moved only enough to escape his touch.

"Madelon. Are you all right?" he said.

Anouk laughed brittlely. "Why shouldn't she be all right?"

Philippe's gaze lashed her. "I don't know."

Anouk's voice sounded solicitous. "I knew Madelon would be home alone. I had no idea you'd leave Ducrot so early. He's a night person, likes to drink and talk with the boys until dawn."

"He doesn't drink with me."

She shrugged. "As I told you. You could be friends with the Vicomte. You simply need to learn the secret."

"What do you want?" he said.

Anouk laughed. "I told you. I wanted to visit your lovely little wife. A delayed courtesy call. What better time than when you were—talking business—with my husband?" She moved her glance to Madelon's pale face. "I've been meaning to visit Madelon. We have so much in common. We could be such friends in this godforsaken place." Anouk's gaze slid over Madelon like a serpent, but her voice turned to ice. "Why do you stay here, when you have so much to lose?"

"You stay here," Madelon said.

"I know what I want. And I'm not going to leave without it."

"How brave of you."

"Yes. Isn't it?" Anouk shrugged. "Unlike you, I know what I want. I know the cost. I'm willing to pay it. It means enough to me that death doesn't frighten me. I'm afraid, my dear Madelon, that you expose yourself to terrible dangers to prove nothing."

"I'm certain I don't know what you mean."

"I think you do. Do you really love your husband so madly, so devotedly, that you were willing to sacrifice your baby for him?"

"That's enough." Philippe's jaw tightened, a hard squared line. "If there is nothing more you want here, Madame Bazaine. . . ."

Anouk spread her hands in a little gesture of amused disdain. "Does it matter what I want? Madelon and I are not talking about me. We're talking about Madelon and the fearful dangers she faces, when she could be safe and secure in Paris."

"Your concern is most touching," Madelon said, chilled.

"I am concerned." Anouk smiled. "It is well known, my dear Madelon, even among the servants in the colony here, that you live apart from Philippe. That you have no marriage at all, except in name."

Madelon's laughter fluted faintly toward hysteria. With a supreme effort of will, she spoke levelly. "One shouldn't rely on servants' gossip. After all, Madame Bazaine, one can see that I am pregnant."

"Yes. There's that gossip, too. Married—what? Three months?—and seven months pregnant?"

"That's none of your goddamn business," Philippe said. "I think it is."

She turned again to Madelon. "Why do you persist in trying to hold on to this man whom you obviously don't even really want? You haven't made any real effort to hold him, you know. He came into my arms because he was starved by you. You are fool enough not to work to hold a man like this, a real man in a world of fakes. You don't have to be fool enough to go on staying in this place—your very life endangered—when you don't have to."

Madelon retreated a step. She stared at Anouk while the full truth of Philippe's betrayal struck her and battered her again. Suddenly, her facade shattered, she cried out; pressing her gray-knuckled fists against her stomach. She shook her head. She looked at Philippe, her eyes losing focus.

Philippe stood helpless. Anouk had her revenge, but this no longer mattered. All his thoughts were for Madelon. He saw the disillusion, the final loss of faith, the deep hurt, swirling in Madelon's eyes.

"Madelon. Please. For God's sake." Philippe reached out to her.

She lunged backward. "Let me alone," she said, her lips pulled taut about her teeth.

"You're my wife, Madelon. For God's sake, listen to me. I love you. I married you."

Her laughter spewed from her mouth, sick with contempt and hatred.

She shook her head, her eyes frantic. She chewed at her

mouth, looking around the room in panic. "Leave me alone!" she cried again. "You don't need me. You've got your whore."

Madelon spun around and tried to run from the room. But she took only a step. It was as if something unseen shoved her abruptly. She staggered and sank to her knees.

Lying helplessly on the floor, she drew up her legs, her face pallid, eyes agonized. She screamed, "Myti!"

Philippe ran to her. He fell to the floor beside her. He tried to take her into his arms. "Madelon. Let me help you."

"Stay away from me. Myti!" she screamed again, pain shattering her voice. The servant came running into the room, amazingly quick and graceful for such a huge woman.

Madelon stretched out her hand toward Myti as if pleading for the woman to protect her. Myti fell on her knees to the floor beside Madelon. Madelon cried out, "Oh God, Myti, I'm in such pain. I'm on fire, on fire, my God, such pain."

Myti held the fragile Madelon as if she were a child. She looked up at Philippe. Her voice was level, but urgent. "Best get doctor. Her water's broke. Madame's in labor."

Stunned, Philippe got to his feet. He ran to the door. Clee stood there. Beyond him, Fanny pressed against the wall, eyes wide. Philippe said, "Clee. Get Dr. Feuillet. At once. Tell him madame is in labor."

Clee didn't hesitate. The front door slammed behind him. Philippe glanced toward Fanny, all his rage concentrating on her. "Damn you," he said. "Get in there. Help Myti. Clean up the floor. Do something except standing there like a goddamn idiot."

Fanny nodded and slipped past him. She ran to where Myti crouched rocking Madelon in her hamlike arms. Philippe followed her. Tears welled in his eyes. "Is she all right?"

"Don't know, *m'sieu*," Myti said.

Philippe knelt beside Madelon. "The doctor will be here. Soon." He touched her face tenderly with the backs of his fingers.

Madelon lurched away, her face twisting savagely.

"Don't touch me. Damn you! Don't ever touch me again."
She pressed herself against Myti's protective bulk.

He made no effort to hide the tears running down his
cheeks. "I love you," he said. "I swear it. God knows, I
love only you."

Wracked with pain which almost overwhelmed her,
Madelon stared up at him. She spoke slowly, the words
spaced by the agony charging through her. "Isn't it funny?
I believe you. I think you do love me in your way. Isn't
it too bad—it's such a low, vile, dirty way?"

[30]

The front door was thrown open and left ajar. Dr. Feuillet, carrying a small black medical bag, hurried in, Clee at his heels. Both were damp, their clothes rain-spattered, their shoes muddy.

It must have seemed a strange tableau to the doctor. Philippe stood immobile beside Madelon and Myti. Madelon's face was blanched with pain. Her fingers gouged Myti's arms, but the big woman did not protest. She whispered reassuringly to Madelon and smoothed her sweated hair back from her forehead.

Anouk Bazaine remained standing in the center of the room, like the eye around which a hurricane swirls. The hood of her gray cape was pushed back from her head. Lamplight cast a wan halo about her dark hair. Her face was expressionless.

Philippe jerked his head toward Fanny. She understood him, ran from the room and returned with towels for the doctor.

Dr. Feuillet stood a moment drying his hands and arms. Then he knelt beside Madelon. Myti said something to him. The doctor nodded and glanced up at Philippe. "Will you kindly lift madame to the couch?"

Madelon stirred, protesting. She shook her head violently, her face deathly pale. "No. I'll manage alone."

"You can't," the doctor told her, voice brusque.

Philippe knelt beside Madelon, but she cried out fretfully, "No. Don't touch me."

"I'll help madame, *m'sieu*," Myti said. She turned easily, placed her arms under Madelon's knees and shoulders and lifted her onto the couch.

The doctor bent over Madelon for what seemed a long time to Philippe. Rain slapped in gusts against the windows, blew in at the open door. Frogs were loud in the darkness. At last, Dr. Feuillet straightened and spoke to Philippe across his shoulder. We must get her to the hospital."

Turning to speak to Clee, Philippe's gaze struck Anouk. "The hell with waiting for an ambulance," he said. "Madame Bazaine's carriage is outside. We'll use that."

Philippe entered the French hospital on the shore north of Colón. He had walked downhill in the rain without feeling its wetness against his face or upon his bare head. He was hardly aware of anything outside himself. When he entered the lighted corridor he recoiled at the pervasive sour-rotted smell.

As he went deeper into the facility, the hackles stood on the nape of his neck. He recognized the odor of death.

He hesitated outside the screen doors which marked the contagion ward. He knew that beyond those doors, men were stacked in cots, waiting to die, most of them victims of yellow fever, Chagres fever, malaria or galloping syphilis. By the time the infected workers reached the hospital, they suffered acute melancholy, the sense that they were doomed. Among the laborers, the hospital, operated by the French, was a place of horror, a boneyard of no return. They believed if a man entered the place without infection, he would contract it at once. Few came out alive, they said. A stop at the hospital was only the last way-station on the way to the cemetery.

Pressing the back of his hand against his nostrils Philippe hurried across the building to the maternity ward. Through a long corridor, completely separated from the rest of the hospital, was the small room where life began.

Philippe prowled the corridor, unable to sit down for more than a minute or two at a time. After a long time, Myti came out of the labor room. She smiled and touched his hand. "Madame has been moved into delivery. She is not having an easy time, *m'sieu.*"

He stood with Myti at a window. Below them the dark bay was littered with the faint lights of ships and boats at anchor.

Dr. Feuillet came out of the delivery room. Philippe saw him in the corridor. He hurried across the room, snagging the doctor's arm in the hallway. "How is she?"

Dr. Feuillet shook his head. "Premature delivery is never easy. A first labor makes it more difficult, increases the risk. There is a slight obstruction. I'm afraid we're dealing with an abruption of placenta, a premature detachment. Instead of an afterbirth it has become an obstruction. Don't worry. These things happen sometimes in the best of deliveries. Eh? Time, that's all. It will take time. She's getting every attention."

"May I see her?"

Dr. Feuillet frowned and shook his head. "She doesn't want to see you."

"I've got to talk to her."

"Not now. I'm sorry. Be patient. Often a primpura—a woman in her first confinement—suffers mild melancholy, depression. This happens. Once the baby is born, everything will be fine. You'll see."

Myti sagged in an uncomfortable chair and slept with her chin sagged upon her massive bosom. After midnight, the pulse of the hospital slowed. The sea lights winked in the dark harbor.

Philippe continued to pace the corridor, hour after hour. No sounds emanated from the delivery room. He stood just outside the thick doors, feeling like an exile. He began to be certain that Madelon had died.

When Dr. Feuillet emerged from the delivery room in the last hour before dawn, he looked even more exhausted than Philippe. He tried to smile. "You've a son," he said.

"How is Madelon?"

"They're both doing well."

Philippe caught his arm. "May I see Madelon?"

The doctor shook his head. "I wish you wouldn't. Give her a little time."

"If I could just speak with her—"

"It wouldn't help. She's had a very bad time."

Myti came across the room and stood beside Philippe. The doctor gave her a tired smile. "You're a good, brave woman, Myti. Your mistress has a son, a beautiful boy."

"Gracias a dios," Myto said.

"Why don't you take *M'sieu* Bunau-Varilla home? Get some rest, both of you."

"I can't leave," Philippe protested. "I've got to see Madelon."

The doctor stopped smiling. "I'm sorry. I've left word. You're not to see her. Not now. I'm truly sorry, Bunau-Varilla, but it's your wife's own request. She does not wish to see you. I must consider what's best for her. As long as she does not wish to see you, it's best not to upset her, best to stay away from her." The doctor sighed heavily. He touched Philippe's arm in a gesture of sympathy, smiled at Myti, and walked away, yawning, stooped with fatigue.

Philippe stood unmoving. Myti closed her fingers on his arm. "We go now, *m'sieu*. Let her rest. We come later. When madame sees your baby, all will be different, I vow. Sometimes it is hard to forgive when one is wronged, but it will happen. Hurt goes deep. *Sí*. But love goes all the way into the bones. You'll see."

Philippe fell fully dressed across his bed in the first pink rays of dawn. His eyes burned with unshed tears, his body ached with self-hatred. Exhaustion overcame him slowly. His last thoughts were that he would take a brief nap—no more than 15 minutes. Then he would bathe and return to the hospital. He would wait outside Madelon's door until she agreed to see him. Maybe Myti was right, maybe love did go all the way into the bones. One didn't throw it off because one wished to. He had to believe this. He had to believe in something.

He awoke abruptly. He sat up, frantic, overcome with a terrible sense of wrong.

He believed he'd slept only a few minutes, but he was undressed, under the fresh white sheets of his bed. He wore a nightshirt. Then he saw that it was dark outside his window. He threw off the covers and lunged from his bed.

He yelled for Clee. Fanny. Myti. The house was silent, like an abandoned place.

"Clee! Damn it. Where are you?"

Clee came from the rear of the house. He moved slowly. Philippe said, "Find a carriage. I'm going to the hospital as soon as I'm dressed."

Clee winced, but said nothing. He nodded and retreated from the room. By the time Philippe was dressed, a hired carriage awaited him outside his door.

The carriage raced downhill from the colony and Philippe leaped out at the hospital entrance. He entered the building and strode through the halls of death to the place set aside for Birth.

He asked a nurse, "Which room is Madame Bunau-Varilla's?"

She looked up at him oddly, then pointed. "That is Madame Bunau-Varilla's room, sir, but—"

"I'll see her, whether she wants to see me or not," Philippe said across his shoulder, already walking away along the corridor.

The nurse got up from her desk and hurried, as swiftly as she could in the starched, ankle-length uniform, through the hallway.

Philippe pushed open the door at the room to which the nurse had directed him. He stopped with his hand on the door facing.

The bed was freshly made, the room empty.

His heart sank. Was the nurse trying to tell him something had happened to Madelon—or to the baby? He forced himself to remain calm. Perhaps the nurse had shown him the wrong room.

As he turned to leave, Dr. Feuillet hurried toward him, the nurse in his wake.

"Where is Madelon?" Philippe said.

Dr. Feuillet drew a deep breath. He spread his hands. "She's gone."

"Gone? On the first day after delivery? What kind of joke is this?"

"I'm afraid it is no joke at all, Philippe. All of us tried to stop her, to reason with her, to warn her. She was adamant. She would not listen. She learned that the S.S. *Lafayette* sailed today for Paris. She was like a woman possessed. She would be aboard that ship. She demanded to be removed from here. She was accompanied by her maid and a nurse. We did all we could to insure her health, to make her comfortable, to transport her carefully. There was nothing else we could do. I'm sorry."

Philippe sagged against the wall. The texture of the materials chewed into his back. He shook his head. "Didn't she leave a message for me? Didn't she say anything?"

"She told me—to say—she hoped you would let her go quietly and finally, as she wished it, and that you would not follow her or try to stop her."

[31]

Philippe walked into a misting rain. The sun shone daz-
zlingly white through the persistent shower, adding heat
to the discomfort, and drawing steam from the ground.
Mud caked his shoes, but he did not care. He felt sick
at his stomach, with a nausea and emptiness which would
not release him.

He stalked along Front Street and out on the wharves.
He stared at the ships anchored in the harbor and tied up
along the docks. The S.S. *Lafayette* had departed; the
bay seemed empty, the world a gray void.

Rain struck him and ran in rivulets down his face,
hotter than tears. He stood for a long time staring out
across the bay to the horizon where storm clouds gathered,
black and sun-crested.

At last he turned away, like a man bereft in a cemetery. He went into the nearest tavern and ordered straight
whiskey. The taste was hot, fiery, but its effect no more
than water. He bought three bottles and carried them up
the hill under his arm.

The house was silent and forlorn. He heard Myti and
Clee in the rear of the house but he did not call to them.

He did not want to talk to them now. He didn't need their pity. He had enough of his own.

He gazed around at the house Madelon and Myti had so lovingly furnished. His eyes burned; his aching throat felt tight.

"The hell with it," he said aloud. "The hell with all of it." He turned around in the room, staring at each separate piece of furniture. "I'll have the draymen up here. I'll clear it out. I'll clear it all out."

He fell across his bed fully dressed. He uncorked a bottle and drank the raw alcohol straight. For a moment he was afraid he would retch. But he did not. He could not. This would be too easy.

"It's not easy," he said aloud. "Nothing's easy." He took another long drink from the mouth of the bottle. This time it was easier.

The hot liquid burned his stomach, but he did not care. He finished off the first bottle, but felt no better.

When Myti came in and begged him to eat, he cursed her. Some time later, how long he had no idea, Clee tried to pull off his muddy boots. Philippe threatened to assault him with an empty bottle. Sadly, shaking his head, Clee withdrew.

Philippe drank. He yelled, raged, wept and shouted. And he drank. He drank until he discovered—as he had once before—that he was not one of those mortals who could find either answers or surcease in the bottom of a bottle.

A note anchored atop the paperwork cluttering his desk summoned him, at his earliest convenience, to Chief Engineer Bazaine's office.

Bazaine let him cool his heels for an hour in his anteroom. Ordinarily, Philippe would have burned with resentment and frustration. Today he did not care. There was nothing Bazaine could do to him now.

Bazaine wasted no time, minced no words. He did not invite Philippe to sit down, but stared up at him malevolently across his cluttered table. "Well, I hear you've run to the director-general with your accusations against me."

"What in hell are you talking about?"

"Don't take that attitude with me. Would you like to walk down and confront the director-general himself with your lies about me?"

"Yes. Let's go. Come on, get up. Let's go."

"Watch your tongue. You can get yourself in trouble, taking that attitude."

"Don't ever threaten me, Bazaine, not with anything, unless you mean to carry out your threat."

"Oh, I'll carry out anything I threaten to do to you, *m'sieu*. But I'll do it my way. On my terms. At my discretion. I've seen ambitious, obnoxious little people, but none as obvious as you. Well, this I can assure you: you can cram your nose up Gallaudet's ass as much and as far as you like, you're still working for me, you'll still answer to me, and your hare-brained recommendations will still go through this office—which means they won't go anywhere. Is that clear?"

"It has been clear since the moment I met you."

"Then do your work, produce on the job, goddamn it, and stop rocking the boat. I won't tolerate it."

"You will sit here on your ass, though, and let the project wash out to sea," Philippe said.

"I follow orders, Bunau-Varilla."

"By whose orders do you let equipment decay, materials rot, excavations be flooded or filled by landslides as quickly as they're dredged?"

"I am not God, *m'sieu*."

"You could come out and see where this project is being allowed to go to hell."

"Why should I? I am busy working here. By the rules. Doing the job I was engaged to do. And I have you, *m'sieu*, to report every little error, every minor failure."

"We don't have *minor* failures on this project any more, sir. Every time a dredge is washed out to sea, there's another savage denouncement of us, this program, of de Lesseps himself, in the Assembly."

"This dismays me no less than it does you, *m'sieu*. However, until we are provided new plans which will help us overcome our present natural and insurmountable obstacles, we'll continue to work as best we can."

"My God! If only we were *permitted* to work at our

best, rather than our most ineffective! What a giant step that would be! How the morale of the men would go up. How the very look of this project would change."

"And how would you suggest we begin this miracle, *m'sieu?*"

"By making our own new plans for developing this project—by not waiting for them to be handed down to us—because they never will be."

"Name one step we could take that we have not taken, only to have it overwhelmed by some calamity, some natural catastrophe."

Philippe stared down at Bazaine across that table. "I would suggest first that we clear the entire surveyed passage of the canal and keep it cleared. Not only would this provide incentive, it would instantly pinpoint those regions where excavation and development could most feasibly be undertaken under present conditions."

"Ridiculous. Clear fifty miles of jungle? It will be twenty years, if ever, that we complete a sea-level canal across this isthmus. The best engineering minds are agreed at least on this. There is no point in wasting money and labor keeping a passageway clear. Why do we need it? To show off to visiting politicians? What would we prove?"

"That we know what we're doing, that we know where we are going, that we are looking for the best way to get there by building now where we can build now. That we have a viable and feasible route across this isthmus. If nothing else it would restore the confidence of the Assembly and the creditors."

"We have an established route. We have innumerable maps of it. Do I have to remind you that our surveyors have followed, almost precisely, the path of the Trans-Panama Railroad built by Aspinwall? The rails follow the ideal canal route. This has been proved by practice and survey."

"Meanwhile, *m'sieu,* the trains run, but we make petty little hacks at the jungle. We reach out to harness a river, and then we fall back."

"No. You lie again. We are *driven* back. But, I'll tell you what, you make me sick to my stomach coming in here with your complaints, running to Gallaudet with your baseless charges against me."

Bazaine stood up and warped his swarthy face into a smile of purest malice and hatred. "I'm putting you in charge of the Third Division. You'll be chief engineer with offices on the Pacific coast. Your section extends from the Pacific at Panama City to the Culebra Cut. That's a distance of 25 kilometers, *m'sieu,* approximately one-third of the total length of the projected canal. It should occupy your mind and your energies fully. By God, it had better.

"You'll be in charge over there, and responsible. I don't want to hear you whining and complaining. If you want to chop out 25 kilometers of canal channel as some kind of cosmetic display, by all means, do it! I don't give a damn what you do on the other side of the Culebra Cut, as long as you keep to hell out of my way, out of my sight."

[32]

Philippe departed Colón on the trans-isthmus train, with, finally, a sense of purpose and no small hangover. Korvache, Burns and Snelling hosted a farewell party at Leone's Bar. They rented the entire saloon, brought in musicians and shapely young females who immediately doffed their clothing to the beating of drums, wailing of reeds and yells of encouragement in half a dozen languages. With too much to drink and too much smoke from cigars rolled with the dried leaves of what Korvache called "the wild tobacco," Philippe didn't recall the end of the party. He didn't remember being helped aboard the railway coach. Clee accompanied him, leaving Colón for the first time in his young life. When Myti wept at being left behind, he took her along as housekeeper.

There was no time to think. For this he was thankful. He toppled into a seat and slept. The loss of Madelon and the son he'd never even seen lurked always on the ragged edges of his conscious mind, awaiting the quiet moment, the lonely hour, the empty night. He wrote often to Madelon in Bris but got no reply.

Clee shook him awake when the train shuddered to a stop in the company depot on the Culebra Cut plateau.

Head aching, Philippe left the train. Legs unsteady, sunlight lancing painfully into his eyes, stomach fluttering, he carried his suitcases, letting Myti and Clee share the steamer trunk. Clee hated this raw and remote settlement —Colón was Paris by comparison. But Philippe found the clean mountain air refreshing and remarkably free of any taint of sewage.

Master of all he beheld he surveyed the company settlement—temporary buildings, huts, lean-tos, workshops, tents and equipment; even the trainload of excavation explosives he'd ordered had arrived and sat waiting on a siding.

He was an exile here—Napoleon at Elba, Grant at Galena, Bunau-Varilla at Culebra Cut. Though he was in command of the Third Division, he didn't deceive himself. Bazaine had him recorded as troublemaker, disrupter, malcontent. Not recorded but equally as damning, possible or potential cuckolder.

He didn't care why he was here. He'd been assigned a section—25 kilometers of the canal route—as his sole responsibility. Bazaine saw it as a chance to be rid of him, to put him beyond Anouk's reach, and finally to write him off as a failure. As yet, no deep or lasting excavation had been completed between the Cut and the sea. This three-hundred-foot elevation had a four-year history of disaster.

Clee thrust open the door of the whitewashed company shack which was to serve Philippe as office and quarters. They stopped, surprised to see not one stick of furniture in the four rooms. Everything was freshly painted, the floors were scoured, but the house was completely bare. They set the steamer trunk down in the small front room. Philippe and Myti sagged upon it while Clee walked about shaking his head, swearing and pushing all windows open.

Philippe had no intention of getting caught in what had become the French trap out here, doing all nonessential tasks first. "Get furniture," he told Clee. "See whoever is in charge. Buy it, scrounge it, beg it. Just remember, if there are no beds by nightfall, I'll sleep on the floor, Myti

247

on the screen porch. But you'll sleep on the ground out-side."

Clee grinned and departed. He returned in three hours with furnishings, work tables, drawing boards, labor aides and engineers to greet their new chief. Clee explained why the hut had been bare. "The furnishings were burned. The chief you replaced, *m'sieu,* he died of yellow jack. People here scared. They burned everything he touched, even the bed he died on."

Philippe surprised Clee—and himself—by laughing aloud. "We just discovered another reason Bazaine as-signed me here. The yellow fever epidemic."

"No epidemic yet," an engineer said. "Chief Réné was the first to die this month so far, since the rains stopped."

"Oh?" Philippe grinned. "The rains have stopped?"

The engineer nodded. "Rainy season is usually thirty or forty days shorter on the Pacific coast. But, Jesus, we got swamps, bad swamp air, and mosquitoes breeding by the billions."

With an exhausted young engineer named Jacques Dorsay, Philippe made his first inspection tour of the Cut. He found little to cheer about. Machinery had been lost in mudslides during the rainy season. "Most of what we've accomplished so far," Dorsay said, "has been res-cuing our equipment from landslides or flash floods, then redoing the excavation destroyed."

"Why has there been no lasting excavation at all?"

"There has been. During the dry season, the land up here is pretty stable and we dig and haul. But even then, the clay clogs every shovel and has to be scraped off each dig. And the mudslides. During rains, land just caves in in thousand-meter hunks. We've dug, shored up and come back in the morning to find the whole hillside caved in, usually on top of heavy equipment."

"Hasn't anybody figured a way to stop the slides?"

"You can't stop a slide when you don't know where it will start. You'll see a fissure in the earth five hundred meters above the excavation. By morning that whole area below the crack is gone—and anything before it is gone with it."

Philippe took up a handful of the mixed volcanic

shales, clay, and limestone which turned blue in rainstorms before it caved in upon itself.

"It's a nightmare," Dorsay said. "A goddamn nightmare. Your site looks solid, then the sandstone shifts, and the clay begins to slough off in huge mountains of earth and rocks and trees—an avalanche. It carries whole sections, the largest steam shovels, everything caught in its path. Even took out a railroad bridge. It was three years before they could build a stable and permanent replacement."

Philippe returned from his tour about dusk. Clee and some helpers had set furniture in the house. Myti prepared a supper of fried plantain, sheepshead and boiled rice. A small, yellow-skinned man slumped in the only front-room chair. "Gentleman been waiting to see you," Clee said, retreating from the room.

"The kid's been scared I'd die 'fore you got here." The visitor rose from the chair, found the effort too taxing, and abandoned it. He waved a saffron-stained hand, the bones of which appeared almost visible through his papyruslike skin.

Philippe felt a twist of pity. This was the first time he'd been so near an advanced case of malaria. The poor devil's yellowing flesh looked flushed and dry with fever. But though he looked as if he were afire inside, he was suddenly shaken by body-wrenching chills.

"Poison swamp air," the man said. "Should never have come near this place. Hellish disease. Doctor told me malaria has been the direct cause of over one-half the deaths of the human race. And now it's got me by the tail." Suddenly he suffered so severe a chill his teeth chattered, his skin showed goose pimples. He pressed his fists against the skull-splitting ache in his temples. He took a heavy dose of quinine and sank back in his chair, wincing in agony.

"You ought to be in bed," Philippe said.

"People die in bed. Got too much to do. Hear you're the new man here to take Réné's job. God help you. Réné was a good man but helpless against the red tape. My name's Von Weiler. Never mind shaking hands. I might be infectious. Who the hell knows for sure? I head

249

my own contracting firm, under Dutch license. I bid in the contract to excavate at the Cut here. The ridge up here is giving us hell and costing us a fortune, three hundred feet above sea level. The limestone soil makes digging like scooping up refined sugar. Nothing to hold it together. It just caves in on itself, and my men. Réné couldn't help without orders. Maybe you can't. But if you can, I need your help, and like you can see, time's running out on me."

"Anything we want to do up here, *M'sieu* Von Weiler, we'll do. We'll explain or ask for permission later."

Von Weiler looked as if he might weep helplessly. "My God. Am I hearing this? Or am I delirious? I've been delayed and stopped and backed up, but in all the time I've been out here, I've very seldom been told unequivocally to go ahead on anything."

"What's your problem?"

"Hell, I got nothing but problems. But mainly I've got a dredge coming from Scotland. The buckets are big enough to take out bites of that limestone and maybe stay ahead of it as it crumbles in on itself. I've spent more than I've got. Either I'm allowed to go ahead, or it's bankruptcy for me and you got to start all over."

"Are you well enough to work?"

"Hell, I'm well enough to direct my men. They're good people. I can run the job from a canvas cot when it gets too bad."

"I tried to get the chief engineer at Colón to try shoring up well behind the digging. Too expensive, time-consuming, made no sense to Bazaine."

"That by-the-book bastard."

"Does it make sense to you?"

"How would you do it?"

"Cut those tall straight Parana pines. Sink them with pile drivers. Dig. Shore it. And dig again."

The sick man nodded at last. "We've wasted three years. The delay cutting and driving, and the cost, are nothing to what's gone down rat holes so far. You order crews to fell trees and deliver them, my men and equipment will make a test."

"When can you start?" When Von Weiler suggested

dawn, Philippe burst out laughing, his blood pumping furiously. How incredible to hear a man speaking positively, even if he was a yellowing skeleton speaking raspingly from his deathbed.

Philippe found himself unable to sleep that night. To know there were men like the Dutchman, Von Weiler, trying to meet the terms of his contract in spite of a crippling—and probably fatal—disease, elated him as nothing had since he'd arrived in Panama.

There was a slender chance to make this project successful, in spite of rain, malaria, yellow fever, limestone soil and bureaucratic red tape. Something about Von Weiler—his indomitable spirit, his hard-nosed determination to drive ahead until he fell dead, reminded Philippe of Guido De Blasio. Once De Blasio was brought to his mind, rest was impossible, sleep out of the question. He became convinced that he could lessen the terrible odds against himself if he could bring De Blasio out here as his assistant. De Blasio never thought in the set, established patterns. When conventional wisdom said something was impossible, De Blasio attacked it by turning his thinking upside-down. With De Blasio, answers came not from the way things had always been done with accepted methods but from finding new ways to attack the old problems.

Philippe got up, scratched a short wooden match and lighted a candle. The fire wavered and then glowed yellowly in the purple tropic night. He scribbled out a message to be dispatched to De Blasio at dawn: "Biggest job in history of man. Need's man's biggest bastard to make it work. Please."

Clee sat up, blinking on his canvas cot. "You all right, m'sieu?"

"I'm all right, go back to sleep."

"Scared maybe you caught malaria from that yellow man."

"I haven't caught anything yet. Get back to sleep."

Philippe had just blown out the candle and moved toward his bed when the night was illumined in every direction by savage fires, roaring suddenly out of control and followed by explosions.

251

Philippe stepped into his trousers, shoved his feet into boots and ran barechested into the garishly lighted night. One explosion followed another as the train cars carrying explosives burned and blew up. The very earth trembled with every detonation, and debris flew like shrapnel fired from cannon.

Philippe ran, joined by every engineer and worker, toward the exploding cars on the rail siding. Then he slowed, feeling helpless. There was nothing they could do now that fire had set off the explosives. Those cars would go up like a chain of firecrackers.

Near the tracks he found dozens of mutilated and dismembered bodies. From the remains they could discern only that they were not workers. "Indians," somebody said. Then they saw others running in the weird yellow and cerise firelight—swamp Indians, wearing only breechcloths and warpaint. The dead warriors had set fire to the cars, not knowing they were loaded with explosives, and had been unable to escape.

Fleeing shadows of Indians running in terror flared wraithlike in the raging firelight and against the gray clouds of explosives which hung over the area. Some of the canal personnel fired at the retreating Indians.

Suddenly a lone Indian appeared, scrambling up on top of the sidetracked engine. He poised, tall and slender, his sleek body sweated and glistening in the eerie fireglow.

Someone fired a gun at the Indian on the top of the cab, but the man seemed unaware, certainly unintimidated by gunfire or the men running toward him. His deeply resonant voice rose strong and forceful even against the crackling fires, the rumbling of explosions.

"See me well, white men," he shouted in Spanish. "Here I am. Quixaltan. King of this land. King of the Darien Indians, whose people you have killed and enslaved and now wish to drive from their homes. My people ruled this land before the Spanish murderers came, before the French pillagers. You will kill us all, or you will never keep our lands."

Most of the workers hesitated fifty yards from the tracks, watching Quixaltan, with his arms out at his sides, his legs apart, his head thrust upward toward the heavens, the very earth heaving and quivering below him, the fires in the cars of explosives raging toward him. Philippe ran forward. He and Quixaltan faced each other in a fiery tableau.

"Get down from there," Philippe yelled. "Or you're going to be blown to hell."

"You—you will blow me to hell, white man?"

"I won't have to. Those explosives are going to rip up every car and that engine before they stop."

Another explosion, half a dozen cars away shook the foundations of the buildings, rattled the huge engine. Atop it, Quixaltan wavered, fighting for his balance.

"You want to live to lead your people, get down fast," Philippe told him.

"You want me down, white man, you shoot me down."

"I won't have to shoot you. Those train cars are exploding as the heat builds up. You have sense enough to lead your people, you ought to have instinct enough to get out of there while you can."

Quixaltan hesitated again. "You leader of these people?"

"Yes. Come on down. You've got something to say, say it to me."

Quixaltan wavered. But another eruption of explosives sent shards and boards and metal and fire showering down around them. Convinced, he sprang outward, landing as light as a puma on the ground beside Philippe.

Philippe caught his arm and dragged him away from the tracks. The other people were already retreating. Quixaltan tried to shake free of his grasp and raged at him, cursing him for daring to contaminate his royal person by touching him with white hands. "They're not that white," Philippe told him. He tightened his grip on the slender, rigid bicep and the Darien king followed in his wake across the train yard.

"You people want peace," Quixaltan told him when they stopped walking. "Get all of your materials out of here. Now."

"To hell with you, King Quixaltan. We made a treaty with the Colombian government."

"That is not my government."

253

"It's the recognized government of the Panama territory. You have a problem, take it up with them. I ought to have you thrown in jail for what you've done here tonight."

"We will go on doing this until you white people leave our lands."

"To hell with your lands. That's my property you and your warriors have blown to smithereens."

Quixaltan only nodded. "And so we shall go on." At that moment two cars erupted simultaneously and the engine seemed to fly apart out on the tracks. The king stood with his mouth open. After a moment he shook his head, but he said nothing more.

By some miracle the main rail tracks and roadbed sustained only minor damage. This destruction was repaired and train service resumed by noon the following day. It was two days before the West Indian Negroes and Chinese had cleared the debris from the explosions. Siding rails were twisted, misshapen and ripped from their ties. Strangest of all was the way Quixaltan and his warriors dissolved like unreal wisps from a nightmare. Those captured were turned over to the Colombian army, but they disappeared during the night. Clee said it was because the soldiers feared Indian reprisals even more than they did the voodoo practiced by the West Indian Negroes. Anyhow, they were gone and the encampment waited, slightly more tense than before, for them to strike again.

Railway laborers were sent in to repair the sidings. Philippe ordered his crews out to fell pines. He found a telegraph message from Guido De Blasio in his office one night. It was brief: "Scared constipated yellow fever. Stop. Don't ask me into that pesthole even in name of stupid friendship."

Philippe felt his heart sink, some of his growing hope dissipating, but he accepted De Blasio's decision. He'd never suspected Guido feared anything on God's earth, but when yellow jack and malaria caused nine of every ten deaths in Panama—and now that he'd seen what malaria was doing to Von Weiler, maybe there was logic in Guido's refusal. If Guido feared yellow jack so terribly,

Philippe would respect his judgment, no matter how badly he needed him.

He spent the next week directing the men shoring up the limestone soil while Von Weiler brought in his big shovels, derricks and pile drivers. There was little resistance as the scraped poles were driven into the soft volcanic soil.

Derricks lifted the poles, men set them straight and pile drivers sent them easily into the ground. Von Weiler's men moved in, excavating and shoring with concrete. The pilings held. The soft, grainy earth did not crumble. Excited and encouraged by this minor success, Philippe's engineers set the West Indians and native mestizos to clearing and burning brush, draining swamps and cutting back the fast growing grasses.

Philippe was pleased that the shoring had held up at Gold Hill, but he saw this task would be almost impossible in salt marshes and in the Chagres River valley. He spent more and more time drawing up plans for larger steam shovels, barges and gondola rail cars. The first order of business had to be heavier equipment.

He was in his undershirt, dripping sweat, working at his drawing board when Director-General Gallaudet arrived.

Gallaudet shook his head. "You look like hell, my boy. Ten years older than when you left Colón. Don't you ever sleep?"

"I don't need much sleep," Philippe said. "There's just so much to do now. It's not working with older methods, but I believe we are making progress."

"Yes. That's one reason why I am here. I got the report that you had put into practice Ducrot Bazaine's plans for shoring up the limestone behind the shovels. He reports it is working up here. That's mainly what I came to see."

Philippe was speechless. But he only nodded. If Bazaine needed to take sole credit for a successful operation, to hell with it.

He went on a rail car with Gallaudet and his staff. He left orders with Myti to outdo herself in fixing a feast for company that night.

Gallaudet got off the rail car and walked to the bottom

of the long excavation gouged out of Gold Hill. He laughed, nodding his satisfaction and delight. "By God, it's not a whole canal, but it's one step. We'll have to get Bazaine some kind of bonus and maybe a citation for this, eh? And you made his plan work, Philippe. I'm proud of you, too. By God, it's going to work, having you younger men—men who won't quit—out here."

Philippe invited Gallaudet and his staff to dinner, and they accepted. Philippe didn't give a damn about the dinner. He sent Clee to the saloon to round up all the wine he could scrounge. In the meantime, while the staff drank toasts to the success of the canal, he spread out his plans for mammoth steam shovels on the drawing board before Gallaudet.

Gallaudet listened with intense interest to the presentation. Philippe's pulse quickened as Gallaudet's only objection to his suggestions concerned the practicability of shipping such monstrous equipment.

"That's part of my plan, sir," Philippe said. "We'll order it built to specification and shipped in crates to Colón. We can move it via train. My engineers and technicians will assemble the equipment on the site. It can be done. It will work. It will prove less costly in the end than trying to dig with inadequate shovels, dredges and excavators. I believe it's the only way we can stay ahead of floods and landslides."

The entire presentation was disrupted when a man came running from the telegraph office. "Message for you, Monsieur Gallaudet," he said, breathless and shaken. "Madame Gallaudet has been stricken. She is very ill. They're afraid she may have yellow fever."

Gallaudet remained outwardly calm but Philippe felt he saw something die in the older man's haggard eyes. Gallaudet spoke very calmly. "I'm very sorry, young man. About the dinner. Everything. I must get back to Colón at once. I'm sorry."

Myti, Clee and Philippe sat down with Dorsay and a couple of other engineers to the feast Myti had prepared. None of them ate very much. Nobody was hungry.

Philippe prowled the encampment for hours after dark, feeling caged in the cottage. Word came that Monsieur

Gallaudet was taking his wife aboard the first ship out to seek medical aid in Paris. Philippe kept seeing her kindly, gentle face, and the lost look in the eyes of Monsieur Gallaudet.

He stood and gazed about the darkened community. Muted sounds of laughter, men playing cards, drinking in the makeshift saloon, or talking in their tents eddied around him. Philippe felt that his work here at the Cut had been set back another five years at least. He wrote out and dispatched one final plea to Guido De Blasio.

"Need someone who can think in new ways. Stop. Someone to make ideas work. Stop. Someone who won't quit. Stop. Hell with yellow fever. Stop. This is biggest job of our lives. Stop. What a way to die."

He walked silently back to his hut, slapping absently at the mosquitoes that swarmed about his head.

$$\begin{bmatrix} 33 \end{bmatrix}$$

*Never before in the four-year history of the French com-*pany in Panama had so much been accomplished on the canal as was achieved under Philippe's relentless leadership in the next few months at Culebra Cut.

Laborers, engineers, masons, hod-carriers, drovers and mechanics fell to, working as if infected by Philippe's enthusiasm and obsessive drive. And as Dorsay suggested one night over beer, perhaps all these men were sick of sitting on their tails. They had lounged in lethargic, heat-numbing inactivity, waiting for some sign from the former men in command. None had come. They had played cards until they hated the sight even of a royal flush. No one could cheat at poker any more; they all knew each other too well. And they grinned amiably, even in grudging admiration, watching Philippe strip off his shirt and join the crew where work was bogged down. He was driven. Each passing day brought them nearer the return of the long rainy season. There was so much to do, so little time to do it. He asked nothing of his people that he wasn't doing himself; he worked harder and longer hours than any other man at the Cut. But even the dullest laborer comprehended that "the chief" was driving himself beyond human endurance and so they established a new lottery; they sold raffle tickets on how long he'd last.

"Hell," one man said. "Hurry and give me a lottery ticket. The bloke may go before we can make the transaction legal."

Everything was against Philippe, and even the men who grew to know him best and admire him most recognized this. Deaths from yellow fever so far were few, and ruinous malarial attacks had struck only lightly but this good fortune couldn't last. The rainy season would bring floods and mire to high-water levels and make excavation impossible. Digging would be like dipping soup with a fork. But the men worked with Philippe as if they believed with him the work would withstand the flash flooding. They joined him in gazing proudly on new cuts winding like yellow arteries through the bilious green of the jungle.

The feverish activity extended northward even to Colón. Men there, also sick of inactivity and delay, made a contest of accomplishment on each coast. No sooner would a report go into Colón of another reinforcement securing an entire section of Culebra Cut than a reply would flash back of similar accomplishment on the Atlantic coast.

Imperceptibly as it might seem to an outsider, the land was cut, the trails blazed which linked a lake with a river valley. The great cedars and cypress were felled, hewn and set up as frames for yet another canal-wall reinforcement.

It seemed to Philippe that the world outside this primitive, sun-blasted area no longer existed. The French went to war with Madagascar. They declared protectorate rights over Annam and Tonkin in Indo-China. This was news without reality. A man named Maxim invented an automatic machine gun; death was now available in wholesale lots. Servia invaded Bulgaria. Great Britain conquered Burma. Pasteur discovered a cure for hydrophobia. But as yet the most learned medical men had no answers for the "vapors" and "bad night air" believed responsible for epidemic yellow fever and malaria in low countries and swampy regions. Events from outside were remote, like messages from another, not very vital planet in some more fortunate galaxy.

His letters to Madelon were ragged exhausted scraps, and yet, though there were no answers, he never stopped writing. But by the time he sagged into a chair before a lamp-lit table to write, Clee already snored on his canvas cot, the camp lay quiet, and Philippe's own mind spun with fatigue. He slumped, hardly able to concentrate or to coordinate his hand to move his pen.

A month-old newspaper described the funeral of Madame Gallaudet. Present were many French notables, including the President, members of the cabinet and assembly, and foremost Vicomte de Lesseps and the outspoken young champion of the canal project, Claude-Bruce Grabralet.

Philippe sagged, overcome by a sense of depression. His eyes burned with tears, but he felt that he wept for all of them as much as for Madame Gallaudet. She had made her choices; she had lived her brief time with her loved ones. But, somehow, even the death of a beloved person in Paris was remote and lacked hard reality in the desperate jungle.

Indian drums had reality of a most harrowing kind. During the hot nights those drums battered out a restless, savage tempo which, with the hundred-degree heat, the ticks and mosquitoes, made the night eternal and sleep impossible.

Quixaltan and his Darien tribesmen were seldom visible, in the jungle or in the settlements along the river, but his frantic drums were constant and nagging reminders that he was out there. Now, every night was fraught with the threat of Indian attacks, of looting, murder or mindless arson. There was the total lack of peace and the continual menace Quixaltan had promised them.

Philippe walked into the settlement saloon and bought beer for everybody when news came over the wires that fourteen shiploads of machinery were due momentarily in Colón.

After the celebration, he bathed, scrubbing off the soil and sweat and stink of Culebra Cut. Standing in the shower, he was surprised to find how thin his arms were. It was like soaping the chest and belly of a stranger, he'd lost so much weight. His pectoral muscles were wirelike cords. The flesh was being sucked dry from his bones by the tropical sun. He grinned, thinking how his mother would react to his weight loss and the sun-blackened flesh of his face and body.

With Clee decked out in his best and looking forward urgently to a visit with the whores of Colón, they boarded the coastbound train. Philippe sat at the open window and watched the strange green land race past. Cinders stung his face. He looked forward to cutting any bureaucratic red tape that would delay their being allotted freight cars and men to load the new equipment. He had momentum. He was moving forward now and god-damned if they were going to stop him!

When the train was within five miles of Colón, it was halted and stood puffing impotently on the tracks. All children, women, the aged, infirm and any who preferred to leave the train, were removed. The men who remained were warned of trouble in the city. Military personnel went through the cars issuing rifles to the passengers. "A native revolt—against the French Canal Company and the Colombian Government," Philippe was told.

The train crept along the tracks into the outskirts of the seaport. The passengers could see the burning city from the hills long before they descended the long incline down onto the coastal plain.

By the time the train faltered into town and the armed passengers were permitted to leave the coaches, gunfire was only sporadic in the streets where pockets of snipers and resisters were hidden.

The town of Colón was a frenzied hell as it crumbled into its own fiery grave. Morality and laws were so precarious that there was no stability even among the leaders themselves. The central government at Bogotá was fearful to trust its own generals in Panama City with armed troops. In the chaos any ambitious man might generate and ignite a *coup* overnight. A trusted ally could become an implacable enemy as the wind changed.

No one knew who was responsible for this latest insurrection—only that it blossomed like some poisonous nightflower, destroying everything it touched. Orange flame blazed against the roof of heaven, screened by a shrouding pall of gray smoke. All over the city, great inverted funnels of smoke spewed the guts of the civilized town into the darkness.

Philippe broke into a run, with Clee close behind him, toward the offices of the Canal Company on the piers in the habor. The streets were ablaze as they trotted through them; it seemed that the uniformed army had restored some semblance of order. Whose order? God only knew, and Philippe didn't give a damn at the moment, because the docks were burning furiously, each separate blaze feeding on another, sparking another, growing and spreading, reflected like a pool of hell in the bay. From the materials and buildings along the wharves towering clouds of fire and sparks shot upward. Colón was burning to the ground and its piers were spilling into the harbor.

All through the night, Philippe and the others of the Company stood helplessly and watched the burning wharves crumple and topple into the crimson bay, filling it with blackened flotsam. Lost in the floating debris were his last hopes of unloading fourteen shiploads of vital machinery and equipment. The Canal Company building must have been a priority target of the insurrectionists; it had gone first. The dry wood erupted, into a thousand grasping red fingers clutching futilely toward the serene clouds and the moon winking playfully beyond. Plans, designs, surveys, drafts, payrolls, everything gone. Some of the men wept. Some cursed. Some were too deeply affected for any words they knew. They simply stood slumped, staring silently, watching the destruction.

Philippe stared with tear-brimmed eyes at the holocaust. His body was wracked by a growing sense of outrage. These people had started this, all of it, the gunfire and the arson, the pillaging and looting, the raping and killing. And what in God's name were they fighting against?

Raging, his hands tightened on the rifle. He wished he might stride through these streets with Mr. Maxim's newly invented automatic machine gun, shooting people indiscriminately. No, not with bullets, with brains, a little common sense that would show them they were fighting progress that might have yanked them from primitive savagery and ignorance into the nineteenth century. The stupid fools!

He watched the drunken looters running happily through the streets. He saw old fires sputter out and new ones flare up because the rioters didn't want the excitement to end.

He could see the ships standing offshore. Ships that could not approach the ruined wharves. Machinery. Equipment. Supplies. New engineering recruits. West Indian laborers. Irish workers. Chinese. Everything brought to a flaming halt by Ogoun Feraille, the voodoo god of war.

Philippe heard his name spoken very softly behind him and he turned to see Guido De Blasio, smoke-blackened, fire-scorched, but grinning.

"Guido!"

Guido caught him in his arms, kissing his cheeks. "Philippe! I knew you'd arrange a warm welcome for me, old man, but *mon dieu,* isn't this a trace ridiculous?"

[34]

Ducrot Bazaine set up temporary offices the next morning
at his home in the French section above the charred and
ruined city.

Walking up the twisting street toward those white
company-built cottages, Philippe swore. "Why is it," he
asked De Blasio, "that disadvantaged people—when they
do riot—destroy their own areas instead of striking first
at the rich, the people they hate?"

"Hell, don't ask me. I'm an engineer, not a mind-
reader," Guido said. He shrugged. The morning sun
blazed intolerably hot and he mopped sweat from his
dark face. "Hell, how should I know? I'm burning up.
Are you sure I don't have yellow jack?"

Philippe laughed, despite his overwhelming sense of
depression. "Don't tell me you've never been in heat like
this before?"

"Heat, yes. I've spent most of my adult life in heat.
But this, *mon cher,* is not heat. It is living inside a steam
bath, or else I'm already dying of malaria."

"Stop bellyaching. We need all our best mental capacity when we get in to see Bazaine. He obstructs on
principle. We must be prepared for him."

264

"Why do you fear this Bazaine? He's on our side, isn't he?"

Philippe laughed and spread his hands. "I'll let you decide that."

Armed soldiers met them at the entrance to the French settlement. They held their rifles at the ready and refused to let Philippe and De Blasio pass. "This area is closed, señores. Come back *mañana.*"

"We're already here," Philippe said. "We have important business here."

"This area is closed, señor, except to those who live up here. If you live up here, let's see your pass."

Guido stared at the guard. "Hell, I wouldn't live in these houses, *muchacho.* But I am thinking of buying them, as rent-free homes for the brave soldiers who defended this city, their families, and families of homeless refugees. Now, put away those rifles or I'll personally see to it that none of you men—or your families—are permitted to move in up here."

Guido's simultaneous promise and threat brought immediate and favorable results. The captain of the guards sent an armed escort to convey them to the home of the chief of engineers.

Once inside the Bazaine cottage, they were stopped in the foyer by a male secretary. The chief engineer was engaged in making a full report of the disaster for release to Paris. There was no chance to see Monsieur Bazaine within the week.

Philippe swore, and loudly. The sound of his voice brought Madame Bazaine to one of the inner doors. She hesitated a moment, staring at Philippe as if he were a vagrant or a rioter from the streets, and then she retreated. Philippe heard Guido whistle under his breath. *"Mon dieu,* such a fantastic creature! Give me one night in her bed, and I'll die happily, victim even of yellow fever."

"Listen to me." Philippe spoke to the secretary, but his voice was pitched to penetrate every wall, to rattle dishes in the cabinets, pictures in their frames. "We've got fourteen shiploads of equipment anchored in that bay out there. We want men to build pontoon docks for unloading those ships. You tell Bazaine we get it, or he'll have a report for de Lesseps that will singe the old man's beard."

"Well said." Guido nodded approvingly. "Now we can catch the next ship out of this pesthole."

Philippe's raging produced the desired results. The door to the study was thrown open and Bazaine bolted through it like an embattled rooster from its perch. He was followed at a more leisurely pace by half a dozen other senior company officers.

Bazaine stared at Philippe, his face purple, his hands shaking. "You—how in hell did you get in here?"

"That's a question I've been waiting to ask you, sir, since the day we met," Philippe said. "I hate like hell to disturb your reporting to Paris. But I can correct part of this disaster if you'll give me men and authority to build a temporary dock of pontoons."

"Impossible. We are busy here on important, upper-level matters."

"What could be more important than trying to save what we've got?" Philippe advanced. "What's more important than fourteen shiploads of equipment with no place to unload?"

Bazaine shrugged. "One day, perhaps, *m'sieu,* you'll learn that each matter is handled in its turn. Now, if you'll excuse me?"

Philippe looked as if he would physically restrain the little man from leaving the crowded foyer. "No. I won't excuse you. We need men. We need authority to commandeer boats, barrels, anything that floats to build a pontoon dock, and then we need every able-bodied laborer in the company to move that equipment to wagons and then to flatcars and freight cars. We don't need it next week or next month. We need it now."

Bazaine ignored everything Philippe had said. He spoke to his secretary. "Réné, if this person does not leave at once, I want you to call the guard and have him thrown out."

Guido spoke in a sarcastic tone of mock servility. "Does this mean you are refusing to let us unload this equipment?"

Bazaine had turned toward the inner office. Now he

266

turned his heels, his face contorted. "Who the hell are you, *m'sieu*?"

"I was another one of your malcontented employees until this moment," De Blasio said. "But I quit. I wouldn't work for such a stupid son of a bitch, even if the pay were good."

Bazaine's face flushed. Then he waved his arm. "Réné, show the gentlemen out."

"Yes, Réné," Philippe said. "Why don't you do that?"

The white-faced secretary looked as if he might vomit.

Bazaine stopped in the doorway of his study. He said, *"M'sieu* Bunau-Varilla, the senior officers of this company are well aware from my reports of your insubordination. This is more than I'll tolerate. I warn you to leave now, quietly. I suggest you await the decision of this conference at Culebra Cut."

"Just a moment, gentlemen."

Philippe's eyes widened. He stared at Monsieur Gallaudet. He hadn't even heard that the director-general had returned from Paris. He had believed that the aging man might retire without making the long ocean voyage. The best Philippe could say now was that Monsieur Gallaudet looked as if he had surrendered unconditionally to his implacable foe, age. There was nothing left in the tall man's graying face; he had nothing left to live for. He had sacrificed a wife, two children and his own health to this canal project.

Gallaudet stepped around Bazaine. Without smiling, he handed Philippe an order hastily scribbled on Company letterhead. He spoke in a gently droll way. "I couldn't help overhearing your request, *M'sieu* Bunau-Varilla. This paper will authorize you to use whatever men and equipment you need to transport the goods from ship to worksite. I'm sure Chief Engineer Bazaine will support my decision."

Their shirts stripped away, Philippe and De Blasio joined Snelling, Korvache and dozens of other engineers who found devising a workable pontoon dock a challenge they couldn't resist. By the following morning, after a night in which no one slept, the first ship was brought

alongside the makeshift wharf and cranes began trans-
ferring cargo. Philippe and De Blasio had spent most of
the first day grinning at each other because they'd managed another victory over the bureaucracy. By dawn, they
were laughing, and their fatigued laughter was tinged with
traces of hysteria.

It was an endless time. For 48 continuous hours there
was a constant stream of Negroes passing crates and
bundles of materials from pontoons to wagons. The
wagons rumbled through the plundered streets to the rail
freight yards. The black men worked steadily, their clothing sticking to their skins, their blue-black faces glistening
in the blazing sunlight.

The fourteenth ship was finally towed into place by
exhausted laborers rowing whale boats. It was tied up and
unloading begun. Philippe felt the backs of his legs
quivering and he was afraid he was going to fall. He
leaned against an old crate. He'd had a total of two hours'
restless sleep since the unloading had begun. He did not
feel mentally fatigued but he knew all his energy had
come from excitement. They had confronted the type of
problem which, in the past four years, had always disrupted their efforts. They had solved it. The first train-
loads of equipment were already crossing the isthmus
toward the Cut.

Through a haze of exhaustion he saw Clee striding
toward him. The boy wore new boots and a fresh white
suit. Clee said, *"M'sieu* Bazaine sent word to the hotel,
m'sieu. Even if you were asleep, he said I was to wake
you. They wish you at his office, without delay."

He found Bazaine alone in his study with Monsieur
Gallaudet. Bazaine did not ask him to sit down. He said
without preamble, *"M'sieu* Gallaudet has something he
wishes to say to you, *m'sieu."*

Philippe smiled toward the tired and aging Director-
General.

"I'm being forced to return to Paris, Philippe," Monsieur Gallaudet said. "There is no point in concealing
from you the reason. I must plead with the Company for
additional financing. You know we are in desperate

268

straits here. I may as well confess that the Company is on the brink of disaster in Paris."

"We mustn't give up," Philippe said. "There is a desperate need for this canal. It can be built. It will repay all costs, many times over. We must not stop."

"I don't know," Gallaudet said. "I have no answers, my boy. Only questions, just as you have. I'll ask those questions in Paris. But I tell you frankly, I fear for the answers we'll get. We are bitterly opposed. In the highest places. Meantime, someone must be left here—responsible for this project—in my place."

Philippe glanced toward Bazaine and winced. He dreaded to think of his own future chances of getting anything done with Gallaudet gone from the isthmus. He wanted to blurt out to the director-general that they might as well close down as to leave Ducrot Bazaine in charge. He held his breath and said nothing.

"Ducrot Bazaine will remain in his present position as chief engineer," Gallaudet said.

"What?" The word burst across Bazaine's lips.

"I thought we understood that, Ducrot," Gallaudet said.

"My understanding was that I would replace you."

"I'm sorry, Ducrot. Because I never said that. I never implied it, or suggested it. Perhaps you expected to hear it, and thus thought you did."

Ducrot's voice shook. "Of course I expected to hear it. Who better than I to be left here as acting director-general?"

"No, Ducrot. I'm designating Philippe Bunau-Varilla as acting director-general with full authority in all matters."

Bazaine stood up. He was white-faced. "You won't get away with it, Gallaudet. I have friends in high placcs. They already oppose you and the company. Why, I could ruin you. I warn you. Don't make this mistake. I am Vicomte Ducrot Bazaine. You can't insult me in this intolerable manner. You cannot ask me to work under a young, trouble-making, headstrong engineer. No. I'll confront you before the officers of the Company. I'll leave Colón on the first ship. I'll fight you in Paris. If you think you can insult me like this, you may have my resignation as of this moment."

Gallaudet exhaled heavily. "Then I accept it with regret, Ducrot. From my first day with the Company, I have done what I believed best. My last act has conformed to that policy. Yet I do regret your decision."

"You haven't yet begun to appreciate the depth of your regret, *m'sieu,*" Bazaine said. "Do you know that this man made improper advances toward my wife, that he attempted to rape her? Is this the man you are placing in charge of this operation? What will a scandal of these proportions do to the Company in its present precarious financial condition? Do you want to sink this company? Go ahead. Elevate this rogue, this rapist above me, and see what happens to you, and to him and to this Company."

Gallaudet remained outwardly unmoved. His voice remained grave and low. "I have made my decision. However, I am not one to leave loose ends. If you insist upon making charges, which could indeed create a scandal in Paris, I demand that you call Madame Bazaine into this room and let her make her charges to Philippe's face. Now."

Bazaine's face was rigid. He sent his secretary to fetch Madame Bazaine. The study was deathly silent until she walked in and the secretary closed the door behind her.

When Madame Bazaine saw Philippe, she stopped as if in a catatonic trance. Her eyes moved from Philippe to her husband and back again to Philippe.

Gallaudet's voice was gentle. "Madame, you know my great love and regard for you. I would spare you any pain. But it has been charged that Philippe Bunau-Varilla made improper, uncouth advances toward you, that he attempted to rape you. I will not pry. I will not persist. But I ask you to be kind enough merely to say where these attacks occurred. Nothing more. I would not think of asking you more than that."

Philippe watched her. He could not believe a woman could be so lovely, so damnably desirable even when viewed from the brink of ruin.

Madame stared straight ahead. She only shook her head. She stood there shaking her head.

Bazaine raged. "Tell them! Tell them! As you told me!"

She did not look at her husband. She only shook her head. Bazaine cursed her. He ran toward her, his hand raised in a fist. She only stood silent, unmoving, as if staring through him. Infrequently she shook her head negatively from side to side.

Philippe watched Bazaine wither before their eyes. He supposed his own hatred had blinded him to the truth about Bazaine before. The high-handed little son of a bitch hid his deep inner terror of being exposed behind that swaggering facade. Bazaine lacked self-confidence because he knew better than anyone else that he lacked ordinary competence, because he fully comprehended his inner deficiencies, because he had to compensate for his superficiality through intolerant hauteur. He was a Bazaine, and that was all he was. Seeing the overweening little bastard stripped of affectation and vanity, one could almost feel pity for that craven hulk who had traded on rank, status and pretension. He was not the first incompetent to trade on degrees, family name, brass balls and amoral trickery to climb to power; he sure as hell would not be the last.

At the moment he happened to be only the most pitiable of the species.

[35]

In the hectic days ahead, Philippe and De Blasio found little time to recall their adventures in Algeria and Tunis. There seemed less and less time for regular meals, adequate rest, or relaxation. This was a different world, a hot, sweaty world where ruin could come unexpectedly from jungle, sea or sky.

De Blasio's first tour of the proposed canal route convinced him that a sea-level canal in this rugged, wild and uncontrollable terrain was not feasible. He said that building canal locks was the only answer to their problem. This agreed precisely with what Philippe had believed for months but had pragmatically refrained from advancing to Bazaine as a viable plan. Now, that obstruction was removed. Mortar, brick, stone and cement-reinforced channels, through which vessels could be propelled or towed, would solve many of the problems created by attempting to utilize natural riverbeds, lakes and valleys for the channel. Dams would not only provide facilities for changing water levels, but would act as safety valves during flooding seasons. Ships could be lowered or brought up from one level to another.

They spent hours discussing the possibility of locks, the

way they'd been used in water navigation throughout recorded history. Often their dialogues ended only when De Blasio passed out from liquor or fell asleep listening and nodding.

Though Philippe had no time to laugh with De Blasio, Guido and young Clee hit it off well. De Blasio loved to hear the ex-pimp's wild tales of adventures with the *putas de Colón.* Clee could talk by the hour. De Blasio was content to rock, to drink, to listen and to throw his head back, raging with laughter. "I don't believe a god-damn thing you say, kid. On the other hand, nobody could make up fucking stories like those!"

Clee's adventures among the yellow jack victims—the stricken, the dying and the dead—filled De Blasio with a terror that anyone could read in his dark face. Philippe had seen enough of Bronze John's victims to know how vile and violent yellow fever death could be, but Clee's descriptions piled horror upon horror—until De Blasio would escape, by staggering from the house, or plunging into drink.

The third day after Bazaine departed from Colón for Paris, Philippe called his first staff meeting. It was the hour of the beginning of the local *siesta,* a routine which most of the newcomers had adopted, but Philippe did not believe he had the time to waste.

The men gathered in the makeshift hall, yawning and muttering, some even suggesting that this had better be a beer bust, a stag party or something else worthwhile, like a pay raise.

Philippe's talk was brief. The machinery was safely ashore, the equipment on its way to work sites. The Colombian government was providing the materials, the Company the labor to repair the wharves in the harbor. Work was being rushed to beat the rain season. He invited suggestions, criticisms, or questions from the engineers. "Old ideas, old methods, old answers have not worked here in Panama," he said. "If you have a new idea, no matter if it is so outlandish you're ashamed to put it in words, bring it to us! If we can, we'll make it work. All we know for sure is that old, tried methods have failed here. We were hired and sent here to find

273

ways to build a navigable canal against incredible odds, not to send back to Paris reports on why we cannot beat those odds or finish our job."

Most of the young men went on yawning, but at least they listened. "My most important announcement is one of excavation goals. Our former goal of fifty million cubic yards per month—"

"Was impossible of accomplishment," someone said and rueful laughter greeted this truth.

Philippe nodded. "That's why I'm setting a new quota. One that is entirely reasonable with the new and heavier equipment we now have and the even heavier machinery which we will be getting down here in the next few months. My new quota is for one hundred million cubic yards of excavation per month. By achieving that quota, we can reclaim much lost time, we can cut long-term costs, we can get ahead of natural disasters which have always wiped out smaller excavations in the past."

Several engineers grumbled aloud. "You're dreaming. Or feverish."

"Not even Bazaine made such demands. As long as we could offer explanations why we couldn't meet the fifty million cubic yard total, he was satisfied."

"Bazaine is in Paris," Philippe said. "Anyone content to work Bazaine's way may join him there."

Korvache laughed. "You've got to start getting more sleep, old man."

"We'll all sleep better when we're digging a hundred million cubic yards," Philippe persisted.

Snelling said, "I think I should remind you, old man, that de Lessep's people took only 75 million cubic yards out a month in Suez, which was a remarkable achievement, and was accomplished under conditions close to heavenly compared with those we enjoy in this jungle sweatbox."

Philippe's voice was hoarse with exhaustion. "I don't want to sound like my immediate predecessor, but I don't want to hear *why* you can't reach your quota. I do welcome ways on *how* to do it."

"So would we all," Snelling said. "Who are we to bitch to, if you won't listen to us any more?"

Philippe nodded. "I'm naming Guido De Blasio chief engineer on this project. He'll hear your bitching as long as your report includes a reasonable effort to meet your quota. God knows I haven't set this goal arbitrarily. It can be done! Old Von Weiler exceeded that quota out at Gold Hill against the rottenest kind of limestone cave-ins."

He paused a moment, but they sat silently. He said, "The Assembly, the government, the financiers are threatening to shut us down. There is only one way we can keep going and that's by showing them we know what we're doing, we know how to do it, and we shall do it."

"I haven't heard a pep talk like this since I left the rugby fields at Eton," Snelling said. "And the god's truth is, those pep talks are the reason I left."

But the engineers were grinning, joking and bitching aloud when they left the meeting room. To the exhausted Philippe this was a favorable omen. They all wanted the same thing, completion of the canal. It was the problem they hated, not him, not each other, not the project.

When the men left the meeting room they walked out into an early afternoon thunderstorm. It was important for only one reason; it was the first of the season. It was not yet May, but the huge, fat-bellied clouds hovered over the isthmus and spilled tons of water within days. It put added urgency in everything Philippe did. He was now fighting time, too.

There was always too much to do. A problem on the Pacific coast which could not be postponed. Only one thing helped. De Blasio was at his side eighteen hours a day. Because of De Blasio, he found himself less driven. When he had to travel, De Blasio accompanied him. De Blasio saw that all Philippe's errands, orders and inspections were implemented. How many orders De Blasio barked without asking anyone, Philippe never knew, or cared. How many people with how many problems were kept out of Philippe's ken by De Blasio, he would never even inquire. He trusted Guido totally and this was all that mattered.

His energies and time were spared for problems of construction and new equipment. Philippe believed that electric power, generated from the Chagres River valley, could greatly improve operations on the canal. He submitted plans for such a plant, worked out with the aid of electrical engineers. He designed an electric dredge which was capable of greatly increased speeds and exceptional economy of operation. He stood over the draftsmen until the specifications for the electric dredge were completed and sent to Paris. Then he heard nothing more about it.

His first victory was in building his gang raft for the dynamite crews. He ordered the rafts constructed at once, huge floating rectangles of logs and watertight barrels. Scores of men could be transported by use of a small steam engine. Workers, engineers, officials and natives stood on the river banks and hooted the first time the heavily loaded raft puffed by, but efficiency increased a hundredfold on rivers and lakes.

Excavations increased in every section. Ever-larger excavators were barged in, assembled on site and set in place along the line in record time. The engineers with whom he worked were a special breed, proud of their renown, and as anxious as he to succeed. Freed to use their imaginations and creative skills, they invented hundreds of ways to improve efficiency, cut costs and speed construction. They learned as they labored. They improvised when old methods failed them.

The contract firms were pleased to test any engineering innovation. Most contractors had come to Panama like adventurers to a gold rush, to make a quick killing. Most were losing their shirts. They found Bunau-Varilla easy to work with, anxious to help them produce and quick to search out new ways to solve old problems.

The air crackled with a new enthusiasm and sense of accomplishment. They began to believe again in what they were doing.

Philippe set thousands of Jamaicans, West Indians and Chinese to cutting a swath four hundred feet wide, which would expose for the first time the exact route of the canal. The first engineer in control of the canal had begged to be permitted to make such a clearing, but he had been constricted to a strip of only fifty feet in width. This was inadequate and was abandoned. Now the crooked line of open space took shape from Colón south.

This project proved to be one of extreme danger. The crews crossed the rushing Chagres River more than twenty times. In rain forests thick with foliage, matted vines, and huge trees, the crews worked only with axes, machetes and dynamite. Poisonous snakes slithered everywhere in that massed undergrowth, dripped from trees like parasitic flowers. Workers lived in terror—they often could see only a few yards in any direction. They charged forward, yelling, singing, swearing, shouting, in waves, against the green citadel.

By May the canal route had been cleared from Colón to Panama City.

Colón came alive with rushing freight wagons, workers, dockhands unloading ships, mechanics assembling equipment and machines. Crates of new materials and supplies reared higher than the buildings along Front Street.

With twenty thousand employees at work—three-quarters of them black—Philippe's responsibilities were unending. He built veranda-type quarters on stilts for the laborers at Matachin, San Pablo and Gatun, putting the laborers out of reach of floods and rats.

The tempo of activity increased a thousandfold under Philippe's direction. The faster the pace of work, the more relentlessly Philippe was driven to stay ahead of the problems. There was real accomplishment, but there were always new, unforeseen obstructions. The constant threat of storms, which would undo everything accomplished, hung over the isthmus in gathering clouds. He set thousands of men to work shoring up every foot of excavation gouged out along the line. Natural waterways were diverted, dammed, or rechanneled.

One thing kept Philippe going without rest. The company and the world would now see where the project was aimed, how that mammoth task could be completed. He was sleepless night after night, and even when he finally fell across the bed exhausted, his mind churned.

He existed in a state of fatigue, his mind turned inward upon problems swarming like angry bees. As workers died, he was charged with finding replacements. He estimated that of every hundred new arrivals, at least twenty died. Many were rendered too ill to work. In addition to labor, he was obligated to furnish equipment and adequate housing for the contractors. Any failure to provide men or machinery gave a contractor reason for breaking his contract.

Culebra Cut remained a hell-spot. Though Von Weiler worked with huge shovels and was contracted to remove seven hundred thousand cubic meters a month, his crews managed less than one-seventh of this. Korvache reported that he had fired a young engineer of great promise for talking in saloons about the imminent financial collapse of the Canal Company. Workers were frightened, dissatisfied, unsure they would be paid. Contractors demanded cash at every transaction.

They hung on by their fingernails. But it was never easy. Equipment ordered came late or never arrived at all. Machinery and men were lost in a tragic accident near Mendoza. Philippe fought and scrounged to meet company obligations but De Blasio was continually critical of the corporate officials in Paris.

"There is only one kind of canal that will ever be successful in this hellish terrain," De Blasio raged. He chewed his cigar, striding up and down in Philippe's office. "That has to be a lock-type canal. Even those stupid bastards in Paris should be able to see that." He slapped at the proposed route map with a ruler. "Look. There. There. There. At the exit of Gatun Lake. At Miraflores. In the Cut where the canal must either be a series of dams or excavated to a depth that lacks all relation to reason. If they're too pigheaded stupid to see this in Paris, then they deserve to fail. If we're smart, we'll sit on our asses, somewhere Bronze John can't find us, and help them fail. It would be our greatest service to them."

"You think I don't want to quit sometimes? But you know I can't."

"The hell you can't."

"No more than you can."

"Oh, I could quit. Just say the word and I fall over on my back and live off Panama Passions."

"Panama Passions?"

"Quinine and wine. You drink it against malaria, against

thinking, against de Lesseps and the Canal Company. Against God Himself. And it works. Your stomach churns, your head spins, your ears ring like a million bells, and you finally have the Panama Passion. You no longer give a shit."

Philippe put his head back laughing. "I don't know what I'd do without you, Guido."

"Don't you? You just stick around on this doomed job, with no help at all from Paris, and by God you'll find out what you can do without me."

Though Philippe received no encouragement from Paris for his canal-lock suggestions, he and De Blasio continued, in whatever spare moments they could arrange, to work on such plans.

The storms broke, bringing floods of sudden ferocity in the middle of sunlit days. Men, materials, and equipment were washed clean as work was paralyzed. Reports of disaster came from every direction. Philippe strode along the line, along the brinks of rivers, watching the land slough off, carrying his equipment with it. He ordered everything lashed down.

Days and nights were without meaning. He remembered neither eating nor sleeping. When at last he was half-carried into the cottage where he had once lived with Madelon he found De Blasio passed out in a rocking chair. Clee snored on a canvas cot and Burns and Snelling lay sprawled across a bed.

De Blasio sat up yawning and eyed Philippe coldly. "Anybody ever tell you you've got to learn to rest? Your own body begins to hate you. You push it too hard. One day it pushes back. It simply refuses to function."

Philippe shrugged. Always he'd felt driven by forces outside himself; he had something to accomplish, something he did not even understand. The drive to achieve had been far more intense on this project. He remembered he'd been warned long ago—while still a student at the Ecole Polytechnique—that he was tamping down worries, fatigue, frustrations that one day would have to be dealt with. The hell with it! He wasn't even 26 yet, and as healthy as a horse. Sure, he'd lost weight. Who wouldn't, living in God's own steambath? "You sound like an old maid," he told De Blasio.

De Blasio cursed him sharply, turned up a bottle, took a long drink and sank back, as if stunned, in the chair, instantly asleep. Philippe grinned. How he wished he had Guido's gift for relaxing.

Philippe sat at the bare dining-room table. He turned up a lamp. He found paper, ink, a pen. He shook his head to clear it but cringed against a violent ringing in his ears, as if from an overdose of quinine. He shuddered, dizzy, nauseated in the pit of his stomach. He wanted to vomit, but could not. He tried by conscious will to force his sickness from his mind. He wrote scratchingly, "My dearest Madelon. . . . " The pen fell from his hand and he collapsed, his face flat on the table.

[36]

Philippe awakened in the hospital at Colón. He sprawled in a narrow white bed between windows, in a room with three other men. He was unaware of it—he was only vaguely aware of anything—but the men changed every two or three days. An occupant of a bed died, he was carted away, a priest murmuring last rites, and in a few hours a new fever victim was shunted into his place.

Philippe alternated between waking fever, and restless sleep. He wakened to blinding flashes of lightning and simultaneous blasts of thunder that shook the building to its foundations. He slept to the staccato tattoo of rain upon the roofing, louder than a freight train roaring through an interminable tunnel. When awake he stared at the opaque sheeting of gray rain against the windows. His dreams were fevered and frantic, his sleep haunted by unnamable terrors.

He retained an image of De Blasio's terrorized face. Whether it was reality or hallucination he could not say. De Blasio stood over him and gazed in abject agony at Philippe's face, contorted and livid with fever. He held himself rigid, barely breathing, afraid to touch or to be touched. It was like running a cruel gauntlet. He could force himself through it only once. He did not come back.

Guido admitted he had attempted to book passage out but had been too late and had failed. He stayed drunk, drinking on the job, during meals, and until he fell asleep at night. All he could say was that he and the swarming mosquitoes drinking his alcoholic blood were the happiest beings in this pestilent place.

"Work?" he answered Philippe's whispered question. "What work? Hell, work's stopped. But, what the hell, we're using our big shovels to gouge out communal grave-slits where they dump the dead. Then our big tractors cover them over as some priest says wholesale mass. No one can say the Company is not contributing to this place. We're burying its dead."

When De Blasio and Clee were gone, Philippe thrashed about on the bed, his mind spinning: work stoppage on the canal, growing cries against the project·in Paris, and he lying helpless. When he fought to get out of bed, huge black orderlies caught and restrained him. He fell back sobbing and sank at last into fevered sleep. Nothing was clear after that.

Though Philippe didn't know it, Panama—the entire neck of land from Mexico south—was in the grip of epidemic. Yellow jack, malaria victims stumbled in delirious fever, fell in their own vomit on the streets. People around them fled, retreating in numb horror. The isthmus seethed with panic. They'd all lived through epidemics, but this was no reassurance; it was another source of terror. Bronze John got you, sooner or later, and before you died, you turned bronze. You resembled your killer. Those few wealthy enough to escape bartered and bid against each other for the right to board any ship sailing from Colón harbor—bound anywhere to escape the pestilence. And then, as news of the plague leaked out—it was too horrendous to be concealed—boats shunned the port. Colón was cut off from all outside sea lanes.

Town and countryside existed in a state of terrorized paralysis. Huge bonfires burned all night to "dry out" the "poisonous night vapors," to heat the "bad air" rising from stagnant and stinking swamps. In the steaming humidity people slept in air-tight rooms, windows nailed shut against the fatal "night swamp breath." They refused to open their doors to anyone after dark, lest a breath of the pestilent vapors intrude. People died in the streets. Others, attempting to flee the contagion of the city, perished in their own black vomitus along jungle trails. The most devout, damp with holy water and weak from prayer, screamed out in delirium for God's help as blood leaked from their nostrils and ran from their eyelids.

Tumbrels, carts ordinarily used to transport manure, now rumbled through streets collecting bodies of those who had died during the night. Those who could force the hospital to admit them were jammed into beds that filled wards and corridors. They died on mattresses rather than in the streets; their deaths were no less agonized. They were injected with ineffectual potions, fed debilitating cathartics. They were bled, purged, ignored. And they died.

Each morning, frightened Negroes scrubbed down the hospital floors and walls with barrels of salt water and foul-smelling disinfectants. The odor of death hung over the hospital. Finally, Indian medicine men and the West Indian voodoo priests were consulted. Strange incantations rolled like evening vespers through the halls. Burning leaves, roots, herbs, in fearful mixtures, were stewed and stirred into vile concoctions and forced down the throats of the infected. The best that could be said for this program was that the dying were happy to escape into death.

New nightmares obsessed Philippe, unlike anything he'd endured before.

He was being lifted from his hospital cot. Pain radiated out everywhere a hand touched his fevered skin. Even the roots of his hair ached. His eyes throbbed and burned in their dry sockets.

Then, he was conscious of movement, the rattle of wagon wheels on rough streets. Name of God! They thought he was dead! They were carting him off to one of those burial grounds.

He writhed, trying to cry out, but if he uttered any sounds, no one heard him; if they heard him, they ignored him.

283

Jesus. Maybe he was dead. Maybe this was death. This faint, final consciousness of an unreachable reality, of the essence without the materiality of living.

But these intense spasms of pain lancing through his body, these waves of agony shooting against his skull. Did pain follow you beyond death?

No. He was alive. But these people had abandoned him to the dead. They were burying him, rumbling him along the street to a common grave, just to be rid of him. But he couldn't let go like this. There was so much he'd left undone, so much he regretted, so much he needed. He had never even seen his own son. And Madelon. Dying would be easier if he could see Madelon's face one last time. He would ask nothing of her, not even forgiveness, but he did need so desperately just to see her. They couldn't just throw him in a hasty ditch and push the wet and slimy mud over him. Not yet. Not yet.

He struggled, but he was unable to move.

Then the wagon had stopped. Clop of hooves against cobbles, rattle of metal and leather, clatter of wheels no longer reverberated inside his head.

Everything was strangely, ominously silent. The room was cool. He was lying on a bed. The mattress was soft, though painful against his sensitive skin.

He kept seeing Madelon's face bending close over his. More hallucination. It was as if someone flashed a light blindingly into his eyes for an instant. A halo burst outward in the painful afterglow. Either he was dead and an angel from beyond emerged from the blinding glow, or. . . .

Madelon bent closely over him. She was trying to tell him something, but he could not hear her through the thunder inside his head. Those flashes of light were too brief, too quickly gone. Her face was there—it was truly there!—and then she dissolved in the darkness. He cried out.

Then, when he did see her bending close, touching his cheek with the backs of her gentle fingers, he shook his head in terror. It must be hallucination. It must not be Madelon in this pestilent hole.

She came close, with cloths to soothe his fever. He, pleaded with her to get out, get away to Paris, outrun Bronze John. . . .

He sagged into exhausted sleep. Moonlight ebbed from the room. Almost instantly, the sun flared through slatted window blinds, like lances impaling his irises.

He opened his eyes, blinked against the savage glare— a glare in which Madelon's lovely face appeared like a mirage inside a painful halo. Beyond her, he saw the walls, the paintings, the familiar furnishings of the cottage they'd shared here in Colón.

"No!" Philippe wailed, shaking his head from side to side.

He struggled to get up but gentle hands restrained him—Madelon's gentle hands. She was here, in this pestilent hole. "You must get away," he whispered. "In the name of God, Madelon, get away."

She brushed his forehead lightly with her lips. Her voice was odd, distant through the fevered ringing in his ears. "Don't be afraid for me, Philippe. Get well. Please. Hurry and get well. I do love you so."

[37]

The touch of her hand was restorative. The vision of her face reached deep inside him and found a will to live. Her gentle kiss *inspired* him, even in the fevered night world where he wandered. Her kisses were reason to recover.

The pain of every spoken word echoed in his skull, exploding like screams in an empty rainbarrel. Yet he lived for her whispered endearments.

He *would* live. He would get well. The odds favoring Bronze John were 99 to one. That one chance was all he asked. There was no known cure for yellow fever. But he had the inspiration of Madelon's presence and Madelon's love. He *would* recover.

A hundred times in the long night the intolerable fire of fever drove him to the brink of madness. He found himself locked inside the prison of his own mind and set upon by his enemies. They flew at him like vultures and he was helpless against them. In ear-splitting voices, they accused him of unspeakable crimes. They sentenced him to death. They would not suffer a defense. He rolled, tossed, burned and shriveled with fever.

In the early morning, in the deep darkness before dawn,

death came in on the mists and tugged at him, drawing him toward the peace and promise of empty, infinite silence without pain.

"Madelon," he whispered. "Please, God, let me live for Madelon." The fever burned higher, the madness wheeled and screeched inside his skull. But Madelon was near and he clung to life and his need for her.

Yet, when she was beside him, her face a blurred vision before his fevered eyes, he could not escape the fear he felt for her in this place.

"Are you sure you're all right?" His eyes searched her face, looking for lines, for fear, for the desperation of fatigue. "Are you sure you're happy here?"

She kissed him lightly. That odd voice soothed him. "I would be happy, if only you were well enough to love me as I love you."

His head rolled back and forth on his heated pillow. "You must get away while you can."

Her voice caressed him. "I won't go without you. When you are well we will go. You and I alone to a place only for you and me."

"And our son?"

She hesitated, then kissed him. "And our son."

He reached up, touched her face with his thin, trembling fingers, felt her tears. She pressed her face against his for a moment. Her cool cheek soothed his fever as a cloud obscures the blaze of the sun.

He needed her so, but remained terrified for her safety. Contagion. Illness. Death. "This does not matter," she whispered. "Nothing matters except we are together at last in this moment. We have this day. We have this hour."

Philippe lay for a long time staring at the overhead fan, bringing the slowly turning blades into sharp focus. His eyes burned, but his vision was clear. He no longer saw only the images of hallucination, he saw reality.

Eyes brimming with joyous tears, he stared at pictures framed on the wall, furniture placed in the remote dimness of the room, the banana trees and palms beyond his window, the sunlight glittering on the blue lawn.

He looked down at his hands. Some of his exultance

287

ebbed. Stranger's hands. Thin, quivering, clawlike fingers, wasted hands. And yet he lived.

"Madelon!"

His call echoed inside his skull and threatened to unhinge him. He pressed his fists against his temples and waited, holding his breath.

After a moment, he called again. "Myti?"

The huge woman appeared at once in the doorway. He could see her only dimly at such distance. But he recognized her, the massive breasts, the bandanna about her head.

He said, voice quavering. "I see you, Myti. I really see you. You are really there."

"Yes, *m'sieu*. Myti is here."

"And Madelon?" He stirred on the bed. "Where is Madelon? I want to see her, Myti, really to see her."

Myti smiled, a faint movement touching only at the edges of her full mouth. "In a moment, *m'sieu*. Soon.'"

He cried out. "Now, Myti. Now."

"She come to you, *m'sieu*. Soon now."

"Where is she?" He struggled against invisible fetters. "I want to see her."

"*M'sieu*." Myti's voice softened. Her eyes brimmed with tears. "I must tell you—"

"She's not ill? She hasn't caught this fever?"

"No, *m'sieu*."

"Then call her. Tell her I'm awake, Myti. Really awake." Philippe trembled visibly. His head rolled back and forth on the rumpled pillow.

"Soon. But first, *m'sieu*, certain things you must know. She has made you well. She alone has made you well."

"God in heaven, Myti. I know that."

"You have been most ill, *m'sieu*. Out of your head."

"Hallucinations." His mouth trembled and tears welled in his eyes. He sagged against the pillow and pressed the heel of his hand against his throbbing temples. "She wasn't real. I dreamed it."

"No. No, Philippe, you didn't dream it," said that odd voice which had lured him back from the brink of death.

Myti retreated and Madelon came slowly, almost reluctantly forward.

He stared, feeling as if he had plunged into nightmare again. It was not Madelon at all.

Anouk Bazaine stood beside his bed. Her eyes brimmed with tears. Her face was Easter-lily pale, drawn with fatigue. Most of all, she looked frightened.

[38]

Anouk wavered slightly. He had never seen her hair mussed before, unless she was naked. Her eyes were shadowed. She recovered her balance with a supreme effort of will.

Philippe swallowed back bitter disappointment. It was not Madelon. His visions of Madelon had been just that, hallucinatory images.

Anouk, and not Madelon, had been with him through this hellish struggle. It was Anouk's voice he'd heard and barely been able to reconcile with Madelon's face. He had seen Madelon's image because, in his illness and fever, he had wanted to see it, he had needed to see it. In her face he found a reason to fight for his life.

Philippe tried to smile. "You? An angel of mercy? You, of all people?"

Anouk smiled wanly, too exhausted to parry his taunting. "It was my fault you were sent to the Cut. My fault you lost Madelon. I love you. I couldn't stand it when I heard you were sick, maybe dying. I could not sit by and let you—die alone."

"Virtue. Self-sacrifice. Martyr. None of these words seem to fit you, Madame Bazaine."

"I suppose not."

"Still, I am alive. Thanks to you."

She shook her head. "Don't thank me too much." She glanced around, as if confused. "I was—where I wanted to be."

"In a pesthole? Taking care of a fever victim? You? The elegant lady?"

She sagged, her energies flagging. "I guess no one is more astonished than I am."

He tried to sit up, could not. "Are you all right?"

"I will be. I'm just overcome with relief about you. I'm just tired."

He gazed up at her. "I do thank you, Anouk, with all my heart."

She wavered again. "For what?"

"For staying with me. It must have been hell for you."

"I told you. I wanted to. I do only what I want to do."

"Still." He bit at his underlip. "You let me believe you were Madelon."

She shrugged. "It didn't matter what you believed. I let you believe what you wanted to believe."

He nodded. He lifted his hand to her, let it fall at his side. "Please rest. We can talk later."

Anouk drew the back of her hand across her eyes. She sighed deeply. "Yes. Maybe if I—just lie down for a little while."

She gazed at him a moment, her glassy eyes bright. She was looking at a miracle that she could not quite believe, even yet. Then she turned and walked away. She paused, glanced over her shoulder, started to speak. Abruptly, her knees buckled and she sagged wordlessly to the floor.

Philippe lunged up in bed. He almost blacked out. The room wheeled and skidded violently about his head. He gripped the mattress to steady himself. He yelled, "Myti!"

Myti came running. She knelt on the floor beside Anouk. She touched her face. Myti looked up at Philippe, her eyes stricken. She shook her head. "Fever. She's burning up with fever."

By morning, Philippe was stronger. The grotesque hollowness in his skull decreased, the constant ringing in his ears lessened. He was still too weak to get out of bed, but he no longer thought of his own illness. All his thoughts were for Anouk.

Myti came in, more withdrawn than he'd ever seen her. Philippe said, "How is Madame Bazaine?"

"She got the bone fever."

"Yellow jack?"

Myti nodded. "All the symptoms. I seen 'em all my life."

"Have you sent for the doctor?"

"No doctor would come for me, *m'sieu*."

"He'll come for me. Send Clee for Dr. Feuillet. Tell him I said at once."

Myti brightened perceptibly. He heard her speaking tensely with Clee across the house. The outer door slammed.

Myti returned. She said, "She didn't want me to tell you about her fever."

"How was she to keep it from me?"

"She think she just tired. She think she be well soon. She don't know how ill she is." Myti shook her head. "While you sick, I learn what a good woman she is. In here." Myti touched her massive breast. "She headstrong. She spoiled. But she a very brave lady. A very great lady. She stayed with you all night, every night."

Philippe nodded. "We'll do what we can. Everything we can. We'll make it up to her."

Myti seemed to be tolling beads in some private confessional. "She left her husband. Easy life. She come back here." She smiled, remembering. "She shave you every morning. So careful. Then she wax the ends of your mustache, so they stick out, so we laugh, looking at you. She live for you, to nurse you. It was her brought you here when the doctors at the hospital gave up on you."

"I swear to you, Myti. We won't give up on her."

"No, sir. We won't."

Dr. Feuillet stared at Philippe. Obviously, he had never expected to see him again in this life.

"What's wrong with you?" Philippe said.

292

"I'm amazed. I don't believe it. We gave you up for dead."

"You're not here to talk about me. Or what you could do for me. Madame Bazaine is ill."

"I've seen her. I've examined her." He spread his hands. "Yellow fever. As soon as I can, I'll send an ambulance. We'll take her to the hospital."

"No."

The doctor flinched, unable to believe the power in Philippe's voice. "Philippe? I see you alive. A miracle. But we are better prepared to make Madame Bazaine more comfortable in the hospital. In this case, we have no choice. She can't stay here."

"She will stay here. People don't go to that hospital to get well. They go there to die."

Dr. Feuillet's face looked gray. "I am too tired to argue that with you, Philippe. But we can't leave Madame Bazaine here. It is not acceptable. Who will take care of her?"

"I shall. Myti and I."

"My God. You can't help yourself."

"I am getting well. I'll be up. In a day—"

"A day? A week or two weeks. Perhaps."

"Whatever time it is, I'll be here. I'll do all I can. Myti—"

"Myti is a good woman. But she's an illiterate, half savage."

"I won't send Anouk to that pesthole to die."

"She is nobility. She will receive every attention—"

"I received every attention. You gave me up for dead. Anouk slaved for me. She faced the hell of yellow fever to help me, even when there was no hope. I won't abandon her to you, to the hospital, to anyone. We will take care of her. You will come here."

"My God, Philippe, I have no time to make calls."

"Then get out. We'll do what we can without you. But we won't send her away. We won't give up on her."

The doctor's voice was low. "I'll come when I can, Philippe. You're right, I don't know much. Nothing. Less than nothing. Still, I'll try to help you. I'll do what I can."

The days grew hotter and hotter. Sudden rains erupted, adding boiling water to the intolerable burdens of failure, disease, and despair.

Myti remained at Anouk's bedside hour after hour, until finally the huge woman sagged against the wall in exhaustion.

Philippe managed to stagger across his room. "Go to bed," he told Myti. "Rest."

"She is in terrible pain. The vomiting—"

"We'll take care of it. Go to bed. God knows, we can't lose you too." He braced himself against the doorjamb. He yelled, "Clee!"

The youth came reluctantly from the rear of the house. Philippe said, "Myti is ready to drop from exhaustion. You'll have to care for Madame Bazaine until Myti rests, until I'm strong enough to stand alone."

Clee shook his head, face gray and rigid. "I can't, *m'sieu*. You know. For you, I do anything. You know, my last master, I revere him, I stay with him in the fever. Beside you, he was as nothing. But I cannot do it again. I have the fear."

"Then get out."

Clee stared at him, shaking his head. He did not believe what he heard.

"Go on. Get out," Philippe said. "We all have the fear. You cannot see the fever and not have the fear. But we do what we can. You can not do anything. Go. I understand. But go. Get out. We don't need you here."

Clee's eyes filled with tears. "I stay. I have no life away from here. I do for madame what I can."

Philippe stared at Anouk's fever-flushed face. In the shadows, she looked gray and pathetic. Her hair was matted across her forehead and on her cheeks. Her fevered lips were cracked and swollen. Her delicate neck was stringy, her voluptuous body wasted. He could find no trace of the radiant, vivacious woman of fashion who had appeared out of the darkness that night on the ship.

Philippe said, "Is there anything I can do, Anouk?"

She threw her appallingly thin arm over her face. "Don't look at me."

294

"Your illness makes you no less beautiful."

"Ah, Philippe, we could have been so happy, but it was already too late when we met."

"It's all right. Don't try to talk. Save your strength."

"I—want to tell you. Remember I said I was a woman on fire inside, and no one man could ever cool me down. Remember? I was wrong, Philippe. After you, I wanted no other man. You—cooled me down, Philippe. You cooled me down."

"It comes out even, Anouk. You set me afire."

Her lips pulled into a painful smile. "I know. You did love me, didn't you?"

"I wanted you, Anouk, with everything in me. All the time. With all my mind. All my heart. I could not get you out of my thoughts."

She sighed deeply and licked with the tip of her tongue at her broken lips. "I'm not really very smart, am I?"

"No. If you were smart, you'd be in Paris now. With Ducrot Bazaine, with half the world staring at you in lust, the other half in envy."

Her head rolled back and forth on her pillow. "No. I'm not smart because I found out I was not what I thought. How I laughed at foolish Madame Gallaudet. At your silly Madelon. They were so gullible. They loved their men enough to follow them into hell. I laughed. They gave up everything—chasing after the man they loved. But I was the biggest fool of all, eh? I was safely away from this place. But I found I could not stay away from you. The man *I* loved, I found I would rather be here, like this, and in hell with you than to be the center of attention at Maxim's."

He closed his fingers gently on her fevered hand. "I find that hard to believe."

"So do I. But it's true. It's true. I laughed at them, Philippe, but I was wrong. I was wrong."

"You'll be back at Maxim's. We're going to make you well. I swear it. As I lived, *you* will live."

Her weakening fingers tightened on his hand. "Oh, Philippe. I wish I had your strength. Your will." She sobbed suddenly. "I wish I had given you that will to live, but I know it was Madelon. It was Madelon."

295

"It was you who were there. In the night. Your hands. Your kindnesses. I will never forget that."

"Please. Please don't forget, Philippe. Please don't. Remember, I did love you. Oh, my dearest Philippe, I have been cruel to you, but even when I tried to hurt you, I loved you deeply with all my heart."

Philippe stayed out of his bed all the next day. He took his turn in Anouk's room. She called for him, she wept his name. But when he went to her, she did not know him.

The hours dragged endlessly through the hot and savage days. Dr. Feuillet came infrequently. He examined Anouk and shook his head. "Let us take her to the hospital, Philippe. It is the best thing we can do for her now. The best we can do for you."

"We'll nurse her here," Philippe said.

The doctor went away. The days blurred one into the other. They did everything they could for Anouk. Finally it came down to keeping her as comfortable as possible. She no longer knew any of them.

Clee brought ice to combat her fever. Myti brushed her luxuriant hair until she could no longer endure the pain. Philippe smoothed fragrant lotions into her body. The three of them traded off as Anouk's nurse around the clock.

They slept, but only for a few hours at a time. Philippe stayed giddy with fatigue. He stared at Anouk's wasted body and wept for the splendid beauty which once decorated the brightest salons of Paris.

The nights were the worst. Darkness pressed inward, a black shroud, the hot breath of death.

Philippe sat each night beside Anouk's bed until Myti came to relieve him in the hours before dawn. He stood up, lightheaded. He scarcely remembered walking to his own bed. He fell across it in the heavy shadows. His mind spun.

He couldn't have slept more than a few moments. He came awake with Myti shaking his shoulder. She stood over him, holding a lamp. The light flickered over his face. He blinked up at her.

Myti was sobbing. "Madame," she whispered. "Madame is dead."

Philippe lunged up from the bed. He ran across the room. Anouk's chamber was dark, but he crossed it from habit, as if it were brightly lit.

Myti entered the room behind him, set the lamp on a dresser top. "Madame died brave," Myti said. "She—did not even cry out."

Philippe sank to his knees beside Anouk's bed. He stared at her. She lay rigid, like a statue on the white sheet. It was as if she had never lived.

He laid his head down on the mattress beside her body. "Oh God, Myti," he said. "Why? What is it she did for me that we couldn't do for her?"

Myti's voice was low. "We did all we could. Bronze John kills most everyone he touches. He took her no matter what we did. We done all we could. Poor madame. She just did not have the will to stay alive that you did."

Philippe clutched the sheets in his fists. "It's my fault."

"No, *m'sieu*, no."

"Yes. The will to live, Myti. You're right. I did have it because she gave it to me. With all her heart, she gave all she could to me. But I couldn't—I couldn't give it to her. I wanted to, Myti. God knows I wanted to."

"Madame knew, *m'sieu*. Believe me, she knew."

Abruptly, deaths from the epidemic fever ceased. With no more reason for Bronze John's departure than for his deplorable onslaught, the plague passed. Survivors emerged, attempting to rebuild their stricken town from its charred ruins. Many who had fled by sea, now returned in trepidation, timidly, but hopeful. The first ships anchored in the harbor, were towed in and secured at newly constructed piers.

Little more than a walking skeleton, Philippe sent word from the cottage that work would resume on the canal.

When De Blasio heard that Philippe had recovered, he showed up at the cottage with half a dozen bottles of champagne.

He grabbed Philippe in his arms, laughing and crying at once, amazed that Philippe had survived, but his loudest thanksgiving and marveling were for himself. He had stayed dizzy-headed with quinine, drunk with liquor, weak with fear, but by God, he had lived!

Even before Philippe could leave the cottage, he and De Blasio were deep in new plans for the canal. They would not wait for approval of the dams and locks and diversionary channels they agreed must be built. They would divert materials, laborers, equipment. Their new excavations would survive the most violent floods and mudslides because the mammoth steam shovels, like those at Culebra Cut, would gouge out greater bites of the earth and concrete would secure the lanes. Waterways would be controlled, nature would finally bend to their will, and the passage opened at last between the seas.

But, as always, there were obstacles which had to be removed before the vital building operations even could be instituted. Reports from all sections were disastrous. Storms and floods had wiped out all progress to date along the route.

Philippe stared, shaken at the reports of natural damage. Despite all the work they'd accomplished, he had not yet improved on Bazaine's poor record. Achievements of the spring were wiped out by the monsoons of summer. From everywhere came reports of trouble, failure, disaster or setbacks, at Frijoles, North Gambia, Summit. He could count on problems in the valley of the Chagres River as he could rely on the sun's rising each dawn from the green belly of the Caribbean.

Philippe dispatched work orders and work approvals all along the line of the canal. One area troubled him. From Culebra Cut alone were there no accounts either of progress or problems. He wired Korvache daily, but received in response only mildly worded acknowledgments: Work proceeded on schedule.

Philippe felt instinctive dread building inside him. He had overseen Culebra Cut. From experience, he was aware things never went well for very long at the Cut. It was almost an equation. Absence of tangible evidence of trouble disturbed him more than would a lengthy recital of misfortunes.

Philippe sent for De Blasio. "We're taking the next train to Culebra Cut," he told Guido.

"You're not well enough to go anywhere."

"Still, we're going up there."

"Why? You've got Korvache up there. A good man. Let him handle it. You can't do it all, Director-General, no matter how many hours you add to a day."

"Our newest, heaviest machinery is up there. I've got

to know it's safe. We must secure it. I trust Korvache, sure. But I want to be there. We lose those new Scot-built shovels, we're dead for at least another year."

They returned to Culebra Cut via the southbound train in a sudden storm of hurricane force. The train slowed in the blinding storm and crept through the darkness.

De Blasio chewed his cigar. He clutched a bottle of whiskey in his fist. He had finished it off long before they climbed the foothills to the cut.

Thunder shook the train coaches; rails and roadbed quavered. Rising wind rattled windows. Rain blotted out the jungle and made ugly mirrors of the panes.

The train struggled at last into the station at Culebra Cut.

Korvache's hut was only a few blocks from the depot but in the darkness and driving rainstorm, they slogged what seemed miles in calf-deep mud.

Korvache met them at the cottage door. He was stagger-ing drunk.

"Goddamn it, Korvache," Philippe raged. "Our new heavy equipment is in the pass."

"I don't think so," Korvache said. "I don't think there's a goddamn thing there by now."

"What in hell are you talking about?"

Korvache stared at himn barely able to focus his gaze. "I saw it, Philippe."

"You saw what?"

"The crack, the break, the fissure in the mountain. Mud turns blue. Land cracks. Then you go back and the land's gone. Just sloughs off and falls. Only when I saw this one I knew it was all over. I came back here and got drunk."

"You saw what, Korvache?"

"I told you. Beautiful blue fissure. All along the mountain. Huge plateau. 'Can't fall,' Von Weiler said. 'Too big. Hell, it's half the mountain,' Von Weiler said. 'Shit, Von Weiler,' I said, 'when land cracks like that up here, it falls. I don't give shit how big it is, it falls. When it's ready, it falls.' One thing to do: Get hell out of way. Two things. Get drunk. I got out of way, I got drunk."

"And the equipment?"

"How the hell you going to move it? Mountain may not even still be there. May be. Haven't heard it fall, but when it goes, won't be a goddamn thing down there. Everything old Von Weiler got done will be washed away."

Philippe found himself trembling. The reinforcements he'd viewed so proudly, the walls, the framing, the structures—but most of all, irreplaceable heavy steam shovels—all washed away.

"One good thing," Korvache said.

"Yes?"

"Von Weiler," Korvache said. "Von Weiler never will know. Poor old yellow-skinned bastard. Died. Son of a bitch finally died. During the night. We gonna bury him, if the rain ever lets up long enough we can put him in the ground."

By midnight, the rain slacked slightly. The wind still whipped violently across the compound. Mud congealed on the gravedigger's shovels. By candlelight, in the tent where Von Weiler died, Philippe read the burial service.

He bit back the sickness. It kept building in him. All the good people sacrificed to this hellhole.

De Blasio stood just outside the lighted tent. But it was not far enough away—he could still see the corpse in the open pine casket. Seeing the wasted, yellow-skinned remains, Guido trembled violently. Korvache tried to support him, but De Blasio broke away and staggered across the compound.

He could not be reassured. His terror was of the sickness, not of dying. Hell, a husband's gunfire held no terror for him. He didn't fear the sudden fatal jolt of heart failure. If he were knifed, or beaten to death, he could expire serenely, a man's death. "But not yellow jack or malaria. To stumble and fall in your own black vomit. To know when you see that black fluid gushing out of you, you are going to die, and nobody can save you, and you'll die, not in your time, but when Bronze John is finally through tormenting you, so you die whining and cringing and begging like a cur."

"If it's any consolation, old fellow," Korvache said. "Von Weiler never whined. Or begged. He died quiet."

301

"Yeah. Well, maybe he was brave. I'm not brave, not like that. Not to die like that." He drank from the mouth of a liquor bottle.

At dawn, Philippe was out with Korvache to inspect the break in the blue mountain. Korvache had not lied. The jagged fissure marked off a vast plateau of boulders, jungle growth and great parana pines.

"It might last a week," Korvache said. "It may go while we're standing here."

Philippe stared through the storm at the equipment abandoned along the brink of the last excavation Von Weiler's men had made.

"We've got to secure that machinery down there," Philippe said.

"Are you crazy?"

"I know we can't lose those big shovels."

"You couldn't force men down there, not with guns," Korvache said. "You're one hell of a fellow, Philippe, but don't be a goddamn fool."

"I'm not asking you to go down there with me."

"Well, for that I'm thankful."

Philippe's plan was simple in theory, perilous in execution. Across the pass from the heavy equipment were huge cedars which might support heavy chains secured to the shovels. He assigned forty men to winching chains around the half-dozen highest giant trees.

Rains increased in intensity, and the winds whipped the largest trees, bending them like reeds. Poisonous snakes wallowed past the porch in rushing water, struggling and whipping, attempting to reach the stoop.

Philippe shot a line across the chasm to the first shovel.

Korvache stood on the high ground above the trees where the laborers fought to secure the huge chains. "And now what?" Korvache said.

Philippe glanced at him. "You may not want to watch this," he said. "I'm going down there and cross the ditch. Then I'll secure the chains to the shovel and you people can winch it across from up here."

"And you're going to do that alone?" Korvache said.

"If I have to," Philippe said. He didn't look at him. "It's just a matter of getting over there, that's all."

"And getting back," Korvache said. "That's the part you can't do."

"The hell we can't," De Blasio said. "There's some way back. We'll find it."

Philippe grinned at Guido. With ropes secured about their waists, they began the slow descent to the chasm. As they went deeper, Philippe saw tons of boulders, uprooted trees and battered equipment blocked the open water course.

"That's the way it is sometimes," De Blasio said. "Hell, if it was easy, anybody could do it."

The hillside became an endless green lake. They swam between the high-piled residue of mudslides. Everything hung suspended. Huge, uprooted trees leaned, as if awaiting the new torrents from up the pass which would carry them into the valley.

They kept as much as possible within the shelters created by the high-piled debris. All around them the rising water rushed furiously, level with the crest of the embankments where the shovel stood. De Blasio and Philippe swam and trod water, fighting to stay as close together as possible in the blinding downpour.

"Like old times in the desert, eh?" De Blasio yelled above the wind.

"How in hell is this like the desert?"

De Blasio laughed. "Because, *mon ami*, we didn't know what the hell we were doing there, either."

The rains slackened slightly as they fought across the water-filled chasm to the embankment. Philippe caught one of the treads of the huge shovel and clung to it. The torrents threatened to sweep them along with the palm fronds and soupy mud swirling past.

"Go up and try to start the engine," De Blasio said. "I'll hook the rope in the winches, and we can start the chains down and across."

Philippe watched Guido scramble up the long arm lined with scoops. He managed to hang on in the fierce gale-force winds and make his way to the cabin. Every-

303

thing was sodden. It took him a long time to start the engine.

He watched De Blasio secure the lines to the winches and pulleys. Philippe pulled on the chain, blowing the steam whistle as a signal to the men across the pass. The sound and steam were lost in the gale.

He engaged the gears, starting the winches. The rope began to wind itself on the huge spools. He freed all the brakes and climbed out of the cab. Lightning snapped around his face. Winds made the heavy chains dance wildly. After what seemed an eternity, Philippe descended to where De Blasio hung on, watching the rope and chain winched across the chasm.

Philippe signaled De Blasio to get off the shovel. He yelled as loudly as he could. "The winch will hold. They can use winches over there to hold it against any floods."

His own voice was lost in what seemed to be thunder, but endless, overwhelming thunder. It was too deep, too sustained for thunder. De Blasio yelled and pointed upward. Rolling down the roadbed toward them was a torrent of blue mud, water, uprooted trees and boulders.

"Landslide." De Blasio spoke in the calmest tone Philippe remembered having ever heard from Guido.

"Let's get out of here," Philippe yelled. The earth around them trembled. It looked as if the whole mountainside was spilling down through the pass upon them.

De Blasio leaped away from the arm and scrambled through the clotting underbrush and swirling water toward the broken face of high ground across the chasm.

Behind them, and far above them, a monstrous ooze descended, covering everything in its path. Clawing their way up the incline became a nightmare. Sodden clay and vines coiled, a viscous mixture, so slippery they could not get a foothold. If they caught vines, the green ropes slid along their hands and broke free. A jutting rock which looked like a rung upward pulled loose at a touch.

Philippe managed to swing his upper torso over the jutting belly of a small plateau. This was no safe haven. The sodden mud would crumble under pressures of the onrushing floodwaters.

He tried to yell at De Blasio, but every sound paled

in the keening, grating roar of sloughing earth. An avalanche of broken boulders and twisted trees, slipped downward under the onrush of new mud and released new torrents of water. For one long breath in time, the mass held and then suddenly, it all broke loose, thundering. Irresistibly the mass oozed forward on the wave of water and mud.

Freed, the avalanche gathered momentum, roaring downward. Huge boulders leaped outward and spun like pebbles in the swift and violent current. Wind and water and thunder choked the passage between the slopes, ripping out everything in its path.

As it rolled and billowed toward him, Philippe crawled and clawed his way upward.

Then, high above the first wave of mud and debris, another roar erupted as vast table lands of blue mud sloughed away, tumbling outward and pushing yet another mass ahead of it.

The gale wailed through the pass. Water rushed downward through the brush, ripping it out. As Philippe felt the pull of the water, his body went weak. The life was being pressed out of his body by the force of the rushing mud.

Climbing upward, he saw tall trees bend like saplings, flutter reedlike, and snap or tear out by the roots under the force of the mudslide. He saw the first wave of mud strike the mammoth steam shovel, inundating it. The great machine quivered and slowly shifted under the pressure of the avalanche.

In horror, he watched the huge machine topple like a toy over the brink of the embankment and thunder, bobbling along in the sliding sea of boulders, trees and mud. The remaining supports collapsed, the great chains snapped like cheap ribbon and then the steam shovel seemed to dance away like a leaf on the tide.

For one second he stood, riveted, watching ruin envelop him. Then, the matter of staying alive claimed his whole mind. He looped his rope about a tree trunk and fell to his knees at the brink of the wild torrent of water. The ground quivered under him. He twisted around, clutching De Blasio's guide rope and hauling it in toward him.

The flood roared louder than ever, suddenly deafening. It was as if De Blasio fought him, trying to yank the rope free from his grasp. But this was not true. De Blasio was caught in the undertow of the swirling torrent and was being hauled away.

Feeling his grip weakening, Philippe cursed De Blasio, pleading with him to fight harder, to hang on. He glanced upward toward safety, but could see nothing except the green curtain of the jungle, the slanting gray fury of the rain.

He stared down at De Blasio caught helplessly in the downrushing flood. Straightening, Philippe tried to leap out to him, but the snub of rope on tree restrained him. He fell to his knees at the brink of the slide.

Boulders and trees and mud struck De Blasio in a mammoth wave. His rope snapped. It was as if De Blasio leaped away in the holocaust.

Philippe toppled backward. He clung to the tree as the water rose around his boots and the small arm of land quivered jellylike under him.

He watched the muddy waters rise, racing past, carrying Guido's body away in a roiling torrent of wreckage, equipment and debris. Even in the fulminating roar, Philippe was unaware of the horrible thunder of it; he was conscious only of unspeakable grief and loss. He crouched, with the ground washing out from under him, in heartsick silence.

[40]

Philippe sagged against the vines and loose rocks, unable to think. The violent ooze continued to rise about his boots, forcing him into action. He fought his way upward again above the thunderous surge of water, mud and debris.

As horror released him, he began to see by what a thin miracle he had been spared. The roadbed below existed only as a raging, torrential river. Around him the very air crackled, charged with static electricity. Lightning turned the world incredibly white, and thunder seemed to loosen the unsteady earth beneath his boots.

Still out of sight of the crest, he climbed up a soft clay slope, making painfully slow progress. Rivulets ran down the ribs cut in the clay. These sluices fanned out in every direction, washing away the dirt, rushing it toward the mammoth landslide below.

He climbed slowly upward to a knoll, the only high ground he'd found in the inundated jungle. His boot cleats helped him dig a purchase into the slippery clay. An uprooted tree, driven downward on sludge, had lodged horizontally between two bent, but upright, cedars.

He crawled in under the log and lay shivering. He kept

seeing Guido's body being swept along in the torrent while he could only crouch helplessly and watch. No matter how tightly he closed his eyes he could not shut out the fearful image. He wept.

He did not know how long he lay in the slime. He shivered with chill and shuddered with horror. The jungle closed over him, impenetrably black in the ropes of rain. After a long time it seemed to him the thunderous upheaval of the slide had lessened.

Finally, he could stay no longer in the dark hole. He had rested enough so he could fight the blinding rain and swift running water again. He crawled out from beneath the log and waded through the tangled undergrowth, heading uphill.

He fell often. His legs tangled in the vines and he had to hack himself free. Rain beat down with such violence that it whipped the surface of the rising water into a misty frenzy. Vines pulled free in his hands, wet mud sloughed away under his weight, sending him toppling. He grabbed wildly, clinging to the banyan roots for support.

He crawled faster. He reached a place where the land dropped off almost vertically from the fanlike precipice above. Rain slashed across his face, blinding him. Clumps, brushes and huge trees shook and bent, palsied in the wind. Every stone he clutched, pulled free in his hand, threatening to send him toppling back down the incline.

He had to find a new way upward, a longer, winding route. He loosened the rope about his waist and let it drop to the ground. Somewhere above him it had broken anyhow, destroying his last contact with the men on the hill.

He laughed sourly. By now they'd given him up for dead and returned to camp. Cursing, raging, no longer conscious of anything except the crest of the hill, like some impossible grail above him, he grabbed at vines, roots, trees, saplings, grasses and rocks to steady himself. He stopped thinking about the force of the storm, the treacherous footing, the vines clutching at his boots. He wormed his way upward.

When he reached the flat plateau at the top of the hill

and pulled himself over the edge, he found no protection, only a fierce and violent abyss abandoned in the black night storm. Wind shrieked, moaned and roared around him.

He came out of the jungle into the clearing of the company settlement. Little remained of the rough structures or the wood and canvas tents. He ran through knee-deep water toward Korvache's hut.

Men, huddled in remaining buildings, shouted to him, but he was not really aware of them.

When he came at last into sight of Korvache's house, he could see the slender figure of the young engineer awaiting him on the stoop. Korvache had been standing in the blowing rain for a long, tense time.

Philippe staggered up the steps. Korvache said, "Where's Guido?"

Philippe shook his head. Korvache winced. "Well, thank God you made it, Philippe. Are you all right?"

Philippe supported himself for a moment against a porch upright. "I'm all right."

He rested there a moment longer and then moved toward the door and the dry, lighted room beyond.

Korvache caught his arm. "Wait a minute, Philippe."

"Let me go."

"Wait minute. Can't you wait a minute?"

"No. Let me alone. I can't talk now. I can't stand up any more. I don't want to stand up any more."

"Listen to me."

"I don't want to talk any more, either."

"Wait a minute, goddamn it." Then Korvache's voice softened, but his grip on Philippe's arm tightened. "Philippe, I've got news for you."

Philippe hesitated. He toppled against the doorjamb and stared at Korvache. He shook his head slowly back and forth. After the shock of watching helplessly as De Blasio died, he could not believe there was any good news left on this earth. He did not want to hear anything Korvache had to say. His mind rejected every sensation except the terror of evil. "Madelon?" he whispered.

"No. It's not Madelon."

"Then let me go. I'm too tired, Korvache."

"In a moment, Philippe. Before you go in there, there are certain things you must know."

"Not now, goddamn it."

"Philippe, I wouldn't torture you. Christ, I know how beat you are. But you must hear this."

Shaking visibly, Philippe shook his head. His eyes glittered, wild. He turned and staggered into the front room.

Korvache caught his arm. "We just got the message, Philippe, relayed to you from Colón. The canal—the whole project has been shut down by Paris. Orders of de Lesseps himself."

Philippe recoiled as if he'd been struck. He wiped his sodden arm across his spattered face. He sagged, weeping against the wall. He pressed his face against the rough boards, beating his fist impotently against them.

"We're to close down, Philippe."

Philippe nodded. He wiped his nose on his wet sleeve. He could breathe only raggedly. His lungs and chest felt tight, his throat was choked. Korvache stepped back and Philippe looked around the ugly little hut. Lamplight in the cluttered parlor was ineffectual against the dank blackness of the raging storm. The wind howled and screeched around the cottage, but inside there was a deathly stillness. All he could think was *Guido is dead.* The project was already closed out before they started down that hill. Guido's death had been for nothing.

It was over. It was all over.

As if in some unreal dream he saw Myti sitting on a kitchen chair, Clee standing beyond her. His gaze came back to Myti, a great dark monolith of strength in the darkness.

Philippe walked slowly to Myti. He sank to his knees and buried his head in her lap, weeping helplessly. Myti caressed his hair gently. She did not speak.

FIVE

Washington, D. C.,
1899–1904

[41]

Philippe stood at the railing of the S.S. Champagne *and* watched the gray-capped sea glide past. The starlit sky loomed remote in the North Atlantic darkness. He should have been tired, but he was not. He was filled with anticipation and determination, mixed with the bitter taste of fear—fear of defeat, which he had learned in Paris over the past few years, and a fear of the unknown.

Ahead lay new opportunity. In the United States he would find a dawn for his ambitions, hopes and dreams. Why should he be afraid? He tried to laugh. "My heart is pure, and I shall fear no evil." Yet, he was chilled deep inside, in a way which had nothing to do with the cold, North Atlantic night.

It would work out. It had to work out. He would make it work out. The omens were good. He had won for the New Canal Company a ten-year extension for the Panama Canal concession from the Republic of Colombia. He was making it work out.

But even this thought led to a sense of depression. He had joined in forming the *Compagnie Nouvelle Canal du Panama,* believing it dedicated to promoting financial support for the completion of a lock-type canal across the isthmus.

How quickly he'd been disabused of this fantasy! The New Company, with capitalization of sixty million francs, was never intended by its organizers to cut one gully in Panamanian soil. The directorate banded together solely to keep the concession from lapsing, and to keep title deeds in hopes of peddling them profitably.

He was stunned and dismally disappointed by this stalemate arrangement. The single affirmative action taken by the directors of the new company was the appointment of a technical committee.

He admitted he was only an engineer, a babe in the world of finance and international manipulation, but he had never encountered a more cynical maneuver by men who shunned publicity, dreaded the spotlight, and attempted to stay as much as possible out of the public press and public attention.

Growing daily more enraged, Philippe waited only until the newly appointed committee made its first report. Then he gathered the necessary credentials and set out to involve the United States in actual canal construction by offering the French concession for sale to President McKinley.

Philippe had returned to Paris in 1886, staggered by defeat. He'd always had, among his assorted daydreams, images of coming home to Paris in a flaring of banners, a tattooing of snares, sounding of trumpets in triumph. Things came easily to him; he believed in success, in his own destiny. But he came home in defeat and despair.

It was a long distance between the tropics of Panama and the harsh realities of civilized France. It was not only a matter of ocean miles; it was entering another planet. Returning to Paris from Colón, discredited and defeated, was a jolting experience; it might truly have been traumatic except for the tranquil interval at sea.

Days aboard ship restored him. Only in the deep darkness before dawn did he find himself tormented—what might have been, what could have been avoided, what had been left undone.

Physically, the sea voyage was uneventful, from the lime-green Caribbean to the savage, shadowy grays of the north Atlantic. The ship embarked on a glittering, languid day, cerulean skies fluttering white pennants in farewell, the wake of the steamer bright and frothy. He idled at the rails and dreaded arriving home. He was returning in failure to Madelon's world, a place from which he had wrested her in highest hopes, a place from which he should never have taken her. He had sacrificed her to the canal. Now he had only discredit and failure, and his loss of Madelon. He could not face her. This was the only decision he was capable of making.

The second day he was in Paris he called upon Vicomte Ferdinand de Lesseps, wishing to make his report to the elder statesman in private. De Lesseps received him with faint smiles of anticipation; one clings beyond reason to hope. Charles de Lesseps was with his father and said at once, "Whatever failures you must report, my father and I understand the obstacles you faced, how bravely you struggled—and at what great cost."

"For a brief time," old de Lesseps said, "when I got your reports, I was encouraged. I believed we may have found answers."

"I think in the lock-type canal we have found the answer," Philippe said. They let him talk, attended him politely. Gradually, he became aware he was talking to himself.

"I could not change our plans," de Lesseps said at last. "Not now. Not even if I believed in a lock-type canal as sincerely as you do. I have staked my reputation, the savings of France, all my hopes on a sea-level canal."

Charles was almost apologetic. "My father and I could not suddenly present a totally new concept for the canal. Even if we believed it to be the answer, we could not do it." He spread his hands. "Is there nothing you can convey which might benefit us politically? For example, solutions to the problems of landslides and flooding?"

"The obstacle which must be removed is a medical one. Epidemic. Malaria. Yellow fever. We could recover

314

flooded excavations, rechannel water routes, but not while our men are dying."

"Are you suggesting we spend millions to do medical research down there while not a mile of canal is dredged?"

"The answer can and must be found to epidemic or the excavation will be nothing but a mass grave."

Charles tried to smile. "We are in deepest accord with your goals. We know of no other man more dedicated to the realization of my father's dream than you. We cherish and respect you for it. That is why it is so difficult for me to tell you that we cannot provide ten francs for research. Frankly, we have already victimized ourselves and imperiled the Company, by dealing with loan sharks. We needed short-term capital immediately. There was nowhere else to turn. We face debts with ruinous interest. Debts to be liquidated with whatever legitimate funds we can get. We believe the state should support the canal if only to save the hundred million francs invested by the French people. But we have powerful opponents. And none more vocal than M'sieu Surrett."

Vicomte de Lesseps sagged in his chair. "We are victims of unremitting attacks from the press. The politicians are terrified of becoming involved, of becoming targets of rags like *The Panama*. And, who can blame them for being afraid?" His trembling hand touched the *Tribune* which lay on the table before him. "Look at this. *M'sieu* Surrett is quoted, 'The ruin'—he means the canal—'is getting along fine. Scarcely more than fifty percent remains to be lost or squandered.' "

Sick at heart, Philippe took his leave. Vicomte de Lesseps said, "Keep your faith, as I keep mine. We'll find a way to dig that canal, if you and I have to do it alone and by hand."

Philippe gripped de Lesseps' hand tightly, trying to reassure the proud Old Lion.

Charles walked out into the corridor with Philippe. "Let us face one last sad truth, my friend. I would do anything possible to spare my father from public humiliation, from the savage attacks of papers like *The Panama*. Any favorable publicity you read in that filthy sheet is just that. Favorable publicity. Bought and paid for. I have been forced many times to pay to stop the cruel slander of my father."

Over the next months, Philippe attended conferences on the canal almost daily. In one of these sessions the idea was conceived of a national lottery to support completion of the canal. With such a lottery, de Lesseps had been able to save the old Suez project. Less than enthusiastically, he embraced the scheme again.

In order to launch a lottery loan, they would have to shepherd enabling legislation through the general assembly. Both de Lessepses believed Philippe to be their most ardent, sincere and knowledgeable supporter. They nominated him to call upon that most implacable foe of the project, the Finance Minister, Monsieur Cecile Surrett.

Philippe arrived at Monsieur Surett's elegant home precisely on time. He was ushered into a sumptuous drawing room and there permitted to cool his polished heels. His gorge rising by the second, he decided at least twice to walk out, and when the corridor door opened at last, Philippe turned stiffly, without smiling.

Monsieur Surrett listened with disdainful politeness, more interested in the fact that Philippe had survived yellow fever than in the canal's future. The finance deputy agreed with obvious distaste that if the project were to be saved, assuming it worth saving, its salvation would have to come through some scheme. A national lottery seemed to him less fraudulent than many which had been presented to him. He was impressed by Philippe's ardor and sincerity. While he would not lift a finger in its support, he would not openly oppose lottery legislation the company might bring to his office.

Philippe, Charles and even the faltering Vicomte de Lesseps canvassed the lobbies. Few representatives opposed the lottery directly. Philippe discovered an incredible number who let him know subtly, or boldly, that they could support the plan for a price.

The company by now had reached its nadir, Charles confessed to Philippe. Though he and others attempted to keep the truth from the Vicomte, old de Lesseps was not deceived.

How painful it was to watch that fiery old statesman making pathetic appeals directly to the public for six hundred million francs to stave off ruin and disgrace. In exhausting public appearances, he offered bonds repayable by lot at double the subscription price. Then *Le Matin,* in a front-page exposé, reported that the Company had to date expended—squandered?—a total of 935 million francs, without a mile of permanent ditch excavated.

To Philippe's astonishment, de Lesseps summoned him. The old man looked gray. He made no effort to smile and did nothing which might expend one extra ounce of his diminishing energy.

At last, de Lesseps said, "I have given thought to your drafts for a lock-type canal, Philippe. Even now, in my heart, I believe a sea-level canal would be best. But I don't have to tell you I am desperate. Perhaps a canal, such as you suggest, with locks, might capture the public fancy, restore lost confidence. At least, I want you to present the idea to the board. It may save us. It cannot now hurt us."

On November 15, 1887, request for permission to create a national lottery was formally made to the government. The parliament refused, ordering its Committee of Eleven to examine the entire lottery proposal before the member bodies would consider it.

When Claude-Bruce Grabralet opened the door of his apartment, he looked at Philippe with a total lack of recognition. Then he stared, eyes widening, and he shook his head in disbelief.

"Philippe! Can it be you? This sun-blackened skeleton? This fried husk of the beautiful man I loved more than my own life?"

Philippe laughed. "Whatever is left of me. Yes. It is I."

"My God, my dearest Philippe, what have they done to you?"

"In Panama? Nothing. Compared to what they are doing to me here in Paris, nothing." Philippe exhaled heavily. "We need help, Claude-Bruce, in the Committee of Eleven. In the Assembly."

The smile died on Claude-Bruce's slender face. "You dare ask me to help you?"

"I know what your principles are, Claude-Bruce. I know that as you once championed de Lesseps, now you oppose him and the Company. But I believe you are wrong now. I beg you, consider in the name of friendship."

"I warned you, Philippe, long ago, not to treat me cruelly, not to turn away from my love. You should have been wiser."

"None of us is wise all the time, Claude-Bruce. On the other hand, none of us is always right. All I ask is that you open your mind to the true goals of the Company."

"An open mind? Me? I wonder now why I loved you at all, Philippe. I think you never understood me at all."

"I understood you, Claude. I understand you now. But I have never been as desperate before. I came to you because you are now one of the most powerful men in parliament. Because I have nowhere else to turn."

"But you turned me away once when I needed you more than anything. You chose my wife instead of me. I hope you are happy with her."

"You know better than that. I haven't seen her. I have been told she is in America."

"Such a shame. The course of true love as rocky as ever. Such a shame."

"Claude-Bruce, please. Don't let your hatred for me blind you to the good, to the true benefits of this project."

"Your project be damned, Philippe. I no longer care about it. But you are wrong. I have never hated you. I have tried. But I never quite learned the trick."

"Then, for God's sake, help us. I know—I have always known you are honest. From the first I knew you, I saw you as President of the Republic one day."

Claude-Bruce shrugged. "Thanks to you I will never achieve that. Still, I have had only my work to live for. All my energies, all my passions, have gone into it."

"As mine have into this canal, Claude-Bruce. My beliefs now are what yours once were. The canal project is necessary. As vital now as the first time you championed it. But the company is about to fail. Without help of men like you, it will fail."

"Then to hell with it."

"Is there nothing I can say to you?"

"Of course, there's much you can say to me. You can have my vote in the committee. My support in the assembly. It's very easy. When you are my love, there is nothing I would not do for you, in my bed and out of it."

"I am talking about matters of great importance—"

"So am I. I am speaking of my love, long denied, and my need, long refused, but never for one moment out of my mind."

"Can't I make you see how vital this canal is to France?"

"I simply no longer care. I want you. If I can't have you, then now at least I have the opportunity to destroy you."

"I can't believe this of you, Grabralet."

"Believe it. You rejected my love, stole my wife, crippled my career, made my life empty. Now I have it in my power to get revenge. But don't look so defeated, my love. I am always here. As I have always been here. You have only to come to me and you will have anything it is in my power to give you."

The meeting of the Committee of Eleven was called to order. Philippe sat, without hope, in the visitor's gallery with Charles de Lesseps. As expected, a preliminary vote was six to five against a favorable endorsement of the lottery.

Charles de Lesseps was permitted to make a final plea for the lottery, for the canal, for the opportunity to fulfill his father's dreams for the glory of France. Few of the members bothered to listen. Most read newspapers or signed routine work from their separate offices. The chairman dozed, mouth sagged open, head resting against the back of his judge's chair. Philippe was aware of Claude-Bruce Grabralet's hooded gaze fixed on him the whole time de Lesseps spoke.

On the second ballot, Claude-Bruce changed his vote. He placed the majority in favor of the lottery. The room was hushed, spectators and members sitting in tense, brittle silence.

On the brink of tears, Philippe pushed his way forward to express his gratitude to Claude-Bruce. The deputy chairman was surrounded by reporters. One said, "Your vote apparently violates all the statements you've recently made concerning the canal company."

Claude-Bruce was looking beyond the reporter, toward Philippe. He shrugged. "I suppose so."

"Would you say why you changed your mind and your vote, sir?"

Claude-Bruce continued to gaze across the reporter's shoulder. "I did it—I would say—for love."

The reporter was perplexed. "For love?"

Claude-Bruce continued to let his taunting smile rake at Philippe. He shook his head. "Let's just say I love my country. That always sounds good, doesn't it?"

De Lesseps moved to launch the national lottery. However, the financial instability of the company itself affected its launching. As soon as bonds were prepared for presentation, pressure was applied from one of the Company's largest creditors. To protect its own interests, Credit Lyonnais forced the Company to launch the full lottery at once, rather than in single issues as de Lesseps planned.

Immediate reaction demonstrated how disastrous and costly this mistake was. The effort asked from the market was too sudden and too huge. While the prizes looked most attractive, French savings were in no condition to permit buyers to respond. A violent campaign in the press was directed against the Company, its directors, its financial condition, and at Vicomte de Lesseps himself.

On the day before the lottery subscription, a bear raid brought the market price of the Company's outstanding securities down to a new low.

On June 26, the day of the issue, a rumor flashed across the provinces and in Paris, as if orchestrated, that Ferdinand de Lesseps had died during the night.

Philippe was among those who sat with the Old Lion during the next two days.

The old statesman shook his head sadly. "When we started, it all seemed so simple. We had only to cross the

Isthmus of Panama. But no. Now they will not stop until they have dragged us through hell itself."

Defeat of the lottery was inevitable. Of the two million bonds offered, only eight hundred thousand were subscribed.

This meant the end of the Company. On February 4, 1889, after a futile attempt to raise money through sale and mortgaging of the personal assets of its Board, the Company expired. The *Compagnie Universelle du Canal Interoceanique* was dead.

On November 21, 1892, a government Committee, looking for scapegoats, accused Ferdinand and Charles de Lesseps of fraud, theft, bribery and other high crimes against the people.

The grandeur of Vicomte de Lesseps' bearing, the imposing figure he presented when he entered the courtroom each day, the dignity with which he faced his accusers, made a deep impression on every person who witnessed his trial.

The defense attorney called Philippe to the stand where he was led through a careful and dispassionate account of the "Acts of God" which, rather than fraud or mismanagement, mitigated from the first against the canal. Deaths from epidemic. Landslides. Hurricanes. Flooding.

The prosecutor stood up with a faint shrug, his face a chilled mask of disdain. "I find no relevance in any of your testimony," he said.

"Nothing else is relevant," Philippe said.

"Were you not an engineer who went to Panama only in 1885?"

"Yes."

"An engineer with less than three years' actual experience?"

"Yes."

"And yet, was not a renowned engineer, with more than twenty years, experience—released so that you could take over as Director-General of the entire project, within a year after your arrival in Panama?"

"Yes, but—"

"That is all. I have no other questions of this witness."

The jury deliberated almost four full days. Philippe took slight heart. He and supporters of the Company believed this delay a hopeful augur.

He sat heartbroken when the verdict was announced. The jury found the defendants guilty as charged, on all counts. Ferdinand and Charles de Lesseps were both condemned to the maximum punishment—five years' imprisonment and three thousand francs fine.

Because of his ill health and advanced years, Ferdinand de Lesseps' sentence was commuted. The court permitted him to retire to his estate at La Chenaie. Common sense somehow prevailed in an atmosphere polluted and poisoned by prejudice—the judgments of the court were quashed on June 18, 1893. On December 7, 1894, Vicomte de Lesseps died.

The determination was that the Vicomte died of old age. But Philippe refused to accept this. "The hell he did. He was still younger than I am—in his heart."

The next day a maid found Claude-Bruce Grabralet in his bed. He had thrust the barrel of a gun deep into his mouth and pressed the trigger.

Philippe realized that these two men, one a victim of time, the other of suicide, had actually died of the same cause—heartbreak because their dreams had eluded them. He grew more determined than ever that somehow he would see a canal across the isthmus—and that he must see Madelon again.

[42]

Philippe sailed into New York harbor in the early spring of 1899. He stood on deck in a blustery chill and returned the greeting of that French lady, *Liberté,* who resided near the Battery.

He lunched at the Ritz, drove in open cabs along cool, remote Riverside Drive, or stood enthralled in the midst of downtown crowds. A tempo throbbed in the atmosphere unlike anything he'd experienced in Paris or any other city. Vigor and vitality were almost tangible; one felt caught up and carried along in it.

He'd never seen so many theaters so brightly and garishly lit. As the nineteenth century ended, the legitimate theatre in America was robustly healthy. Over four hundred dramatic and stock companies were on tour. Vaudeville, burlesque, minstrels, operas and musical extravaganzas were all popular. Almost fifty legitimate theaters, plus six vaudeville houses brightened Manhattan alone. *Cyrano de Bergerac, Barbara Fritchie* and *Ben-Hur* were the big attractions. Long lines stood outside Weber & Field's Music Hall. Bernhardt starring in *L'Aiglon,* William Gillette, Anna Held, Lillian Russell, William Warfield, Maurice Barrymore—these names all glittered in glory. And, in nickelodeons, the new moving pictures flickered, leaped and lunged.

In Central Park, Spanish-War veterans, now displaced and restless, huddled on benches beneath as many copies of the *Times,* Pulitzer's *World,* or Hearst's *American* as they could salvage from refuse cans during the day.

In the serene park by night, the city appeared a place of witchery, of shimmering lights rising unsupported against darkling skies.

Philippe returned to his Waldorf-Astoria suite around midnight. He saw as he approached along the corridor that his door was ajar, his lights burning, a yellow rectangle spilling into the dimly lit hallway. Troubled, he hesitated, then entered the room warily.

A slender, dark-skinned man leaped apologetically to his feet, smiling and bobbing his head. The most significant detail about the visitor was not the advanced age and worn appearance of his clothing, but the obvious original elegance and quality of material.

"I am Isaac Seligman."

Philippe exhaled and smiled. He extended his hand. Isaac was a member of the powerful financial family of New York. "I have a letter of introduction to you from Charles de Lesseps," Philippe said.

Issac nodded. He spoke diffidently, with a slight stammer. "I have had letters from my good friend Charles about you, and your aims here. I hope if there is anything I, my family or our firm can do for you, you will call on us."

Philippe laughed and spread his hands. "I am a helpless pilgrim. I need all the help I can get."

Isaac bobbed his head. "I determined this. And so, I took the liberty of arranging your first appearance in America. It will secure you most helpful and widespread newsprint exposure. And it will put you immediately in touch with the right people. It will provide the platform for your explaining to Americans why you are here and what you hope to accomplish."

"I'm ready, eager, to go anywhere, do anything,"

324

Philippe said. "I suppose you've set up this meeting in Washington?"

"In Cincinnati."

"Cincinnati? What's that?"

"A city in Ohio. The heart of Republican America. They call in Mark Hanna country. They call Mark Hanna 'the kingmaker.' Many say he is solely responsible for McKinley's election as President. I especially want you to meet Mark Hanna."

Philippe nodded. "Then we're off to Cincinnati."

Isaac Seligman shook his head. "You are off to Cincinnati. Alone. It would be less than wise for me to appear in public with you. Or for you to appear in my company. I don't have to remind you that Jesse Seligman, before he died, was involved in Ferdinand de Lessep's *Comité Américain*. The aims of this committee were quite honorable, but . . . our family's reputation for strictest integrity was . . . stained. Jesse was summoned to appear before Senator Morgan's committee. There was a matter of the three-hundred-thousand-dollar fee our firm was paid for helping to enlist American financial and political support behind the canal project. Nothing serious but . . . I want to do nothing which might compromise the integrity of your mission."

Philippe sat in the coach seat, listening to the almost hypnotic click of wheels on rails. He watched the Jersey meadows, the flatlands of Pennsylvania slip past on the wind. He had consciously to control the impatience, nervous tension and fear of failure which had driven him since de Lesseps' death. He was almost forty now; he no longer believed he would work miracles. But he was unable to rest.

There was so much to do, with time running out, and nobody really listening any more. The world rushed headlong toward its destiny in the new century, but the Panama Canal project was shunted from the mainstream. Sometimes he felt only he cared, only he was spurred by furious urgency.

The huge dining room was brilliant with lights illumining French and American flags. Gilt signs informed the world the sponsors were members of the Cincinnati Commercial Club. The fat-bellied men and their perfumed wives in boas and silks looked completely satisfied with life. Philippe sat throughout the meal without touching his food.

He was introduced, by a toothsome master of ceremonies, with a brief recital of his career in Panama, his efforts in behalf of the failed canal, his hopes of locating support for "de Lesseps' vision" in America.

Philippe began hesitantly. His slight French accent was just enough to flavor his speech with the winning exotic touch. He spoke with conviction, with clarity and simple honesty.

"I represent no private interests. I do not come to you as salesman for the new Panama Canal Company. I come only to defend the grand and noble conception of Ferdinand de Lesseps, one of the most heroic men of our time. I went to Panama because of my admiration for him. I come to you now from my love for his memory. I lived in Panama in struggle and in danger. I did not despair then. I do not despair now.

"I come to a great nation which wants, needs and totally understands the value of a canal in Central America. But sentiment, I am warned, leans heavily toward digging that canal in Nicaragua.

"I must say to you that a Panama Canal would be one-third the length of a canal across Nicaragua. It would have fewer curves, require less total excavation, need fewer locks. It would cost less, it would serve better."

He spoke eloquently and sincerely. He won this audience, he converted any doubters among them. When he thanked them for their courtesy to him, they leaped to their feet in an uproarious standing ovation.

Isaac Seligman had not exaggerated. Cincinnati was the ideal place to meet the right people. Republican personages swarmed forward to grasp Philippe's hand, congratulate him on a "great little talk" and to promise him their total support.

He was introduced to Myron T. Herrick, a close friend

326

of President McKinley's. Herrick was a man who obviously had been an extremely handsome youth and had grown even more so with age. He greeted Philippe warmly.

Mark Hanna came forward and grasped Philippe's hand in both of his. "You got us fired up, Bunau-Varilla. You got us all fired up."

A cigar-smoking man in a black suit stretched over a paunch, Hanna was gray-faced with illness. But he spoke with exuberance.

"Stick with us, Bunau-Varilla, and we'll help you get what you want. Anything I can't get for you, Myron Herrick can. Our party controls Congress, the country is prospering, the Democrats may well be finished as far as any real clout is concerned. They were out yelling all over the country and we elected Bill McKinley, with Bill sitting and rocking on his front porch right here at home. We have the power."

Philippe felt abruptly caught up and carried along by the boundless confidence of these Midwestern Americans. It was not an unpleasant sensation. He began to hope again. The ice was broken, as Isaac Seligman had promised, under the most cordial conditions.

He heard Hanna talking of putting through a telephone call to President McKinley at the White House. "Talk long distance, without even shoutin'," Hanna said. "And I want you to meet Bill McKinley. You'll like Bill. He'll like you. Bill likes people. And we all love a man who loves his great cause."

More letters of introduction were promised, to party leaders in Cleveland, Boston, to McCormick in Chicago, to the biggest names in Washington, D.C.

Hanna grasped Philippe's hand and said, "You are a fine young man, Bunau-Varilla, and a handsome fellow to boot."

"Thank you," Philippe said. "I only wish my looks were enough to build us a Canal."

"A man's looks are never enough!" The handsome, silver-haired Herrick laughed. "But a woman is another story. For example, your countrywoman, Philippe, the beautiful young widow Madelon Grenet, over at the French Embassy."

"Oh, hell yes," Hanna said. "Madelon Grenet. Hair like pampered gold! We mustn't let *her* looks carry the day. She's a good friend of Senator John Tyler Morgan, that bastard Democrat from Alabama."

"His *very* good friend," Herrick said, laughing and clapping Hanna on the shoulder.

Philippe felt as if a chilled wind had blown through the crowded, flag-bedecked room, chilling all ardor, shattering all expectations like fragile glass.

[43]

It was a long, circuitous route Philippe traveled from Cin-
cinnati to Washington, D.C.—a banquet in Boston at the
New Algonquin Club; guest of James Deering in Chicago,
who introduced him to Marshall Field, Robert Lincoln
and Cyrus McCormick; appearance before the New York
Chamber of Commerce. But Madelon was in Philippe's
mind every mile of the hectic journey.

Arriving in Washington, Philippe registered at the
Willard Hotel, that huge gray monolith, already aging and
world-famous, looking grandly out over 14th and Pennsylvania.

His first reaction to the Capitol was disappointment.
The town was provincial after Manhattan, raw and new
after Boston, slow and lethargic after Chicago. Congressmen and senators one met resembled red-faced farmers.
Most spat tobacco globs juicily into the spittoons which
sprouted everywhere.

Philippe sent his credentials and letters of introduction,
gathered along his lecture trail, to Secretary of State John
Hay. Then he walked out to the French Embassy, ostensi-
bly to enlist a deputy to accompany him on his first formal meeting with Hay.

His heart pounding in a frenzy, as it had not since he was a student, he stood in the lobby, watching for any sign of Madelon. Surely, even after thirteen years he would know instinctively if she were near. But she was not there.

On the ride to Lafayette Square, Philippe asked the deputy, "Is there a Madame Grenet working at the Embassy? I believe I may have known her."

"Yes, you may well have," said the deputy. "Her husband worked on the canal. He died of yellow fever in '86."

"Yes, I did know him . . . I should like to meet Madame Grenet."

"She isn't at the Embassy now." The deputy paused. "But I could get her address for you, if you wish."

Philippe exhaled, but said nothing. *She was not at the Embassy. She was the good friend, the very good friend of Senator John Tyler Morgan.* What did he have of Madelon after these thirteen eternal and empty years? Not much; memories mutilated by time. Nothing. Less than nothing. His strongest claims were only the wistful fragments of old dreams. He shivered with a sudden chill of loss and a wave of regret surged through him. With a somber reluctance, he relinquished her.

He was astonished to find Secretary Hay an old man not so much in years as in physical frailty, failing health and waning energy. At 61, the secretary had been in poor condition for some years. The two men found much in common to discuss. Hay congratulated Philippe on the success of his whirlwind tour and on the powerful friends he had made.

Hay had a fantastic career. His first law offices had been next door to young Abraham Lincoln's and they become close friends. Hay became a member of Lincoln's household at the White House, serving as his secretary during the war years.

He had been two years a part of the American legation in Paris, and spent an hour questioning Philippe about mutual friends in that city where he had been happiest.

Hay and his staff heard Philippe's presentation politely. But Hay warned that many factors mitigated against the French proposal for assuming the canal concession in

Panama. "We've just concluded a costly war with Spain. We find an isolationist reaction among the people. New international problems. New possessions ceded from Spain. Territories in the Caribbean and the Pacific."

"This makes interoceanic communications more urgent, not less."

"These communications problems must be solved." Hay nodded. He recounted the record-breaking run of the cruiser *Oregon* around the tip of South America. While lying at anchor in the San Francisco harbor, the *Oregon* was ordered to take part in the battle of Santiago de Cuba. She steamed around the Horn in ninety days. Hay spread his hands. "The public was amazed. Only 90 days around the Horn, but to all of us the run revealed the weakness of our communications between the two oceans."

Philippe spoke enthusiastically. "A Panama Canal would chop seventy-eight hundred miles off the voyage from New York to San Francisco. The trip would take less than half the time."

"I'm sure President McKinley will be most enthusiastic. We'll arrange a meeting at the earliest," Hay promised.

Philippe did not deceive himself. Powerful men like Mark Hanna worked behind the scenes. He was summoned to Secretary Hay's office a few weeks later. The slight, ailing man smiled. "Something has happened which I wouldn't have believed possible even six months ago. President McKinley has ordered a committee to France with offers to buy your concession in Panama."

Philippe's first disappointment came when he was informed that the New Company asked $109,141,500 for the concession.

His second disappointment came on September 6, 1901. By that time, the asking price had dropped to forty million dollars, but all progress was suspended when President McKinley was shot at Buffalo, New York. He died September 14, and Theodore Roosevelt became President.

T.R. strode in like a giant where McKinley had moved like a shadow. Sweeping changes followed his inauguration. Though McKinley and Roosevelt were members of the same party, they were totally unlike. McKinley followed orders sent *down* from somewhere to the oval office;

331

he was accommodating; he deferred to others' opinions; he was easily managed by influential leaders.

At 42, the youngest President in history, T.R. was his own man from his first day in office.

With Hay's aid and Mark Hanna's sponsorship, Philippe found access to T.R.'s White House office comparatively easy.

"Heard about you. Heard about you. Bully work you're doing, Bunau-Varilla. You've some powerful detractors, but you've friends here in the White House, I can assure you. I've favored a canal in Panama for many years. A canal controlled, operated and fortified by the United States. If we spend millions to build that canal, by Gad, we've got to be able to fortify it so it can't be used against us in time of war. If that canal is fortified by us, it becomes one of our most potent sources of possible sea strength. I favor the canal. I favor the route across Panama. I favor buying the French concession. But there are many people lined against me in the Congress. I'll tell you, the most formidable of all is that Democrat from Alabama, John Tyler Morgan. He wants that canal in Nicaragua because Nicaragua is closer to Alabama than Panama is. He'll fight any treaty to death, and he's not going to give an inch. You've been winning over this country with your charm and dedication. I think you'd do well to turn your sights on John Tyler Morgan. He's certainly your most formidable foe, and you must never underestimate him. Never."

Philippe admitted he'd kept his distance from the Senator from Alabama because of the whispers that there existed some secret relationship between Morgan and Madelon. He could not believe this, and yet he dreaded learning the truth.

But he had now reached the place where he had at least to attempt to reach Morgan and convince him of the superiority of Panama as site for the canal.

This proved easier to plan than to carry out. Morgan cavalierly refused to see him. According to friends, Morgan openly called Bunau-Varilla "that clown French adventurer, not to be taken seriously."

332

On the floor of the Senate, Morgan had said that the "odd" manner in which the Compagnie Nouvelle had been established, convinced him that the whole organization was nothing better than an assembly of crooks. "How was the Compagnie Nouvelle formed?" he demanded in his whining cracker twang. "All French contractors who had worked on the canal during the French years, and who had managed to remain solvent, were told they could either invest in Compagnie Nouvelle or face prosecution for fraud and breach of contract. Two-thirds of the new company's capital, eight million dollars, was raised in this way. Plainly, there would be no Compagnie Nouvelle asking us to deal with them without this basis of blackmail. No, we will never deal with criminals and adventurers."

However, Philippe was getting under the senator's sensitive hide. His effective exploitation of the Nicaraguan volcano dangers in speech after speech aroused Morgan's ire until the senator publicly called Bunau-Varilla a "lying son of a bitch."

Philippe almost despaired of meeting Morgan on any reasonable plane. But in May of that year, his good friend and associate Isaac Seligman came excitedly into his room at the Hotel Willard. "I've arranged through very important people your meeting with Senator Morgan. An intimate and friendly meeting. You're invited to his home for a party."

Philippe prowled Washington, his mind in turmoil. If he went to Morgan, he could no longer deny whatever alliance existed between the senator and Madelon. If he did not go, he relinquished an excellent and likely final opportunity of getting his facts before his strongest opponent.

Finally, the hour arrived and he found himself driving in the early dark up Pennsylvania Avenue toward the illumined Capitol. His cab turned on John Marshall Place and stopped before a tall brick row house.

As Philippe pressed the doorbell, he knew that his strongest enemy was behind that door. Was his wife there too—as this man's mistress?

A black butler, in polished shoes, expensive black coat

and ruffled white shirt, answered the door. When Philippe gave his name, the butler nodded and took his hat and cape. Beyond the large foyer, open French doors revealed a room brilliant with lights, decorated for a festive evening. In a corner, three black musicians tuned their instruments.

"Mista Morgan ask that you come right into his study, suh. Mista Morgan say you have opportunity for some talk before our party begins, suh."

Philippe was ushered into a book-lined study, with deep windowseats, heavy leather-covered furniture, a mammoth old mahogany desk. Eight or ten men sat at ease, wreathed in blue cigar smoke, in deep chairs. They were laughing, and abruptly ceased laughing when Philippe was announced.

John Tyler Morgan came out of a deep leather-covered chair with the alacrity of a man of thirty, though Philippe knew the senator to be at least sixty. Philippe gazed at him in some trepidation—one of the most powerful figures in American politics, an equal rival of Hanna himself.

Though small of stature, Morgan was keen-witted, energetic and the most intellectual of the Democrats in congress. Despite his age, he remained fiercely uncompromising, and unforgiving. Crossing him in any way could still cost a man his career, reputation and even his livelihood. Morgan loved to work—he spent eighteen hours a day on Senate affairs—and he most enjoyed a good fight.

"Asked some friends in to meet you," Morgan said, shaking Philippe's hand and dropping it abruptly. He introduced Philippe to senators or congressmen from Alabama, Mississippi, Louisiana and Texas, cronies, Philippe saw, men whose states would be revived when the Mississippi River became a major waterway of the world again. Morgan admitted an ocean passage at Nicaragua would mean a return of prosperity to the South, because Nicaragua was closer to the American Southern ports—Galveston, New Orleans, Mobile—than any canal at Panama. These men could be counted on to share Morgan's opinions, prejudices, doubts and suspicions.

Morgan laughed and waved Philippe to a chair, offered him bourbon and branch water, "the national drink of the South, suh. Asked you here early, Bunau-Varilla, so's we could get acquainted before the party, air our differences."

"I don't think our differences are so great, sir," Philippe said. "We both want that canal built with all our hearts."

"But in different places and for mighty different reasons." Morgan winked at the men around him. His hair and mustache were cottony white, his neck lean inside an oversized wing-collar. His faded blue eyes were piercing.

He gestured with his cigar. "I tell you, suh, and every gentlemen in this room—and they're all gentlemen, all honorable gentlemen—" he waited while his guests laughed appreciatively, "—will tell you I have championed a canal in Nicaragua since I first arrived in Washington more than twenty years ago. This here canal has been the dream of my life, the Nicaragua waterway, suh, is the *American* route."

"The Nicaragua canal will be a monument to John Tyler's public service," the gentleman from Texas said.

"Only damned kind of monument I want," Morgan said. "Now, suh, against my lifelong career of working—selflessly, suh—for a Nicaragua passage, let's consider you. What are you in this for? You gettin' rich? You expectin' to get rich?"

"I believe I am as honest and dedicated as you are, sir."

"Honesty and dedication, along with patriotism, the refuge of scoundrels."

"Is this why you asked me here, to insult my integrity?"

"No. Hell, it ain't your integrity I question. It's you, son. Your mustache. Jesus, down home, you'd be laughed out to the chickens wearing a waxed job like that. Them pointy waxed ends—don't mind my sayin' so, but they makes you look like the villain in some cheap melodrama. Every cartoonist in the country is drawin' you, waxed mustache an' all, as stealing all the eggs from the henhouse you was set to guard. Hell, why wouldn't I question you? You could cut off the mustache and at least *look* honest!"

The room rang with the savage laughter of Morgan's

cronies. Philippe smiled and shrugged. "I could laugh this off, Senator, as I laugh off the cartoons in the newspapers. I know what I am. I know what sacrifices I have made. I do not give a goddamn what scurrilous lies you, or anyone else, spread about me. I know who I am."

"They're calling you a schemer, a lobbyist, an adventurer," Morgan said in that taunting drawl.

"If one calls a man an adventurer who sacrifices his time, his own money, and all his capacities to the aid of his poor nation and to the eventual service of your country, sir, I am then an adventurer. Otherwise, I am not."

Some of the men cleared their throats. Morgan laughed again. "Just joshin' you, Bunau-Varilla. Havin' a little fun. Breakin' the ice. Way the boys do down home in the barbershops."

Philippe shrugged.

"All right, you're in the house with your goods," Morgan said. "Let's see what you got to peddle. From where I sit, suh, not very much. In the first place, the price of forty million dollars demanded by that bunch of crooks—pardon me, by your associates at Compagnie Nouvelle—is entirely unreasonable. You'll never sell the American people on a swindle like that, bub."

"There is a considerable move in sentiment toward the Panama Canal," Philippe said.

Morgan looked about at his friends as if their guest had taken leave of his senses. "If there's been a penny's switch in sentiment from Nicaragua to Panama, I haven't heard a bush crack in the woods about it."

Philippe smiled. "Maybe you just haven't been listening, sir."

"Oh, I been listening, cousin. Do I have to remind you, they voted in the House—308 to two—to proceed with the Nicaragua canal? Does that sound like a switch to Panama? Maybe you're the ole boy who ain't listening for nothing except the sound of money that can be pushed in his own pocket."

Philippe managed to control himself, kept his voice on the precise level with Morgan's. "You then represent honor and I thievery?"

"Couldn't of said it better myself, friend. The facts

336

show Nicaragua superior to Panama from every engineering standpoint and from all political considerations. Unlike Panama, Nicaragua is a stable country, politically, with a great potential for development. It offers on a canal route, fifty miles of lake, sixty miles of navigable river, the lowest pass in the entire region, Mexico to South America. It's a land relatively free of disease while Panama is a place of pestilence! Pestilence. Look at Bunau-Varilla, gentlemen, for proof of what yellow fever can do for the pitiful few who survive its onslaught. Look at him! Bunau-Varilla is a walking survivor. And he would *send* us there. No, he wouldn't *go* there again, he would send us—for *only* forty million dollars *American*."

"Panama would not be the same now as when my poor country struggled to construct there. Malaria and yellow fever were controlled, almost eradicated in Cuba, by the U.S. This can be done again in Panama."

Morgan looked as if he would spit in disgust. "Panama! A job which has disgusted France. Villainies perpetrated by its own people upon its own people by men like Bunau-Varilla. An affair gangrenous with corruption. That's what you would turn over to us, a program of no value, assets virtually worthless, stockholders a passel of common thieves, paid schemers and adventurers. This is what you would palm off on us for *only* forty million dollars *American*."

Morgan had a characteristic of glaring at people even under ordinary circumstances. The way he now watched Philippe suggested that if he removed his watchful gaze even for an instant, the Frenchman would be up to chicanery.

Philippe's rage rose. He was unaccustomed to accepting so much vilification without retort, but he saw a powerful foe not one whit converted, as full of prejudice as the day he closed his mind on this subject. He tried to speak, but Morgan would not permit it.

"I'll tell you, Bunau-Varilla, I wouldn't give you 37½ cents for your *Panama* canal, and all you've done down there."

"Are we to be denied just payment for our surveys, our material, our work, our sacrfices in men, time and money?"

337

Morgan shrugged. "Not at all. You misunderstand me. If you find a buyer, I hope you get your forty million dollars. It's just that I want no part of the arrangement, even if I got the whole shootin' match for 37½ cents. I wouldn't take it."

Morgan's cronies snickered and nudged each other. Philippe could see his venerable foe was enjoying himself enormously.

"I don't believe the reasonable men and women of your great country feel as you do, Senator."

Morgan laughed and waved his cigar. "Any of those who changed from Nicaragua to Panama because of Roosevelt charm and Bunau-Varilla lies, I see as little less than treasonous, suh. Hell, General Walker was the strongest proponent of Nicaragua exceptin' me, until Roosevelt came into office. Suddenly Walker is a Panama man. Hell, it's common knowledge. Roosevelt offered Walker directorship of construction of the canal to get him to abandon us."

"Perhaps General Walker was persuaded by the truth."

"Perhaps the sun won't come up in the East next Thursday, too."

Philippe forced himself to smile. He said, "I don't care for your jokes and insults, sir. Just as I do not care for money. For wealth. You believe I do this for some greedy motive of profit? Well, how little you know me, how little you care for truth. I know the good and decent people who died to make that canal in Panama possible. Each one—each one!—worth more than that entire, ugly, hot and backward land. That canal is an international necessity. Someone will build it in Panama, where it belongs. You think I will stop because you laugh and accuse me of crookedness? I will never stop, *m'sieu*. Never. The canal *will* be dug. In Panama."

He turned and strode toward the corridor.

[44]

"Philippe!"

Stalking toward the street door, Philippe stopped in mid-stride. He looked about at the sound of her voice and stared stupefied at the vision, the unreal reality of Madelon in the French doorway. Behind her, the party droned, with Washington's elite laughing and smiling and showing its teeth even when it was not really amused.

Philippe stared at Madelon. Servants and guests swirled unseen about them. He was suddenly assailed by one brutal thought which wiped away all others: She did belong in this house. The persistent rumor which submerges but does not die, surfaced and swept over him in all its implications. She did belong in this man's house.

She hurried toward him, her slender arm outstretched. Light in dazzling prisms from chandeliers fragmented and spun in her hair. She looked as young as she had the last time he saw her. She was as fragilely beautiful as always. She was an unquenchable thirst. She was an old man's mistress.

"Oh, Philippe. It's so good to see you." At the peal of her voice, he responded as worshippers do to vesper bells. A wave of tenderness went through him.

She caught his hands. "You're not leaving?"

"Yes."

"Why? Where are you going?"

"I don't know. Out. To New York. To Paris."

She bit her lip, her violet eyes shadowed. "You're enraged."

"I met your lover."

"What?"

He shrugged. "You look lovely. You haven't changed."

"Your words are so charming. Why do they sound so cruel?"

"I don't know." He looked around. "This is a difficult time."

"Can't you stay? A little while?"

"I'm sorry. I wasn't thrown out or ordered out by my host, but I don't think he'd welcome me, a vile and villainous adventurer, among his guests."

Her lips pulled into a gentle smile. She caught his hand and led him across the foyer. She closed the door of a small sitting room behind them, and the music and laughter and mindless chatter abruptly ceased. The room was lamplit and cozy, with couch, love seat and large easy chair before a fireplace. A large bay window jutted out almost to the street. Philippe glanced around, somehow hating this retreat.

Madelon seemed completely at ease. There was a composure about her that was more chill than tranquility, more resignation than self-possession, more passive acceptance than expectancy or pleasure.

He exhaled deeply. There was no reason she should remain the enchanted girl he'd known; she'd waded through disenchantment to whatever refuge she'd found. Of course, she was no longer the virginal young girl he'd loved on Ile St. Louis, no more the sad, betrayed little wife, pregnant and distressed in an alien land. Time had thundered forward for all of them. Still, the years had been more than kind to Madelon. She was one of those fortunate women who, in her late thirties, looked to be in her twenties.

He wanted to weep for her, as she stood here now, and for all they'd lost.

He thought back over all he'd heard about her over the years in America. She was reputed to be Senator John Tyler Morgan's single greatest asset in dealing with out-of-chambers politics, which was actually where most Washington political matters were resolved—cloak-halls, hotel suites, restaurants, bed chambers.

She had appeared on the Washington scene like a late-opening flower which bursts delayed into full bloom. She spent her days and, obviously, her nights in activity designed to provide the senator all the opportunities he coveted to exercise his incredible power. She brought people hurrying to him who would ordinarily have avoided a mean-talking old curmudgeon. She involved herself with her whole heart and with such innate good taste that everything she did proved charming and unaffected.

The way it sometimes happens in Washington, Madelon had become one of the most sought-after people in town.

She had attracted first the attention, then the interest and imagination, and at last, the devotion of the town's volatile society. Madelon's parties were written about in the newspapers. Diplomats, congressmen, publishers, business tycoons, vied for invitations to her pleasant dinners, dances and informal evenings.

It was suggested that more actual diplomacy was practiced in Madelon's parlor than in dozens of estates along Embassy Row. More accommodations and concessions were effected at Madelon's gatherings than in Senate cloakrooms. Secrets were spilled, traded, bought in one way or another, exploited, over her wine glasses. She burst like a brilliant comet over the dull, bureaucratic-gray skies of the District of Columbia.

Madelon did more than bring the right faces to Senator Morgan, they said. She rendered guests impotent to resist her charm, anxious to be invited again, driven to please her, to earn her smile. Through it all, she remained coolly self-possessed, assured of who she was, unaffected, enchanting, displaying genuine interest in them all. With grace and bewitching wit, she collected those people Morgan needed at the moment. Every effort she made, the whispers said, was directed toward helping him achieve his goal.

341

In a frenzy of despair, Philippe shook his head and turned toward the door.

"Please don't go," she said. She exhaled tautly. "Unless you are afraid my conflicting interests will compromise you and your mission. I wouldn't want people to think you are selling out to me, any more than I would want them to think I am surrendering my beliefs to your mistaken values."

"What in hell are you talking about?"

She laughed. "The only safe subject for us, my dearest. The canal. As devoutly as you wish it placed in Panama, I desire to see it where it should be, in Nicaragua."

He stared at her in total disbelief. "For God's sake, why?"

"I've been to Panama. I've also been to Nicaragua. They are two different worlds—one clean and lovely, one a pesthole. You should see Managua, Philippe."

"I suppose you saw it with the senator?"

"Yes. As a matter of fact, I did."

His hands clenched into gray-knuckled fists at his sides. She made no secret of her relationship with Morgan. "I have nothing more to say to you."

She laughed and touched his arm. "Why, Philippe, I do believe you're jealous."

"You're goddamn right I'm jealous."

"On what grounds, *mon chéri*?"

"The usual. You are my wife."

"Am I? After thirteen years, Philippe? I doubt even my church would hold me to such a union. There are words to cover our situation. Desertion. Abandonment. No. I lived in agony. I recovered. I made a new life without you in any part of it."

"Don't talk desertion. I made a home for you. You walked out of it."

"A home? A hovel in a pestilent hole. I left, praying you would follow me and our son. Well, you didn't. We survived. I hate Panama with all my heart and soul. For the misery I saw there. For the misery I suffered there. There'll be no American canal in Panama. Not if I can stop it. I believe John Morgan can defeat it, and I shall try with all my energies to help him."

342

"What you really hate is not Panama. It's me you hate with all your heart."

"Shouldn't I? You taught me to hate, Philippe. You. You alone. Even poor Claude-Bruce never taught me to hate. I loved you with all my heart, and if I hate you, it is with all my heart."

He gazed into her lovely, tear-wet eyes, like spring violets. She spoke of grief, but she was surrounded by glamour and affluence. She looked so lovely he was afraid fully to trust in her protestations of sorrow. All these years she'd had other preoccupations, other interests, and always the option of calling his name.

She shrugged, speaking as if of some inconsequential matter. "I hate you for what you did to me."

"And if there must be hate between us, why not mine? I hate you for running away. Even when I forgave you that, I hated you for refusing even to see me in thirteen years."

"When I left you, you didn't need me. You had your whore."

"Thank God I had someone after you ran out."

"Well, then, you must understand how I feel about John Tyler Morgan."

"No. I can't understand that."

"But at last, and at least—you know."

"I know what?"

"What it is to be jealous."

He glanced about, feeling helpless, almost as if disoriented. He drew a deep breath, exhaled it. "Our son," he said at last. "How is he?"

"He's all right. He's quite well. I have only had to look at Etienne over these past thirteen years to be forcefully reminded of the hell you made of my life."

"I—I'd like to see him."

She shook her head. "You need not see him. He has lived well without you. He can live without you. He does not know you. He does not need to know you."

"Maybe I need to know him."

"Then you should have thought of that, thirteen years ago."

"Are you being purposely cruel? Does it please you?"

343

"I suppose so. You made me cruel. I wear cruelty as a shield against hurt. No one can hurt me if I'm cruel to them first."

He tried to hold her gaze, his own eyes anguished. "Madelon, does nothing we had together mean anything to you?"

But, even as he asked this, he read the answer in her dark eyes. Even those things which had seemed good when they happened were nightmarish to her in retrospect. No happy memory but was chilled with the touch of horror.

He spread his hands, his voice hollow with despair. "I'm sorry, Madelon. I won't keep you any more."

She remained unmoving, her eyes wet with unshed tears. Again, the memories of what he'd wanted their life together to be swept over him like a blurred montage, all out of focus because the reality of what had been was too hurtful to face squarely, even across this chasm of time.

"Don't go," she whispered, her words choked in her taut throat. "Stay. Just a few more minutes."

"What will he think?"

"Who?" Her chin tilted defiantly.

"Your John Tyler Morgan. Your guests. Your servants."

She spread her hands. "I don't know. They—none of them connect you with me."

"I know," he said with chilled irony. "Your husband died in a yellow-fever epidemic in Panama in 1886, didn't he?"

"Senator Morgan says that a lie is an abomination unto the Lord and an ever-present help in time of need."

"Why did you need this particular lie?"

She smiled. "I doubt if you'll believe me, but—to protect you. I knew what you were trying to do promoting the canal in Panama. I was—involved with Senator Morgan, an unalterable foe to Panama. I didn't want to harm you or your mission. I think you wrong, but I know the Panama Canal to be your life. I knew that if your own wife were fighting vigorously for the canal in Nicaragua, it might fatally weaken your case for Panama.

You could not be linked with me and the senator. I could not do that to you. I never wanted to hurt you, Philippe."

"You did a fine job of it, without wanting to."

Her eyes brimmed with tears. She blinked them away savagely. "Nobody ever wants to hurt anyone else, I suppose. Not really. But they can't help it. Nobody can. Nobody ever can."

His hands trembling, he touched her shoulders. An electric charge of desire surged through him. "Oh God, Madelon, you'll never know how I've wanted you."

She turned away, not looking at him. She spoke to the backs of her hands. "I'm sorry, Philippe. Truly sorry. With all my heart."

Irony rimmed his voice. "But there's nothing you can do about it."

"Nothing."

"Because of that bastard Morgan?"

"Philippe, whatever is between us, right or wrong, is between us. It does not concern John Tyler Morgan. Suppose we did return to each other? I would ruin your chances with Panama. What sort of marriage would we have now, after all these years, all that's happened? Could you forgive me John Tyler Morgan?"

He stared at her, torn between love and jealous rage. She could not belong to that wicked old man. She could not care for Morgan. She could *not*. She belonged to him as she could never belong to Morgan or anyone else. Their lives were linked by a hundred raveled threads. She had borne his son. They had belonged, even if the memory were distilled and distorted in her mind. Even when he'd lost her, she still belonged to him in all those remembered ways, and in God's sight. She could never change that, never deny it, any more than she could forget.

She glanced up at him, face taut and sad. "You see, you couldn't forgive me. Any more than I could forgive you Sahyin or Anouk Bazaine. Do you think I can ever forget that I ran away and she returned to you, died for you? No, Philippe, it's too late for us. I've been down too many tired roads ever to turn back."

"He can't have you," he burst out in sudden savagery. "You're my wife. You have been from the moment I first looked at you. You always have been. You always will be. Nothing he can do, nothing you can do will change that."

"My poor Philippe." She spoke as she might to their son. He supposed in his anguish that he did appear baffled.

He swung out his arm, as if warding off blows about his head and shoulders. "Is all this easier for you? Is that it? Entertaining his friends? Lying with him—here in this room? In his bed? Naked in his bed?"

She stiffened. Her eyes darkened. Her chin tilted. "Poor Philippe. We've finally changed places, haven't we? Once my jealousy blinded me, as you are blinded now. Please. You'd better go. You are spoiling what little we did have."

"Am I? Or have you chosen the highest bidder? The brass ring? The free ride? A virgin in Paris. A whore in Washington."

His gratuitous cruelty stung her. She retreated half a step. She blinked back tears as if he'd struck her physically, tears she refused now to shed. "Get out," she whispered.

He nodded. Then, his face pallid, his body trembling, he turned to leave. Suddenly he spun around and faced her again, his eyes savage.

He caught her in his arms. She struggled against him but he held her fiercely. "Just a farewell kiss," he said in anguish. "Something to keep you warm in that old man's cold bed."

He pressed his mouth over hers. Her lips were icy, but he felt them warm, felt them part. It was as if he drank from her mouth to quench an infinite thirst. They kissed for a long, hungry time, everything outside that room forgotten, denied.

She sagged against him, defenseless. He held her body to his own as if they were a matched set, long separated. There were only their quivering, heat-wracked bodies, the pressure of her full breasts upon his chest, the upthrust of her fevered mound upon his aching rigidity. Ecstasy flooded through them.

When at last he released her, the room spun. She almost fell, steadying herself against the loveseat.

He stared down into her eyes for a long time, bewildered, challenging, troubled, accusing, helpless, pleading, raging. He turned suddenly and walked out.

The world looked dark and cold and empty, an abandoned place. It was not that he was finally losing her. He admitted now, he had lost her a long time ago. This was just another of the small catastrophes that they could not conquer, as if the world itself were comprised only of small, hurtful, interconnecting catastrophes.

Philippe walked across Lafayette Square. The very air crackled around him with the incessant shouting of news-boys: Senator Morgan demands impeachment of Roose-velt, cites treason, betrayal and high crimes against the nation.

As was frequent on fall days in the low-lying, tidal-basin Capitol, chilled afternoon rains slanted in on sudden devastating winds. Constitution Avenue, which had been the unsightly Tiber Creek until 1880 when it was finally covered-over and paved, returned to its natural state, a gushing torrential stream boiling west toward the Potomac.

Philippe looked forward with dread to this meeting with Hay. It had been a long and desperately busy two years. Whatever gains Philippe made for the Panama concession, they were stalemated or erased by John Tyler Morgan's counteractions.

Characteristically, Roosevelt ignored Morgan and pro-ceeded in his plans to work out the Panama program. However, from the first, Roosevelt and Hay found it im-possible to deal with the Colombian dictatorship, which ruled Panama as one of its "departments."

In 1898, Colombian President San Clemente had been

imprisoned by Vice President Marroquin. On July 1, 1900, Marroquin had declared San Clemente "absent" and seized power. He had governed since as absolute dictator, even adjourning the Congress. When he was obliged to convene Congress to discuss its treaty with the U.S. in 1903, it was the first meeting of that august body in three years.

Negotiations with Colombia began in Washington where the Hay-Herran treaty was signed. The Compagnie Nouvelle agreed to transfer all rights, privileges, properties, materials and concessions, as well as the Panama Railroad, to the United States. Colombia agreed not to interfere in the building or operation of the canal, to cede a strip of land six miles wide on the isthmus. While maintaining theoretical sovereignty, Colombia granted the U.S. the right to administer, police and protect this zone, as well as to set up special law courts. In return, the Colombian government was to receive indemnity of ten million dollars at once and, beginning nine years after ratification, an annual rental of $250,000.

The lawmakers in the Colombian congress reacted violently to their limited sovereignty over the canal zone. They expressed outrage at the indemnity, claiming they should receive fifteen million dollars from the U.S. and an additional ten million dollars from the Compagnie Nouvelle for permission to transfer the concession.

The Colombian press, enjoying sudden access to "freedom of speech," called the Treaty a "shameful contract" and in splenetic editorials demanded the gallows for the traitor Herran.

United States citizens, too, whipped to a frenzy by impassioned speeches in the Senate and around the country by John Tyler Morgan, protested against involvement of U.S. money and politics in the volatile Department of Panama.

Emotionally and physically exhausted, Philippe despaired of ever pushing the canal project through either the U.S. Congress, dominated by an implacable Senator Morgan or the intransigent Colombians. Whatever amount of indemnity was offered, the Colombians decided they should get a few millions more. Philippe felt too tired to fight Morgan and the Colombians. He admitted the old Alabaman was too formidable a foe for him.

But President Roosevelt grinned and waved his arm. "We'll build that canal. Only the United States is rich enough to build it, so the United States *must* build it. To me it's that simple and hasn't one damned thing to do with gunboat imperialism or Yankee greed . . . in spite of what John Tyler Morgan is shouting. The whole world will benefit from that canal. I've kept things moving so far, and we'll keep moving."

There were a hundred arguments against the validity of the Colombian dissent, and the Morgan opposition, and Philippe made them all. However, it all abruptly slammed to a halt when on August 8, 1903, the Colombian Senate rejected the Hay-Herran Treaty by unanimous vote.

Philippe now reached the place where he must either retreat in surrender or strike from some new position. "Damn it, Mr. Hay, this is war," Philippe said to the Secretary of State. "If Morgan and the Colombians want all-out war, I'll give it to them. I'm damned if I'll stand by and see twenty years of hard labor defeated in so many days."

"Panama must secede," Philippe told any who would listen, and his audiences grew. Foremost among his converts were Manuel Amador Guerrero and Dr. Omar Alonzo Martez. They agreed to join with him and a group of dissidents to break Panama away from Colombia.

With Guerrero as commander, Philippe recruited soldiers for the Panamanian Army of Secession. He pledged one hundred thousand American dollars of his own money to pay soldier wages. Guerrero, Martez and others promised like amounts. They could not afford to permit an outsider to display greater patriotism in public.

Philippe found himself wishing for Guido De Blasio and his reckless schemes for saving every lost cause, no matter how bleak its prospects. Recalling Guido brought back Guido's old laughter, his theory that a good engineer faced his problem squarely and found his answer in the quickest, most direct fashion. "Make an equation of it," Guido laughed. "The ends justify the means."

Suddenly now, Philippe was able to laugh. "You forget,

Señor Amador, your country—Panama—has a protection pact with the United States."

Martez laughed uncertainly. "Does it not seem an irony—the United States aiding a Colombian department to secede—when only recently the U.S. fought one of the bloodiest wars in history to keep the confederated states from separating from the Union?"

"Let's not get involved with ironies," Philippe said. "They only cloud the true issue. The U.S. is indeed bound by treaty to protect property and people and to preserve order in case of any attack on the isthmus." He nodded fiercely. "I believe they will support you. It is the chance we must take."

Saying a brief prayer to whatever gods Guido De Blasio had worshipped, Philippe scribbled a message in Spanish and gave it to Dr. Amador to send by cable to Washington:

> John Hay, Secretary of State, Washington, D.C.
> We have intercepted top-secret Colombian intelligence which reveals a planned armed invasion of Panama to suppress and murder those friendly to the United States and its aims and interests in Pan-America. Fear attack imminent.

U.S. response was immediate and unequivocal. The gunship *Nashville* was ordered to proceed to Colón. The *Boston* was sent to San Juan Del Sur, Nicaragua; the *Atlantic* sailed into Guantanamo, Cuba, and the *Dixie* received orders to sail for the isthmus from League Island.

Orders to ship commanders were clear and without ambiguity. Ships were to maintain free and uninterrupted railway transit on the isthmus, to land and occupy the line if trans-isthmus service were threatened by armed force. They were instructed to prevent landings of any armed forces, either Colombian government or insurgent, at any point within fifty miles of Panama. If, in the judgment of the commanders, any force approaching the isthmus might precipitate a conflict, they were to use force to prevent such approach or landing.

Colombian gunboats standing in the harbor were informed that the revolution had been effected, the independence of Panama achieved. Two gunboats acquiesced and departed, but the commander of the third sent official word that unless the Colombian officers held prisoner in the garrison were set at liberty within two hours, he would shell the city.

At the expiration of this time limit, he fired two rounds, one of which killed a Chinese man on the streets near the barracks. But when the base fort returned fire, the gunboat steamed out of the harbor. On November 6, the new State of Panama was recognized by President Roosevelt.

Thousands of Panamanians who had not even realized they had been living under the rule of distant, faceless men in Bogotá, now rejoiced that their soil was their own—freed forever, as Amador's message promised, from yoke of foreign oppression and domination. They began a wild night of celebration. Their very lives were impermanent. Much that was given them with one hand in the past had been snatched away with the other. They'd learned to live only for this moment. This joyous fiesta was to be enjoyed while one could—while drums beat wildly, the trumpets flourished and people danced the tamborita in the streets.

The frenzy increased in savage intensity. Barrels, kegs, bottles and hogsheads of rum, beer and tequila appeared, along with makeshift tables of roast chickens and hams. Only late in the night did the celebration turn to burning, looting, raping, all those pleasures reserved to a victorious people.

One of Dr. Amador's first official acts was to reward Philippe, appointing him Panama's accredited agent to President Roosevelt, with the pretentious title of Minister Plenipotentiary, which authorized and empowered him to conduct negotiations in the name of the new government. Amador cried out, "Without our good and selfless friend, Bunau-Varilla, there would be no independence of Panama."

However, greed is not unknown even in the newest and most ardent governments. Immediate dissatisfaction among Dr. Amador's cabinet arose with the terms and conditions of the Hay-Herran Treaty, amount of indemnity, and U.S. control of the canal zone. The dissent was the same as that expressed in Bogotá, only the faces and the voices were different.

Still, Philippe was unprepared for the news brought him by Dr. Martez. Amador and his cabinet had had second thoughts; they regretted having appointed a foreigner to such high position as Minister Plenipotentiary. They decided the title was nominal only. They determined to act in their own behalf. They left Colón by ship to discuss in Washington new terms and conditions for a canal treaty.

Philippe arrived in the District of Columbia to find the atmosphere of the humid tidewater basin already static and crackling, the very air bristling with hostility. Charges of "conspiracy" between the American White House and the revolutionists in Panama surfaced as soon as news of the *coup d'état* was circulated. Morgan demanded an immediate inquiry into the actions of the President and the manner of acquiring proposed canal rights of way, through secret fomenting and overt support of revolution.

Secretary Hay welcomed Philippe warmly into his office, though he was too ill to get out of his chair, which by now seemed to have outgrown the frail and dying man.

Hay assured Philippe he found no problem in dealing with him as authorized representative of the new Panamanian government, nor could he foresee any difficulty inside the Executive branch. Hay accompanied Philippe to the President's office in the White House.

They found T.R. jaunty, animated and stimulated by the recent victory. He was even intrigued by the violent reaction in the U.S. against the secession.

"I see no crime in anything we did," T.R. said. "I haven't time to give history lessons to my opposition, but the facts are that since Panama joined Colombia, Panama has not had *one* governor or representative from among its native people, only those imposed from outside by the bandits who grabbed Colombia. Why don't Morgan and those others yelling for my scalp admit that the Colombian congress has convened *one time*, in God knows how many years, and this once was for the sole purpose of rejecting agreements between our nation and Colombia, and upping the ante? Those rascals didn't give a snap for what was best for Panama. They had one aim, and one aim only, in mind. They meant to demand more millions in plunder, for their own booty, and to hell with what was best for Panama and the rest of the world."

Roosevelt swung his arm and grinned without mirth. "If we had acted otherwise than we did, we'd have caught hell from these same jackals now yapping at our heels. They would have called any inaction folly and weakness, a crime against *our* nation, and that time they would have been right." He shrugged his heavy shoulders and now his smile was genuine. "The position Morgan and his cohorts presently take is all wrong, that's all, and we've only to keep our tempers in check and hang on to our sense of humor."

"And carry a big stick," Secretary Hay suggested in a dry tone.

Roosevelt put his head back, laughing, his pince-nez lenses reflecting the brilliance of the chandeliers. "That too," he said, nodding vigorously. "That, too."

Philippe left the White House and walked along muddy Pennsylvania Avenue in a chilled drizzle to the Willard Hotel. His teeth chattered with cold on the short walk. He was too tired to be moved by the hostility crackling against him in the lobby. He did not bother with people who couldn't snub him because he was too exhausted to glance their way. Hell, he'd not started out to make friends. He had intended all along to build a canal across Panama.

That afternoon, November 18, 1903, eighteen years after Philippe joined the fight to build a canal in Panama, President Roosevelt had signed the Hay–Bunau-Varilla Treaty. Panama was now committed to almost the exact terms and conditions of the Hay-Herran Treaty.

At that moment he believed his job, his long ordeal, was over. A reaction of total fatigue had washed down through him.

He entered his room overlooking 14th Street, undressed and fell across his bed. Sounds of carriages, an occasional horn of one of the new automobiles, laughter of passersby on the street, shouts of newsboys, mixed together and rode in the open windows on chilled mists of rain. He was too tired to care. He fell asleep. He slept for two days, lying on his bed, or lounging in a deep chair set at the window with its rectangular view of the bustling Southern town. He ordered meals and mail sent up to him.

He slept, waking only from nightmares in which he cried after Madelon and she moved forever just beyond his reach. She lived in his mind in the hours when he was awake. Even the faint recall of her cologne stirred him unbearably. Breeze-wafted laughter of some girl walking below his window brought Madelon into the room, flooding his mind and accelerating his heart. Nor could he escape her when he slept. Madelon haunted his dreams, with a hurtful loss that he could not dispel. Not even total fatigue could erase his overpowering need for Madelon. In fact, the more tired he became, the more intense was his desire for Madelon's arms and lips. But one thought washed over all others. It was too late for them.

He was sprawled in his chair, his eyes fixed on nothingness in some middle distance, his mind plodding after Madelon across the chasms of time, when the knock rattled his door a dozen times. He answered at last and was handed the note which summoned him urgently to the office of Secretary Hay.

He found the ailing Secretary slumped in his chair behind a desk stacked high with paperwork. Hay said, "We've missed you around here. Wasn't like you to run out when the shooting started."

"I was exhausted."

"We all are."

"Has something happened to the Treaty?"

Hay spread his hands and stared at the papyruslike flesh of his slender fingers. "Depends on what you mean. The Panamanian Government has agreed to the provisions of the Hay–Bunau-Varilla Treaty. They are ready for us to build and control a ten-mile Canal Zone. Our trouble is coming from within this country. From John Tyler Morgan. The old man seems to have lost all perspective now that Nicaragua is losing favor, and Roosevelt is winning the day for Panama. Morgan claims to have evidence of Presidential conspiracy in the revolution. Now a Mr.

Duque, whom I seem to have met once briefly and never visited alone, reports through John Tyler Morgan and the Pulitzer papers that I told Duque that the Panama Revolution was to have taken place on September 23, but that I opposed this date because I felt it was premature and should be deferred. I really don't care what they say about me, but it is humiliating to have this Administration sullied by such scurrilous lies.

"Where slanderers are of foreign origin, I have no concern. Our criticism comes from Americans. For them I have deepest contempt and indignation. In wanton dishonesty and malice, a man like John Tyler Morgan abandons a lifetime reputation for almost saintly regard for truth and principles to destroy progress on what can be the greatest work of its kind ever attempted. A project which will despite them all benefit and reward *them* beyond their wildest dreams, in this country, in every country, and especially that deprived, backward and bloody state of Panama."

"What precisely is Morgan charging?"

Hay glanced up, questioningly. "Haven't you seen the Washington papers?"

"I've seen no papers at all. I've read nothing except the most urgent of my mail."

"You've lived an ideal existence." The Secretary smiled wryly. "But in a fool's paradise, I'm afraid. Do you recall the article you wrote for *Le Matin*? The essay concerning U.S. plans for development in Panama?"

"What possible fault can be found with my report to the French people—in a French periodical?"

"Few see it as a *report*. Morgan sees it as a blueprint, an outline, followed to the letter, the dotted *i* and the crossed *t*, by the White House and the State Department. He charges the ugliest conspiracy of all, that you advised not only the revolutionists in Panama, but that you led the President and me by the hand through a vile and nefarious scheme."

"I should have killed him."

"The Yankees should have shot him at Chickamauga, but it's too late for that now."

"How is the President taking this slander?"

356

"He's standing up under it better than I am. Or he was until this latest attack on his family and friends in the *World*." Hay shook his head. "God knows, not even Lincoln—and I was there with him, too—at the darkest hour of the Civil War was reviled as Roosevelt is today. Roosevelt's *crime,* as I see it, is that he *acted* while others debated, and for this alone, he has been brutally abused and slandered. No national enterprise of my knowledge was ever subjected to more persistent and scurrilous assault."

They joined President Roosevelt in his office in order to attend a conference with him. They found T.R. livid and ready to smash every item of bric-a-brac in the White House simply to relieve intolerable inner pressures.

Roosevelt shook a copy of the New York *World* before their faces. "John Tyler Morgan originated this story, Bunau-Varilla, with the cooperation of that shabby journalist Mr. Joseph Pulitzer. I agree with Mr. Pulitzer that freedom of the press is a precious right. But unknown, or unimportant to him, is the fact that *every* right carries with it a balancing obligation and responsibility."

The *World* claimed to have information concerning the acquisition of the Panama Canal which proved the Roosevelt Administration far more corrupt than the Republican Administration of the hapless Grant, more corrupt than one could possibly foresee the party could become again in a hundred years—"if, after these facts are aired, there exists a Republican Party at all. Roosevelt may well, this time, pull the Grand Old Party down forever with him."

Pulitzer's newspaper charged that an American syndicate had secretly acquired title and property of the Compagnie Nouvelle du Canal from its perfidious representative Bunau-Varilla. This syndicate then, the newspaper alleged, resold this title to the U.S. Government at a "huge" profit to members of the syndicate and at the expense of the American taxpayer.

The newspaper named the members of this fraudulent syndicate which, it stated, included the President's brother-in-law, Douglas Robinson, and Charles P. Taft, brother of William, whom Roosevelt favored as his successor in office.

"Do you want my word under oath, Mr. President?" Philippe asked.

"My oath on this ugly business is strong enough for both of us," Roosevelt said. "We have begun a total investigation which will spare no one. Though these stories are totally without foundation. They are lies. Against me. Against my friends. Against my family. And by damned if I'll tolerate that.

"But even more serious, these stories are wholly, and in form, a libel upon the United States Government. I do not believe we should concern ourselves with the particular hired individuals who wrote these lying and libelous stories and editorials. The real offenders are Senator John Tyler Morgan and Mr. Joseph Pulitzer, editor and proprietor of the *World*.

"While the criminal offense of which Messieurs Morgan and Pulitzer are guilty is a libel upon individuals, the great injury is the blackening of the good name of the American people." He spread his hands, his eyes glittering. "All I can say to you, gentlemen, is that in a moment, we shall face Mr. Morgan, and Mr. Pulitzer, among others, across a conference table. And I ask of both of you only one thing. Help me, in the name of God, to control my rages. Do not allow me, I beg you, to sink to the depths of slime and evil of these two vermin. We shall smile at them. We shall shake their hand. And so help me God, we'll see them in hell."

A dozen congressmen and senators, among them Hanna, Herrick, Lodge and Morgan, along with several magazine and newspaper publishers, gathered at a conference table in a White House meeting room.

Hay sank quietly into his chair near the President's. Philippe sat at the end of the long table. The room was quickly filled with cigar smoke. Many of the Congressmen bent awkwardly and frequently to spew tobacco juice toward strategically placed spittoons.

Senator Lodge spoke first. "Without expressing my own opinions, bias or concerns on this matter, let me state as dispassionately as possible the situation we face because of charges promulgated in newspapers and in the Senate by Senator Morgan. My able colleague, Senator Morgan, has quoted extensively from an article written by Philippe Bunau-Varilla in *Le Matin* of September second last. Morgan points out that Bunau-Varilla represents not only the Compagnie Nouvelle du Canal of France, but acts as Minister Plenipotentiary for Panama, that he has been an ardent lobbyist for U.S. intervention in Panama for the past eighteen years. Further, that he was at one time placed in charge of building the failed canal under the French. That he is, in short, a man with many conflicts of interest, of questionable repute, a man totally involved in every aspect of this situation, with every hope of profiteering handsomely from it. But more than that, he is directly delegated the responsibility of recouping at least forty million dollars from the U.S. for rights to a defunct project in a neutral Central American state, this money to accrue to the accounts of a company of questionable legality."

"Don't let your impartiality, New England dispassion and complete objectivity choke you up, Senator," Hay suggested in a mildly taunting tone. Laughter rippled along the table.

Senator Lodge smiled, but his voice and manner remained chilled. "Senator Morgan charges that Bunau-Varilla's article in *Le Matin* of September 2 foreshadows precisely the course followed by this Administration in dealing with the Panama uprising and subsequent declaration of independence. From this *precise* outline, Morgan and others deduce that Secretary Hay, or you, Mr. President, must have inspired that coarse of action so minutely detailed by *M'sieu* Bunau-Varilla. Wayne McVeagh, as well as Senator Morgan and others, profess to be able to produce telegrams from Bunau-Varilla which will show an exact knowledge of secret U.S. movements in this affair, even our intentions as regards sending ships to the isthmus, keeping order there, and recognizing a revolutionary government. This seems to these critics, at least, Mr. Hay, to prove that Bunau-Varilla had prior assurances from this government, and that he not only acted on and profited from such assurances, but that he so advised the revolutionaries based on his intimate knowledge of our intentions and planned actions."

"Have you, Senator Morgan, or you, Senator McVeagh, or any of you other gentlemen seen such telegrams? Can you produce them? When may we expect to see them?" Hay asked. A low rumble volleyed along the table.

Senator Lodge shrugged. "The *existence* of such telegrams is the salient point here, Mr. Hay. As Senator Morgan will tell you, such telegrams *do* exist in which Bunau-Varilla asserts that he *does* have these very assurances—gunboat movement, protection for the revolutionaries, recognition of a revolutionary government, reparation plans—all from inside this Administration."

"But you have not personally seen any such telegrams, Senator Lodge?" the President inquired.

Senator Lodge shook his head negatively. "No, sir, I have not. Not personally, but—"

"Well, I haven't seen any such telegrams, either," Roosevelt said in the mildest of tones. "But I can state to all of you here, and in the presence of *M'sieu* Bunau-Varilla, that neither John Hay, nor I, nor anyone speaking for us, either privately, directly, or indirectly, gave such assurances or such information in any shape or form to the gentleman."

Senator Morgan spoke now, suspicious eyes glittering, drawling voice rasping. "But don't you see, Mr. President, that this begs the main issue? It just don't slop the hogs. You do not deny that Bunau-Varilla's *Le Matin* article is a remarkable forecast of what actually transpired in the months and weeks since last September second?"

The President nodded, voice polite and almost gentle. "I do not deny it. It is indeed remarkable. But what this exposé reveals is that this forecast was prepared and published six weeks *before* Bunau-Varilla saw either Hay or me on this matter. It appeared one *week* before I called John Bassett Moore to Oyster Bay, and, *for the first time,* definitely formulated my policy, even in my own mind.

"Gentlemen, you of the opposition have proved too much. You have proved that Bunau-Varilla may have advised, led, supported, even inspired, the revolutionaries in

360

Panama, but you also prove that he did not gain his assurances or information from us. Simply because *we* didn't have it at that time. He was already writing what he believed, six weeks before I myself believed it. You have proved that Bunau-Varilla, after eighteen years of devoting his life to the subject, was able to forecast what the U.S. was going to do in Central America at least *six weeks* before he even saw or talked to people in my Administration, and some little time before I had even made up my mind what I should do.

"I don't know what Bunau-Varilla told the revolutionaries in Panama. It is not my place or my duty to know. But I do know that he did not base his advice on prior assurances from us. This administration acted in the best interests of this nation, and of Panama and, we believe, of the world. We did what we had to do in Panama. If this action followed a campaign or program coincidentally laid out in speculation by Bunau-Varilla, it proves only that Bunau-Varilla is a hell of an able fellow."

The President hesitated in a way he had, which could prove either flattering or disconcerting, of meeting the gaze of each man along both sides of the table. One of the senators spat into a spittoon. Otherwise no one moved until John Tyler Morgan growled, "It still don't slop the hogs. It still don't answer questions. It don't take the rag off the bush. It don't square with what John tole Mary. It still don't git you out of the woods, Mr. President. Not with me, and not with the American people."

"Are you speaking for them now, John?" Hay inquired.

"God knows somebody's got to in a pack of hounds like this."

President Roosevelt stared across the table at the old Alabaman. He said in a soft, unrelenting tone, "What do you want of me, Senator Morgan? I have answered you the best I know, from motives as honest as your own, I think. No more. No less. What is it I should do? I could have followed traditional methods. I would then have submitted a dignified state paper on the Panama situation of probably two hundred printed pages to Congress, and the debate on it would be going on for the next five years.

But instead, I took the Canal Zone and while the debate goes on, so shall that canal."

"That's where I believe you totally wrong, sir," Morgan said.

"Oh? Who's to stop me?"

Morgan's voice shook, but from suppressed rages and not from any hint of weakness, age or infirmity. "Sir, never in 26 years serving my folks in Congress, never once in the most evil of my nightmares have I ever imagined talking to a President as I must speak to you. I find your actions, all your actions, sir, deplorable, little less than treasonous, and totally a betrayal of decent American principles.

"Sir, you have lent your support, and the weight of your great office, to a canal in a country which has been repeatedly rejected as an unsuitable site by reputable engineers—and you have done so for private profit. You have permitted scoundrels, adventurers and thieves to profit from your actions which will endanger U.S. neutrality, and may well bankrupt her before you and your cronies are through.

"You come to the Senate now with a so-called Hay–Bunau-Varilla Treaty which will permit you to build a Panama Canal. You ask Congress to ratify this evil document. Well, that's where I'll stop you. In the name of the American people, I'll stop you. I can tell you sir, here and now, you'll never get that treacherous paper, that treasonous piece of conspiracy ratified by the Senate. No, suh. Not as long as I have breath. Not as long as I can take the truth to the American people. I'll tear you down first before I'll permit this foul betrayal to proceed another mile into iniquity."

[46]

Philippe went by hansom cab directly from Lafayette Square to 315 John Marshall Place. He told the driver to wait and swung out of the carriage. He strode across the walk and mounted the stone steps. The day was just clearing.

Senator Morgan's black manservant opened the heavy oak door almost before the echo of Philippe's rapping the brass knocker ebbed. The elegantly attired butler smiled in recognition, but shook his head. "The senator ain't here, suh. He ain't nevah here this time of day. He always over to his senate this time of day."

"I don't want to see the senator. I'd like to see Madame Grenet."

The stout black man frowned and shook his head again. "No, suh. Madame Grenet, she ain't here, suh."

"Do you know where I might find her? It is urgent."

The butler hesitated, chewing at his underlip. "Senator ain't partial to me givin' addresses of his friends to strangers." His face brightened. "But you—sort of friend of the family, I reckon."

"Sort of. It is urgent."

"Yassuh. Well, you might try Madame Grenet's home."

He gave a number on M Street. "She do have a right pretty little cottage. Overlooks the Potomac, it do. Mighty pleasant, where madame live. Out in Georgetown."

Philippe told the hack driver to move at top speed across town northwest to M Street. He sat back, watching the cars, cabs and pedestrians borne past in quick, vague glimpses. He felt troubled. Of all the whispers he'd heard about Madelon he had not once heard that she had a cottage overlooking the Potomac in Georgetown. How wrong had he been on how many scores? His face burned. He stared down at his trembling hands.

The driver pulled into the curb before a row house, recessed slightly from the cobbled walk behind a low stone fence. For a moment, Philippe sat unmoving. The driver turned on the carriage boot. "This here's the number what you tole me. Yas, suh. You want I should wait, suh?"

"No." Philippe paid and dismissed the driver. He crossed the walk, went through the grilled-iron gateway and rapped with the heavy doorknocker.

After a brief pause, the door was unlocked noisily from within and opened hesitantly. Philippe stared at Fanny LeBeau's comic-valentine face. He had not seen her in eighteen years, but he knew her instantly.

Fanny recognized him, too. A look of mild panic flared in her bulging eyes and, for an instant, she appeared ready to slam the door and flee.

"Hello, Fanny. Is madame at home?"

"Not now, *m'sieu*. Maybe you could come back?"

"Maybe I could wait, Fanny."

"I don't know when madame will return." The panic was less mild.

"Is Etienne here?"

"That boy? No, no, he's not home neither. I don't know when he'll be home."

Someone spoke behind Philippe and Fanny looked trapped. "Why don't you know when Etienne will be home, Fanny? I come home every day at this time."

Philippe turned, at the sound of his own voice. He stared incredulous, unable to believe his own eyes. The

364

years spun away and Philippe felt he looked at himself as he had come first to that courtyard apartment where he'd met Madelon on the Ile St. Louis more than 22 years ago.

The boy's hair was dark, thick about his ears and over his collar. His eyes laughed, and the boy himself, actually a young man, was rakishly good-looking, defiant, jaunty and reckless. Philippe *was* looking at his own past.

"Etienne," he whispered.

"Father?" Etienne said, grinning.

Philippe smiled though his eyes blurred with unashamed tears of pleasure and discovery. "What is left of me. Yes, I'm your papa, Etienne. God knows, there can be no doubt of that."

"I never entertained the faintest skepticism about it. That's university talk, Papa, for saying I never doubted it." Etienne laughed. "Every time Fanny is mad with me, she cries out, 'You're just your papa made over!' "

They laughed, and swallowed back all the sentiment rising in their taut throats.

"Come in, Father. Please. My God, I can't believe Fanny didn't invite you in."

"Dear Fanny hasn't changed," Philippe said.

"Wasn't proper," Fanny mumbled. "Alone in the house with him."

They sat at a small table in the courtyard at the rear of the house. Philippe, lounging in the shade of an elm, with a view of the river and Virginia's rugged palisades beyond, felt a deep serenity, a restfulness he'd not even glimpsed in eighteen hectic years. Madelon, through her magic, had transformed this brick townhouse into a narrow strip of France overlooking the Potomac. She had evoked Paris upon this alien soil.

He sagged in the pillowed, wrought-iron chair, aware that Etienne studied him closely. "I've wanted to meet you," Etienne said. "I've always wanted to meet you."

"And I you."

Etienne smiled. Philippe remembered his own teasing smile a long time ago, recreated now in Etienne's young face. "Mother and Fanny have told me much about you."

"I'm not really all that bad."

"You couldn't be."

"And you, Etienne?"

Etienne shrugged. "I go to Georgetown. I study engineering."

"And how do you feel about me?"

Etienne laughed. "I love you. You're my father."

"In absentia."

"Then I've loved you in absentia. As I told my mother, when the United States starts building the canal in Panama, I shall be there. As you were."

Philippe's eyes filled with tears. His throat felt choked with his pride. He sat for a long moment in the lacy dappling of sunlight. At last, he said only, "You should be at home. In Paris. In school."

"Why?"

"How will it be, a son of mine whose second language is French?"

"I don't care about that. I do care about the canal. All you did for it. All you have tried to do for it. The way you have sacrificed your—your life for it. You see, I don't happen to share Senator Morgan's view that you're prompted by greed."

"Thank you, Etienne."

"You aren't, are you?"

They both laughed.

Philippe sighed. "I want you to know, Etienne. I don't give a damn about the rest of them. I do care about you, what you know, what you think, what you believe. I came to the canal because of my inexpressible admiration for a very remarkable man."

"De Lesseps?"

"And then I saw other magnificent young men and women, selfless, dedicated people, die for what de Lesseps dreamed could be accomplished in Panama. I tried, after we were shut down, to put it from my mind, admit we had failed. But I could not do it. Not and live with myself. I was driven to insuring the construction of that canal, if not by the French, by somebody. In de Lesseps' name. In the name of Guido De Blasio and the thousands like him who never thought once of personal profit, but died trying to bring about completion of a vital and necessary sea-link against impossible odds. I'm sorry. I never meant to make a speech to you. God forbid. But this is the truth, Etienne. The only truth."

Etienne swallowed hard. He nodded, then laughed. "As Senator Morgan says, you're not really a rascal. You just look like one."

Philippe tried, but could not smile.

"Your friend—your mother's friend—Senator Morgan has won, I'm afraid. But it will prove a costly victory. He has waged a campaign of villification and destructiveness which threatens to impeach President Roosevelt. There is only a hundred-to-one chance that the new Panama treaty which Roosevelt signed will be ratified in a Senate dominated, intimidated, and deceived by Senator Morgan. I have come to plead with your mother to use her influence, her rationality, her good sense, to stop this reckless and violent man before he destroys all we have worked so hard to achieve."

"What do you think Mother could do?"

"I don't know. I'm desperate. I pray she'll talk sanity to Morgan. Make him see that his victory will not be worth its fearful cost. He will destroy a good and honorable man. He may well throw this government into the kind of panic and chaos it faced when Andrew Johnson was impeached."

Etienne stood up. "I support your views, almost totally. I know you hate Senator Morgan. I know he despises you. I know he means to have that canal built in Nicaragua, or not built at all. But you are blinded, one to the other, by hatred. He sees no good in you. He feels that whatever evil he does you, and to President Roosevelt, is justified by the honorable ends he seeks. On the other hand, he is a man of great intelligence and wit, a pleasure for his friends and underlings to work with. In his own mind, his motives are noble and patriotic. He believes he is right and you are wrong, as well as a scoundrel. I don't see how my mother, or anyone else could influence him otherwise than the course he is set upon, just as you could not join him or believe good of him."

"I was there today. In that White House room. I heard

367

the savage attack he made on the President. I know he will not stop. Just as I know he then must be stopped."

"As your hatred blinds you to Senator Morgan's virtues, your love and admiration for President Roosevelt also blind you to Roosevelt's—humanity, his human failings, weaknesses, the faults for which he is cordially hated—self-glorification for one thing. Intolerance of any view but his own. Craftiness and arrogance. No, don't look like that. I feel as strongly as you. Roosevelt is a great man. A noble and magnificent leader, but not without his faults. Senator Morgan sees only faults. You see only virtue. Senator Morgan sees his attack, which you call scurrilous, as a Godly crusade."

"My God. Whose side are you on?"

"Yours. I told you. But I refuse to wear halters to blind myself to facts. Senator Morgan believes himself as honest and right, and on the side of God, as you do or as President Roosevelt does. But, you *are* right, Father. You and the President. Yes, T.R. is a remarkable man. As was de Lesseps, I'm sure, but you are as remarkable as either of them . . . and you are right."

From his jacket pocket, Etienne removed his wallet and took from it a small bright postage stamp. He extended it on the tip of his index finger. "Have you seen this latest evidence of how right you are, Father?"

Philippe took the small colorful one-*centavo* Nicaraguan stamp. It showed a railroad wharf in the foreground and, in the background, Momotombo, in violent eruption.

Etienne's laughter was incredulous. "Can you believe any country would be rash enough to issue a postage stamp, an official seal, with a picture of an erupting volcano as representative of its nation?"

Philippe shook his head, staring at the stamp. "And yet, Senator Morgan proceeds doggedly to persist in declaring Nicaragua as the suitable site for the American canal."

At this moment, the glass doors from the living room were pushed open and Madelon came out upon the sunlit flagstone terrace.

As Philippe and Etienne stood to receive her, Madelon stopped and stared at them, shaking her head. She gazed first at Philippe and then at Etienne and back again. Her eyes brimmed with tears. She put out her hand. "Oh, Philippe."

At last, Philippe was able to get Madelon alone in the parlor. He locked the door to the corridor. She watched him, frowning faintly, but said nothing. Beyond the doors the night closed in across the river in cloudy mists. She still looked golden and fragile and as desirable as the first day he saw her.

Philippe's heart pounded, his hands ached to close on the loveliness of her breasts, the gentle curve of her flawless throat.

He managed to keep his voice calm. "Etienne—is a beautiful boy."

She watched him prowl before her. "Yes. He looks exactly like you at eighteen."

"God knows I hope he doesn't look like me at forty."

She bit her lip, her voice oddly empty. "Perhaps he won't have to go through hell. As you did. When Etienne was a baby, I looked at him and hated you because he was a constant reminder of all our hurt and loss. But now, in these last years when he has grown to look so like you did, it is haunting. It is like looking at you, as you were, young and strong and beautiful. As if, sometimes, you are here, in this room with me. Reminding me how deeply I loved you. How deeply you loved me in your own way."

"And yet, you still fight me. You still think me wrong. About everything. Even about Panama."

She looked up now and her eyes met his. "I shall lose both you and Etienne to that place of pestilence. Oh God, he's so like you! He says he'll be among the first there to work, the moment construction starts."

"No," he answered. "He won't go there. There'll be no construction in Panama. That's why I came here. To plead with you, no matter your hatred for me or Panama, to use your influence with Morgan. Stop him before he destroys everything around him in his malice."

She smiled gently, and with compassion he had not seen in her eyes before. "Do you really think I have so much influence with him?"

"I don't know. I hope so. Somebody must stop him."

369

She sighed, stood up and walked to the darkening doorway, the night beyond it pressing in upon them. "You know him so little," she said.

"I think you can make him do what you want."

"You flatter me, Philippe, whether you intend to or not. He would not listen to me on Panama any more than he would to you. His mind is closed on it. He is determined to build that canal in Nicaragua. He has worked for it even longer than you have for Panama. No one can change him on that."

He took a step toward her. "You mean you won't help me?"

She turned, her face pale and sad. "Philippe, I mean I cannot."

His voice rasped in the room. "If you have no influence with him, who in God's world does? What has it bought you then, to be at his beck and call, all these years?"

She bit her lip and looked around the room as if it were a cage, as if the world were a cage.

"Philippe?" Her voice was soft and empty. "I know what you believe of me. I know what most of Washington believes of me. I'm sorry. I have no control, no power over Senator Morgan. I'm sorry. There's no way I could stop him."

His eyes bored into hers. His fists clenched at his sides. "What it adds up to is that you won't. Are you even with me now for all hurts, Madelon? Are we quits at last? Are you finally and totally revenged against me?"

Her gaze still held his. A veil seemed to fall down in them. "I think you had better go now," she said.

He did not even hear her, so wrapped in agony was he. "You alone could help me stop that evil old man, and you refuse. Then to hell with you. Go back to his bed. Laugh with him about how I came pleading to you, how I came to you in my weakness, in my need. And finally you could repay me, get even at last, for everything."

"Philippe—"

"All right, madame. We won't meet again. I am beaten. This can be good for delightful jokes between you and your lover at the last. You can laugh with him about my defeat."

"Are you finished?" she said.

"No. We are not quite quits, Madame. Not yet. I think if you want so badly to hate me, I should give you a memory truly to hate."

"Don't, Philippe."

He stood gazing at her, the pressures expanding inside him. "Why not? Are you afraid your senile old lover will come through that door? Well, he won't. It's locked."

She tried to walk past him toward the door.

He seized her arm and pulled her back savagely into his arms. She turned, trying to break free, but he held her brutally. He caught the back of her head in his hand and forced her face up to his. Her eyes were large and round, and swirled with shadows. His mouth closed over hers. His hands moved tautly, roughly through her hair which shook loose and tumbled about her shoulders.

"No," she whispered, "If I scream, Fanny will come."

"I hope she does."

Something swirled in her eyes, and he saw it was laughter. But she fought him again. "Wait," she begged. "Please wait. For Etienne's sake?"

"Why should I? Etienne knows how deeply I love you. Only you have ever been fool enough not to know. Why don't you tell the truth at last?"

She breathed heavily, pressed against him, staring up at him. "What is the truth?"

"That you're afraid your—your lover will find out."

"Oh, you're such a fool," she raged. "Such a damn fool."

He clutched the neckline of her dress in his fist. He yanked downward, the tiny buttons popping loose, snapping free and flying out on the carpeting. He shoved the loosened fabric down over her shoulders. The dress toppled along her thighs and fell in a heap about her feet.

"Oh, Philippe, please."

"It's too late for begging, too."

He broke the straps of her slip and removed it, tearing it downward along her body. Her breasts burst free. Suddenly she sagged against him, no longer resisting. He stared, eyes brimming with tears, at the mature perfection

n-standing breasts, her rigid nipples. His
over her breasts, caressing and fondling.

she was naked, he held her body against him,
himself to her, his own rigidity throbbing. His
...ds moved hungrily, fiercely over her. His mouth
covered hers and after a moment her lips parted. They
kissed for a long, breathless time. His body trembled with
longing.

They sank to the carpeting, sinking in embrace upon it,
her thighs opening to him. Their hearts pounded with
incredible savagery. She closed her eyes for a brief instant
and when she opened them, they were hot with a wildness
he'd never seen in them before.

Her arms went up under his to his shoulders, pulling
him down to her. Her fingernails dug into the flesh of his
shoulders. The pungent fragrance of her heated body
swept over him. Her body molded against his. Her mouth
locked against his. He thrust himself into her and felt her
body moving under him, frantic. She was burning hotter
than the sun of Panama, searing him as that furnace never
had. He stroked passionately, in anger, in rage, in madness. Sensations too bitterly sweet to be borne racked him.
Their frenzy mounted and burst in a savage, mindless
unison.

He fell away from her and she opened her eyes and
watched him move away in dim shadows, standing above
her, rearranging his clothing.

He stood, drained, the backs of his legs weak, his
body trembling with agony of need and loss. All he could
think was how desperately he loved her. He had always
loved her. He would love her forever. It was just too bad.
He could not make her care.

Her head was turned away, her hair wild against the
flooring, and she was crying. He said, "Good-bye, Madelon. I won't bother you again."

"Oh, Philippe," she whispered after him in the darkness. "Oh, my poor Philippe."

[47]

Philippe was among the first in the visitors' gallery when debate began on the Hay–Bunau-Varilla Treaty.

John Tyler Morgan took the floor early and kept it long. The old Alabaman was no orator despite 26 years of haranguing the Senate chambers. But this debate was his kind of fight. This treaty was so controversial that none could discuss it calmly. Morgan and Hoar, of Massachusetts, led the assault on the treaty and on President Roosevelt's conduct.

The debate flared passionately, one of the fiercest in the history of the Senate. Every slander, every suspicion of intrigue, was aired. Morgan passed around cartoons from New York newspapers depicting Bunau-Varilla in every manner of secretive maneuver and escapade, but always greedily clutching French canal stock in one hand behind his back.

As the debate raged on the Senate floor, one fact emerged that heartened the pro-treaty forces. Little real fault could be found or manufactured against the treaty itself. Spooner, Cullom and Lodge led in supporting the measure. The man most missed by treaty proponents was Mark Hanna. Word came from his room at the Arlington Hotel. The 65-year-old Kingmaker lay dying.

Philippe supplied Spooner and others invaluable aid with clever diagrams which he had designed. Each displayed Panama's essential engineering and navigational superiority. All were based on the canal commission's own statistics. They were as simple as a child's primer drawings, as easily grasped and understood. They conveyed their message at a glance and were easy to remember. They made a dramatic impact. Spooner called them "inspiration." Few people, he said, understood or bothered to read technical reports. The only advantage Panama could claim over Nicaragua was technical superiority. The most backward and casual auditor could immediately grasp the meaning and content of Philippe's diagrams.

Further, Philippe supplied arguments against the Nicaragua route because of the danger of volcanic eruptions. This was the last straw for John Tyler Morgan. This one issue, hammered at repeatedly, inflamed the old Senator beyond endurance. He lunged to his feet, shouting that "a scurrilous French adventurer continues to call the shots for my unworthy opponents, just as he has led them all these years. He dictates from the gallery yonder every word mouthed by these orators on the floor. He is still preaching his damnable libel about seismic disturbances in that lovely country!"

Morgan refused to permit any hint of sentiment or generosity toward his old "railroad foe" Marcus Alonzo Hanna to contaminate proceedings on the Senate floor. Even when Hanna died on February 15, Morgan limited time and length of eulogies in the chambers. "We will keep our eyes on the main issue," he shouted. "And the main issue is defeat of this treasonous paper!"

When Morgan sensed instinctively any sign of the tide turning against him and his opposition to the treaty, he would arrange for new tirades, new charges, new delaying tactics by his cohorts, refusing to permit a vote, he said, "Until the climate is ready."

Finally, the vote could be postponed no longer. No further delaying tactics would prevail. Philippe felt ill, helpless, impotent. He questioned everyone. Few held out any hope for ratification of his treaty.

When vote was called, John Tyler Morgan forced a voice vote on the floor. He wanted to see the traitors who would stand against him and America, he thundered. Final voting began after a noon recess.

The voting began badly for the treaty. Then, for Philippe and proponents of the Panama Canal, everything was suddenly and stunningly reversed. The final vote ratified the Hay–Bunau-Varilla Treaty by a margin of 66 to fourteen.

John Tyler Morgan slumped unmoving in his aisle seat on the Senate floor. He seemed unaware that the visitors' gallery had erupted in cheering, singing, yelling. Reporters raced to the few telephones available to them in the building. The cavernous corridors echoed with shouting, running feet, yells of victory. The place was bedlam.

Philippe walked through this madness in a daze. He still could not believe it was true, it was over, he was victorious. It was like a dream which was simply too wonderful to be real.

Senator Spooner met him in the corridor and threw his arm about his his shoulder. "That stamp!" Spooner shouted, laughing and shaking his head. "That stamp! A stroke of true genius, Bunau-Varilla!"

"Stamp?" Philippe stared without comprehension at the Senator.

Spooner winked. "Of course. Of course, you wouldn't know anything about that little stamp caper, eh, you sly French fox!"

Spooner handed Philippe a sheet of bond paper upon which was pasted one of the bright one-*centavo* Nicaraguan stamps. Under this color rendition of huge Momotombo in eruption was printed:

Look at the coat of arms of the Republic of Nicaragua. Look at Nicaraguan postage stamps. Nations put upon their coat of arms what best symbolizes their native soil. What have the Nicaraguans chosen to *characterize* their country on their coat of arms, on their postage stamps? Volcanoes.

Spooner laughed heartily. "Every congressman, every Senator, got one of these stamps and this note. Today. At the eleventh hour. Before the voting began. Exactly before the voting began. As T.R. said of you, Bunau-Varilla, you're one hell of a fellow."

Philippe walked along the vast echoing corridors. John Tyler Morgan spoke his name twice before Philippe became aware of the old Senator standing in his path.

"That stamp. A truly masterful stroke of planning and execution. Eh?" Morgan said.

Philippe shook his head, still numb. "I had nothing to do with it. I wish to God I had, but I did not."

"I know you didn't. Your best couldn't defeat me. But I believe this stamp business turned the tide. I'd have bet my life that I had the votes to beat your treaty. All your chicanery and secret dealing and skulking around, now you can go home to Paris and collect your profits."

"I'm too numbed, Senator, to fight with you now."

"Oh, it's easy to be generous in victory. When you collect as a Compagnie stockholder, which, by God, I know you to be, you should be an extremely wealthy man."

Philippe shrugged. "I know you won't believe it, Senator, and I don't give a damn, but the fact is, I have written to the Company. You may check with them. Whatever my profit from the sale of the French concession will go toward erecting a statue to de Lesseps in Panama."

The old senator smiled coldly and shook his head. "Hell, I believe you. And I believe almost nothing any more."

"Whether you do or not, it's true."

"Never claimed I had the *entire* corner on patriotism, or honesty. I admire you. I don't like you, but I admire you."

Philippe laughed with a memory of his old *élan*. "I don't like you, either."

Morgan laughed with him. "You've been a foe worth the fight. What will you do now? Twenty years at one job and suddenly you're out of work. You going down and run Panama for them natives?"

Philippe shrugged again. "As soon as the treaty was ratified, I cabled my resignation as envoy extraordinary to President Amador. Whatever salary they owe me, it too will be held for erection of the monument to de Lesseps."

"Cuttin' bait all around, are you?"

"Yes. I'm going home, Senator. To Paris."

"Good. But before you go, you ought to express your gratitude to Madame Grenet. You may not have been ratified in there today if it had not been for those stamps and that letter she sent out at just the right moment."

[48]

Philippe walked slowly through the wrought-iron gateway
at the brick townhouse where Madelon and his son lived.
His heart pounded. He had not thought he would ever
come back here, and yet he'd returned in his thoughts a
hundred times.

Fanny LeBeau answered his knock. She didn't smile,
though she curtsied; for her, almost a sign of respect.
Seeing her pasty-white face set and rigid reminded him
that some things had not changed.

"They are not home," Fanny said. But then she added,
"You can come in and wait if you wish."

Philippe paced the patio outside the living room. He
was relieved that neither Madelon nor Etienne were at
home yet. He still needed time to compose himself, to
find the right words to say to her.

He stood at the small fence. Afternoon shadows laced
the walls and accented the undersides of the flowers in
their dark beds. A chill breeze stabbed upward from the
river. Until now, he had not truly known how exhausted
he was, mentally, physically, spiritually. Forty-four years
old! Was it possible? Where had the time gone?

He looked about and grinned wryly. His life, his

family, his career and his dreams, all gone with the landslides, the epidemic fevers, the flash floods and the wild winds of hurricanes across the isthmus. His life and energies, all expended on that canal. It had been such a long journey—such a plodding, tiresome struggle on uncharted byways which led nowhere directly, following detours and tangents, trying to hurry through mud and alligators up to his hips. He thought of his friends, lost in that struggle against the jungle, of all the hatreds and intrigues, the jealousies and betrayals, the cowardices and the ignorance.

Hearing light steps on the flagstones, he turned and gazed at Madelon. Her lovely face flushed, her violet eyes touched at his, fell away, returned and met his gaze squarely. His heart lurched. How lovely she was; how desirable and, oh God, how he had failed and hurt her. He knew he could never find the right words. He wanted to go to her, to take her in his arms, but he didn't move.

They stood looking at each other, two people in the garden shadowed by an elm. Beyond them the rocky slope fell to the wide dark river. Across the Potomac the rugged escarpments of northern Virginia loomed like parapets. The atmosphere was thick with silences, as if the world and everyone in it waited. There was so much he had to say, and yet he could not find the words. He could not stand to lose her again, and yet he did not know how to get her back where she had always belonged, in his arms.

Madelon smiled and said. "You've won."

He nodded. "Yes. It's over. Nothing seems as good as the fact that it is done. I got out of it alive and now I can put it behind me."

"It seems wonderful to me and I'm proud of you."

"Are you, Madelon? At last?"

Suddenly she was crying. She came near him. "Oh, Philippe, I've never stopped loving you."

He drew her to him and kissed her gently. "I'm going home, Madelon. To Paris. Will you go with me?"

She sniffled and nodded, then she laughed. "Yes. Oh, yes. I want to go home, Philippe. With you. And Etienne.

379

That's all I want." She bit her lip. "But there's something you must know."

His heart sank. He steeled himself. "What is it?"

She gazed up at him, her violet eyes caught the sunlight, drowning it in her tears. "I'm pregnant again."

He lifted her from her feet and swung her around. She laughed. "We aren't twenty any more, Philippe."

He grinned down at her. "You may not be."

Etienne came across the flagstones from the shadowed house. "Is this a private celebration, or may I join in?"

They put out their arms and caught their son inside them, holding him close. They laughed and they cried and they clung to each other, and the past with all its hurt and loss fell away from them. Or most of it.

ALISTAIR MacLEAN

Alistair MacLean is known throughout the world as one of the great storytellers of all time. Many of his novels have been made into highly successful movies.

☐	THE BLACK SHRIKE	13903-4	1.75
☐	FEAR IS THE KEY	13560-8	1.75
☐	THE GUNS OF NAVARONE	X3537	1.75
☐	H.M.S. ULYSSES	X3526	1.75
☐	NIGHT WITHOUT END	13710-4	1.75
☐	THE SATAN BUG	14009-1	1.75
☐	THE SECRET WAYS	14010-5	1.95
☐	SOUTH BY JAVA HEAD	13800-3	1.75
☐	BEAR ISLAND	23560-2	1.95
☐	BREAKHEART PASS	22731-6	1.75
☐	CARAVAN TO VACCARES	23361-8	1.75
☐	CIRCUS	22875-4	1.95
☐	FORCE 10 FROM NAVARONE	23565-3	1.95
☐	THE GOLDEN RENDEZVOUS	23624-2	1.95
☐	ICE STATION ZEBRA	23234-4	1.75
☐	PUPPET ON A CHAIN	23318-8	1.75
☐	THE WAY TO DUSTY DEATH	23257-3	1.75
☐	WHEN EIGHT BELLS TOLL	23506-8	1.75
☐	WHERE EAGLES DARE	23623-4	1.75

Buy them at your local bookstores or use this handy coupon for ordering:

FAWCETT BOOKS GROUP, P.O. Box C730, 524 Myrtle Avenue, Pratt Station Brooklyn, N.Y. 11205

Please send me the books I have checked above. Orders for less than 5 books must include 60¢ for the first book and 25¢ for each additional book to cover mailing and handling. Postage is FREE for orders of 5 books or more. Check or money order only. Please include sales tax.

Name_____ Books $_____
Address_____ Postage _____
                                        Sales Tax _____
City_____ State/Zip_____   Total $_____

Please allow 4 to 5 weeks for delivery

Taylor Caldwell

☐ NEVER VICTORIOUS, NEVER DEFEATED	08435-9	1.95
☐ TENDER VICTORY	08298-4	2.25
☐ THIS SIDE OF INNOCENCE	08434-0	1.95
☐ YOUR SINS AND MINE	00331-6	1.25
☐ THE ARM AND THE DARKNESS	23616-1	2.25
☐ CAPTAINS AND THE KINGS	23069-4	2.25
☐ DIALOGUES WITH THE DEVIL	Q2768	1.50
☐ THE FINAL HOUR	23670-6	2.25
☐ GLORY AND THE LIGHTNING	23515-7	2.25
☐ GRANDMOTHER AND THE PRIESTS	C2664	1.95
☐ GREAT LION OF GOD	22445-7	1.95
☐ THE LATE CLARA BEAME	23157-7	1.50
☐ MAGGIE—HER MARRIAGE	23119-4	1.50
☐ NO ONE HEARS BUT HIM	23306-5	1.75
☐ ON GROWING UP TOUGH	23082-1	1.50
☐ A PILLAR OF IRON	23569-6	2.25
☐ THE ROMANCE OF ATLANTIS	23787-7	1.95
☐ TESTIMONY OF TWO MEN	23212-3	2.25
☐ WICKED ANGEL	23310-3	1.75
☐ TO LOOK AND PASS	13491-1	1.75

C-1